The smile o

With the lantern dous
absolute. Cass battled
despite her sister's softly breathing presence just ~~~~
away. Preacher Pernell's face swam into her mind's eye.
Sometimes, when he was looking off into the distance,
his expression set into lines that made him look hard as
nails—contemplating the sins of the world, no doubt.
Those arresting black eyes could put the fear of God into
almost anyone. But his smile—well, his smile seemed to
belong to a different man. It wasn't fearsome at all, but
slow and lazy, sometimes crooked, and made her heart
warm with the notion that it was purely for her. Of course,
it wasn't. The ladies were just teasing when they suggested he had eyes for her. He was a preacher, after all.
And the tingly sensation she got in the hollow of her
stomach when she saw him was only because he brought
to mind righteousness and redemption and all the other
holy subjects preachers spoke about.

She was sure that was all it was . . .

**"Readers know that if they desire a humorous,
but entertaining story, they turn to the works of
Emily Carmichael."**
—Harriet Klausner

Jezebel's Sister

Emily Carmichael

JOVE BOOKS, NEW YORK

JEZEBEL'S SISTER

A Jove Book / published by arrangement with
the author

PRINTING HISTORY
Jove edition / March 2001

The Penguin Putnam Inc. World Wide Web site address is
http://www.penguinputnam.com

ISBN: 0-515-12996-8

A JOVE BOOK®
Jove Books are published by The Berkley Publishing Group,
a division of Penguin Putnam Inc.,
375 Hudson Street, New York, New York 10014.
JOVE and the "J" design
are trademarks belonging to Penguin Putnam Inc.

PRINTED IN THE UNITED STATES OF AMERICA

10 9 8 7 6 5 4 3 2 1

Chapter 1

The mercantile was a seedy-looking place—not exactly the sort of rich target to make a thief's mouth water. Hardly a prize, Nathan Stone thought, to rate the attention of five self-styled badmen. Nathan didn't feel good about this piece of work, and not just because thieving was no way for a Tennessee gentleman to make a living.

"The place don't look like much." Peter Frost looked around and scratched the fuzz on his chin. Of the five of them who rode in Eliot Jennings's band, Peter was the youngest and the cockiest.

Steve Ford pulled out a wicked-looking knife, stabbed it into the pickle barrel, and plopped his catch into his mouth. "This whole town ain't worth much, if you ask me."

"No one asked you." Eliot Jennings glanced at the storekeeper, who was busy rearranging bottles of patent medicines along the wall behind the counter. "There's gotta be some cash in the old man's till. Enough to buy us all a big steak, a bigger whiskey, and a turn with a whore up in Marysville."

"There's another customer." Nathan nodded in the direction of a young woman examining yard goods in one corner.

Ford snorted in contempt. "What's the matter, Stone? You think the little lady's gonna pull a pistol and break up our party?"

"I think she's going to holler loud enough to alert the whole town if you pull a gun on the old man over there."

Jennings rolled his eyes. "Well then, take your pretty face over there and distract her—close enough where you can make sure she don't make no noise."

"Wait until she leaves."

Jennings spat a gob of brown tobacco juice onto the plank floor. "Damn but you're gettin' to be an old woman, Stone. You were always whinin' about something, even back when we rode with Quantrill. Let's get this over with and get outta here. I'm hungry." He pulled his neckerchief over his face and swaggered up to the store counter, where the bald little clerk raised his eyes to peer at him over his glasses. "Pops, you got any cash in the box today?"

The man stiffened. His bloodhound jowls began to shake with indignation as he moved his hand beneath the counter.

"Ah-ah!" Jennings cautioned, a finger wagging in reprimand. "That better be the cash box you're reachin' for, Pops, and not a pistol. 'Cause if there's slugs whizzin' around here, they're gonna be mine, not yours. Understand?"

The proprietor's face darkened to an angry red. "Git outta here, rat bait. I'll spit in your face before I give you a cent of this store's money."

The young woman in yard goods looked up at the clerk's strident declaration. Her mouth formed an O of alarm. Nathan pulled his own scarf across his lower face and interposed his broad body between her and the little drama at the counter.

"Lady, get out of sight behind those hats, and stay there until this is finished."

Jewel green eyes swept Nathan with contempt. "Just what do you scoundrels think you're doing?"

"Do as I say. Now." He took her arm and pulled her behind the hat display, away from the attention of his fellow thieves.

Freckles swarmed across her nose and cheeks as the color left her face. "Don't touch me, you swine." She jerked free, and he grabbed her again, not so gently this time.

"Just show some sense, will you?"

Apparently not the sensible type, she took a swing at him with her reticule. Nathan grabbed the handbag and pulled it from her grip. He should have known from the glaring red of her hair that the girl had a temper. Holding on to her was like wrestling an octopus. She landed more than one painful blow before he managed to wrap an arm around her waist and clamp a hand over her mouth. Under his breath, Nathan cursed Jennings, the war, the town, the clerk, the fractious redhead, and himself in equal measure. This really was no way for an ex-gentleman from Tennessee to make a living.

Jennings drew his gun and waved it at the stubborn clerk. "Quit arguin', Pops. Give us what we want, or you'll be real sorry."

With an eager gleam in his eyes, young Peter Frost drew his gun as well. "Just go behind the counter and fetch the money, Jennings. Gramps there isn't gonna make a move while he's lookin' down the barrel of my pistol."

The girl struggled indignantly against Nathan's restraint. Her teeth sank into the hand that sealed her mouth, but didn't make it past his leather glove.

"Damned viper!" he growled. "Behave, or I'll use that rope over there to hog-tie you."

Ford gave Nathan a twisted grin from where he lounged against a shelf of boots. "Have your hands full there, Stone?"

Ted Kane, the other member of their little band from hell, stood in the doorway to watch for trouble coming their way. "Hurry up, Jennings," he urged. "There's another couple of customers headed this way."

"Okay, okay. Hear that, Pops?" Jennings vaulted over the counter. The old merchant growled, his jowls flapping indignantly as he grabbed for whatever it was he had stashed beneath the counter. Peter, nervous and eager to prove himself, jerked in alarm and fired. His first shot went wide. The second shot, more carefully aimed, would have sent a slug straight into the old man's chest if Nathan hadn't tossed the girl aside and launched himself forward, knocking the boy to the floor. Peter consigned Nathan to hell in vividly colorful terms, and the storekeeper staggered against the counter with a bloody crease in his thigh. Bottles of Mrs. Winslow's Soothing Syrup and Doctor Brown's Woodland Balm rained down around him. From behind the hat display came the virago of the red hair and green eyes, wailing an alarm of truly operatic volume. She fastened herself to Nathan like a prickly burr.

"Look what you've done, you pig! Give me back my reticule, and leave that old man alone! Help! Robbers! Help us! Help us!"

For such a small woman, she had a voice that could wake the dead. If the gunfire hadn't told the whole town that something was wrong, her shrieks would have left no doubt.

Desperately, Jennings rummaged beneath the counter to find the cash box. When the wounded clerk tried to grab his arm, he turned and cold-bloodedly knocked the old man over the head.

Peter waved his pistol toward the door. "Let's get outta here!" Ford and Kane were already heading for the horses.

The hellcat batted at Nathan with her lethal reticule. Heftier than any ladies' handbag had a right to be, it crashed against his temple and knocked him off his feet. He recovered and lunged for her as she turned her attention to Peter, who didn't hesitate to swing his gun in her direction. Nathan knocked the pistol from Peter's hand, jerked the bag from the girl's grip, and hauled her behind the counter, where he pushed her down beside the clerk.

"Stay there, damnit! Do you want to get yourself shot?" What was wrong with women these days? he wondered. Didn't they know when to be terrified?

"Give me back my bag, you wretch!"

When she started to bounce up, he threw her bag into her lap, which landed her on the floor again, backside first. Before she could get up again, he ran.

On the street, people had stopped what they were doing and stared at the commotion. A few men ran toward the store. One had a rifle, and another had a shotgun tucked beneath his arm.

Ford and Kane galloped through the gathering crowd while Nathan and Peter climbed into their saddles. Jennings struggled to stuff cash into his pockets and mount his horse at the same time.

"Forget the money!" Nathan yelled to Jennings. Nathan kneed his mount forward as Peter galloped down the street in front of him. A rifle shot cracked through the air. Peter jerked, cried out, and slid from his saddle. He hit the ground, bounced to his feet, and ran, clutching his shoulder. Just behind him, Nathan leaned down to help the boy swing up behind the saddle, but angry hands reached up to pull them both down. Before he was forced to the ground, he saw Jennings pulled from his horse, coins and greenbacks spilling from his jacket and shirt pockets, landing in the mud as a hefty man with a badge sat on him and tied his hands behind his back.

Nathan figured the three of them were going to be calling a jail cell home for the foreseeable future. But he was wrong.

There is nothing like a hanging to liven up a drizzly spring day, or so thought the good citizens gathered in the street in front of the church. Silas was a very small town. Entertainments were few and far between, and the most noteworthy events of the last few years had been less than entertaining. While the War Between the States raged, little Silas had suffered at the hands of both proslavery and Free State guerrillas. Even the notorious Quantrill had paid them a visit, leaving fire and blood in his wake.

When the war ended, the trouble hadn't. Ex-guerrillas turned to outlawry, wreaking havoc out of anger, desperation, or simply for the joy of it. Scoundrels hardened by the violence of war found easy pickings among plain, hardworking people who wanted only to work the land and raise their families in peace.

It was little wonder, then, that the people of Silas found satisfaction in witnessing the end of three of the jackals that plagued their lives. Farmers, bankers, storekeepers, the old blacksmith who'd lost his son at faraway Gettysburg, the aging widow whose husband had died in a Confederate prisoner-of-war camp—they were tired of being ridden over, spit upon, and robbed.

The miscreants who sat gloomily atop their horses beneath the town's one oak tree had been caught red-handed robbing Samuel Keller's mercantile—the only business in town with enough cash to attract a bandit. They deserved to be sent to their Maker with nooses around their necks. Marshal Goodman, a part-time constable who had never apprehended anyone more dangerous than old Charlie Tibbs, the town drunk, had distinguished himself by capturing the villains. Silas didn't have a jail tight enough to hold such dangerous gunslingers, so the town council had voted unanimously to proceed immediately with the business of hanging. To hell with waiting for the circuit judge to come to town.

While Preacher Evans offered up a prayer to God for the salvation of the sinners' souls, the citizens of Silas congratulated themselves on ridding Kansas of bad seed. The first outlaw was little more than a boy, but he was the scoundrel who'd shot poor Keller. The rope around his neck had tamed his cocky defiance to a terrified silence. The second devil was more villainous in looks—mean-eyed and greasy-haired, with a stare that said he'd just as soon shoot a man as look at him. The third outlaw was a sad case indeed, a sorry soul who would surely end up in hell for wasting the gifts that the good Lord had given him. He was a well-made fellow with good looks and straight teeth, but his eyes spoke his true nature. Bitter, they were. Almost as black as his hair. Those flint-hard eyes made the rascal look as old as evil itself, and the grim line of his mouth could have come from pure cussed meanness or disgust with a life ill-spent. A witness to the robbery, Miss Cassidy Rose McAllister, claimed the black-eyed fellow had knocked the gunman's aim aside and saved old Sam's life. As the lady had been in the store at the time, she'd been in a position to see. But everyone knew Cassidy Rose was "*that* kind of woman," so decent people didn't pay much mind to what she said.

Not that it would have mattered if the McAllister girl's claim was true. In their present mood, the people of Silas didn't care. The world would be a better place without these rogues.

Nathan sat astride his horse and contemplated the downward spiral of his life. Since that life was about to end, such reflections seemed grimly appropriate. He had seen nothing but bad luck since the damned war had started, and today was no different. Today, in fact, was the culmination of bad luck, the summit on a mountain of the most foul, stinking, rotten luck ever known to man.

He admitted that hanging probably served him right, seeing that he'd been nothing but stupid since the day he'd left his Tennessee home to strike his blow for the Southern cause. He'd been a naive idiot, expecting heroism and noble battles. Instead, he'd found blood, violence, and the discovery that the world was a more vicious place than he'd ever suspected. He'd ended up finally in "Bleeding Kansas," raiding with Quantrill, sick in his soul at the sights he saw and the things he did. Finally, he'd told Quantrill to go to hell, where the man would no doubt feel right at home, and turned tail for Tennessee, or what was left of it.

No refuge had awaited him there. Tennessee was a way of life as dead as his family and friends. His home was destroyed, his father and brother dead, his mother broken in spirit. She had died within weeks of his return. He supposed he shouldn't hate the Yankees for what they'd done, considering the scorched earth and blood that he himself had left behind in his part of the war. But he hated them anyway.

The war had ended by the time he left bleak Tennessee. He'd wandered aimlessly, finally ending up in Kansas, with former comrades his genteel mother would have named "bad company." No more Tennessee gentleman, now, just a scavenger who rode with others of like mind, bitter ex-soldiers with nowhere to go and nothing but trouble on their minds. They exacted revenge on the Yankees and the scum who had profited from the war. That's what Nathan told himself, but he knew in his heart that they were no better than common brigands. Plain, hardworking folk too often got in the way of their "revenge"—hardworking folk like the angry citizens of Silas who were so anxious to watch him die. Hardworking folk like that stubborn old clerk and his hell-cat customer with the red-headed temper. If that damned girl hadn't joined the fight and yelled her silly head off, the three of them might have gotten away, in spite of their own stupidity.

Hadn't she been a sight, though, that pint-sized whirl-wind with hair flying and freckles all but glowing with anger? If Nathan weren't looking at the world from the inside of a noose, he might have found some humor in the incident. But his sense of humor had simply up and left when that pudgy marshal had hauled out three hanging ropes. The citizens of Silas were just about cranky enough, Nathan figured, to hang a dog for pissing on the wrong post, and there wasn't much question in their minds what to do with three no-goods who shot up one of the town fathers.

With an ignoble end staring him in the face, Nathan dis-covered that life was precious. He wanted to live. He wanted to live so much that the wanting ached.

Preacher Evans's long prayer ended, and the silence was deafening. Nathan's heart hammered in his chest, and blood rushed through his veins in muted thunder. He muttered his own prayer, a simple plea that he wouldn't piss his pants or disgrace himself in any other way while waiting his turn. He'd seen other men hang, and it wasn't a way he wanted to go.

Young Peter Frost was the first to swing. If these up-right citizens had an ounce of mercy, they'd have hanged them all at once. But they wanted them to die one by one, slowly—a cruel final torment. Peter didn't die easily. The rope was old and frayed. The boy's neck didn't break. His face turned blue before he finally stopped twitching.

When the marshal gave Jennings's horse a sharp slap on the rump, Nathan's horse, Tiger, snorted and jumped. The fellow at Tiger's head yanked back on the bit and cursed. Nathan heard Jennings's neck break, as loud as a dry stick cracked across a man's knee. He didn't look at the body swinging next to him. Jennings had been lucky. He went fast, not like Peter. Nathan felt his bowels turn to water and his stomach cramp in fear. He wished the man holding

Tiger's bridle had let the horse bolt. The agony would be over, and he wouldn't have to endure these last few seconds of trying to face his fate like a man.

The crowd turned expectant faces his way. They merged in a wavering blur. He could feel their hunger for his death. With a loud thwack, the marshal's hand landed on Tiger's rump. The horse, contrary as usual, snorted and backed a step instead of bolting forward. The noose tightened, and spots swam before Nathan's eyes. This was going to be bad, very bad.

"G'wan, ya stubborn mule! Go!"

At the second slap, Tiger lurched forward. Feeling as though the world had slowed to the sluggish pace of a nightmare, Nathan felt himself come off the saddle. The noose sawed at his throat. Pain turned his vision red. The need for air pierced his chest like a burning spear.

Then the world spun. Dirt came up to meet him. He sucked in air and shook his head to clear it. Above him dangled the frayed end of the rope. For a moment, silence descended, then broke around him in a babble of voices. Miraculously, Nathan was the one who recovered first. He launched himself to his feet and whistled sharply. Tiger wheeled about and pranced over to him.

"Get him!" the marshal cried.

Hands snatched at him, but he kicked out with his booted feet, connecting with a stomach here, a groin there. Unnerved by the chaos, Tiger unwittingly helped by doing a bit of kicking of his own. The marshal's helpers quickly decided that laying hands on the prisoner wasn't worth a steel-shod hoof to the head. The marshal pulled a pistol, but he didn't dare to fire into the crowd.

Telling himself it would never work, Nathan hooked his left boot in the stirrup and desperately launched himself upward. As he threw his right leg across Tiger's back, the horse was already moving. With hands tied behind him, balance was precarious. Almost impossible, in fact. The saddle horn dug into Nathan's stomach as he bent forward and tried desperately to stay on.

"After him!" Marshal Goodman shouted. "To your horses!"

Reins flapping free, Tiger galloped wildly down Main Street. Nathan didn't turn his head to look back. It was hard enough to stay aboard facing forward. He heard the drum of pursuing hooves, but in spite of that, a bubble of elation expanded in his chest. He knew that the Tennessee stud—the only thing he'd managed to salvage from a home ravaged by war—could outrun any nag those farmers could be riding. If Nathan could stay in the saddle, he'd be free. Free, and alive. Once he managed to get the cursed noose from around his neck, he'd run to the ends of the earth, if necessary, to make sure that a noose didn't get put there again. One hanging was enough for any man.

Twilight approached by the time Nathan's lathered horse faltered to a stop. But if Tiger's endurance was severely strained, Nathan's was near exhausted. They had maintained a grueling pace, and pursuit had fallen well behind. He could have stopped an hour earlier, most probably, but Nathan wasn't sure the marshal had given up. With his bad luck, he would crest the next hill and turn to see a posse galloping toward him. It wasn't likely, though. The rolling hills and sparsely timbered stream valleys had provided some cover, but Nathan's saving grace was Tiger's speed and great heart. Even now, if Nathan asked for more effort, the horse would give it.

"Enough, old friend." Nathan wished he could give Tiger's neck a grateful pat, but his hands were still tied behind him. Mounting the horse had been a miracle. Staying on during the hell-bent-for-leather flight had been another one. He was going to need yet another to get out of this situation with both his hair and his neck intact. With his hands tied behind his back and a noose around his neck, he was a sitting duck for both kinds of unfriendlies that roamed these parts. The Indians around here weren't much more friendly than the lawmen.

The smell didn't hit Nathan until they had come to a complete stop and his breathing calmed. The first quiet, unstrained breath he drew made him grimace. Something nearby had died and was getting ripe. Very ripe. Tiger rounded a low hill of windswept grass and descended into a brushy hollow. A low growl warned them off. Tiger stopped and backed a step.

"Jesus!" Nathan groaned. Since he'd walked out on Quantrill's bunch, he'd forgotten how to look at death unmoved. Maybe he'd never fully learned. But Quantrill himself might have blanched at the sight of the ripening piece of meat that once had been a man. A few days had passed since the fellow had died, but no scavengers had gotten to the body—probably because of the beast who stood guard a few feet away and rumbled in warning every few seconds.

"Take it easy, there, dog. Your friend's past help, I'm afraid."

The animal regarded him suspiciously. He was a sorry-looking mutt—painfully thin, with a dull gray, spiky coat that looked more like unkempt hair than proper dog fur. Most noticeable, however, besides the ominous growl, was the dog's size. Sitting, its nose would be level with a tall man's belt buckle. Even half starved, the beast looked as if it could break a wolf—or a man, for that matter—in two.

If Nathan had possessed a lick of sense, he would have backed away. Tiger's nervous tremble told him the horse wanted to do just that. One thing tempted him beyond good sense, though. At the corpse's belt was a thing of life-and-death value—a knife.

Awkwardly, Nathan dismounted, drawing a snarl of frightening volume from the dog.

"Back off, mutt! You hear?"

Nathan hoped he sounded authoritative. Confidence was difficult to project when one's knees were trembling from both exhaustion and fear. He took two steps forward, and the beast's snarl grew louder.

"Back off! You heard me! Git!"

The dog looked ready to spring. He was lean and long-legged, the stuff of some child's shaggy nightmare. But the knife beckoned.

Nathan said the first thing that came to mind. "Sit!"

The dog blinked at him.

"Do as I say, you stupid animal. Sit!"

The dog sat.

"Down!"

The dog slowly lay down.

"Well, I'll be damned."

Even the dog looked surprised.

"Stay! Got it, dog? Stay!"

Nathan sidled warily over to the body. He turned his back to the dead man and squatted down so his numb hands could grasp the knife. After a few moments' fumbling he was able to slide it from the sheath. The dog watched suspiciously. Nathan wasted no time in sawing the ropes that tied his wrists. Blood rushed back into hands, making his fingers tingle painfully. He ignored the discomfort and set to work cutting the noose that circled his neck. When the rope parted, he hurled it away as far as his numb arms could manage. A cautious exploration of his neck showed it to be somewhat raw, but thankfully free of lacerations serious enough to produce a hanging scar that would forever brand him. No matter what, now matter how, he was never going to wear a noose again.

Now that he was free, Nathan looked more closely at the dead man. The fellow was middle aged and pudgy. There was little doubt about what killed him. His chest sprouted three arrows, and his head was a bloody mess where hair had once been. Sioux, Nathan guessed. Their territory was far west of here, but it wouldn't be the first time a war band had roamed east into Pawnee territory. They'd no doubt taken the man's horse as well as his hair. Nathan was surprised they hadn't taken the dog. But then, the animal was too thin and stringy to be much use in the stewpot.

"Well, friend," Nathan told the corpse, "since you got me out of a bad fix with that knife of yours, I guess the least I owe you is a burial."

He didn't have a shovel, so he dragged the body to a natural depression between the roots of a lone oak, holding his breath in an effort not to gag. It took a good hour to find enough large rocks to cover the body, but finally, as the last of the twilight disappeared, the job was done. Feeling a bit quixotic and not a little silly, Nathan fashioned a crude cross out of deadfall and propped it at the head of the rock mound. He had no name to carve in the wood.

Whoever the fellow was, no one would know he was here except the mangy dog who still watched Nathan's every move.

"Well, dog. That's that. Your friend's buried right and proper. Go kill a rabbit or something. You look like you could use a meal."

Whining, the dog got up. Nathan tensed, but the shaggy beast merely walked over to the leather jacket that Nathan had rescued from the corpse. A man with nothing to call his own except a horse and the clothes on his back couldn't afford to be picky, and the dead fellow didn't have any more use for it. The dog nosed the jacket, then threw back his long-snouted head and let loose an unearthly howl. A shiver went down Nathan's spine.

"Okay, okay. You can have the jacket."

The dog nosed it again, and a dirty, creased envelope fell from an inside pocket. Cautiously, Nathan approached the garment, keeping a wary eye on the dog. The beast merely looked at him as he picked up the envelope. Inside was a folded letter. By the light of a sulfur match dug from his saddlebag, Nathan could just make out the faded script. The message was addressed to a Reverend Homer Pernell.

Before he passed on to his reward, our beloved and well-respected Reverend Hines recommended you as a God-fearing man possessing qualities of Moral Steadfastness and Courage. How fortunate for our community of Christian Brothers and Sisters that you are willing to guide our little band in the ways of Righteousness during our upcoming Adventure. We see the Lord's hand in the happy coincidence of your desiring to travel to Oregon at the same time our little Community decided to undertake the journey. We grieve the loss of dear Rev. Hines, but rejoice that such a Worthy Person as yourself is willing to shoulder his Responsibilities. It is true that our Lord never closes a door without opening a window somewhere else.

If you will present yourself in Shelby, Missouri, before the first of May, we will ensure that you are out-

*fitted with all you need for the trip. We plan to em-
bark with our families, livestock, and all we possess
by May 5. May God be with us during the coming
Endeavor.*

The letter was signed by a Mrs. Jedediah Jacobs and
dated March 13.

Nathan regarded the rocky grave with some sympathy.
"I guess God had other plans for you, friend. Looks as if
you'll never make that trip to Oregon. I don't understand
what would make a man want to go out there anyway, unless he's on the lam from the . . ." He trailed off, a smile
growing on his face. "Unless he's on the lam from the law.
Damned if an idea didn't just hit me in the head."

He looked down at the letter again. The woman who'd
written it apparently had never met Reverend Pernell, and
he'd be willing to bet that no one else in the little "community of Christian Brothers and Sisters" had either. All
they required of him was moral and religious guidance, and
in return, they would give him a complete outfit to travel
west.

Hell, Nathan thought. He could provide moral and religious guidance with the best of them. Hadn't his mother
forced him to attend Sunday school and church services
every week while he was growing up in Tennessee? As for
the preaching—he could manage it. He'd preach up the devil
himself if it would give him a new start in life.

Carefully, Nathan folded the letter, put it back into the
envelope, and slipped it into his shirt pocket. Then he went
to work with Homer Pernell's knife to carve a name in the
cross he'd propped at the head of the grave. The name he
carved was his own. When he was done, he tied the dead
man's jacket onto the rear of his saddle—cold or not, he
wasn't going to wear the thing without washing it first.

The dog pricked his ears as Nathan swung into the saddle.

"Well, dog, are you coming or staying? Where I'm going,
I figure at least we'll get three square meals a day."

The big beast trotted over to Tiger, his tongue lolling in

an amiable canine grin. Tiger threw him a nervous look, but stood his ground.

Nathan took one last look at the grave. In the bright moonlight, the bare mound of rocks seemed to glow eerily. "Don't worry about your name, friend Pernell. I'll treat it right. I'll be as moral and righteous as a sack full of saints." He smiled and gave a wry salute. "Rest in peace, Nathan Stone. Long live Homer Pernell."

Chapter 2

Webster, Kansas
May 1866

Living in a whorehouse wasn't exactly an entree to polite society, even in an end-of-the-road place like Webster, Kansas. Therefore Cassidy Rose McAllister wasn't surprised to be excluded from Ethel James's nineteenth birthday party. Ethel would have invited her, despite the certainty of raised eyebrows, but Cass had told her she didn't care to mingle with all those holier-than-thou priggish matrons and their nose-in-the-air daughters. That was a lie, of course, because she wanted very much to be part of that starchy crowd— an impossible dream, for everyone in Webster knew Cass lived at Lila's Place, and they also knew exactly what went on in the handsome white clapboard house that passed itself off as a boardinghouse for young ladies of refinement. Ethel's father would have a fit if he knew that his daughter had befriended Cass, and he'd likely have shut poor Ethel in her room forever if Cass had shown up at the party.

All the same, Cass couldn't resist a peek through the windows of Community Hall, where Ethel and almost every respectable citizen of Webster were sipping cider, eating birthday cake, and dancing to Olin Mathers's fiddle. She wasn't spying. Not really. She had to walk right past Community Hall on her way back from visiting Mrs. Oswald, whose new baby had done nothing but toss up her meals until Lila sent over milk from their goat. Mrs. Oswald couldn't afford to turn up her nose at Lila's help. Babies had to eat to grow, and this baby wasn't eating anything but what came out of a goat's teat. It wasn't the goat, after all, that was soiled. It was Lila and her "ladies."

Cass pulled her shawl more tightly around her, for the evening was chilly for the month of May. Her breath fogged the window, giving the scene within a dreamlike patina. For Cass it was a dream—a world of genteel manners, respect, and propriety. She imagined herself inside, socializing with Webster's finest, a green dress the color of spring matching her eyes, a green ribbon twined through her hair. It was a shame that her hair wasn't a more respectable color, blond like Frenchie's or soft, rich brown like Lila's, but at least her shade of red, flamboyant as it was, was the color God gave her—not like the bright crimson that Greta got from a bottle.

But this was Cass's fantasy, so she decided that her brazen hair, set off by the green dress and matching ribbon, was the pinnacle of fashion. Men would push each other aside to converse with her, bring her cider, feed her cake, and beg her to dance. Puffed-up matrons would lecture their daughters to learn from Cassidy Rose McAllister's example. Her manners would be very proper, her virtue unquestioned. And somewhere in the crowd, a very respectable man—a storekeeper or, better still, an earnest farmer—would see the genteel Miss McAllister and ponder what an eminently acceptable lady she was. He would seek out Ethel and beg her to present him, and—

"Hssst! Cass!"

Cass blinked. Her fantasy, like fragile glass, broke into a thousand shards as a plump figure frothed with ribbons, lace, and bows appeared beside her.

"Cass!"

"Ethel?"

"Cass! What are you doing here?"

"I'm on my way home from Mrs. Oswald's. What are

you doing here? You're supposed to be in there with your guests!"

"I saw you looking through the window."

"Shoot! Did anyone else see me?"

"I don't know."

"How embarrassing!"

"You told me you didn't want to come."

"Well, I don't."

Ethel cocked a brow skeptically.

"I don't! I was just passing by and decided to see how your party was going."

"All right. All right." Ethel's tone was unconvinced. "Do you want some cider and cake? I could sneak some out."

"No!" she snapped. "I don't want cider and cake. What do you think I am, some sort of poor relation?"

"I'm sorry. That's not what I meant."

Ethel looked so crestfallen that Cass couldn't help but smile a wry admission. "The cake's not what I was dreaming about, anyway. I was thinking about dancing at a party like this without anyone looking down her nose at me."

"It could happen." Ethel's plump cheeks dimpled in a smile.

"It will happen," Cass said. "Someday."

The two young women sat down together on one of the benches along the side of the building. Ethel batted at her hooped skirt as it ballooned around her.

"What are you doing with all those bows on your hips?" Cass chided. "How many times have I told you that you need clean lines to smooth out your figure?"

"The only way my figure will ever be smooth is to take a carving knife to it. Mother picked out the dress. I wanted to wear the one that you made me for Christmas. It makes me look positively ravishing. You really have a way with a needle."

"It's a good thing. I have to keep Lila in dresses." A horrible thought flashed into Cass's mind. "You didn't tell your mother that I gave you the dress, did you?"

"Of course not. I told her that I made it. She was so proud she nearly busted her corset. Of course, the problem with that is, now she thinks I can sew like an angel."

Cass laughed.

"I'm sorry I didn't invite you, Cass."

"Don't be sorry. I wouldn't have invited me either."

"Well, it doesn't seem fair. You aren't a . . . you know. *That* kind of woman. But people treat you like one, just because . . . well . . ."

"Just because my sister is a madam and the family business is a brothel?"

Ethel nearly choked. "You shouldn't say that word."

"I live in that word."

"Why don't you leave?" Ethel asked with an airy wave of her hand. "You're only twenty, and you have your whole life to build a new reputation. You could open a seamstress shop somewhere, or work as a schoolteacher. I hear some places out west are so desperate for teachers they'll take absolutely anyone."

Cass drilled her with a look, and Ethel colored bright red. "I didn't mean it that way! You'd make a wonderful teacher. You can read and do sums better than anyone."

"I know you didn't mean anything."

"And I'd think that living with your sister would be . . . you know . . . not very safe, with all those rowdy men around."

Cass laughed. "Are you kidding? Lila would likely shoot any fellow who so much as turned an eye in my direction. I'm safer at Lila's Place than locked in a convent. And don't you worry, Ethel James! I'll be leaving Lila's Place, and Webster too, as soon as I can persuade Lila to come with me. I'm going to be respectable, you know. And I'm going to make my sister respectable, too. Just see if I don't."

"What if she doesn't want to be respectable?"

"Everyone wants to be respectable, deep down inside. She feels responsible for the girls who work at her place. That's why she's dragging her feet about leaving. But she promised me she'll give it up. I just need to pin her down on the timing. That's all."

"Well, if you're still here in autumn, you can come to my wedding."

"Wedding?" Cassidy's eyes grew round. "Ethel! You're getting married?"

Ethel smirked. "Tom Wells proposed last night. As soon as he talks to Father, it'll be official."

"How wonderful!"

"A September wedding would be just perfect, don't you think? That would give me all summer to plan a huge celebration. And maybe you could help me make a dress."

Cass would be as likely as Lila's goat to get an invitation to the wedding. Less likely, perhaps. But none of that was Ethel's fault. "I'm very happy for you, Ethel. Really very happy."

"Thank you." Ethel giggled. "I'd better get back, before Tom thinks I'm walking out with another fellow. Will you be at church tomorrow?"

"Of course. Why wouldn't I be?" She grinned wickedly. "Reverend Tidwell can huff about it all he wants, but I have the same right as anyone else to attend services." The respectable folk of Webster were scandalized by having to rub shoulders with her in Sunday services. When the preacher had asked her to find her religion elsewhere, she'd threatened to convert all the ladies of Lila's Place into regular churchgoers.

"You are a wonder," Ethel said. "I could never stand up to people as you do."

"Oh, piffle! I wouldn't give up church. That's where I met you."

More important, church was the place where Cass could best pretend that she was as staid and solid as the other people who sat in the hard wooden pews listening to Mr. Tidwell lecture on the wages of sin.

Ethel continued eagerly. "My parents invited Tom to sit in our pew at services tomorrow, so that almost makes it official. Oh, Cass! He is so handsome!"

"Then get back to him, you goose. Besides, I have to get home. I have Lila's account book to do tonight."

"I'll wave at you Sunday."

"And give your father a fit? Don't you dare."

Ethel stood and straightened her bows and flounces. "When I'm a married lady, I won't have to care about what Father thinks. You'll be invited to all my parties." She crooked her fingers in a little farewell wave and disappeared around the corner toward the door. Cass suffered a pang of envy. Not for Ethel's handsome boyfriend. It was Ethel's future that Cass envied—marriage, children, quilting bees, ladies' benevolence circles, and a family pew in church. Respectability, and all it encompassed. For Ethel James, it was a birthright. For Cassidy Rose McAllister, it was merely a dream.

From the hour of seven in the evening until the small hours of the morning, Lila's place was never without customers, or gentleman callers, as Lila and her ladies called them. Tonight was busier than usual, however, for the day was Saturday. Hardworking men from the surrounding area came to town to relax, let off steam, and enjoy some obliging female companionship. Townsmen told their wives they had to clean up at the store, or check figures at the office, or meet with friends for a friendly game of cards, and instead took themselves into Lila's parlor, where "refined" young women with knowing eyes and inviting smiles kept them company as they sipped Lila's good whiskey and listened as "the professor," as all such musicians were called, tinkled away at the piano.

Lila herself, dressed in a gold gown that set off her warm hazel eyes and rich brown hair, presided over the evening's entertainments. Holding court on a plushly upholstered brocade settee, she bantered with one gent who'd had a bit too much to drink and surreptitiously signaled the barkeeper to cut him off. With another fellow, whose spirits were down, she flirted outrageously, then tactfully handed him off to Mary, a Chinese girl who could make any man feel ten feet tall. Still another customer required a dose of feminine sympathy. His business was going badly, and his wife, the shrew, cared only that he work longer hours to bring in more money. Lila said the appropriate words, made the proper noises, and jotted a mental note to be sure the gent paid his bill at the end of the evening.

She could do it all with her eyes shut, with her ears closed—in fact, sometimes she thought of trying just that. It would make things more interesting. Not that her life wasn't good. Every time she walked through the opulent parlor with

its veloured wallpaper, velvet draperies, thick rugs, and marble fireplace, Lila marveled at her good fortune. This very
profitable "boardinghouse" was a far cry from the broken-
down dirt farm in Iowa where she'd spent her first fourteen
years. When her parents had died within weeks of each other,
she'd been an unwashed, ignorant orphan with nothing but
the clothes on her back and a hungry five-year-old sister. Now
she was a successful businesswoman with more cash hidden
away in her mattress than most women saw all their lives.

"Miss Lila." Ephraim Masters presented himself with an
old-fashioned elegant bow. "You're looking very fetching
tonight."

"And you are extremely handsome, sir. Is that a new set
of teeth you're wearing?"

"Yes, ma'am. There's a new dentist fellow over at
Lawrence. Fitted me with these new choppers. Thought I'd
sashay over and show them off to you ladies."

Lila's smile warmed her eyes. Ephraim was seventy-five
if he was a day. About the most he could do with the girls
was enjoy an evening of lively conversation and bask in
their attention, but he showed up every Saturday night. The
ladies loved him for his polite respect and lively sense of
humor. They actually competed—in a refined sort of way,
of course—for the privilege of listening to his stories and
enjoying his grandfatherly advice. Lila thought she would
steer him toward Steamboat Sue tonight. Sue had been looking peaked lately—or perhaps it was simply that she wasn't
as young as she would have them all think. In any case, a
night of doing nothing more than coddling old Ephraim
would do her good.

Ephraim was pronouncing his fervent approval of the
opening of an actual university school in nearby Lawrence,
and Lila decided to let him run on a bit. He was warming
to his subject when a deep voice cut in.

"Well, aren't you as pretty as a rose blossom, sweetheart.
Can I buy you a glass of this fine whiskey?"

The intruder was a tall, lean fellow with a neatly trimmed
mustache and slicked-back hair. Lila hadn't seen the man
before, and she didn't care for the rude way he cut off the

old man. Still, she was too much the businesswoman to let her vexation show.

"You're very kind, sir. And very generous in your compliments, considering the number of beautiful roses to choose from here. May I introduce Mr. Ephraim Masters, an old friend and Webster's resident haberdasher."

The stranger turned his gaze briefly to the old man and dismissed him with a flick of an eye. "How about that whiskey, sweetheart?"

"The residents here do not drink, sir, though Mr. Talbot at the bar has a selection of fine liquor for our guests' pleasure. I'm Lila McAllister, the owner of this establishment. I'd be happy to introduce you to some lovely young ladies who would be delighted to entertain you while you enjoy a drink. If you fancy music, the professor can play just about any piece you'd care to name, and in the next room there are several friendly card games in progress. If you would like to join one of them, I could arrange an entree."

"I'd be more interested in spending time with you." His eyes traveled to her décolletage, which was quite modest, given her profession. Lila didn't allow her ladies to dress like trash, and she didn't either.

Ephraim harrumphed, clearly annoyed by the man's intrusion. "Plainly you haven't been here before, son. Miss Lila owns the place. She's not on the menu, if you catch my meaning."

"Why don't you just mind your own business, old man? Maybe the lady—"

"Now, gentlemen." Lila gave them a soothing smile. "The misunderstanding was a natural one, Ephraim. But Mr. Masters is correct, Mr. . . . ?"

"Chalmers. Henry Chalmers."

"Mr. Chalmers. My days of taking an active part in the entertainment are past." She smiled winningly. "It takes a young thing to keep up with you gentlemen. Once you've met Greta, you'll forget every other woman you've ever met. I promise." She signaled a statuesque woman whose purple-tinged hair was the only discordant note in a superlatively composed symphony of luscious curves and abundant flesh. Greta's watered silk gown sported lace and flounces strategically placed to emphasize features of her figure that needed very little emphasis. She undulated her way toward their group in a manner designed to have every red-blooded man's tongue hitting the floor.

"Mr. Chalmers, meet Greta, who I'm sure you will find a delightful companion for the evening."

Chalmers gave Greta an appreciative inspection.

"Greta, Mr. Chalmers is a newcomer to Lila's Place. Ask Mr. Talbot to give him a free whiskey, or any other refreshment he desires."

Leaving Chalmers with the capable Greta, Lila escorted Ephraim toward Steamboat Sue, who, along with another girl, listened raptly to young Gerald Porter's story about his adventures in the war. Everyone hereabouts knew Gerald had seen more action pushing a pencil than firing a gun, but the girls listened with wide eyes anyway.

Once Lila had Ephraim established in Sue's company, she went to fetch a soda water from the elegant oak bar that occupied one corner of the parlor. During business hours she didn't allow her girls to drink, smoke, chew tobacco, or take snuff, and to set a good example, she followed the strict rules herself. But her throat was parched and her mouth hurt from too much smiling. A cool drink was just what she needed.

She didn't reach the bar before a curly-headed Anita intercepted her. The scowl on her doll-like face would have sent a customer running the opposite way, despite the charming dimples and fetching swell of bosom.

"Mrs. McAllister, I must speak with you."

The "Mrs." was a form of respect Lila demanded from her employees, even though the closest she'd been to marriage was the night long ago when she'd entertained a customer in a bridal gown made completely of see-through lace. The man had paid richly for both the fantasy and the dress.

"Can it wait until morning, Anita?"

"No. I'm upset, and you know when I'm upset I don't bring in half as much as when I'm feeling more sociable."

"It's your job to be sociable."

"How sociable can a girl be when her personal treasures

are being destroyed intentionally by that malicious, uppity old witch in the kitchen?"

Lila sighed. "Now, Anita . . ."

"Come see! Just come see."

Lila followed Anita up the crimson-carpeted staircase, down a spacious hallway livened by paintings of nude women reclining in evocative positions, and into Anita's bedroom. It was decorated in a girlish style, with a pink ruffled counterpane and matching draperies. A dressing table was crowded with vials of perfume and bottles of lotions, and a gaily flowered screen walled off one corner for dressing and undressing.

"Look at this! Just look at it!" Anita picked up a hand mirror from the dressing table. It was ivory, with an ornately carved handle that matched an ivory comb and hairbrush of like design. "Mama Luce broke this when she was cleaning my room. Elias Trevor gave this to me."

The fabled Mr. Trevor, Lila thought with strained patience—the rich North Carolina planter who supposedly had been all set to marry Anita when the war had inconveniently interrupted their plans. Though Anita pursued her profession with a gusto that raised doubts as to the extent of her grief, the late lamented Elias was trotted out whenever she felt put upon or in need of sympathy—which was often.

"What makes you think Mama Luce broke it?"

"It was whole this morning," Anita huffed. "I found it broken when I came back from shopping. Luce had been in here to clean. Who else could it have been?"

"Did you ask her about it?"

"I did more than ask about it. I demanded she pay for it, and the old witch denied she'd touched it, of course. What do you expect? That mirror is worth at least ten dollars."

"Ten dollars?"

"It's real ivory."

Lila felt a brief flash of nostalgia for the days when she had been one of the girls creating such problems, not the one expected to referee. Sometimes she felt like a mother with a herd of squabbling children. "I'll talk to Luce."

"Back before the war, she'd be whipped within an inch
of her life."

A honeyed voice with the lassitude of the Deep South
interrupted. "Back befo' the war, miss nose-in-the-air hussy,
I was free as you was. Freer, mos' likely, 'cause I wasn't
obliged to get on my back and spread my legs for any Jack
Jump Up with a stiff tool."

"Who're you calling a hussy, you fat troublemaker?"

"I calls 'em like I sees 'em, honey, and if you ain't a
hussy, I never seen one."

"What're you doing sneaking around up here, anyway,
when you should be down in the kitchen?"

Crossing arms across an enormous bosom, Luce turned
toward Lila with an air of indignant innocence.

"I saw this lyin' piece of trash drag you up here, Miz
Lila, and I done knew she was gonna spin you a tale about
that mirror. So I took myself up here to defen' myself."

"Piece of trash? Why, you uppity old bitch. . . !"

"You watch yore mouth, girl, or I'll. . . !"

Lila sighed as the two women continued berating each
other, wishing for Cass to come through the door and save
her. It was Cass who normally kept the peace. Luce's bluster didn't scare her and the ladies' complaints and moods
didn't move her. A lifted brow from Cassidy Rose could
stop a catfight midscratch.

Cass was off visiting Mrs. Oswald, though. She disliked
being in the house while the ladies were working, and Lila
didn't blame her. Her living in a house of ill repute was
bad enough, without sticking her nose into what went on
downstairs when the men got randy and the girls started
earning their pay. Lila had tried to get her to live elsewhere.
A few years ago she'd tried to send her off to a fancy school,
but Cass had refused to go. More recently she had offered
to set her up in her own clothing design business—Cass
was terrific with a needle and thread—and a year ago she
nearly persuaded her to move to Denver with a girl who
had once worked at the house. It wasn't that she wanted to
be rid of Cass, but having her sister painted with the same
brush that tarred her had never been part of Lila's plan.

Still, she would have been all too happy to have Cass walk in and take these two battling cats by the tail.

"Enough!" Lila shouted above the melee. "Be quiet! Both of you. Mama Luce, tell the truth. Did you accidentally break Anita's mirror?"

"No, Miz Lila!" Luce held herself above the rule about calling Lila Mrs. McAllister. She called people whatever she pleased.

Lila turned to Anita. "Are you sure your skirt didn't knock it off the dressing table sometime when you didn't notice?"

"Of course I didn't knock it off! What kind of looby do you think I am? She's lying, and I want my ten dollars!"

"Mama Luce don't lie. If you want ten dollars, hussy, you better take yourself downstairs and git to work."

Anita growled and curled her fingers into claws. Only a timely commotion from below kept her from lunging for the cook. A sudden outbreak of shouting was punctuated by a sharp thud that might have been a heavy object—such as a body—hitting the floor or a wall. A chorus of feminine screams followed hard on the heels of the thud. Their own embroilment forgotten, Lila, Anita, and Mama Luce rushed the doorway, momentarily got stuck in the passage due to Luce's bulk, then shot out and down the stairs.

Lila stopped at the bottom of the staircase to send Mama Luce after the shotgun she kept in the kitchen. Fights were not common at Lila's Place, because the men thereabouts knew the quickest way to get barred from the house was to start a ruckus. The newcomer hadn't gotten the message, however, because he and Tucker Harris were squared off inside a ring of agitated women. The professor had abandoned his piano to act as referee—to no effect. A thread of crimson ran down Tucker's chin from the corner of his mouth, and a somewhat dazed look in his eye made Lila speculate that his body had been the heavy object bouncing off the wall.

Blond, statuesque Frenchie La Fleur, evidently the cause of the hostilities, stood a little to one side, screaming at the combatants to "knock off this shit!" The rule about "lady-like tone and demeanor at all times" obviously had been forgotten along with her French accent.

"*What* is going on here?" Lila demanded as she strode into the room.

Tucker Harris was the first to answer. His words were slightly slurred by a fat lip. "Thish here Fancy Jack is hornin' in on my woman, and when I called him on it, he tells me to go fu— uh, bug off."

Tucker hadn't forgotten the rule about language, even if the one about fighting had slipped his mind. Lila didn't bother to remind him that Frenchie was a sporting woman, and therefore scarcely his private property. Tucker had a powerful hankering for Frenchie, and as long as he was on the premises, he didn't let anyone else buy a piece of her time, or any other part of her, for that matter. As long as he was willing to pay for Frenchie's services, and Frenchie herself didn't object, Lila let the arrangement stand. Unfortunately, Henry Chalmers had taken a liking to the girl, and he wasn't about to recognize another man's claim on public property. That French accent, fake as it was, did pack a powerful punch to a man's ardor, not to mention the silky blond ringlets, flawless skin, and bodacious curves.

Lila gave Greta a black look. She was supposed to be keeping Mr. Chalmers busy. The girl shrugged and rolled her eyes.

"Mr. Chalmers, we have a very strict rule about fighting in this establishment."

"Back off, sister. My money's as good as his, and I was sitting with her long before that sonofabitch came in."

"We also have a rule about foul language, sir. I realize you're a newcomer, but—"

"I said back off." He threw a glance at Frenchie. "You coming upstairs with me?"

"Sure." Frenchie said with a shrug.

"She's coming with me," Tucker blustered.

"Like hell." Chalmers threw a punch. Tucker staggered backward, then recovered to charge like a bull into Chalmers's stomach. Chalmers brought his knee up in a lethal blow to the groin. Tucker's shriek drowned out the pleas for peace from both Lila and Frenchie.

"Luce!" Lila demanded. "Give me the shotgun!"

Mama Luce bustled over and slapped the old double-barreled twelve-gauge into her hands. Lila leveled the weapon at the contenders. Her purpose was to get their attention, not to fire it. So when Tucker lunged once again for Chalmers, the explosion of a gunshot took her by surprise.

Frenchie screamed, and seconds later the other ladies joined in the shrieking. Horrified, Lila saw a blossom of crimson growing on Tucker's shirt. In Chalmers's hand was a pocket pistol. The barrel still smoked.

At that inconvenient moment, Marshal Eddie Myers burst through the front door.

Cass sat for a long while after Ethel left. She no longer looked through the window, but she could hear the music, the laughter, and the buzz of happy conversation. Ethel was probably dancing with her beau even as Cass listened. The thought inspired a smile. Ethel would no doubt be very happy with Tom Wells, very happy planning her autumn wedding extravaganza. Cass just hoped she wasn't around to watch that party in the same manner as tonight.

She and Lila needed a town where they weren't known, a place where the stench of a lurid reputation couldn't follow them. They'd been in Webster three years now, since Quantrill's sack of nearby Lawrence had made that town no place to be in the business of pleasure. In the years before Lawrence, Lila had worked houses in a string of towns from Iowa and Illinois to Kentucky and Missouri. She had claimed they had no choice. When their parents died of the flux, Lila had shouldered the responsibility for feeding both of them, and for the just-blossoming girl she'd been, there was no other way to make a living.

Lila had learned to accept the life, sheltering her younger sister from as much of the nastiness as she could. But Cass had always hated it—hated it for Lila, and for herself as well. She hated the looks decent people gave them, the speculation and leers from the men, the snubs from the women. Early on in Webster, she'd taken to driving the few miles to Silas to shop, thinking she would be anonymous in that town, at least. But her reputation followed even there. Not long ago she'd been shopping for dress goods in the Silas mercantile and had become embroiled in a robbery, of all

things. She'd spoken up in defense of one of the thieves—
a man who, scoundrel though he was, had tried to prevent
a shooting and had probably saved the old clerk's life. The
angry citizens had completely discounted her testimony. She
was "*that* kind of woman," they'd said, so of course her
opinion counted for nothing and her truthfulness was gravely
in doubt.

They'd dragged the fellow to the hanging oak along with
the others, and more than one of the vigilantes had looked
her way, wondering why she had spoken up, speculating
that she might be in league with the bandits. Cass hadn't
stayed for the hanging, and she didn't think she would return to Silas for shopping any time soon.

She longed to move on to greener, cleaner pastures, and
somehow she was going to drag Lila with her. Her sister
didn't entertain customers any longer, but being a madam
was almost as bad. Lila had sacrificed herself to keep them
both alive and out of a workhouse, and now Cass was going
to save her from herself. Just as soon as she convinced Lila
that she needed saving.

Ethel's party was still going strong when Cass headed
toward home. A block away from Lila's Place, she knew
something was wrong. Only one light shone in a back window, and no music drifted into the night from the professor's nimble fingers. The hour was much too early for the
house to be so quiet.

Cautiously, she opened the front door and stepped into
the dark entrance hall. Dark? On a Saturday night? "Hello?"

A voice came from the back of the house. "Miz Cassidy.
Izzat you?"

"Mama Luce?" Cass hurried into the kitchen, where the
little round woman gave her a fervent hug.

"It's me, honey. I's the only one that uppity marshal
didn't drag down to the jailhouse."

"Jailhouse? Omigod! What's happened? Where's Lila?"

"She in the calaboose with the rest of 'em. That's where
she is. That woman's got a mouth on her when she gits
mad. Yes, she does. And Marshal Eddie didn't like it one
bit."

The marshal didn't like Lila one bit, either, Cass knew.

Or rather, he had once liked her quite a lot. He'd done his darnedest to weasel his way into Lila's bed, but Lila had wanted no part of him. She didn't whore for a living any longer, and a fat marshal with greasy hair wasn't her idea of romantic recreation. Unfortunately, the marshal wasn't the sort of man to be a good sport about a rebuff. He'd been making trouble for Lila ever since, fixing a vulturine eye on the house and everyone in it, waiting for some opportunity to shut them down.

Mama Luce didn't have to be asked twice. She brimmed over with the story. The details spilled out with a speed that set Cass's head to spinning—the fight, the shooting, the marshal's untimely entrance.

"That Chalmers—he bad news. He belongs in jail. Yessirree."

"Okay, there was a shooting. Poor Tucker Harris is getting a bullet dug out of him and the fellow who shot him is in jail. What about the others?"

"Well, that good-fer-nuthin' marshal was gonna drag Frenchie to jail for startin' the fight, and Miz Lila—you know Miz Lila! She takes up on Frenchie's side, and then Steamboat Sue gits in there and starts battin' at the marshal, 'cause now he's draggin' Miz Lila away too. The professor, he jumps in to help—you know that man has his eye on that Frenchie gal! An' befo' you know it, honey, the whole house is ashoutin' and aswingin' away like the war is startin' all over agin! Me, I take myself back to the kitchen, but I hear Marshal Eddie tell Lila she's gonna be behind bars till you-know-where freezes solid. That's what he say."

Cass lowered her head into her hands and groaned.

"That ain't gonna help, honey, 'cause I been moanin' and groanin' fit to make the angels cry since the bunch of 'em left, and nuthin's changed."

The silence of the house settled ominously around them, a quiet so deep that Cass could almost hear her brain ticking. This situation called for some creative thinking. Every disaster contained the seeds of opportunity, somewhere. The trick was in finding them.

Chapter 3

"You stop pickin' at yore food, Miz Cassidy! If you ain't gonna eat them good biscuits and gravy I made, I'll throw 'em out back for the stray dogs. Least they appreciate fine cookin'."

Cass refrained from pointing out that Mama Luce hadn't eaten much breakfast, either. "It's not your cooking, Luce. I'm busy trying to think. That's all."

"You think better if you eat first, honey. That poor brain of yours needs some fuel if you want it to heat up with ideas."

"My brain is heating up just fine. It just needs a little time to think of a plan."

"Well, I hope yore brain is in better fettle than Miz Lila's. That girl's stubborn when she mad, and she madder than a wet cat, ain't she?"

Lila was indeed madder than a wet cat. When Cass and Mama Luce had visited the jailbirds early that morning, bringing them fresh-baked biscuits, maple syrup, cold ham, fresh milk from Lila's goat, and a pot of strong coffee, Lila had been all but spitting. Cass didn't blame her. Marshal Myers was milking the situation for all it was worth and enjoying every minute of it. The ladies were crowded into a cell that stank of urine and vomit and crawled with lice.

They had no privacy from the men. Chalmers and the professor occupied a second cell, along with a couple of rowdy drunks and an old fellow who'd been caught stealing a horse from the livery barn. Neither did the women have any respite from Myers himself, who enjoyed strutting into the cell room and taunting the ladies with whatever piece of humiliation he could devise.

Cass got an earful of Lila's complaints. Three of the ladies, including purple-haired Greta, had cut deals with Myers and left. Left the jail, left Lila's employ, and left town. Six remained, out of either personal loyalty to Lila or a lack of anywhere else to go. They all pleaded with Cass to find a solution to the mess.

Myers probably didn't have legal grounds to hold them, strictly speaking, but this far west, legalities were less important than power, and the marshal had all the power in this situation. Lila was no help. If she'd been willing to humble herself a bit, soften her manner toward the marshal and feed his pride with a little humility, he might have been more reasonable.

But, as Mama Luce noted, when Lila was mad, she was as stubborn as a Missouri mule. Cass had come away from the jail wanting to turn her sister over her knee with one hand and with the other, stuff the marshal down an outhouse.

She would eventually think of a way out of this. Cass was sure that she would. But so far no workable plan had come to mind.

"We could sneak in there in the middle of the night and let 'em out," Luce offered with belligerent enthusiasm.

"There's always someone on guard."

"We hit 'im on the head with a rolling pin."

"And then what?"

"We . . . uh . . ."

"Right." Cass heaved a dispirited sigh. "I suppose I could try to find a lawyer. With all that money stashed in Lila's mattress, we could afford to hire a good one."

Mama Luce snorted. "You think some lawyer's gonna speak up for a passel of sportin' ladies? He'd jest as soon speak up for me, honey. That's no plan."

"We ought to be able to find someone who'll overlook Lila's profession when he's offered a fat fee."

"How many lawyer men in Webster?" Luce asked with a sniff.

Cass thought for a moment, then grimaced. "One, I guess."

"Tha's right, honey. One. Mr. Griffin. Mr. Griffin whose wife stirred up all the town ladies like a nestful of hornets and went to the town council about Miz Lila's house. Lucky for Miz Lila that half the town council shows up at her place on Saturday nights."

"Yes." Cass sighed. "*That* Mr. Griffin. Mrs. Griffin raised a stink about me going to church services, too. And that reminds me. It is Sunday, isn't it?"

"Yes'm. This is the good Lord's day, no matter how stinkin' a day it is. And I'm gonna hear some preachin' today."

"Where are you going to hear preaching?"

The local church would rather shovel brimstone in hell than have a black woman attend their worship service. They muttered indignantly about Cass, tainted as she was, but at least Cass was white. Mama Luce sitting in the pew beside her would have led to tar and feathers or a lynch mob.

"There's a wagon train camped jest outside of town. I hear tell they gonna stick around for a couple days 'cause they got a lady that jest delivered a sickly chile. It's a whole church goin' west, bless their brave souls, an' they got their own preachin' man. Now, folks in that fancy church house up the road can squawk and moan if I set foot inside, but no one can tell ol' Mama Luce she cain't set her backside in the grass and listen to a preacher who's preachin' out in the free outside air." She took the plate of biscuits and gravy from in front of Cass. "You had long enough to eat those biscuits, Miz Cass. By now they're soggy as a cow pie."

"I'll clean up," Cass said dejectedly. "You go listen to your preaching. If you're too late, you'll miss it."

"No, ma'am. Those people be carryin' on all mornin', likely. You not goin' to church, Miz Cass?"

Usually Cass refused to miss a service, not so much because she enjoyed Reverend Tidwell's sermons as because the congregation didn't want her there. Lila wasn't the only one in the family with a stubborn streak. Today, however, she didn't think she could face the hostility. Everyone would know about the shooting and the mass arrest, and no doubt they'd be smirking behind their hymnals and quoting Bible passages about sinners getting their due. Ordinarily, she could turn her nose up at that sort of thing, but today she wasn't in the mood.

"I don't think I'll go," Cass admitted.

Luce cocked her head sympathetically. "You down in the mouth, honey. I don' blame you, but sittin' home sulkin's no way to keep your brain workin' and plannin'. You come to the preachin' with me, an' mebbe some miracle come down an' smack us right on the head. My momma used to tell me, when we was livin' in a little shanty cabin on Massa Fremont's plantation in Carolina, 'Luce,' she say, 'ain't no problem so big that prayin' won't help.' So you get yore bonnet'n' shawl, honey. We gonna do some loud prayin'."

Nathan grimaced into the little mirror that he'd hung on the side of his wagon, scraping the last whiskers from his chin and nicking himself for the second time that morning. Nerves were playing holy hell with his usually steady hand.

He dabbed at the blood, muttered a word that no self-respecting preacher would think of using, then glanced guiltily about to see if anyone had taken note of his unholy lapse. The only one watching him was the huge creature he'd dubbed Dog, and Dog didn't seem to care whether his language was fair or foul.

"Don't you go telling anyone, hear? Or you're out on your own."

The beast gave him a tongue-lolling canine grin, got up, stretched, and padded off toward the stream.

"There goes my moral support," Nathan muttered.

He needed all the support he could get. This morning was the first time he would face his expectant congregation with a Bible in one hand and the word of God supposedly spewing from his mouth. A session with the dentist's pliers would be a happier way to spend the morning.

Transforming himself from a hard-living desperado to a

platitude-spouting preacher was harder than Nathan had expected. The prospect of preaching wasn't the only problem. Cussing was a habit that was hard to break, and turning a lustful eye on fine-looking women was even harder to forsake. Not that his little group of saints boasted a bevy of fine-looking females. These women were virtuous to the core, and some, he swore, took pure delight in making themselves plainer than they really were—which was certainly contrary to female nature as he understood it.

On the whole, however, these God-fearing Christians from Shelby, Missouri, were a good lot. The men were tough and disciplined, hardworking and responsible. The women were caring and patient. Good people, even if they were a bit obsessed with finding sin in themselves and others. Old Jed Jacobs, the acknowledged leader of the pack, could sniff out sin quicker than a hound could scent a hambone, and his wife was just as sharp.

Nathan wiped the shaving soap from his face, scowling at himself in the mirror as he did so. If he let his guard down for one minute, he would likely be out on his ass, with nothing but himself, his horse, and Dog, who was a dubious companion at best. He had wallowed in sin often enough that the stink still remained, even if he had changed to a new and righteous suit of morals.

"Morning, Brother Pernell!" Effie Brown gave him a smile as she walked from the direction of the creek. Each hand gripped a bucket so full that water overflowed the brims with every stride.

"Sister Brown, let me help you with those buckets."

"Oh no, Reverend. You'd slosh your Sunday clothes. Can't have that with you about to preach, can we?"

She cheerfully went on her way, humming a tune that Nathan recognized as a hymn. His nerves jangled. He didn't want to make a jackass of himself in front of these people, not only because this wagon train and new identity were a damned good cover, but because he didn't want to disappoint the forty-odd souls who'd accepted him with such trusting warmth. Without having to prove himself in the least, he'd been welcomed like a brother, given lodging in a family's home, and supplied with a wagon and complete outfit for the trail. When he'd told the tale of being set upon by robbers, the group had taken up a collection to buy him two sets of store-bought clothes, even down to a couple of union suits and an extra pair of boots, and most of the families had donated personal items—an old watch, a handy little pocket knife, a comb, razor, and mirror—to replace the items he'd supposedly lost to the thieves.

Nathan did not want these people to learn that he belonged with the bad guys. He was becoming too accustomed to their respect and friendship. He could get used to being a pillar of the community.

He swung up into the dim interior of his wagon and for the tenth time that morning took a Bible from a storage locker. There had been no time for formal religious services before they left, other than a bit of singing and a lot of praying, so until now, he hadn't been asked to prove his worth by preaching. The prospect was daunting. He'd spent the whole night poring over the Good Book, trying to recall his mother's favorite verses and the numerous Sunday school lessons he'd ignored, wishing he'd paid more heed to his family's church doings. Verses and chapters spun around his mind like mosquitoes. Commandments, proverbs, psalms, sayings, do's, don'ts, verilys, wherefores, and whatfors—how was anyone supposed to keep everything straight?

A shaft of sunlight stabbed into the wagon as the canvas end flap was pushed aside. The bearded, serious face of Jed Jacobs peered inside. "Reverend Pernell. The church is gathered, sir."

"Uh . . . good. Good. Very good."

Jacobs glanced at the Bible held so tightly in Nathan's hand. "I see you're making good use of my aunt's old Bible. A more upright woman never graced this side of Heaven. She'd be happy to know you were using it."

Nathan cleared his throat. Supposedly, his treasured Bible had been stolen by the same bandits who'd taken everything else. "I'd be lost without it," he said truthfully. "I thank you for the gift, Mr. Jacobs."

"I'll see you at services, then."

"I'll be right along. Just need to say another couple of prayers."

The prayers, heartfelt as they were, helped very little as Nathan climbed up onto the bed of a supply wagon whose canvas cover had been raised like the curtain of a stage. In a flash of pure stage fright, he wondered if another hanging party could be much worse than this. The group of emigrants were dressed in their somber Sunday best, the men's hair slicked back, faces washed, and beards freshly trimmed, the women's aprons put aside and their dresses clean and pressed. The faces turned toward his glowed with anticipation.

Nathan took a deep breath and let it out. "Brothers and sisters . . ."

The expectant hush seemed almost unnatural. Words stuck in Nathan's throat. "Uh . . . let us sing?" He gestured lamely to their one source of music—a man with a fiddle— and named the first hymn that came to mind. "Rock of Ages, Brother Clyde."

Clyde sawed away at his fiddle, and the voices of Nathan's congregation rose in enthusiasm if not harmony. What would this stiff-backed group think, Nathan wondered, if they knew what he really was? Maude Atkins would drop her wooden teeth if she knew she'd broken bread with a man whose likeness was reproduced on wanted posters throughout Kansas and Missouri, and her scrawny husband, George, would run for the shotgun. Jed and Eliza Jacobs would have twin strokes, but not before they called the law to haul him off. Alice Scott and Hope Perkins—a virtuous widow and her spinster sister—would fetch a shovel and drive him off like a hog that had gotten into the vegetable patch. The exception might be pretty little Faith Scott, who chafed constantly at her mother's restrictions and might be wild enough to think an outlaw fugitive was romantic. That girl would land herself in trouble without much encouragement at all.

And Charlie Morris—there was a piece of work! The so-called guide the group had engaged in Independence was more scoundrel than trail guide, in Nathan's opinion, and he'd run with enough scoundrels to know one when he saw one. Scoundrel or not, however, Morris would gladly turn

Nathan over to the law if he knew there was money on his head.

The hymn ended, and Nathan promptly invited the gathered faithful to pray for those of their number who were troubled—Simon March and his wife, Virginia, whose newborn baby was growing stronger, and whose frailty was the reason they had called a halt for several days; and the Crespin family, whose youngest boy had fallen and been crushed by the wheels of a wagon just two days after the start of their journey. Nathan asked the group to pray silently, and while they did, he girded his loins, so to speak, for the sermon ahead.

He had dreaded this moment for days, but when the first words left his mouth, he felt the spell begin to gather. He began slowly, but his audience stood rapt, like children waiting patiently through the beginning lines of a ghost story, eagerly anticipating the big scare and screaming to come. The scare these good Christians awaited was hellfire and damnation, the calling down of holy wrath and warnings to repent.

Before the holy folk could become restless, Nathan hit his stride. He himself had been brought up in a church full of Tennessee gentry more interested in socialization than salvation, but he'd heard enough from frontier preachers to know what was expected. Inspiration came from desperation, and he was desperate enough to be downright galvanized. Comparing the travelers to the Biblical tribes wandering in the desert, he wove together a spiel of courage, sacrifice, and danger along with idolatry, lust, heathenism, prodigal sons and daughters, and a fatted calf or two. His listeners didn't seem to mind his mixed metaphors and mixed testaments, and when it came to sin, Nathan was truly inspired. Talking about sin was easy when one had so much firsthand experience committing sin, and he'd been through enough hell on earth during the war to speak with authority about damnation.

With his audience eating out of his hand, Nathan felt a rush of relief. Lightning hadn't struck him, and the earth hadn't opened to swallow him whole. Apparently God didn't mind that the one calling down hell and torment on the unrepentant was the one most likely to be treated to a personal interview with Old Nick. He began to actually enjoy himself.

Just as he started to expound upon lust—one of his favorite sins—two women joined his little group of worshippers. One of the pair was a Negro woman, round as a dumpling, with white grizzled hair and a pair of chins that wobbled every time she moved. The other was a young white woman, and to a man whose intemperance of character was exceeded only by his capacity for trouble, she was an irresistible invitation to the sin that was the current subject of his harangue. In fact, her entrance onto the scene could have been choreographed by the devil himself. A bonnet hid her hair and shadowed her face, but her form alone was enough to set a man's blood singing. She wore a simple shirtwaist and tailored walking skirt that showed off her slender waist and trim hips. A shawl draped her shoulders and hugged generous breasts. She wrapped it more tightly around her to ward off the chilly spring breeze.

Nathan's imagination easily pictured his arms replacing that flimsy shawl, circling her slender body and warming her with his own heat. The image was so inviting that his words faltered for a moment, his tirade against lechery derailed by the distraction of his own ripe fantasy. He'd been without female companionship for entirely too long, Nathan decided.

It was then that a gust of prairie wind knocked the girl's bonnet askew. She slipped it from her head to straighten the gewgaws and ribbons, and Nathan's heart nearly stopped beating. Of all the women to walk in upon his preaching! No two women could boast hair in such a brilliant shade of red, and even thirty feet away he recognized the deceptively sweet-looking face now revealed in the bright glare of the sun. He could almost imagine the freckles swarming over her pert little nose and indignation compressing her soft lips.

A sense of terrible unfairness tightened Nathan's throat and dried up the flow of his words. His luck was running true to form. The interfering little harridan who had gotten him hanged in Silas was making an encore appearance just in time to make a hash of his new life.

Faces turned up to him expectantly, including hers. He waited for her cry of recognition, her shout of denunciation, but it didn't come.

"Hallelujah!" One of his little band exclaimed into the silence. "Amen!"

Nathan groped for something to say—the Ten Commandments, parting seas, burning bushes, Sodom and Gomorrah—anything biblical to throw into the silence. The girl's bonnet still swung from her hands. Her hair blazed in the sunlight. Her eyes—even from a distance he could see their green fire—met his with curiosity. No recognition lit her face.

During the fiasco in Silas, he had covered his lower face with a scarf before he'd actually confronted the girl. Had it been enough of a disguise?

The tension inside him relaxed enough to free his vocal cords. His mother's favorite psalm sprang into his mind.

"Yea though we walk through the valley of the shadow of death . . ."

And have I ever been there!

". . . we will fear no evil. Likewise, when we journey across the Great American Plains in the shadow of the great Rockies—what should we fear? We are good souls who will reap what we sow."

In which case, I'm in a shitload of trouble.

"God's angels will shelter the righteous and smite the less worthy—the red savages and other dangers that challenge the pilgrim—sickness, drought, raging rivers, and unholy evildoers of all kinds."

Except that one evildoer was going to get away without being smote, it appeared. At least for today. Because the redhead had joined the rest of the congregation in a final hymn, and her sweet oval face held not so much as a hint of suspicion.

"Hallelujah and amen!" Nathan shouted with the rest of the congregation at the end of the hymn. And he meant those words from the bottom of his heart.

• • •

"Amen," Cass whispered in accompaniment to the congregation's shout. She sagged with relief, and a bit of letdown, as the service ended and the congregation pressed forward to receive the preacher's blessing. When that man's gaze had suddenly riveted on her, Cass's breath had caught. She had wanted to look away, but she couldn't. The fellow had the most extraordinary eyes—dark and deep, black as sin even as they blazed with holy purpose. They grabbed a person's very heart and held on with steel resolve. When his words had faltered, Cass had feared that he somehow knew she and Luce were from the local brothel. He looked vaguely familiar. Had he wandered through town and seen her come or go from Lila's Place?

But no. They were safe. She had waited breathlessly through his warnings about the evils of lust, expecting any moment for him to denounce her in a very personal condemnation. But his eyes had jerked away, as if by effort, and the sermon moved to safer ground. Perhaps he'd simply been shocked that she'd taken off her bonnet in public. When she became respectable, she would have to remember that ladies with uncovered hair were considered inadequately dressed.

"Tha's what I like!" Mama Luce declared, smiling and nodding at the people in the congregation as if they were old friends. "A preachin' man who gits to the bottom of a body's soul and makes it itch with the fear of the devil."

"It was lively, all right." Cass risked a glance at the preacher as he talked to several of his congregation. He certainly didn't fit Cass's idea of a churchman. Tall and broad-shouldered, he possessed a fluid tension of posture and movement that seemed to indicate more time spent in physical pursuits than spiritual ones. His hair was glossy black, and the sunlight struck steel blue sparks from it as his head moved in emphasis of his words. The fist with which he'd pounded his Bible was big enough to serve him well in a bar fight, if he ever decided to follow the ways of sin rather than talk about them. He was certainly more entertaining than dour Reverend Tidwell. Reverend Tidwell's sermons were more effective than chamomile tea for putting a person to sleep, but no one was going to sleep through this preacher's verbal fireworks.

The preacher wandered away, in earnest conversation with several men. The rest of the congregation was dispersing as well, some remaining in little groups to talk, others heading for their wagons. Mama Luce was exchanging pleasantries with a young Negro man from the train, so Cass took the time for a curious glance about her. She had been a small child in Iowa during the time of the Great Emigration of the '50s, and she'd taken little note of the families who pulled up their Iowa roots to move west. After the death of her parents, she had listened to Lila's wistful fantasies about leaving their dreary, precarious existence behind and traveling to a land of golden opportunity, but of course Lila's wishes had been only dreams, quickly evaporated by the light of harsh reality.

As their lives grew more comfortable, Lila had quit talking about such dreams, but Cass had never quite forgotten the lure of a new start in a new land. During the war, the flood of people and wagons going west had slowed to a mere trickle, and now that peace had come, the stagecoach offered a much easier and faster means of reaching the western territories. Every day the stage from Atchison rattled through Webster on its way to Denver and Salt Lake, and coaches went to California as well. Just the year before, a woman who'd worked at Lila's Place had traveled west that way.

But there were still some travelers who chose the old way. The prairie outside Webster often hosted camps of wagons following the overland trail beside the Kansas River, on their way to the Platte River and points west. More than once Cass had cast a curious eye their way, but until today she had not ventured to visit.

The group camped outside town on this Sunday was a tightly knit little community of church folk. Twenty covered wagons and other miscellaneous carts, buckboards, and one rather fancy carriage were circled into a corral that confined the livestock. Outside the circle, cookfires burned, a few dogs nosed about the campsite, and children chased about the wagons, releasing energy pent up during the long

church service. The adults were returning to their chores,
for on a journey such as theirs, Sabbath restrictions had to
be eased to accommodate necessity. Already the sound of
hammering and the smells of cooking drifted through the
encampment.

Reminded that she had chores of her own, Cass tapped
Luce on the shoulder. "I'm going to head home, Luce."

"Don' do that, honey. Let's you and me look around
some. It ain't like we have somethin' to do back in that big
empty house."

Cass sighed. Mama Luce spoke the truth. Going back to
Lila's big, empty house suddenly didn't seem all that inviting.

"All right. Just for a bit."

They wandered through the wagon camp, curious about
the families who were undertaking such a journey. But most
of Cass's mind still brooded on the situation with her sister and the marshal.

"While you were listening to the preaching, Luce, did
some miracle fly down from heaven to smack you in the
head?"

"No, ma'am. It sure enough didn't."

"How are we going to make the marshal see reason?"

"Ol' Eddie Myers ain't gonna see reason, honey. He's
had his dander up ever since Miz Lila tol' him to keep his
fat hands off'n her. Now he's got the upper hand, he ain't
gonna give in till Miz Lila beg."

"Lila wouldn't ask Eddie Myers for a drink of water if
she were dying of thirst in the desert. By the time the circuit judge gets here in two weeks, the marshal will be so
mad that he'll have Lila doing the shooting instead of
Chalmers."

"Well now, honey, Miz Lila, she was holdin' that shotgun."

"Luce!"

"Yes, ma'am! And that ol' Judge Carter is pals with Marshal Eddie. He likely go along with whatever the marshal
say. That marshal, he a proud man. He ain't worth his weight
in goat turds, but he proud, an' Miz Lila, she prick his pride

like only a woman can. He gonna get his own back, one way or another."

"There's got to be a way out of this."

"Well, if there is, Miz Cass, you'll think of it. You always do, honey." She paused to peer into a wagon. "Hooeee! Lookit that fancy stove there. These folks is takin' the whole homestead with 'em. And there's a right pretty brass bed with a feather mattress."

"I guess when you travel by wagon, you can take all your goods with you. When Martha Tremaine went out to Denver last year on the stagecoach, she could only take what she could stuff into two big carpetbags. Not that she owned much more than that."

"You ever hear from that gal?"

"I got a letter four months ago. She likes Denver. Married a man who adores her."

"That's good. She's a good woman, that Martha."

Martha Tremaine had worked for Lila briefly when her first husband had died, leaving her destitute. She'd not taken to the work, being a virtuous woman at heart, but Lila had kept her on to help Luce in the kitchen, even though Luce didn't really need the help. Lila knew what it was to be hungry and desperate.

Lila was a good woman, too. As good-hearted and true as any woman in this town. And she didn't deserve to be stuck in a filthy jail.

The next wagon had no fancy furnishings packed inside. It was packed instead with children. They seemed to be having the time of their lives, playing chase around the big wagon wheels and shouting at the tops of their little lungs. The mother and an older daughter were kneading bread dough on a makeshift table made from boards laid across two barrels. They greeted Cass and Luce with friendly nods when they walked up.

"Morning, ladies. Would you care for a cup of coffee?"

Cass declined, but stayed a moment to talk to the women. The Campbell family, as they introduced themselves, were excited about their journey. Their community, united by religious faith and a church that had become much like an extended family, had decided to move to the Willamette Valley in Oregon Territory. The farmland there was so rich they could bring in twice the yield with half the work—or so they'd heard—and opportunity abounded for anyone with a good head and a willingness to work.

Cass and Luce exchanged pleasantries with Mrs. Campbell and her daughter and wandered on. There were twenty wagons, about twelve of those big canvas-covered rigs decked out as both moving accommodations and fortresses, and the rest supply wagons and carts of various kinds. All belonged to families of the church group. One of the wagons boasted three generations—from small children to grandparents. It had a coffin packed in with the barrels of flour and salt pork, the beds and cooking pots. The old grandmother—Mrs. Decker—confided to Cass that if she had to be buried on the trip out, she surely wasn't about to be put in the ground without a proper box to hold her earthly remains.

Cass suffered a pang of envy for them all—all these brave families who had packed up their children and belongings, their whole lives, in fact, and were on their way to a new start. A new start—what a lovely idea. No past to haunt a person, and a future built with imagination and hard work.

Most of the emigrants were willing to visit as Cass and Luce wandered by. But one wagon nearly shook with the violence of an argument going on inside. Cass turned away, not wanting to eavesdrop, but the words rang out plainly for all to hear.

"I won't go on, I tell you, Howard Crespin. I won't! I don't have the heart for it after . . . after little Howie . . ." The words trailed off into a sob. Cass guessed this was the family she'd heard about from several of the others. Two days west of Independence, their three-year-old son had fallen from the wagon and been crushed beneath the wheels. They had three older children, and the bereaved mother had taken to tying them in the wagon all day to prevent a similar tragedy—hardly the way for lively children to spend the time crossing the continent.

"I don't care what you have to do, Howard. If you leave here tomorrow with this wagon train, you leave without me and the children. Sell it all. Dump it on the prairie, for all I care. I told you from the outset that this idea was madness, but you insisted. And now it's cost me my baby."

The husband's reply was clipped and angry. "Dump it all, you say? How're we to live, then? Every cent we have went to buy the wagons and provisions. Would you have us starve, woman?"

"Sell it! I don't care! I can't face another two months, waking every morning to wonder if one of my children will fall under a wheel, or find a snake in the brush, or catch the sickness, or end up scalped and skinned by some Indian. I don't care what you do! I can't go on. I can't!"

The woman's sobs almost drowned out the husband's last words. Cass just managed to hear him grumble, "Cain't sell the outfit. Who'd buy it? Ain't like there's an army of folks wantin' to go west these days."

Who would want the Crespin outfit? Who indeed? Inspiration hit Cass like a brick. Impetuous madness. Impossible insanity. But perhaps a little lunacy was the only answer to an impossible situation.

She stared toward the western horizon, eyes shining and face suddenly bright. "Luce, I've got a plan. I've got a great, brilliant, save-the-day sort of plan."

"Hallelujah and amen!" Luce's face lit up in a wide smile. "Miz Cass's got herself a plan! Heaven save us all!"

Chapter 4

May 14, headed west along the banks of the Kansas River—

I can't believe I am here—Cassidy Rose McAllister on a wagon train headed west, just like the pioneers of twenty years ago. If someone had told me a week ago that my life would be so rearranged, I would have laughed. Not that I haven't wanted it to change, because I have, with the most intense longing. And now, here I am. I am astounded that I was able to talk Lila into this adventure, though I suppose she had little choice. It was either leave Webster permanently or endure her jail cell.

To shorten the convoluted events and endeavors of the past few days, suffice it to say I purchased a complete "outfit," as it is called, for the westward journey from an unfortunate, disheartened family that had recently lost a child to misadventure. I then persuaded Marshal Myers to relinquish my sister and her employees on the condition that they would leave not only the town, but the entire area, and be out of his hair forever. The marshal, I'm sure, would have rather kept Lila incarcerated until she could be persuaded to accept his attentions, but he must have known that she had friends in Webster who, in the short run, held their peace about her treatment, but would soon start a rumble of dissatisfaction.

So here we all are, traveling west along the banks of the Kansas River. Our outfit includes two sturdy wagons—a roomy prairie schooner and a smaller covered conveyance for supplies. We have two teams of mules, weatherproof tents for sleeping, flour, beans, bacon, saleratus, salt, salt pork, coffee (no tea, to my dismay), corn meal, dried beef, sugar, and all other necessities for keeping us comfortable on the journey, though in this modern age of stagecoach travel and conveniently spaced military establishments, resupply along the way should not be a problem. In addition, we possess a very detailed guidebook concerning the trail west published seven years ago by a Capt. Randolph Marcy.

I do regret leaving behind Lila's faithful goat, but Mrs. Oswald and her newborn would have been in terrible straits without the milk. Lila will miss the creature, though. She is a bit cranky over these changes to her life. But she will soften once she realizes what a Great Adventure this journey to a new and respectable life will be.

Mindful of the momentous nature of the Great Adventure, I have begun this journal to preserve an account of the happy transformation of our lives. Lila and I are not the only ones who have decided upon this journey toward respectability. Mama Luce is with us, of course. She has been family to us since we all were unfortunate enough to live in Madame Suzette's establishment in Missouri, so many years ago. Rachel, Steamboat Sue (though I suppose she must drop her sobriquet now that she is to be a decent woman), and Frenchie (sadly enough, I don't know Frenchie's real name. I wonder if she remembers it herself) have joined us on our endeavor. Anita also, to my surprise. She is remarkably truculent about the changes the past week have brought. She could have departed, as several of Lila's other ladies did, to find familiar em-

*ployment elsewhere, but she chose to join our little
band of adventurers. The professor, our music man
and a good friend, is also with us. He expounded that
we helpless females would need masculine assistance
on the journey, but in truth, I believe every one of us
women are more competent with the wagons and mules
than the well-meaning pianist.*

*Our journey began without fanfare—except in my
heart. I sit on the wagon box of the "big wagon," as
we call our prairie schooner. Beside me, Lila holds
the reins of the plodding mules. The air is very cool,
and the sky threatens rain, but in my soul is such
warmth. Oregon beckons. A new life awaits. All these
years since our parents died, Lila has taken care of
me, sacrificing her very honor and virtue so that we
would not go hungry. Now I am determined to make
things right again and to help my sister on the road
to a better life. It is her money that bought our outfit and is hidden away in our wagon to purchase a
house and necessities at our destination, but it is my
determination that will hold us to this path. Everyone
in our group feels the rightness of our new direction.
After two days on the trail, Sue and Frenchie still joke
and tease like schoolgirls as they ride in the shelter
of our big canvas roof. Rachel hums a tune as she
drives the supply wagon, and beside her, Anita hasn't
complained for a whole hour, which is a great improvement in her usual habit. The amiable professor
takes joy in trying out the new saddle horse he purchased for the trip.*

*All is right with my world. Even this exasperat-
ingly stumpy, boggy, mosquito-infested bottomland beside the Kansas River cannot cast a pall upon my
keen anticipation of what is to come.*

The greeting of a masculine voice broke Cassidy's con-
centration on her composition. She looked up to see the
preacher riding beside their wagon on a long-limbed, high-
stepping horse. Keeping pace with the horse was the biggest
dog Cass had ever seen.

The preacher touched his hat. "Ladies."

Cass smiled. "Good afternoon, Reverend . . . uh . . ."

"Pernell, ma'am. Homer Pernell, at your service."

Holy preacher the fellow might be, but his eyes were made of sin, Cassidy noted, not for the first time. So dark they were almost black, they possessed an intensity that made her want to squirm. Intense, and a bit wary. Perhaps it was merely the shadow of his flat-brimmed hat that made them seem to brood. Surely a holy preacher had little to brood about, unless it be his flock's sins. And from what Cass had seen so far, his flock had few sins to weigh down a conscience.

"Are you ladies coming along all right? The going these past two days has been a mite rough, what with the rain and the stream crossings."

Frenchie and Sue had peeked from around the wagon canvas to eye their visitor.

"We're doing a lot better since you stopped by," Frenchie cooed. "If I'd known they made preachers like you, Reverend, I'd have gone to services more often."

Cass gave her a quelling frown, then smiled her most ladylike, virtuous smile. "We are doing wonderfully, Reverend Pernell. Thank you for asking."

"If you need any help, we've got plenty of menfolk who would count it a blessing to lend a hand."

"I'll bet," Sue snickered, garnering a chastising look from Cass. On the wagon box beside her, Lila only smiled in amusement.

The reverend seemed inclined to keep them company for a time, despite Sue's and Frenchie's forward manners. He told them something of his flock, some who had introduced themselves in a pleasant way, but many of whom seemed reserved. He related several innocent but amusing stories of their adventures before the ladies had joined the train and expounded a bit on the local color. Sue and Frenchie continued to hang out the front of the wagon, listening to him with winsome smiles and flirtatious eyes. He seemed oblivious to their wiles, which befit a man of his calling, but Cass longed to smack them both. At the same time, she could understand their interest. With those broad shoulders and dark good looks, he was a magnet for any woman's attention. She liked his voice. It was a good preaching voice, deep, resonant, and rich. It sank into a girl's flesh and vibrated in her bones. It made her insides turn warm and liquidy and gave her chills. He could probably talk an angel into sin with that voice. But of course he would never, because he was on the side of the angels, not on the side of sin.

"We'll be up to the Frenchman's ferry tonight, and we'll cross the Kansas River there in the morning. Across from the ferry is a creek named Soldier's Creek. It's named supposedly for a troop from Fort Leavenworth that caught up to a band of whiskey smugglers there and knocked in all the whiskey barrels."

Sue groaned. "What a waste!"

The preacher grinned. "I'm sure the smugglers thought it was."

Cass reflected that the reverend had a rather worldly sense of humor for a preacher. "Have you made this trip before, sir, that you know all these things?" Cass inquired.

"No indeed." Smiling, he turned and dug a little hardcover publication from a saddlebag, holding it up for them to see. "Guidebook."

"Ah. We have one also. Though I believe by a different author."

"I'm glad to hear you have one. The fewer mysteries on the trail, the better. If you ladies need anything, just give a holler. We've all vowed to pull together to get where we're going."

He trotted off, the big dog matching pace with the horse.

"Whooee!" Sue breathed, leaning on Cassidy's shoulder to steady herself against the roll of the wagon. "Ain't he sumpthin'!"

Frenchie snickered. "Little Cassidy thinks he is. Look at the roses in her cheeks. That's not from the sun, honey, because we ain't seen the sun in two days."

"Oh piffle!" Cass felt her face grow warm, turning her cheeks an even brighter shade of revealing rose. "I haven't given the man a single thought."

Luce joined in the fun, chuckling. "Izzat why you looked

like you been bit by an angel itself when you was soakin'
in his preachin' t'other day, Miz Cass?"

"I was not! I mean, I did not! And I haven't been bit-
ten by anything."

"Lust," Sue speculated with a smile. "She's been bit by
lust."

"I most certainly have not! He was being neighborly, and
I was being polite."

"There's polite," Frenchie teased, "and then there's *polite.*"

"He's a handsome hunk of man," Sue said. "Hell, if he
wanted a piece of me, I wouldn't even charge him. I'd count
myself lucky. Isn't often a gal gets to lie down with a gent
who not only doesn't smell but has a full set of teeth. I bet
he's a good roll in the blankets. Lordy, did you see those
muscles?"

Cass was aghast. "Sue! You shouldn't talk about a
preacher like that!"

"He's a man, ain't he? They don't cut it off when a man
becomes a preacher. Though I'll admit, a lot of the preachin'
men I've laid eyes on act like they're missing a few parts."

"Now that there's enough," Mama Luce said. "It ain't
fittin' to be talking' such about the Lord's servants."

"It isn't fitting to be talking such about any man," Cass
instructed. "We're headed for new lives as decent, upstanding women, and decent, upstanding women don't discuss such things as this."

Frenchie gave Lila a wry smile. "I'd still like to see that
one upstanding, if you know what I mean."

Lila shook her head, but her mouth lifted in a droll smile.

Cigar smoke lay in a blue fog above Marshal Burris Goodman's head as he tilted his chair onto its back legs, propped
his boots on his desk, and exhaled more smoke with a sigh.
"Ain't often we get a gen-u-ine U.S. marshal through our
little town here. Could'a used a couple of you fellows a
time or two this last year. Seems every piece of trash who
can put his trigger finger to a pistol thinks us Kansas folks
is easy pickins. Some of 'em learned that this town don't
roll over belly-up to no one."

John Lawton turned from examining the wanted posters pinned to the wall and regarded Marshal Goodman with patience. The man was a dolt, who oozed small-town braggart from every pore, but Goodman was the law in this town, so he needed to both pick his brain and plant a seed in it. Someday all the brains picked and seeds planted would bear fruit. Someday. Lawton was a patient man as long as he believed that someday was an attainable goal.

"Had some trouble off and on, have you?"

"Might say that. Given some trouble of our own to a few."

"Sometimes that becomes necessary. I'm looking for a man."

"Kinda figured you was, seein' the way you were lookin' at those posters. Anyone there?"

"No. The man I'm looking for rode with Quantrill during the war. I think he's still in this area causing trouble. A couple of people have described one of your local hellraisers as looking a lot like him." Lawton pulled a dirty, creased paper from his shirt pocket, unfolded it, and handed it to Goodman. "A wanted poster I came across in Lawrence."

"Looks like a lot of fellas."

"It's not a very good likeness. His chin is more square, and his nose isn't that broad. The line of the brows is a bit straighter."

"Sounds like you know this hell-raiser pretty well."

"A lot better than I want to know him. He's a few inches over six feet. Good-looking sonofabitch that all the ladies look at twice."

"Does he ride a high-bred–lookin' blood bay stud horse that likes to kick the bejesus outta any poor cluck that gets in range?"

"Don't know what he rides."

Goodman snorted and swatted at the drawing. "Well, this looks somethin' like a fella we tried to hang a few weeks back. Good-lookin' bastard. A real hard case—you could tell just by lookin' at him."

Lawton stilled. Even his breathing paused. "You *tried* to hang him?"

"Yup. We tried. Sucker got away. Rope broke. He managed to climb aboard his horse and outrun the whole damned posse. Got to give the bastard credit. He had a good horse, and he can ride, even with his hands tied behind his back."

Lawton let out his breath. Stone had gotten away. So close. He didn't know if he was glad or sorry. Hearing about the man's death wouldn't give the same gut satisfaction as seeing it. "How long ago?"

"Well, I don't recall the exact day, but it was back in April sometime."

"Any sign of him since?"

Goodman leaned farther back and puffed his cigar. He regarded Lawton with the air of a man who holds a trump card. "Sit down, Marshal. Have a smoke. This could be your lucky day."

Lawton narrowed his eyes. "Is this man still around here?"

"You could say that. Oh, sit down, man. The Injuns did your job for you, looks like. The fella's dead. Some surveyin' man found him a couple of days after we tried to hang him. Said the spot was loaded with Injun sign. He got outta the noose just to run into the savages."

"Did the surveyor bring him in?"

"Nah. He found the grave. Had his name on it, even. We figure some of his partners must've found him and buried him. Two of the gang got away after the robbery."

"How do you know it's him in that grave?"

"No reason to think it's not. He'd got clean away. No reason for him to pull no shenanigans. Besides, those rough riders ain't the type to go in for clever tricks. They'd rather shoot than think, if you know what I mean. I ain't worryin' about it enough to dig up some stinkin' corpse, that's for sure."

The marshal pulled his feet from the desk and let the front legs of his chair thump down upon the floor, a clear signal that he'd said what he had to say on the subject. "If you want to see for yourself, old Vince Nelson can tell you how to find it. He runs cattle out there. Most likely you'll find him over at Lucille's boardin' house around suppertime."

The sun was two hours above the horizon next morning when Lawton reined his horse to a halt and looked down into a brushy hollow where a pile of stones and a crude wooden cross marked the last resting place of Nathan Stone. Or so the story went. He urged his horse down the slope, his stomach churning with more than the grim anticipation of exhuming a disintegrating corpse. If this was the end of his search, would it satisfy the burning inside his gut every time he thought of Stone? Was revenge as sweet when someone else does the job for you? Would he go back to his life with the sense that some sort of justice had prevailed?

He didn't know the answer to those questions.

Lawton stopped his mount close enough to the grave to read the name carved into the dead piece of oak that was the crosspiece of the cross. Nathan Stone, it said. Lawton regarded the mound of rocks grimly as he drew leather gloves over his hands. This wasn't a job to any man's taste, but it had to be done. He sure as hell wasn't giving up the chase until he knew for certain that Nathan Stone was rotting in his grave, where he would cause innocent folk, and especially innocent women, no more grief.

Cassidy Rose was not having a good day. The crossing of the Kansas River had gone without a hitch, although the raft had rocked and swayed in an alarming manner, and she'd thought the mules, senseless creatures that they were, were going to bolt over the side and drag them all to a watery grave. They'd kept their wits about them, though, and the second wagon carrying the extra supplies, as well as Rachel, Anita, and the professor, had crossed in equally fine shape. But scarcely an hour after the wagons were on their way again, the big wagon had broken a wheel in one of the annoying stream crossings that proved that small, trickling streams were every bit as dangerous to wagon travel as big raging rivers.

She had broken the wagon wheel. Now she sat on the tailgate of the supply wagon and fretted. She herself had broken the wheel. It had been her driving the team, not Lila, and somehow she'd gotten the wagon down the bank crooked, with too much weight on the right rear wheel, and crack! Two broken spokes and a cracked rim.

"Oh! I feel so miserably stupid! The whole train has stopped moving just because I can't drive a wagon."

"Well, honey, you don' sweet-talk those mules like Miz Lila does. Tha's for sure. But I don' see none o' them useless females you're hauling along wit' you offerin' to help, either. So I wouldn't listen to no whinin' or complainin' from that direction."

Anita smiled like a cat basking in the sun, which was exactly what she and the other women were doing, sitting on a canvas tarp with their skirts spread around them like the petals of bright flowers. "You don't hear complaints from us, you old windbag. After two days of cold and wet, I don't mind sunning myself for a few hours."

"Quit fretting like an old woman," Frenchie advised Cass. "We've got plenty of help, and they'll have us rolling again in no time."

Rachel chuckled. "Just don't come back and try to drive our wagon, Miss Clumsy."

Cass huffed out a dissatisfied snort. The broken wheel wasn't half of it. What was really tweaking her temper was her traveling companions. They were headed for clean, decent lives, or so they said. Yet here they sat, displaying themselves without hats, corsets, or ladylike inhibitions while menfolk from the entire train buzzed around their wagons like flies around honey. They'd had curious visitors from the start—mostly men. But the visits had been friendly neighborliness and introductions. At least, if the motives had been less than aboveboard, no one had done any blatant leering or drooling.

Given the excuse of the broken wheel, however, it seemed that every man under the age of seventy was camped on their doorstep, or more properly, their wagon tongue, competing for the privilege of repairing the damage and offering advice to Preacher Pernell, Ed Campbell, and the professor, who were doing most of the work. At least Mr. Pernell and Mr. Campbell were making progress. The professor, for all his effort, was more a hindrance than a help. The ladies were flirting like shameless harlots, which was, after all, the behavior they knew best. Even Lila wasn't above smiling at Charlie Morris, the trail guide and wagon boss who had come back to investigate the delay. Cass knew she wasn't really interested in the fellow. But habits years in the making couldn't be broken without serious effort, which all of them seemed eager to forget.

Rachel was the only one not making cow eyes at the group of admirers, but then, Rachel had always affected a haughty reserve, even when working the crowded parlor at Lila's Place. With her café au lait complexion and willowy figure, she possessed the kind of exotic beauty that had made quadroons and octoroons the belles of the Southern demimonde, and her aristocratic reserve merely served to make the men pant after her even more desperately.

The fish who dangled on her hook was a handsome Negro who was the hired man of one of the Shelby families. Rachel sat apart from the others on a tree stump, her silk skirts arranged about her just so, looking like a queen on a throne, and the fellow sat on his heels in front of her, hat in hand, gazing up at her with the expression of a small boy admiring a basket of candy sticks. Rachel didn't seem at all interested in her catch, however. His conversation and friendly smiles met with only minimal courtesy, and when his employer called him to help with the broken wheel, she scowled at his back as he left.

Curious, Cass left her perch on the tailgate of the supply wagon and sat down beside Rachel.

"Who was that?" she asked.

Rachel sniffed. "Name's Ben Holden. Says he's called Banjo Ben, because he can play banjo better than anyone in the whole state of Missouri."

Cass raised an admiring brow. "He's very nice looking."

"I suppose. He's a hired man, and look—his master's making him do most of the work replacing our wheel while the rest of them stand by and ogle girls."

"That man is not Mr. Holden's master. Slavery's dead."

Rachel snorted. "You just keep thinking that, baby girl. There's all kinds of slavery. I was never anybody's slave, and I'm not going to be wasting myself on someone who fetches and carries and yessirs and nosirs just so he can be spit upon when they toss a few crumbs his way."

In a surprisingly short time, the new wheel was secure and the broken one stored in the supply wagon. Ben apparently had long experience of such tasks, and with a bit of help from the preacher, who'd rolled up his sleeves and propped his broad back beneath the heavy wagon beside several of his flock, they were ready to be on their way. Ben's "master," as Rachel insisted on calling the man, clapped the tall Negro on the shoulder when the job was finished. Ben said something to the man and laughed, and the man smiled back.

"They look like friends to me," Cass said.

Rachel scoffed. "Baby girl, when it comes time for you to pick a man, you don't ever look at the underlings, you hear? You aim your eyes right at the top. Because that's where you and I deserve to be."

Cass made a face. "Would you stop calling me baby girl? I'm not a baby, you know."

Rachel smiled at her. "Baby girl," she said deliberately, "in some ways you're as old as that old oak tree over there, and in some ways you're just starting to crawl. So I'll keep calling you baby girl just to remind you to be careful."

She rose, brushed the wrinkles from her skirts, and left Cass to her own thoughts, which were a mite indignant. Just starting to crawl, indeed!

That night there was a definite chill in the air that had little to do with the clouds that had once again rolled in to threaten rain. They were camped along the bank of Cross Creek a few miles east of the little village of St. Mary's. The professor and the preacher had hitched up a pony cart to take the broken wheel to the village smith, and the rest of them did camp chores. Lila's ladies gathered around their cookfire, while the Shelby wagons shared a communal fire on the other side of camp. The circled wagons provided both a corral for the livestock and a physical barrier between the two groups. The social atmosphere had been getting cooler and cooler since Lila's group had joined the wagon train, and tonight it was downright frosty.

In Webster, when Cass had bought the wagons and filled

them with her feminine crew, the reception from the Shelby families had been reserved but polite. Once on the trail, common courtesy had prevailed, even if Lila's ladies did get more than one look askance from the brothers and sisters—especially the sisters—of the little godfearing community. Cass had hoped that exemplary behavior and the common experiences of the trail would create acceptance and even friendship, but today had dashed her hopes.

Lila's ladies simply didn't know how to talk to a man without giving a come-hither, and the brethren of the little church community, staunchly virtuous though they might be, would be going against nature itself if they didn't ride by the wagons or stroll alongside for a curious look. Their wives were gathered around their fire like so many witches mixing up a brew, casting sour glances toward the newcomers. Daughters were told not to look their way and sons were practically tied to the wagon wheels so their innocence would not be tempted by women whose virtue was in question. At least that was the picture Cass imagined from the almost palpable chill emanating from the opposite side of camp.

If only she could persuade her friends to mend their ways. Didn't they realize that becoming respectable involved more than not taking payment for their favors? If they would learn to curb their flirtatious looks and their suggestive conversation, modify their dress, their carriage and deportment, perhaps the virtuous Shelby women would welcome them as friends. Was that so much to ask?

"The devil got your goat, honey?" Luce asked. "You is lookin' sour enough to turn those nice fresh potatoes black."

Cass took a vicious swipe at the potato she was peeling. Sitting on a stool not far away, Luce mixed biscuit batter in a tin bowl. Stopping for the night didn't mean the end of work on the wagon train. On the contrary, the work was just beginning. There was water to be hauled, a fire made, supper cooked, clothes mended, harnesses cleaned and oiled, equipment repaired, and on and on. The tasks were endless and were becoming a source of complaint for the ladies, whose customary work was done lying down.

"I'm just tired," Cass replied.

"Huh! Ain't we all?"

"And I wish that the others would try harder to fit in. That's all."

"What do you mean, fit in?" Rachel queried. She had just hauled two buckets of water from the nearby creek and didn't look happy about it as she examined her hands for calluses.

"I mean that we're headed for a new life, and maybe we should leave some old habits behind—like cozying up to everything in trousers and cussing like a muleskinner to punctuate every sentence."

"I don't cuss," Rachel said.

"I do," Frenchie announced boldly. "I like to cuss. I can cuss in French, too. That really lights a man's fires."

"Lila didn't let any of you cuss during business hours at Lila's Place, so I know you can speak decently. Besides, Frenchie, you're not supposed to be lighting any more fires!" Cass reminded her.

"*I* never said that," Steamboat Sue told her. "I don't know what anybody else said, but I never said that. A girl's got to earn a living, and some of us have got no choice but to do it on our backs. If a girl's not married, doesn't sew, doesn't dance, doesn't sing, doesn't cook, and doesn't have much book-learning, what else is she to do?"

"You could learn to sew, or cook, or do ciphers."

"When did you get so holier-than-thou?" Sue asked. "You had a sister to take care of you. You were lucky."

Cass felt her face heat. Sue was right. But she was just trying to help, not sermonize. Surely everyone wanted to improve their lot.

"Yeah!" Anita agreed. "That preacher making eyes at you has you thinking you're better than us. But you listen to me, Cassidy Rose. He's got the same thing on his mind as every other man in this world, and if he has a brain in his head, he can tell that with this group he can buy the milk without taking on the cow. So don't get your hopes up, sweetie pie."

Cass bit her lip, and Anita blew her a triumphant kiss. "Don't be such a prim little prig. The business ain't so bad. Who wants to slave away sewing other people's clothes or cooking their food or waiting on prissy old ladies in a store when you can wear silk dresses and have men giving you jewelry?"

"When was the last time some man gave you jewelry?" Rachel asked contemptuously.

"Elias Trevor—"

"Oh, bullshit on Elias Trevor," Frenchie said with calm contempt. "If he ever existed at all, he had to be the world's biggest milquetoast to slobber after you like you say he did."

"He was so real! And he knew that I was more than a common harlot! You—"

"Oh, sure," Frenchie interrupted with a snicker. "That was real discerning of the gent, I'm sure."

"He was a hell of a lot more of a man than any of these stiff-backed toad-asses that were ogling us today. Every one of them would have to use starch to get it up. It would be a frigging good deed to loosen 'em up a bit if you asked me."

Mama Luce put an end to the conversation. "Them what wants to eat had better stop flappin' their mouths and start usin' 'em to make these fried potatoes and biscuits disappear. There's beans in the pot and beef and barley in the stew pot. And save some for the professor to come back to. If'n that man don't start fillin' out that skinny frame of his, he's just gonna plumb disappear." She darted a sly glance at Cass. "And mebbe that good-looking preacher man might be hungry, too. Ain't no reason for him to miss his supper just 'cause he hauled our broke wheel in to be fixed, is there?"

Preacher Pernell took Luce up on her invitation to supper when he and the professor got back from St. Mary's with the repaired wheel. At least around the preacher, the ladies tried somewhat to behave. No one wanted to flaunt sinfulness in front of a man who might possibly have a direct pipeline to God. Once he left for his own wagon, however, the comments that flew around the cookfire were graphic enough to bring a blush to Cass's cheeks. There was no doubt that the ladies admired him greatly, in a purely physical sense. Frenchie and Anita weren't quite sure that a preaching man, someone who regularly decried lust and fornication, could be truly talented in a carnal sense.

Anita gave Cass a sly look. "We could take bets. Then Cassie should give him a try and report back. I'd do the job, but he seems to have eyes for her. I can't imagine why."

"Because she looks like she has some class," Frenchie sniped.

"Well, if he wants class, that would leave you out, wouldn't it?"

Lila intervened before the fur started to fly. "Anita, button your mouth. You too, Frenchie. And you ladies quit teasing Cass. I swear, with all the caterwauling around our fire, our godfearing friends over there are going to think we're Indians on the warpath. Let's get these pots washed and turn in. The mornings around here always come earlier than we want them to."

Later, in the tent that Lila and Cass shared, Lila said a few words of caution to Cass as they climbed into their blankets. "You're expecting too much of the girls, Cassidy Rose. They said they wanted to get out of Webster. They never said they wanted to start singing hymns and starching corsets."

"Can't they see that this is their chance to lead a new life?"

"Not everyone wants a new life, Cassidy."

"You do. Don't you?"

Lila reached out and patted her hand. "I promised, and I meant it, baby sister."

With the lantern doused, the darkness in the tent seemed absolute. Cass battled the feeling of desolate aloneness, despite her sister's softly breathing presence just inches away. Preacher Pernell's face swam into her mind's eye. Sometimes, when he was looking off into the distance, his expression set into lines that made him look hard as nails—contemplating the sins of the world, no doubt. Those arresting black eyes could put the fear of God into almost anyone. But his smile—well, his smile seemed to belong to a different man. It wasn't fearsome at all, but slow and lazy, sometimes crooked, and made her heart warm with the notion that it was purely for her. Of course it wasn't. The ladies were just teasing when they suggested he had eyes for her. He was a preacher, after all. And the tingly sensation she got in the hollow of her stomach when she saw him was only because he brought to mind righteousness and redemption and all the other holy subjects preachers spoke about.

She was sure that was all it was.

The blaze of an idea lit her mind. If Preacher Pernell inspired her with the righteous fear of God, he could do the same for Lila's ladies. All she had to do was convince him to speak with them, to perhaps make them a project.

First thing the next morning, she vowed, she would seek the man out. She would explain the situation and enlist his aid. Together they would bring her friends to see the light. Together.

Finally she drifted off to sleep, and she was smiling.

Chapter 5

Dawn never caught the little group of emigrants sleeping, for there was much to do before the day's journey began. Cass wasn't accustomed to rising early. Lila's Place had always jumped with activity late into the night, and breakfast for the residents had seldom been served before noon. Since Cass had scheduled her life around the needs of Lila's business, she and the morning sun had been strangers before the start of the great adventure.

As she made her way along the circle of wagons and carts in the predawn light, Cass decided that this early hour might become her favorite time of day. Just above the eastern horizon, a line of clouds glowed brilliant orange to herald the still hidden sun. On the grass beneath her feet, dewdrops garnished every blade, and in the trees that marched along the creek, birds tuned up for the morning symphony. The world was new and fresh, infecting all creatures with the longing for a similar rebirth.

At least, that was how it affected Cassidy Rose McAllister, and she was sure that the rest of her group would soon feel a similar influence. But just to make sure they didn't get the lot of them banished in the meantime, she meant to act upon her vow to solicit the help of Preacher Pernell.

The preacher's wagon wasn't hard to find. It was the one that had the finest horse in the whole company tethered to the tailgate and munching oats from a feedbag. Strange that a preaching man should have such a fine animal. Weren't men of God supposed to be humble in their possessions as in all other things? Preacher Pernell didn't strike Cass as being particularly humble about anything. In truth, he was the most unpreacher-like preacher she'd ever seen. He moved like a predator, not a peacemaker. And his eyes were downright unholy. In a moment of uncertainty, Cass wondered if those eyes struck her with the fear of God—or did they infect her with something much more down-to-earth? Was her motive for seeking him out really to help her friends, or was she making an excuse to see him alone? Could she trust him with the truth about their little group?

She stopped in the concealing shadow of a wagon, undecided. Before she could drum up her courage, the preacher's dog ambled out of the wagon and showed all his teeth in a yawn. Behind him, yawning just as hugely, came the preacher himself.

She froze, paralyzed, and stared. The man was half naked. Ragged towel draped around his neck, he went to the side of his wagon, propped a small mirror against the canvas top, and commenced to shave. Cassidy's breath stopped at every sensuous stroke of the straight razor down his cheeks and up his throat. The interplay of supple muscle in his arms, shoulders, and chest made her heart constrict. Then he went to a bucket of water, dunked his head, and came up dripping rivulets that poured from his hair, onto his broad shoulders, and down his naked chest to pool in his navel and send liquid fingers into the forbidden territory past his waistband. Cass shivered with a sensation that was cold and hot at the same time.

She was not spying, Cass assured herself. Not at all. But she couldn't possibly call attention to herself now, for the preacher's sake. No respectable man would want to be seen in such a state—nearly naked and looking like a savage that had jumped from the pages of some lurid five-cent novel. If Cass came forward now, he would no doubt be mortally embarrassed.

And he should be embarrassed. It just wasn't right that a man who went about preaching morality and righteousness should look like the devil's own version of Adam.

The crack of a twig behind her made Cass jump. She whirled to discover a grinning young Amos Byrd approaching. A six-foot beanpole at sixteen, Amos had straw-colored hair that stood up in at least eight different directions when it wasn't smashed beneath his hat, which he promptly snatched from his head. Amos had frequently appeared at Lila's wagons in the last few days, ambling by in a manner both respectful and awestruck.

"Hey, Miss McAllister! Isn't it a great—"

Cass shushed him with a firm hiss, but it was too late. Preacher Pernell turned and saw her standing there. Her face caught fire, and her tongue twisted into a mute knot. His mouth lifted in a half smile that looked not offended at all, merely amused. Mortified, Cass turned and fled, feeling every bit the nincompoop. So much for inspiring Lila's ladies to reform. She should start acting like a decent woman herself before looking to others' behavior, she scolded herself.

She had almost reached the refuge of her own wagon when a shriek cut through the peace of the morning. It was followed by a second, and a third, rising in volume until the heart-stopping sound finally ended. The silent aftermath was heavy with menace.

For a moment the whole camp seemed to hold its communal breath, then chaos erupted. Men reached for weapons while women fluttered about like agitated hens, flocking into little knots to reassure each other and speculate.

Cass didn't need to speculate, because that scream had been hauntingly familiar. Distant though it had been, it had a strident volume she knew only too well.

Before she could run to her wagon and confirm her fears, she was grabbed from behind. Letting out a shriek herself, she twisted to defend herself, but it was only the preacher. Still shirtless and damp, his fingers closed spasmodically on her arm.

"That wasn't you," he said in a relieved voice.

"The screaming? No! Of course not." She extricated herself from his grip, rubbing her arm. Her nerves jangled alarmingly at his touch.

"Sorry. You took off like a rabbit, and I was afraid you'd taken off for the woods instead of the wagons."

Steamboat Sue hurried out from between the wagons. "Cass! Oh, lord! We couldn't find you, and we thought that caterwauling was— Oh, howdy, Reverend." She cocked a knowing brow. "Now I know where you were."

"I wasn't—"

Sue waved her defense aside. "We can't find Anita, either. You go that way, and I'll go this way."

Rachel joined the group. "Don't even bother looking, because the ninny's not in camp. Luce told her to light the cook fire, so she huffed off for a stroll. Said she wasn't hauling wood for no black woman."

"Everyone was warned to stay close to the wagons," the preacher said. "This country's not as peaceful as it looks."

Rachel shrugged. "That's Anita. She doesn't let warnings cramp her style."

The search party was gone for half an hour. In their absence, Jed Jacobs, Aaron Sutter, and Clyde Dawkins, who stayed to protect the women, hurried everyone into breaking camp and hitching the teams.

"Just in case we need to move fast," Jed told them. "The Lord favors those who keep themselves prepared."

Lila's group was glum. Lila snapped at Frenchie for letting Anita go off alone, and Frenchie snapped right back with the opinion that she wasn't Anita's keeper. Luce moaned that she had a bad feeling because the sun was coming up as red as blood, and Rachel warned her to keep her superstitions to herself. Cass tried to calm the churned emotions by suggesting they stop blaming each other and change the subject until they knew for sure what had happened. Frenchie promptly cooperated.

"Just what were you doing with that manly hunk of a preacher before the sun was up, Cassidy Rose? Besides getting an eyeful of all that naked skin?"

Everyone stopped what they were doing and stared. Even the two mules that Sue was leading to the hitch gave Cass quizzical looks.

"Yes, missy?" Lila inquired in a big-sister voice she rarely used. "You were doing what with Reverend Pernell?"

"Nothing! We were talking is all!"

Luce sniffed. "That kinda talk lead to trouble, if'n you ask ol' Mama Luce. You watch out you don't let yore brains turn to mush like some others I could name."

"Oh, leave her alone," Sue urged the rest of them. "Let her have some fun."

"We were not having fun," Cass denied.

"None of us are having fun," Rachel agreed.

The attempt at conversation died a jittery death. The other women of the train kept their distance, though a few sympathetic glances came their way. The only one who actually bothered to express her concern was Granny Decker, who was traveling with her son and daughter-in-law and a pine coffin, just in case she didn't last the journey west.

"If the gal's alive," Granny said, "the men'll find her. That guide we hired—Charlie Norris—claims he's a gen-u-ine mountain man, so it stands to reason he can track down one little girl. If she's alive, they'll find her, and if she's not alive, then she's safe with God. No use frettin' yourselves sick."

"We appreciate your prayers," Lila told her.

Cass had formed no great opinion of Mr. Charlie Norris in the short time they'd been with the train. The man had so far been content to amble along on his horse and sip from his bottle of "medicinal" whiskey, letting the men of the wagon train figure out the stream crossings and camp procedures. Neither did she think most of the men of the train knew much beyond farming and praying. Never one who enjoyed the passive role, she chafed to search for Anita herself. The minutes dragged by. The women waited, tasks completed, beside the wagons. The mules stomped and fidgeted in their traces. Children whined, fretful from the tense atmosphere but not understanding it. Cass stared up the tree-shrouded course of Cross Creek and wondered if anyone else remembered Anita's comments about the benefits of fresh spring water on the complexion. Were there springs along Cross Creek? Had the girl gone looking for them and perhaps fallen in? Perhaps right at that moment she was drenched and shivering, sitting on a muddy bank with a broken ankle. Surely she should catch up with the search party and tell them to look along the stream.

"Don't you do it, girl."

Granny Decker had come up beside her. Bent and white-haired, she was still bright-eyed.

"Do what?"

"Do what you're thinking about doing. I can see it sticking at you like a burr on a woolen sock. They'll find your friend just to turn around and start looking for you."

Cass deflated. "You're right."

"It's a burdensome thing to learn, my girl. Doing—that's what men are for. Waiting—that's what women are for. It's the harder lot, and that's why God gave it to the stronger sex."

Cass took the old woman's hand. Her skin felt like tissue paper, but the warmth of the contact gave comfort. "Thank you, ma'am. You're a wise woman."

"When you're this old, you'll be wise too," Granny said with a smile. She returned Cassidy's hand squeeze. "It doesn't make being old worth it, but it's something."

"They're coming!" someone shouted.

Cass's hopes soared, then plummeted when she saw the looks on the faces of those who came. Matthew Brown, who'd left on horseback, now led his horse, and over the saddle was draped a limp body. Injured? Dead?

Lila gripped Cass's arm. "Oh, no. No."

The professor broke away from the returning group to try to keep the women back, but Cass was having none of it. She brushed past him, then froze as the blood seemed to drain from her entire body. She opened her mouth to say Anita's name, but no sound came out.

The other women stared but had the sense to hang back, where details were not visible. There was no friendly arm to lend Cass support as she came face-to-face with a savagery that was beyond her comprehension until now. The world swayed beneath her feet as mortal chill gripped her very spirit. Before she could resist she was on her knees in the grass, spewing bile onto the dew-soaked ground.

When everything but the gasping was over, someone

handed her a handkerchief to wipe her face. It was the
preacher. She took it mutely, not trusting herself to speak.

"It's not as bad as it looks," he said softly. "She died
before she was . . . was . . ."

"Mutilated," she croaked.

"Yes."

"How do you know?"

"An arrow to the heart doesn't leave you alive. We would
have heard much more than a couple of screams if she'd
been aware when they—"

"Don't say it. Please."

He was silent. People were looking at them curiously,
Cass noted, but she didn't care.

"I don't believe she's dead. Just last night she was . . .
laughing, and complaining that her skin was . . . was drying
out because of the wind, and . . . and . . . It just doesn't seem
possible that she's dead. It's not fair."

"It's never fair," he told her.

Nathan Stone's properly solemn mien was no pretense as
he conducted the brief service over Anita's grave. But he
felt more a fake than he had since he'd first presented himself to his little flock back in Shelby, Missouri. Preaching
was one thing. He could preach up a storm, and no one was
hurt by him being in league with the devil instead of the
angels.

But planting the dead was serious business. He hoped
his being a fake preacher didn't send the poor woman's soul
to the wrong place. How did he know what verses to read
over the body of a dead whore? Or what words to say. Not
that any of the group of silk-clad, colorful "ladies" had admitted to the oldest profession, but Nathan had trafficked
with whores enough times to recognize one when he saw
one. If Lila McAllister and her little group were decent
women traveling west to meet husbands and fathers—which
was the lame tale Cassidy McAllister had spun for Jed Jacobs, then Nathan Stone was the pope.

But being a fancy lady didn't mean flashy Anita Barbour
wasn't entitled to a proper burying. And it didn't mean her

friends weren't entitled to the comfort of seeing her sent off with the right words.

"I shall lift up mine eyes unto the hills
Whence cometh my help.
My help cometh from the Lord . . ."

One of his mother's favorite psalms. Dalia Sutherland Stone had been a generous and tolerant woman. She wouldn't have been insulted to know that Nathan dredged up the memory of her beloved verses to read over the body of a dead harlot. Or so he hoped.

The group of travelers stood in glum silence as he read.

"The sun shall not smite thee by day
Nor the moon by night . . ."

The sun and the moon, sure. But look out for the Indians. Death always shocked, especially if that death presaged danger for others. They'd known that Indians were out there. The last few years had seen Indian tempers running high, and men and women had died because of it. Indians had died also. Massacre was a sport all races played at.

Anita's death made realities all too clear, even to brash Cassidy McAllister. She stood listening to him, pale and still, holding her sister's hand on one side and that of the old Negro woman on the other. Nathan found it odd to see so much of the boldness leave her. He remembered how she'd fought during the robbery. Stubborn, strong-willed, foolishly fearless. She'd brought them all down, Nathan included. And now she brazenly marched her little band of soiled doves into the midst of a straitlaced troop of church-goers, heedless of both the dangers of the trail and the pos-sibility that she and her tarnished friends would be spit out like so many watermelon seeds.

None of this had daunted Miss Cassidy Rose McAllis-ter, but death stripped her of her bold confidence and left her subdued and quiet, as vulnerable as any other woman. Oddly enough, it made Nathan sad to see it.

Few lingered at the grave when the service was over.

Granny Decker offered heartfelt condolences, and a few other women did as well. Eliza Jacobs, for all practical purposes queen of the little church community, said a stiff word or two of regret. Effie Brown gave Lila's hand a sympathetic squeeze, and her husband, Matthew, hat doffed and head bowed, apologized to the ladies as if he were personally responsible for having found Anita in the state they had. Young Amos Byrd also stammered regrets. The boy seemed to have aged ten years in a mere hour. The sight of death did that to youth, Nathan remembered. He'd been older when it happened, and there had been a hell of a lot more than just one death. But the principle was the same.

Charlie Morris didn't allow them much time for mourning the dead. He rode the circle of wagons, shouting, "Move 'em out, people. There's probably Injuns watching us right now. Let's get crackin'."

As the others left to go to their wagons, Cass approached Nathan with a rather diffident air. "Mr. Pernell, thank you for reading such a nice service. Anita would have liked the words you read. I hope she heard them from . . . from someplace nice."

The wagons were moving out, breaking from the circle in a line that headed west, like a huge snake uncoiling in slow motion. Cass paid no mind. She shifted her weight uneasily from foot to foot, staring at the ground. Then her jaw squared. She raised her gaze and looked him in the eye. "Do you believe in heaven, Preacher Pernell?"

"Uh . . . of course I do." Hoped for a heaven, at least, Nathan added silently.

"And hell?"

He sighed. "Sometimes I wonder if hell isn't right here on earth."

She looked up abruptly. "You're not like any other preacher I've ever known. You're not self-righteous and holier-than-thou like so many. I admire that."

Damned right he wasn't like any preacher she'd known, Nathan thought wryly.

"That's why I feel as if I can tell you the truth. The Bible says the truth will set us free, and I'm hoping the truth will let you see your way clear to being even kinder. The truth is . . ." She hesitated as chagrin stained her cheeks.

Nathan already had a good idea of what the truth was concerning the McAllister group, but he let her search for the right words.

"Let's walk," he suggested, taking her arm. "Young Amos is driving my wagon, but we don't want to be left out here alone."

They moved along with the wagons, which now were strung into a straight column pulling steadily along the muddy trail. There were no stragglers today, and no complaints about the brisk pace set by the Jacobs' wagon in the lead. Everyone was more than willing to leave Cross Creek behind.

Cass sighed. "Do regular preachers have to keep confessions secret like Catholic priests do?"

"Regular preachers don't take confession, but I certainly wouldn't reveal anything told in confidence."

That earned him a fleeting smile, but she instantly grew serious again. "I would appreciate you keeping this conversation to yourself, then. I'm sure you'll understand when you've heard what I have to say." She bit her lip. "The truth is . . . well, the truth is that we're not quite what I told Mr. Jacobs we are. My sister, Lila, who is the best-hearted, most honest woman alive, ran a brothel in Webster. Mama Luce was our cook. The rest of the ladies were in . . . uh . . . Lila's employ. All of us are heading west to start new, clean lives. We're going to be as respectable as Sunday school teachers."

"Well, I'm sure that's commendable." Ironic, Nathan thought, that the little reformed tart was talking to probably the one person on the wagon train who could understand the difficulty of changing one's life, and she didn't know it.

"The trouble is, that a couple of the ladies still cling to the old ways, if you know what I mean. It's hard for them, because they've never known anything else. And they just laugh at me when I try to talk to them about being modest and respectable, minding their language and not flirting with the men. I thought . . . you being a preacher . . ." She looked up at him with those jewel green eyes, and Nathan found himself thinking very unpreacher-like thoughts. Cass's friends weren't the only ones having trouble breaking wicked habits. What a shame that the feisty little red-haired siren was determined to reform.

The minute the thought entered Nathan's mind he regretted it. Everyone deserved a second chance. She did. Her friends did. He did. Cass McAllister deserved something more than a wanted gunman sniffing after her like a randy hound. She wanted and expected him to be an upstanding holy man. Another irony.

"You want me to talk to them?"

"You're very good at preaching up hellfire and damnation."

He smiled wryly. "My specialty. I've had more experience with hellfire and damnation than some."

"It would certainly be a kindness on your part."

The spring was coming back into her step and the lilt to her voice. Nathan wanted to reach out and touch her, for, in spite of her confessed profession, she was fresh and alive, and the brightness of her eyes was simply a window to the brightness of her whole person. How did a woman lead the life she had and retain that sparkle?

"You can see why I'm concerned. I don't think some of the rest of the train would be as understanding about past sins as you seem to be."

"You're probably right about that. I'll do what I can, Miss Cassidy."

"I thought you were an open-minded, understanding man. When I heard you read those beautiful words over poor Anita, I was positive. I didn't want her to be sent on her way under false pretenses."

"Miss McAllister, you don't need to worry about me spilling the beans on you and your friends. I'm a big believer in second chances."

She smiled, and the sordid shadows of the morning seemed to dissolve. "You can call me Cass if you like. All my friends do."

"And you can call me—uh, Homer."

"Such a good, solid name," she said. "Homer."

The train plodded on, everyone subdued by the new awareness of the Indian threat. Conversation was quiet. Mothers kept their children close to the wagons instead of letting them run to and fro as usual. Men kept a wary eye on the passing landscape, paying particular attention to trees and brush that might hide attackers. Suddenly the journey west was more than just an arduous trek to a new land. It was a pilgrimage that could end in death for any one of them. Anita might not have been all that she should have been, but she'd been young and vital. If her life could be snuffed out by such an innocent bit of foolishness as wandering too far from the wagons, then any of them were vulnerable.

They rolled through the little village of St. Mary's, past its smithy and its log-cabin Catholic mission. There Nathan saw Cassidy and her sister, Lila, duck into the old church. No doubt they would solicit a candle or two to be lit for Anita's soul.

"Wise of them to hedge their bets," he commented wryly to Dog, who ambled along beside Tiger.

Dog didn't voice an opinion. And that, Nathan reminded himself, was the great advantage in having a faithful dog beside you rather than a woman.

The village was well behind them when Jed Jacobs rode up on his shaggy sorrel to ride beside Nathan. "That was a right proper service you read this morning for the girl," the patriarch began. Nathan had learned that Jed Jacobs seldom stopped without delivering a sermon. He generally continued talking whether or not he had anything to say.

Today was no exception.

"Yessir. A right proper sermon. A shame that she was so foolish, but it'll serve as warning to the rest of the group. We won't see any wandering or straggling from here on out, I'm thinking. I thank God that it wasn't one of our community that met with such an end. This may have been God's warning to us."

"I think it was more likely the Indians' warning to us," Nathan said.

Jed nodded gravely. "That too. I wonder, Brother Pernell, if we have been wise in permitting that wagon of women to join our party. I may have committed an error of judgment. The younger Miss McAllister, when she first presented herself to me, seemed a decent young woman. But now I have grave suspicions that the virtue of the women in her group is not all it should be."

"Really?" Nathan commented innocently. If there was any question at all in old Jed's mind about the nature of those women, then he'd had his nose in the Bible entirely too long.

"Yes, and I'm sorry to say it. I should have known better, for women alone can be depended upon to fall prey to the devil. Their spiritual fiber is fragile, which of course is why God set men to rule over them. When women stray, they are dangerous to devout, godfearing men, just as Eve was a danger to Adam. And now I fear I have opened the door to just such women. I'm sure it would be a good thing for you to devote your next few sermons to the dangers of temptations of the flesh, for I've seen the glances some of our brethren have cast upon those daughters of Eve."

"Perhaps I'll have a talk with the women," Nathan volunteered.

"You are a generous man," Jed noted, giving Nathan a suspicious look. He wasn't quite as naive as Nathan had thought. "Just bear in mind, Brother Pernell, that the flesh of all men is weak, and being a preacher obligates you to even higher standards of conduct."

"We all do our humble best," Nathan said piously. As the patriarch rode off, he gave in to a wicked smile. "I ought to be on the stage, Dog. What do you think?"

Dog didn't comment. He was much easier to talk to than Jed Jacobs and a good deal less judgmental—the perfect confessor.

"That Cassidy Rose is a peach," he told Dog. "If I weren't such a holy man, I might have my head turned by that one."

Dog whined.

"You're right. That's just plain crazy." Nathan was in no position to be thinking of a woman. Any woman. Much less a redhead with a temper and a damned dubious history. Cass McAllister was a woman who got under a man's skin. She was dangerous, because she made a man want something more than just a night's entertainment. Nathan had never before thought of a woman in such a light, and now was a damned awkward time to start. Or was it? He was a new man, a man with a future. Didn't he have a right to want what every other man wanted?

Dog gave him a look.

"Well why not?" Nathan demanded of the animal.

Was it so crazy? From here on out, he intended to be as straight as an arrow. There was no reason he couldn't offer a woman a home. It might even be a good idea. A preacher with a wife and family was as far removed from a wanted Kansas outlaw as he could get. No one would have to know about his past.

It didn't hurt to think about it, Nathan decided.

The train stopped that evening well before dark and circled the wagons more tightly than ever before, not only to make sure the stock didn't wander, but to provide themselves with a barrier of defense in case they should need it. The tents and cook fires, as usual, were outside the circle, though there was some discussion about everyone sleeping in their wagons for safety. Charlie Morris scoffed at the danger, however.

"Those redskins ain't gonna attack the full train," he assured them, then spat tobacco into a clump of grass. "Jest like wolves, they pick off the stragglers. So if'n you want to keep your hair, don't wander off."

The tents went up and cook fires were lit. As she helped Luce with supper, Cass hoped that Charlie Morris was right.

"Miz Cass, if'n you keep beatin' that biscuit dough like that, it's gonna cook up like shoe leather. Give me that spoon, gal."

"Sorry. I wasn't paying attention."

"We all got bad feelin's 'bout what happened today, but you don't have to take it out on my good biscuits."

"Good biscuits my ass," Frenchie jeered. "They've tasted like ash for the last two days."

"That's true enough," Rachel agreed. "And the beans don't just taste like ashes, you can pick the ash out of your teeth after eating."

"I don't want to hear any complaints from you lazy

layabout hussies. I didn't hire on to cook over no open fire. I'm used to a modern woodstove and proper oven. If any one of you gals don't like ashes in your beans, well then, you can take over the cookin'."

"Give it a rest, everyone," Lila said mildly. "We're all a bit jumpy tonight. And we aren't the only ones. Look at that."

Cass followed Lila's pointing finger to where the men of the train were congregating a short distance away, all carrying rifles, shotguns, or pistols.

"Well, now," the professor said. "It looks like a bit of target practice is about to commence. I think I'll join them."

Frenchie chuckled as he left. "Like he knows one end of that pistol from the other end. He should stick to pianos."

"That's what practice is for," Cass reminded her.

"Exactly," Lila agreed. She dug a Winchester from a chest in the back of the wagon, which had come equipped with enough firepower to rout the entire Sioux nation, at least to Cass's way of thinking.

Cass flinched as her sister tossed her a pistol.

"Come on, baby sister. It won't hurt you to learn how to defend yourself."

Handling the gun gingerly, Cass grimaced. "I suppose not."

Frenchie followed to watch, but the other ladies stayed at the fire. Rachel refused to consider "becoming a gunslinger." It was unladylike. Steamboat Sue bragged that she could already shoot the eye from a squirrel at fifty paces, and Luce just waved them away and shook her head.

As they passed the big community cook fire, Cass attempted a few friendly words to the women there. "Aren't you ladies coming to the target practice?"

Granny Decker gave her a friendly smile. "Not me, dear. I can't hardly see the side of a barn with these old eyes, much less shoot at one and hit it."

Effie Brown also smiled, but shook her head. Eliza Jacobs gave Cass a disapproving look. "It's not a woman's place to be fooling with firearms. Decent women leave such things to men."

Frenchie snickered. "When those Injuns come riding in, ask them if it makes a difference if you're a decent woman, missus."

Eliza huffed indignantly. Cass and Lila grabbed Frenchie's arms and pulled her after them.

"Just couldn't resist, could you?" Cass reproved.

Frenchie and Lila both laughed. "I don't think the old battle-ax needs a gun to defend herself," Lila commented. "That scowl of hers could give any man a heart attack."

The men of the train gave the women surprised looks when they joined them, but the looks turned to respect when Lila proved she could hit the targets—an assortment of bottles and a couple of flour sacks cut into squares—better than most of the men there. That wasn't saying much, however, because many of the men might have made Granny look like a sharpshooter. Preacher Pernell wasn't any better than the rest of them, Cass noted with amusement. But then, one didn't expect a man of God to be adept with weapons of war. The professor put slugs everywhere but the target, but Cass figured she had little room to criticize, because the first time she fired the .44 Lila had given her, she nearly landed on her behind from the recoil.

Finally, when it was nearly too dark to see, Charlie Morris called a halt to the practice. "I ain't never seen a worse group of greenhorns," he complained. "We're gonna do this every damned day until at least some of you can hit a target. If'n the Injuns are watchin' this, they're probably laughing themselves silly. They'll figure they can waltz in here whenever they want to lift a few scalps and we'll be shootin' each other when we aim at them. It's downright disgustin'!"

"He's got a point there," Lila said as they started away from the group. "You keep that gun with you, Cass. And learn to use it."

"I'll keep it in the back of the wagon."

Lila scowled, and Cass gave her a look. "I'll know where it is that way."

"Keep it loaded."

"It might go off. I'll remember where the bullets are."

Lila heaved an exaggerated sigh. "We'll talk later about

this. What is Rachel doing with that bucket? I told her we didn't have water to waste like that."

Lila hurried on ahead, and Cass let her go, glad to have just a moment to herself. In fact, she was rather hoping that the preacher might be walking the same direction, and maybe he just might catch up to her. She turned about to see that several men had stayed behind to gather up the targets, most of which hadn't been in any great danger of being shot up. Preacher Pernell was one of them.

She lingered, telling herself that she was merely enjoying the night air. But she kept her eye on the little group. Two of the men left. The preacher followed. But not before he'd taken his pistol from its holster and rubbed a cloth down the barrel. Something about the simple task piqued Cass's curiosity. He sighted down the barrel and wiped it again. Then he twirled the pistol on his finger and settled it neatly in its holster.

A very curious talent, Cass thought, for a man who couldn't hit a fat cow at ten paces.

Chapter 6

Sunday had become a blessed day for Cass, not for any religious observance on her part, but because the Shelby people had declared that Sundays would be spent in camp, a day of worship and rest. The rest part was mostly symbolic, because everybody had a load of work to keep them busy—washing and mending clothes, baking bread for the coming week, mending harnesses, repairing wagons, doctoring livestock, and on and on in an endless list. Still, a day spent without eating dust, slogging through mud, jostling on a wagon box, or trudging beside the mules was a respite to be treasured.

On the ladies' second Sunday with the wagon train, Cass sat in the warm sunshine beside her tent and sewed. The dress goods she'd packed were coming in handy as yet another part of her plan to prod her companions along the road to a decent life.

"You're very busy," Lila remarked as she sat down on the grass beside her. "What are you making?"

Cass grinned impishly. "Bloomer costumes."

"Lord help us!"

"I'm making them for everybody. It's a very practical mode of dress, Lila. It preserves a woman's modesty, but she gains much more freedom of movement, not to mention comfort. And this fabric is very durable. These costumes could last the entire trip if we're careful."

"I'm sure they'll last the entire trip, because no one but you will wear the blessed things." She chuckled. "I'm too old to wear ruffly trousers under a skirt that barely comes to my ankles."

"Old, piffle! You're barely thirty. Besides, you'll like it," Cass insisted stubbornly. "Some bloomer costumes have skirts just past the knees, but I decided that would just be a spectacle, certainly not what we want."

"Oh no, of course not."

Lila's mock seriousness elicited a sideways look from Cass.

"Don't give me the eye, baby sister. And don't get your hopes up. Bloomers may be practical, but practicality isn't something our girls are used to considering, especially where dress is concerned."

"But what they're wearing is entirely inappropriate, Lila. The cut of Rachel's bodices are impractical for hard physical work. Frenchie's lace is so worn that it's about to come to pieces. And Sue isn't much better. Even you, Lila. That silk is all the latest fashion back East. I should know, because I made it for you. But do you really think something that flashy is suitable for a journey like this?"

Lila fondly fingered the silk material of her skirt. "I haven't been concerned with suitable for a long time, Cassie."

"Well," Cass said brightly. "Now is the time to begin, isn't it? We must all have suitability as our first concern. No more causing trouble with low-cut bodices. Poor Matthew Brown nearly ran his horse into a tree yesterday when Rachel bent over to get water from the stream. And no more tripping over long voluminous skirts. Sue twisted her ankle this morning doing just that, which means she'll be stuck riding in the wagon for a week."

Mama Luce clumped up to them, hands on her hips and a scowl turning her face blacker than it already was. "One of you better git over here, Miz Lila, Miz Cass, or we gonna have a catfight with hissin' and spittin' to call up the devil hisself. An' on a Sunday, too, after that nice preacher man

give his sermon about peace and ever'body lovin' ever'-
body even if they are a pain in the behind. You all better
git over here."

"What now?" Lila sighed as she and Cass both got up.

They found the "cats"—Rachel and Frenchie—arguing
over an empty water bucket. "I filled the blasted things yesterday," Rachel complained to Lila. "It's Frenchie's turn,
but she's too busy sitting in the shade to do a lick of useful work."

Frenchie rolled her eyes. "Oh, sure. This morning I've
mended two goddamned harnesses—one of which, by the
way, was covered in muleshit because Miss High and Mighty
here left it lying in a heap last night after unhitching. If she
didn't wash every goddamned inch of herself every goddamned day, then we wouldn't need to haul half the water
that we do. Would someone tell her this is a wagon train
and not some fancy Louisiana parlor, or wherever it was
that she brags about living."

"Would you two settle down?" Cass chided. "You need
every ounce of your energy, so why are you wasting it spitting at each other?"

Rachel and Frenchie eyed each other in sullen silence.

Cass huffed out a frustrated sigh. "Frenchie, I'll help you
fill the casks. And Rachel, if you must take a complete bath
every day, please do it in the creeks. Lord knows we have
to slog across enough of them. Just stay close and make
sure you have a gun with you." She grabbed a bucket in
one hand and Frenchie in the other and headed toward the
creek.

"Take your pistol," Lila reminded her.

Cass grimaced. "It's not loaded."

"Then take the Winchester."

Frenchie grabbed the rifle. "I'll take it. It's no wonder
Cass is afraid to load her pistol. Every time she practices
she's as likely to blow her own boots off as hit anything
useful."

Sue came strolling up and grinned at them. Sotto voce
she teased: "Typical virgin. She's afraid if she touches it,
it'll go off."

Frenchie and Rachel laughed while Lila scowled and

Cass turned red. She stuck out a pugnacious chin, though, and got her revenge. "As long as you're here, Sue, you can grab the other bucket and carry water."

Sue groaned.

The luster had definitely worn off the adventure of going west.

The reluctant water-bearers walked toward the creek, Lila headed for her tent, and Rachel went back to her tatting, which Frenchie had interrupted with her tirade about the empty water casks. Rachel's mother, Genevieve, had believed that such fine handwork was a talent that marked a woman as a lady. That was back in the days when her mother was mistress to a wealthy planter in Louisiana, and they could afford to spend time on such ladylike pursuits. They hadn't lived at his plantation, of course, but they had stayed in a very nice house in New Orleans, where Genevieve had trained Rachel in manners, dancing, social conversation, fashion, and other necessities of making her way in a world where success was measured in gaining a wealthy protector rather than a husband.

Times had changed drastically. Rachel's mother had died birthing a stillborn baby. Rachel's father, her mother's protector, chose not to acknowledge his mixed-blood daughter, and the highly complex social world for which Rachel had been trained fell apart in war. Rachel had made do with what talents she had, which had eventually led her to Lila's Place in Webster, Kansas—many notches below the kind of life she had been groomed for. The situation was only temporary, she had always told herself, and she was determined not to let such things as tatting and dancing and her fine looks slip just because her life had taken a rough turn.

She really did have to find something to smooth her rough hands, she thought irritably. Hauling water, building fires, and handling the leather reins of the mule team had turned them entirely unsuitable for fine work.

"Hello there."

She didn't look up at the rich bass greeting. Only one man on the train had such a resonant voice.

He continued undaunted. "You look busy."

"I am busy."

"I haven't seen anyone do that since I was a boy. My master's wife was known in the whole county for her lace."

"Tatting is the mark of a lady. Or least that's what my mother thought." She looked up at him then and felt a strange compulsion to put him in his place. She didn't want this man sniffing after her, even if he had such strong, engaging features and shoulders like an ax handle. "My mother and I—we weren't slaves."

Instead of backing off at her haughty tone, the man known as Banjo Ben just grinned, flashing white teeth that made his skin look like ebony in contrast. "My folks were," he said without a hint of shame.

Aggravated, she focused once again on her work.

"If you ladies need any help around here—with the mules or wagons or whatever else—feel free to give me a holler. I work for the Sutters, but they wouldn't mind me helping out over here a bit. It has to be hard on you ladies to be doing all this work."

Rachel sighed. Manners drilled into her as a child demanded at least a minimum of courtesy. "It's very generous of you to offer. I'll admit that sometimes the constant chores wear a body down."

"You ladies have a lot of courage to tackle this trip alone."

She set aside the piece of lace that would eventually become a delicate scarf—something suitable to grace the life she hoped one day to lead. She didn't want to encourage the man, but it was so very tempting to exchange a few words with a friendly face, someone who was neither sniping at her about doing chores or glaring at her with a look that consigned her to hell. Though frankly admiring, this man's eyes held no calculation of what her price might be, and that alone was worth a courteous word or two. "We have the professor," she said, "but the poor man, he's not much help. He tries, but his talents with the fiddle and piano haven't prepared him for a wagon trip across half a continent."

"Why do you call him the professor?"

She shrugged. "That's just what piano players in . . ." About to reveal that the professor had been a piano player in a bawdy house, she caught herself just in time. "Uh, itinerant piano players—they're always called professor."

As if not noticing her gaffe, Ben just smiled slightly. "I've talked to him a time or two. He's a good man."

"Yes, the professor's a good man, but he's certainly not up to this kind of adventure." Her voice became bitter. "None of us are. None of us should be here. We're not cut out for this kind of life—honest work, up before the sun in the morning and asleep at night before the evening's well started." She shook her head and sighed. "Not us."

For a moment Ben looked thoughtful, and Rachel feared he might ask just what kind of life she was cut out to lead. She'd given him the perfect opening. Had it been deliberate? Did the open admiration in his face grate on her cynical nerves? Did something inside her want to show him how very misplaced that admiration was?

He didn't take the bait, however, but kept smiling his affable smile and treating her as if she were the kind of woman that Cass wanted them all to be. "You know, Miss Rachel, smart people like you and me, we don't have to lead the lives that other people think we're cut out for. We change ourselves, and then we change the path we take through this world."

She didn't like the "you and me" part of that, as if she and a hired man with a face as black as coal had anything in common.

Ben wasn't discouraged by her silence. "If you can get yourself out of the blankets before the cock crows tomorrow morning I'll show you one of the nice things about getting up early."

From any other man Rachel would have taken that as a proposition, but Ben's words held no innuendoes. The only thing in his friendly tone was challenge, and though the reaction was silly, some childish part of her wanted to take him up on it. "Of course I can get up before the cock crows, as you put it—if I think it's worth it."

"This would be worth it."

A man tossing out a mysterious invitation that wasn't merely words wrapped around lust. What a novelty. Losing a bit of sleep might be worth finding out if she was wrong about his intentions, Rachel decided.

A call came from across the circle of wagons. "Ben! We're goin' out to hunt! Come on!"

He grinned. "I'll be by for you in the morning."

She looked down the patrician blade of her nose. "Maybe. I'll think on it."

He didn't cajole, as she expected, just chuckled and went off to join the hunters.

What an annoying man, Rachel thought. She most certainly would not meet him the next morning.

The next morning, however, Rachel was dressed and ready to take on the day before the first stirrings from the other tents. Ben Holden and his silly proposition weren't the reason for her early rising, she told herself. She'd been restless. The ground beneath her blankets was unusually hard. The cold air that leaked through the tent flap kept her awake. She had any number of reasons for getting up, and as long as she was up, she might as well see what the man had in mind. His motives for this early morning meeting were a question mark in her mind, and if she didn't go along, they would always be uncertain. Rachel hated uncertainties.

So she climbed to the wagon box of the big wagon and sat idly, watching the slow blanching of the eastern sky as day approached. The camp stirred, disturbing the silent predawn with low voices, the clatter of a pot, the bark of a dog. And Banjo Ben didn't come. Rachel vacillated between castigating herself for being made to look foolish and worrying that she hadn't risen early enough to catch him. The rush of exhilaration when he finally did show up was almost alarming.

"Good morning!" he greeted her in his deep bass voice. "Isn't this time of day beautiful?"

"I'm always up this time of day," she fibbed, "and I don't find anything rapturous about it."

"We'll fix that."

She accepted his help climbing down from the box. "What is this wonderful thing you have to show me that can't be seen in the light of day?"

"Oh, she can be seen in the light of day. But early mornings are when she receives visitors."

"She?"

"Yes ma'am. She."

The mysterious she was a great disappointment when Rachel was led into her presence. "I got up in the middle of the night to meet a cow?" She turned the full force of her disdain on Ben. "Your little joke is not funny."

"No joke, Miss Rachel. Mary here has got to be milked, and I tell you, milking a cow first thing in the morning, when the air is still and cold, the whole world is peaceful, and you're still a little drowsy—it puts the whole hard-workin' day in a new light."

Rachel commented with a rude sound.

"You won't feel that way once you've tried it."

"I am not, absolutely not, getting anywhere close to that cow."

Ben just smiled.

"Not. Absolutely."

A few minutes later, Rachel still didn't understand quite how she came to be sharing a little three-legged stool with Ben and becoming entirely too intimate with the warm underside of a cow. The stool wasn't really big enough for them both, but she certainly wasn't going to attempt this feat without Ben's help, and sitting between his spread legs was fun. She had to admit it.

Contemplating the cow was not fun, however. "I'm not going to touch *that!*"

"Of course you are. I just washed it. It's very soft and clean."

He guided her hand to the distended udder. "Ick!" she complained.

"Put your fingers so—like this."

It was soft, and Mary the cow smelled of warm animal.

"Squeeze gently."

She did, but nothing went into the bucket. The cow swung her head and looked a question at Rachel.

"She doesn't like me."

"Sure she does. There's a trick to this."

He demonstrated, then showed her again with his hand

guiding hers in the required motion. Callused from hard
work, his hands were nevertheless clean. They felt good on
hers. Too good. He was so gentle with Mary. Would he be
as gentle with a woman?

A stream of milk shot into the bucket. Rachel jumped,
and Ben laughed.

Milking a cow wasn't too bad a job, Rachel decided some
time later. The steady beat of the milk splashing into the
bucket, the quiet tempo of Mary's breathing, the feel of
warm cow against her cheek.

The warmth of Ben pressing against her back also might
have had something to do with the peculiar peace that came
over her. Almost reluctantly, Rachel moved aside to let Ben
finish the job. "My hands are cramping. They're no good
for this kind of work."

Ben took one of her hands before she could withdraw
it. His strong fingers massaged the sore muscles. "You're a
smart woman, Miss Rachel, and a capable one. You can
teach your hands to do any task that you set for them."

The massage felt so wonderful that she had to force herself to pull away. She stood, brushed a few pieces of hay
from her skirt, and tried to regain her composure. This en-
counter was not going as she'd imagined. "What are you
after?" she asked sternly.

He turned back to the cow, but his smile was for Rachel.
"All I'm after is friendship. You don't need that suspicious
look in your eye."

"Friendship?" She chuckled dubiously. "Right. You're not
as clever as you think, Mr. Banjo Ben. And I wasn't born
yesterday. And neither were you." She had a sudden need
to end this farce. Rachel might be a woman of a certain
reputation, but she had never until now pretended to be
something she was not. "Ben, you know exactly what I am.
What we all are. Of course you do. Everyone on this wagon
train knows, in spite of Cass thinking she can pass us off
as decent women."

He nodded slightly, without drama or surprise, and continued sending streams of milk into the bucket. He didn't
seem any more interested in the revelation than Mary was.
His lack of response was annoying.

"Admit it," Rachel demanded.

"Admit what?"

"That you think I'm easy pickings. The pretty words, the friendship—all blarney. What you want is sex."

He gave Mary a final pat and moved the full bucket out of range of her feet. Then he looked at Rachel and gave her an unruffled smile. "Not guilty."

"But you knew."

"It's not hard to figure out where you ladies come from."

"Then why were you treating me like a decent woman?"

"Isn't that what you are?"

His illogic took Rachel aback. For a moment she just scowled down at him. Then she blew out a puff of frustration. "You're crazy, Ben Holden. I don't know just what you're doing, or what you want, but I'll tell you one thing here and now. I don't have a price anymore. And even if I did, I wouldn't lie down with some upstart like you. So you can just quit being nice to me, because there's nothing here for you." She started to walk away, but he reached out a hand and stopped her.

"We all do what we have to do to survive, Rachel. I haven't been a slave since I ran away when my mama was sold. I was twelve years old and dumb as a rock, but I made my way west and made myself a life."

She shook off his hand, but didn't leave. "Then what are you doing here on this wagon train?"

"I came back after the war to find my family."

"Did you find them?"

"No."

Rachel fought down a wave of sympathy. She couldn't afford to give any feelings to this all-too-attractive man, because that might put them at the same level. "I'm not like you. I was never a slave, and neither was my mother or grandmother. They were ladies, and that's what I am. I'm going to find myself a rich man to marry, someone who'll treat me right and take care of me the rest of my life."

"Does a man have to be rich to do that?"

"Yes," she insisted, looking down her nose. "He does."

He cocked a brow and gave her an enigmatic smile. "Miss

Rachel, I don't think you know nearly as much about life as you think you do."

Cass absolutely did not understand how nature arranged it that the ground beneath them was either dust or mud. The wagon wheels were either mired to the hub, making every foot of progress hard-won by the poor mules, or they threw up billows of choking dust. One would think, logically, that there would be something in between.

This day they were plagued by dust, and being the last wagon in the twenty-wagon line made their dose of dust the worst to be had. She walked beside the small supply wagon, carrying on a desultory conversation with Rachel and Frenchie. The first hour of the morning she had driven the big wagon while Lila had read out loud from Jane Austen's *Pride and Prejudice*, her favorite novel. But halfway through the morning she'd turned the reins over to Lila and elected to walk. If her backside had spent one more minute on the hard wooden seat, her butt bones were going to come right through her skin. And that wasn't the only sore spot on her aching body. Her back ached from sleeping on the ground. Her shoulders and arms complained from muscling a team of stubborn mules, lifting buckets of water, and hauling wood. She had new respect for people who earned their bread doing manual labor.

Not that the effort wasn't worth it. She and the ladies were on their way to respectable lives, and soon she would get used to the tasks that gave her such trouble now. Wasn't Rachel just now saying that a woman could learn most anything she set her mind to, if it was needful?

"Did I tell you I milked a cow this morning?" Rachel asked.

"About three times," Cass replied.

"I think we should get a cow," Frenchie said. "Then we could have milk in our coffee. I used to milk Lila's goat. I don't understand why we didn't bring it with us."

"A cow is better," Rachel proclaimed. "Lila's goat would butt you every time you turned your back on her. She was nasty. Cows are . . . well, friendly."

Cass decided that Rachel had been in the sun too long

without a hat. She was about to question her sudden attachment to milk cows when Preacher Pernell trotted up on his fine-looking blood bay. Cass's aches and pains and Rachel's cow obsession suddenly faded to unimportance.

"Good morning, Mr. Pernell." Frenchie tossed her crimped blond ringlets and greeted the preacher in her most fetching voice. Since leaving Webster, she'd given up her trademark French accent, but she could still use her voice like a hunter used a snare. Cass shot her a warning look.

The preacher touched his hat. "Good morning, ladies. I hope you're all in fine health this morning."

"We are feeling fine as fine can be. And you're looking in mighty fine fettle, sir."

Frenchie oozed charm, the next thing to simpering, Cass noted irritably.

He patted his horse's neck. "Tiger here needs a bit of exercise, so I'm taking him out for a while. Miss Cassidy, I noticed you walking for the last few miles."

"I need the exercise, too." Not for the world would she tell him her backside was sore.

"I was wondering if you would care to join me in a ride."

Rachel and Frenchie looked at her expectantly, and out the rear opening of the big wagon Steamboat Sue, the professor, and Mama Luce observed as well.

"I don't know how to ride," Cass admitted, disappointed. She imagined riding knee to knee with handsome Preacher Pernell. "And I don't have a horse, even if I did know how."

"The professor has a horse," Frenchie said, loudly enough to be heard in the big wagon. "He'll let you ride it."

"You really should learn how to ride," the preacher advised. "In the far West roads are few. Carriages and wagons can't get in to some spots. You'll want to know how to ride a horse."

Was that a twinkle Cass saw in his eye?

"That's probably so." She sent him a smile that was inviting without being too flirtatious. Preachers probably weren't allowed to flirt. "Perhaps I could find someone to take on the chore of teaching me."

"It would be a pleasure, not a chore, Miss Cass. I would be honored to teach you to ride."

"You can use the professor's horse," Frenchie repeated, grinning broadly. "Can't she, professor!"

The professor waved at Frenchie's shout.

"Perhaps tomorrow we can find some time," the preacher said.

He touched his hat and smiled at them all before trotting away—so polite, Cass noted. Even after she had told him the truth about their deception. Could it be? Was it possible? Might he be courting her, in his preacherly way? Her heart sped. Suddenly the dust wasn't so choking and the day became an adventure rather than a chore.

"Look at that sucker smile on her face," Frenchie chortled. "Our Cassie's in love. Ooooh-la-la!"

The professor and Sue hopped down from the big wagon to join them. "You're welcome to use Traveler," the professor said. "She's a good old mare. You won't have any trouble with her."

Sue laughed. "The one she'll have trouble with is the preaching man. I'll bet riding a horse isn't the only thing he'd like to teach her."

"Sue!" Cass scolded. "He's a preacher!"

"He's a man, isn't he?"

"You've got to be more flirty, baby girl." Frenchie demonstrated. "Ooooh, my," she simpered. "I can't climb aboard this big ol' horse. Could you give a boost to my backside, Homer? That's right," she cooed with an ecstatic wriggle. "Put your hand riiiight there."

"Frenchie, quit! He's teaching me to ride. That's all!"

Sue chuckled. "Don't have kittens, Cass. There's no harm in a little flirtation."

"You need more than flirtation." Frenchie nudged the professor, who had climbed to the wagon box beside Rachel. "She needs to loosen the corset strings a bit, eh, Prof? Have some fun. You aren't getting any younger, baby girl, and it's a pure waste for any woman over twenty to be a virgin. Or a man, for that matter." She cocked a brow toward the professor, who managed to look embarrassed and annoyed at the same time.

Rachel disagreed. "I think it's rather sweet that she's waiting for the right man."

"Sweet my foot! It's a sin to waste your best years. At twenty, Cass should be looking to the future. Once you hit thirty, things start to dry up and sag; the hounds don't come howling up your tree anymore."

"Speak for yourself, Frenchie!" Steamboat Sue shot her a peeved look. "Some of us still have it after thirty."

"And some of us don't know when to start taking in laundry instead of men," Frenchie shot back.

"Would you two cats retract your claws?" Cass demanded. She didn't want to jump off her cloud of daydreams to break up female fisticuffs. Sue's sensitivity about her age was always irresistible to Frenchie, who loved a good mix-up almost as much as she loved men. "No one's going to be taking in laundry, and no one's taking in men anymore, either. Remember?"

"That's right." The professor's pointed look targeted Frenchie. "You're all headed for the straight life. Conventional ladies don't brawl, do they, Cass?"

"No, they don't."

"Well, la-te-dah!" Frenchie told them both.

The professor scowled. Cass scarcely noticed the exchange. Female fisticuffs avoided, her thoughts elevated once again to the preacher and landed firmly in the clouds.

Chapter 7

June 1, camped on the banks of the Red Vermillion—
  Our trail has turned northwestward. We have left the Kansas River, which so far has been our guide across the prairie, and now we are bound for the River Platte, at which all trails merge to cross the Great Plains. The Platte is still far away, though, for though it seems that we have endured an eternity of mules, dust, mud, and hungry mosquitoes, our journey has only just begun.
  Mr. Morris tells us that the Red Vermillion River, where we are now camped, is the old boundary of Pawnee territory. I say old boundary because with the unrest of all the tribes, boundaries have been blurred. Poor Anita's death has served to make us wary of the natives, but harassment of civilized travelers is not the only war games the Indians play. The Pawnee seem to suffer much from the Sioux, who are very fierce and invade their territory without compunction. Mr. Brown and Mr. Pernell, who rode ahead of the wagons most of the day, reported seeing evidence of a burned Pawnee village a short distance east of our camp.
  This morning before the wagons rolled we had a

*battle within our own ranks, or perhaps I should call
it a skirmish, since no bloodshed resulted. Our usually peaceful professor was the instigator. He has become increasingly cross with Frenchie as our journey
wears on, and this morning he confronted her like an
outraged mother hen pecking at an erring chick. She
had enticed Aaron Sutter, a rather handsome middle-
aged Shelby man, to help her gather firewood, and
as the pair returned to the wagons, Frenchie was flirting outrageously. (Preacher Pernell promised to coun-
sel the ladies about this sort of behavior, but he has
not yet found the opportunity.) To summarize a lengthy
battle, suffice it to say that the professor took Frenchie
to task and Frenchie responded in kind.*

*The reason that I trouble to write about this is that
the professor said some very profound words to
Frenchie when she insisted that she was a whore, and
no one should expect her to behave any differently
than a whore would behave. The professor replied that
whoring was how she had earned her living, not what
she was. I saw those words register not only with
Frenchie, but with the other ladies, who watched and
listened. Of course Frenchie bounced back with a
caustic inquiry as to just what he would like her to
be. A schoolteacher, a clerk, some man's wife? She
claimed to like being a whore, but I didn't believe her
for a moment. She is afraid, as are we all, of forging
ahead into an uncertain future.*

*I was about to add my own persuasions to the pro-
fessor's when Lila pulled me aside. She had read my
intentions—as sisters sometimes can— and warned me
quite strictly to leave them to settle their own problems. "You cannot live their lives for them," she
warned me. I have never attempted to live anyone's
life but my own, but I will admit at times I am tempted
to meddle. Lila says I should pay more attention to
my own affairs and leave others to sort out theirs. No
doubt she is right.*

*At this mention of my own affairs, I must write of
Mr. Pernell, the Shelby preacher. Because no one be-*

sides myself will read these words I can be frank about my emotions. This journal is the only one I will tell, for I fear I am being a silly fool, carried away by my dreams of a solid and respectable life. Who indeed could be more solid and respectable than a preacher?

Of course, Mr. Pernell is much more than just a preacher. As Elizabeth would say in Austen's Pride and Prejudice, he is a most amiable gentleman. And very nice looking. In fact, since this account is only between myself and this written page, I may safely confide that though his looks are a bit rougher than the current fashion of male beauty, they produce in me a reaction similar to dizziness. The ladies tease me about it, so I gather that my heart is upon my sleeve. One would think that a sensible woman like myself would know better.

I do dare to hope, however, that Mr. Pernell has conceived some interest in me as well, despite his knowing about my less than pristine upbringing. He very kindly offered to instruct me in the science of horsemanship, and this very afternoon was our first session. I had hoped to present myself as a competent and intelligent woman, but the professor's mare, which I borrowed, did not cooperate. The professor assured me that she was a very even-tempered, sensible horse, but I beg to differ. When I attempted to mount the saddle, I vow the horse decided to mock my incompetence. She swung her great huge head around to observe my attempt to climb aboard, so startling me that my foot missed catching the stirrup and I hung ludicrously from the saddle horn as the stupid beast turned in a circle. I believe the devious horse was having a very fine time.

My second attempt to mount met with more success in that I actually got atop the horse. In order to get me there, Mr. Pernell accidentally (I'm sure it was an accident) boosted me with a hand in a rather inappropriate place. I'm sure he was as embarrassed as I, so I didn't mention it. Once I was in the saddle, the horse responded to my directions with a slow plod,

*slower even than the wagons that were lumbering
along the road beside us. I admit I was not a picture
of maidenly grace as I tried to adjust to the very awkward gait. I gather, however, from the amused looks
Mr. Pernell gave me and the number of times poor
Traveler swung her head around to glare, that the
horse was not the one being awkward. Mr. Pernell
had instructed me to ride astride—not quite proper
for ladies, but he claims the sidesaddle is a menace
to both horse and rider. The sensation of sitting astride
the saddle was wickedly disconcerting, and to that I
attribute my apparent lack of aptitude. After a short
time, Mr. Pernell suggested we go "back to the very
beginning." He handed off his horse to young Amos
Byrd, who was watching with an impudent grin on
his face, and told me to dismount. I won't go into details about that humiliation—just to say that he was
quite a good sport when I landed upon him and top-
pled him into the dust.*

*The next part of our lesson was much more suc-
cessful, and I have hopes that I may yet become a
competent horsewoman. We rode bareback on Traveler, who with Mr. Pernell at the helm became a perfect lady. Even the mare is smitten, you see. With him
mounted behind me, making me feel secure, I immediately adjusted to the horse's motion. Mr. Pernell
says it was because the lack of saddle allowed me
closer to the horse. I contend that it was him holding me in place and moving with me in the correct
rhythm. A truly proper young woman would never
have allowed him to press so close, and she certainly
wouldn't have so enjoyed his arm clamped about her
waist, guiding her in the strange and almost sensuous dance between horse and rider. But Mr. Pernell
already knows I am no proper young woman.*

*We rode together for almost an hour, until the horse
felt almost natural beneath me. We talked, and of
course, I talked too much, as I often do. I was much
more free with stories of my past than Mr. Pernell
was, though he did say he was raised in Tennessee*

*on a horse farm. That would explain his taste in fine
horses. Would that also explain the flamboyant jug-
gling (I can think of no better term for the display I
witnessed) of his pistol? I didn't ask, submitting to a
strange reluctance. If Mr. Pernell has some talents in-
congruous with his present calling, who am I to question him? What do I know of the clergy, after all? I
have always thought them stiff, formal, and disapproving figures, and Mr. Pernell is not that at all. Indeed, I was surprised to note that he is as humanly
male as any of the gentlemen that came calling at
Lila's Place. Tucked near to him as I was during our
ride together, I couldn't help but note his reaction to
our close contact. What a surprise that preachers are
subject to such things, though to think they aren't is
a bit silly. Just like other men, they marry and have
children.*

*Still, I was a bit embarrassed. And perhaps flat-
tered. Since no one else will read these words, I will
admit to that. Flattered, and intrigued. I pray that I
am not being the world's greatest fool.*

Little Ruth March had been born three days before the
Shelby wagons reached Webster, but not until a hundred
miles west of Webster was the baby strong enough for proud
Virginia March to show off to the admiring throng of women
that gathered around the Shelby cook fire. Of course most
of the women had already met the baby, treading cautiously
into the March wagon to look upon the frail addition to
their little community, but the baby's first venture beyond
the shelter of the family wagon was a cause for celebration. There is nothing that causes quite so much of a buzz
among women as a baby.

Even the women from the "outsider wagons," as the
Shelby community had come to call Lila McAllister's group,
were lured from their side of the circle by the sound of the
cooing and gurgling—this from the women, not the baby.
Cass was the first to approach, followed by Lila, Sue, and,
behind them, Frenchie. Eliza Jacobs, queen of the Shelby

sisterhood, regarded the newcomers with a closed face. To Cass's smiled greeting she gave only a stiff nod.

"Oh, how sweet!" Cass exclaimed as she spied the infant, who was being passed around the circle for all to cuddle and admire. Just then the baby was in the arms of Faith Scott, a pretty fifteen-year-old who looked as though she feared the squirming child might break like fine china. Cass drew near to touch the baby's delicate hand. With a relieved sigh, Faith started to hand her the baby.

"No!" Mrs. March cried. "I'll take her." Shouldering Cass aside, she took the infant from Faith's arms and stalked back to her place in the circle of women. Far from being apologetic for her rudeness, she glared. Some of the other women turned a literal cold shoulder toward the visitors, shutting them out with frozen silence.

Frenchie responded with ruffled feathers. "Well, if you hens aren't the biggest pieces of—"

"Shush!" Lila commanded, cutting her off mid-insult. "Come along, ladies. It's rude to go where you're not invited, and this is obviously a private gathering." She took Frenchie's arm and pulled her back along the circle toward their own wagon, and when Frenchie started to object, Lila gave her the look that she'd honed in years taking charge of fractious, independent females who followed few rules but their own. Sue and Cass followed more quietly. Only Cass looked back over her shoulder.

Among the Shelby women, Effie Brown shook her head at her friends. "That was poorly done. They weren't causing any harm. Where is our Christian hospitality?"

A few nodded heads in agreement, but Eliza Jacobs hissed her disapproval. "Those who would remain wholesome should not risk associating with persons who might be a bad influence."

"We won't know what kind of influence they are if we refuse to speak to them," Effie replied.

Amelia Byrd sniffed, as if Lila's ladies had left a foul odor. "They're loose women. Look at the way they dress and talk. Not an ounce of modesty in the lot of them. And did you see the younger McAllister girl riding with Mr. Pernell? Of all things! They were riding together, astride! I can't imagine what Mr. Pernell was thinking, but I'm sure I know what the girl was up to."

Mrs. Jacobs agreed. "It's the work of the devil, if you ask me. To corrupt such a good man—the power of a wicked woman is fearsome."

"It's true," Alice Scott, Faith's widowed mother, agreed. "They're a disgrace. Those women are no more decent women than I am the queen of England."

"Oh, stuff and nonsense!" Grandmother Decker scoffed. "Judge not, ladies. That's what it says in the Good Book, in case you've forgotten. Alice, if you're so concerned with misbehaving females, you should look to your own daughter." The old woman gave Faith a stern look. "How many times have we seen her cozy up to young Amos junior like Eve with an apple in her hand?"

Alice's mouth thinned to a tight line. She shot a look at her mortally embarrassed daughter. "It's true, I know. Faith has a stubborn streak and a wickedly worldly curiosity. She's a sore trial."

"Mother! You talk about me like I'm not even here to listen!"

"Just take heed, young lady, that my eyes aren't the only ones that see your behavior."

Faith sent her mother an outraged glare and flounced away from the fire.

"There's one who needs a strap across her saucy behind," Mrs. Byrd declared.

Granny's bright eyes darted toward Amos's mother. "You might save that strap for your own boy, Amelia. He hangs about the McAllister wagons every chance he gets, following Cassidy McAllister around like a pup after a hambone."

"He's only sixteen."

"Old enough to get himself in trouble."

"He's a good boy, and he's not looking for trouble. I'm his ma, and I keep a good eye on him."

"Don't lie to yourself, Amelia. You've been so busy clucking over the speck in your neighbor's eye that you don't see the logjam headed toward your boy," Granny said with an emphatic nod.

While the Shelby hens clucked away on one side of the

wagon circle and Lila's ladies nursed their indignation on the other side, Nathan Stone sat in his wagon struggling to remember he was Homer Pernell, a pure-minded preaching man, not Nathan Stone, a horny hell-raiser with a woman on his mind. He sat on a hundred-pound sack of flour and rested his elbows on a wooden storage chest that doubled as a desk. A lantern illuminated a Bible and his scrawled notes, but inspiration for his next sermon refused to come. All that came to mind were sins of the flesh and his own chances of committing a load of such sins before the trip was over.

He guessed that his chances were pretty good, given a little cooperation from Cassidy Rose McAllister. She was under his skin but good, and the itch was worse than poison ivy. That riding lesson had been a big mistake. He could still feel the supple waist where his arm had rested, the soft cushion of her backside resting between his legs. Her laughter was music, her smile a glow of warmth. She was temptation itself, and Nathan Stone had never been much for resisting temptation.

What he ought to do was grit his teeth and stay away from the girl. She and her flamboyant friends weren't part of his flock, and he had no call to be sauntering by their wagon, tipping his hat and playing the part of a smitten fool. He had no call getting on a horse with Cass McAllister, rubbing up against her until he was ready to haul her off to the woods for a riding lesson that had nothing to do with horses. He was making an ass of himself for old Jed Jacobs and all the rest to see.

The hell of it was, one part of him cared that his flock was beginning to give him the evil eye, and another part of him didn't. This preaching was ruining him for being a normal human being. He needed to stay a preacher and above suspicion until he was far enough west that no one had heard of outlaw Nathan Stone, but at the same time, he needed a woman. Not just any woman would do. He needed Cass McAllister, with her fiery hair and emerald eyes, her freckled little nose that wrinkled pertly when she laughed, her siren's smile, all the more tempting because she seemed unaware of its magic.

Lordy but he ached. He more than ached. He pined. The thought of his Cassidy Rose lying with other men made his jaw clamp with anger. Never before had Nathan felt possessive of a woman. But this woman made him want to cage her where she couldn't even look at other men, much less ever again sell her body to them.

The snap of his pencil tip diverted Nathan's frustration. He'd pressed the thing so hard against his makeshift desk that it had broken. A series of aimless doodles decorated the page where he'd started to take notes for his sermon. Most of the doodles had curling hair and a come-hither mouth. Nathan crumpled the paper and with a wry shake of his head, tossed it into a dark corner.

Before he could take out another page, a scratching on the wagon canvas heralded a visitor. "Brother Homer?" Jed Jacobs called. Without waiting for permission, the old man stuck his head through the opening. "There you are. Didn't know if you'd be here or not. I see you're studying the Good Book, brother—man's anchor in a wicked world, his salvation in these times of peril."

"Are we in peril, Brother Jacobs?"

"Man is always in peril for the safety of his soul. Mind if I step up?"

"Come on in. Make yourself at home." Nathan stifled a sigh.

Brother Jacobs pulled himself into the wagon and found a seat on a sack of beans, from which he regarded Nathan with a paternal eye. "I've come with a purpose, Brother Homer."

Jed Jacobs always had a purpose, and his purpose usually involved a lecture of some kind.

"You're a good man, Brother Homer. And I know that as a man of God, your reputation is of great concern to you. Therefore I feel duty bound to bring to your attention a certain dissatisfaction among our brothers and sisters."

Nathan knew what was coming, but he asked anyway. "Yes?"

"About your behavior with the younger Miss McAllister."

Speak of the devil and he appears. Or, in this case, she

appears. Nathan figured the less he said, the better. He could only say the wrong thing, and Jacobs rarely listened to anyone else once he got talking.

"Now, Brother Homer, I know your intentions are pure, and I admire your efforts to save a lost soul, but you are a young man, and young men sometimes become prey to wickedness even though their motives are innocent. Let me tell you about women, brother. . . ."

For the next fifteen minutes Nathan endured a dissertation on the spiritual frailties of women and the dangers ungodly women presented to godfearing men. Nathan assumed that much of the man's warnings about subtle charms leading the unwary into temptation were based solely upon hearsay. He couldn't imagine the formidable Mrs. Jacobs employing subtle charms, much less leading any man into temptation.

"Sometimes a preacher needs to listen to his own preaching," Jacobs counseled. "A man with his heart striving after God may be too innocent in the ways of the world to recognize the traps a daughter of Eve might lay for unsuspecting prey. I hope you take no offense at this, Brother Homer, but all are concerned that, in innocence, you may stumble down a path that leads to destruction."

Nathan smiled. "Thank you for your concern, Brother Jacobs. I will take heed, and be assured that innocence is not going to make me prey to wickedness."

Because he had no innocence left, and wickedness had claimed him long ago, in the blood and destruction of war.

A week later they camped at Alcove Springs, just above the crossing of the Big Blue River. For Cass the days had taken on a sameness—the mornings a hurried frenzy to get on the road, the day an endless string of weary miles, and the evenings a tiresome round of chores. Daily riding lessons relived the tedium, but none were quite like the first one, for Mr. Pernell strictly observed the proprieties and rode his own horse while Cass struggled along on Traveler. By the third lesson she had lost the fear that the horse was going to clamp down on the bit and run toward the far horizon, and by the fourth she was able to enjoy herself even at a trot or canter, though her balance in the saddle was still uncertain and her legs had a tendency to flop about awkwardly. Her enjoyment might have owed more to her growing acquaintance with Mr. Pernell than her increased familiarity with the horse. They talked about inconsequential things, but somehow the very act of talking deepened their intimacy, or so Cass fancied. He was reticent about his past, claiming a dull conventional upbringing that would hold no interest for anyone. She also abandoned the past for talk of present and future. Mr. Pernell was a respectable man of delicate conscience. Cass wouldn't risk offending him with tales of the rough places and characters that had touched her life.

By the time they reached the Big Blue River and Alcove Springs, the daily effort of making fifteen to twenty miles no longer drained Cass of energy by the end of the day. Her hands sprouted new calluses. Her endurance for both walking and riding over the uneven ground grew to the point that her muscles, not to mention her backside, ceased their complaining. The mules were still balky and difficult, but as she'd done with other less than amiable acquaintances in her life, she mixed sweet talk with enough firm resolution to keep them at their work. She most often handled the big wagon, and Rachel, who now protected her soft hands with a pair of sturdy leather gloves Ben Holden had given her, drove the supply wagon.

All in all, the group of ladies was weathering the trip quite well, Cass believed—in spite of the difficult stream crossings, the frequent rain, the endless work, the monotony, and the sometimes open hostility from their traveling companions, they were coping.

Alcove Springs was a pleasant break in the monotony. The train halted for its usual Sunday break, and they anticipated staying several days longer to wait for lower water. Because of daily rainstorms over the past week, the Big Blue was dangerously high. They must either wait or build rafts to ferry the wagons and livestock across.

The second day of the halt Cass and Lila borrowed Traveler and rode double to view the springs themselves. The spot was just over a mile from where the wagons were camped.

"We could have easily walked," Lila mentioned from behind the saddle as Traveler plodded along the well-worn trail.

"I've done enough walking in the last few weeks to last a lifetime," Cass said. "I'm glad Mr. Pernell taught me to ride."

Lila chuckled. "Truly? Is that what you two have been doing?"

"Quit, Lila! You're as bad as Frenchie and Sue. Homer Pernell is a very nice man."

"I don't doubt it, sweetie. I think he's absolutely the perfect man for you, if you can pry him loose from that flock of prigs."

"Really? You like him?"

"The question is, do you like him?"

Cass smiled dreamily. "I think he's perfect."

"There you go, then."

Their trail guidebook assured them Alcove Springs was a lovely sight that would gladden the heart and encourage the weary soul. The spot was indeed worth seeing. Lush vegetation softened the bright sunlight to a soft, mellow green in a pretty little dale where clear spring water cascaded over a rock ledge and splashed musically into a quiet green pool. Just when Cass and Lila had slid from Traveler's back and stood admiring the little waterfall, the sound of someone coming brought them both around in alarm.

"Good morning to you, ladies," came a cheery voice. The intruder huffed down the trail, breathing hard and flushed with the effort of her hike. "Ain't this a pretty sight?"

"Granny Decker!" Lila exclaimed. "Did you walk all the way here?"

"'Course I did. Got two legs, don't I?"

"Alone?" Cass marveled.

The old woman chuckled. "I'm old enough to walk out on my own, missy. My son Cory was cutting firewood, and Pamela needs a few hours without her mother-in-law looking over her shoulder, though she'd never say as much. She's a good girl, that Pamela."

Lila took the woman's arm. "You look tuckered. Come sit on this nice big rock—oh, my."

"It's a gravestone," Granny noted calmly. "Look at that. Sarah Keyes, died May 29, 1846, age 70." She parked herself on the gravestone without a flinch. "Sarah won't mind me resting here a bit. Pretty spot for a grave. She picked a good place to die."

"There's another grave over here," Cass said. "John Fuller, age 20. Died April 29, 1849. How sad."

"People die," Granny said with a nod. "It's a part of life. I'm surprised I've lasted this long. That's why I brought along a good solid pine box. I'm not going to be planted in some foreign dirt without a nice box to rest in."

"You won't be needing that box for years," Cass assured her.

"Maybe so, maybe not," Granny said with apparent unconcern. "Look at that pretty waterfall. Makes you feel sorry for people who live in one spot all their born lives, don't it? They never get to see new sights like this. Never get to see what's over the horizon." She stood up. "Suppose I'd better get moving before my old joints rust in place. That would be a fine howdy-do."

Cass helped her up. "Why don't you take our horse to ride back, Granny? We can certainly walk."

"Keep your horse, missy. The day I can't walk a mile or two without keeling over is the day they get out that pine box of mine."

The women weren't the only ones with a hankering to see the springs. A short distance up the trail, Nathan trotted along on Tiger, lost in his own thoughts, when he heard voices ahead. He reined in and loosened the pistol in his holster. Dog had also heard the sound. His shaggy ears pricked forward, then relaxed as he looked up at Nathan, tongue lolling happily.

"Right," Nathan agreed. "Women." He dismounted and led Tiger through the brush that closed in on the trail. When they came into the open, Granny Decker greeted him with a gap-toothed smile. With her were Lila and Cass McAllister.

"Howdy, Reverend," the old woman said. "Come to see the sights, eh?"

Actually, he had come hoping for some solitude, and the last person he wanted to find here was Cassidy Rose McAllister. He'd done some serious pondering since Jed had expounded upon the evils of Woman and the dangers in particular of one redheaded green-eyed hussy of his acquaintance. Much as it went against the grain, he decided to heed the old patriarch's warning. He couldn't afford to do anything that might make the Shelbyites suspicious that he wasn't what they thought he was. Soon their trail would join with the cross-country stage route, with its posting stations and links to civilization. Somewhere close by there might be a wanted poster bearing his likeness. Or a stage passenger who might have seen one. No one would look twice at a preacher man shepherding his flock to Oregon. Everyone would cast cautious eyes on a man traveling alone, without baggage and without family. That's what he would be if he got himself expelled from the Shelby group.

Cass, he decided, wasn't worth the risk. During her riding lessons he'd kept a polite distance, and soon he planned to forgo all but the most casual contact. And yet here she stood in the soft light of this beautiful glade. Her hair was a splash of flame in the quiet green. Her color was high—from the surprise of his bursting upon them so unexpectedly? From pleasure at seeing him? He wanted it to be so. His resolution to do the right thing was weak.

He doffed his hat. "Hello, ladies. I didn't mean to startle you. I was curious to see this place and had some idle time on my hands."

"We're glad it's you and not an Indian," Lila told him. She looked from him to Cass.

With a conspiratorial smile, Granny Decker took Lila's arm. "My dear, I'm going to take you up on your offer after all, I think. Not to take your horse. Oh my, no. These old bones can't climb aboard a horse anymore. But if you would walk me back to camp it would be a kindness."

"I'll help," Cass responded.

"No," Granny and Lila both said. Lila continued, "You bring the professor's horse back when you come. Give us a little while, so if we need help you'll be coming behind us."

Nathan knew very well what Granny and Lila were up to, and Cass knew also. Hands on hips and a wry twist to her lips, she looked after the two schemers as they made their way up the trail. For someone supposedly needing escort, Granny looked remarkably spry.

Cass turned toward Nathan with high color in her face. "They're conspiring, those busybodies. I'm embarrassed."

She looked more pleased than embarrassed, however. He wanted badly to take advantage of that. He wanted to touch her, draw her close, see her eyes blur with passion and her mouth soften with wanting. But he held himself still, reminding himself that he couldn't afford this woman, no matter how tempting she was.

His silence made her frown. "What is it?" she asked uneasily. The jewel green eyes grew sharp and probing. "Is something wrong?"

"No. Nothing's wrong. I didn't see you riding yesterday."

"We were washing clothes, and it took most of the day."

"Well, you're getting quite good. There's no reason for more lessons, I suppose. From now on it's just practice you need."

Those sharp eyes sliced right through the weak excuse. "There is something, isn't there? They've warned you not to have anything to do with me, haven't they?"

Nathan tried to think of a plausible lie, but nothing sprang to mind. She took his hesitation as confession.

"Of course they did." Her voice grew sharp as her eyes brightened with unshed tears. "I'm not worthy of a decent man's attention. Right?"

"You're worthy of any man's attention, Cass."

Her eyes flashed. "That's a lie. And you know it. Preachers aren't supposed to lie. But I suppose that's a minor sin compared to socializing with a woman who has lived in bordellos since she was five years old."

Even Nathan was shocked by that revelation. Dog whined and nudged her hand with his big head. She immediately sat on the ground and put an arm around him, and he willingly leaned against her. The mutt was a sucker for the ladies, and Cass in particular. He had been ever since she had first tossed him a biscuit at the beginning of one of their riding sessions.

Something in Nathan's heart turned. It didn't seem right that a woman as beautiful and spirited as Cassidy Rose McAllister should be so forlorn, reduced to hugging a smelly dog for comfort.

"Cass . . . don't look like that. You've got to understand. No one means any insult to—"

"Hah!"

She shot up, and both Nathan and Dog jumped back. She wasn't forlorn at all. She was angry.

"Do you see the injustice of this?" she demanded. "Men can drink themselves senseless in saloons, gamble and cavort and carry on, and everyone winks about men being men and having their fun. But a woman—shoot! A woman can't even peek into a saloon without having her name painted in mud, and any woman who's walked through the doors of a brothel, no matter what her reason for being there, is ruined forever. No redemption. No second chance."

"Well, now—"

"Don't 'well, now' me, you . . . you . . . you . . . hypocrite!" She poked him in the chest with an index finger more deadly than a pistol. "You people read the Bible, but you don't listen to what it says. It talks about leaving judgment to God, about forgiving sins. But you holier-than-thou church people with your prayers and sermons, you never forgive. Not if the sinner is a woman. Maybe there's no way for a woman to scrub off the tarnish of being an outcast. Maybe it's just hopeless."

With a furious sniff, she marched to her horse, jerked the reins from where they were tied to a bush, and vaulted into the saddle—a little too impassioned a vault that carried her over the saddle and left her clinging to the other side with her arms hampered by an upended skirt and her legs flailing in their attractively ruffled bloomers. Displeased with such antics, Traveler impatiently turned in a quick circle, which cost Cass the rest of her balance. She landed hard on the ground, practically beneath the horse's belly, and squawked as the horse nervously stepped all around her.

Nathan grabbed the reins and guided the horse away from the fallen girl, who glared up at him as if he had been the one threatening to step on her with a steel-shod hoof. "Are you all right? Did she kick you?"

"No. And no."

He offered her a hand. She turned up her nose. "I can manage."

"Of all the stubborn, hardheaded . . ." Reaching down, he took her hand anyway, and when she jerked away, he grabbed both her arms and pulled her up. Sticks and leaves tangled in her hair and trimmed her dress. Her skirt refused to fall into place, and she furiously kicked it down.

"Let go of me!"

"No," he said mildly. He couldn't let go. Not for the life of him. Face tear-streaked, hair wild, eyes spitting fire, and bloomers still flashing white, Cass was as irresistible as any woman he'd ever known. More.

He hauled her closer, clamped her head in a gentle lock, and lowered his aching mouth to hers. As their lips met, he knew he was in trouble.

Chapter 8

Fireworks exploded somewhere in the region of Cassidy's heart. The incredible intimacy of a man's lips caressing hers, his tongue probing and feinting, then boldly exploring, catapulted her into a dreamlike yet intensely aware state. Surrounded by the scent of him, the heat of his body, the steel of his strength, she floated, helpless in a foreign universe, her anger transformed to desire, every part of her springing to life in an unfamiliar, disconcerting way. She longed to become a part of a man, to melt into his flesh, join forces with his very soul. If he'd tried to swallow her whole, she would have helped him.

When he finally released her, Cass plummeted toward the earth. With a cry, she latched onto his arm. He spoke her name softly and reached out to touch the tears coursing down her cheeks. She hadn't realized they were there. Weeping made no sense. She wasn't sad, but lost in rapture. Who knew kissing could be so wonderful? Wonderful, confusing, unsettling, and breathtaking.

"Cassidy Rose McAllister"—he kissed the tip of her nose, then the point of her chin—"you are incredible."

"I am?" Not for the world would she tell him this was her very first kiss.

"You are. And . . . you win." With a quiet sigh, he enfolded her in his arms and buried his face in her hair. She melted against him and closed her eyes with a smile, wondering just what exactly had she won.

Lila leaned against a wheel of the big wagon, a picture of nonchalance in spite of the angry group that had gathered a hundred feet away, haranguing poor Jed Jacobs. The man had been peacefully repairing a harness when a troop of women commanded by his own redoubtable wife had marched up and surrounded him. Lila cared only slightly that the inspiration for their march was she herself—or, more accurately, she and the less than respectable members of her little group. All her life she had been gaped at, spat upon, insulted, and cold-shouldered. Women pulled aside their skirts to avoid the least brush in passing. Any decent woman would cross the street rather than share a walkway with a soiled dove.

Lila had long ago learned to disregard other people's opinions about her. She had always done what she had to do to get by. If that made her a pariah, then so be it. Lila knew her own worth, and a pack of prigs from Missouri couldn't dent it. Her priorities were clear: take care of herself, her sister, and her girls, and do it well. The rest of the world could go to hell for all she cared.

Which was exactly where the Shelby women consigned her, to hear them talk. Jed put down his harness and tried to calm the distaff delegation, but they were having none of it. Even his own wife harangued him. Lila almost felt sorry for the man.

"The time has come, Jedediah," Eliza Jacobs declared. "We have a Christian duty to keep our feet on the path of the Lord and suffer no man or woman who would lure us from that path."

"Now, Eliza . . ."

"Don't 'now, Eliza' me, Mr. Jacobs. You are too generous a soul for your own good. The time has come to wield the sword of righteousness. We must cut the cancer from our midst before it poisons the entire body of our community."

Lila gave Eliza points for speechifying. If women could

be preachers, the old bat would have done a better job even than Mr. Pernell.

Jed tried to pacify. "My dear, emotion is the enemy of reason. Tell me what the problem is, and we will discuss it calmly."

Now Amelia Byrd took up the sword. "I'll tell you what the problem is, Jedediah. The problem is those daughters of Satan you allowed to come into our midst. The she-wolves cut out the weakest among us—the young and the lonely. And they lure them along the paths of temptation."

"Well now—"

Eliza cut in. "Those jezebels will draw down God's wrath upon us, husband. Mark my words. He might aim his lightning at them, but we'll get fried as well. By tolerating their presence among us, we are accountable for their sins."

Jed sighed as more women took up the complaint in an unhappy chorus. He couldn't get a word in edgewise.

Sue came from behind the big wagon, pulled up a stool, and sat down to watch. The lines of age on her face, Lila thought, seemed to cut deeper every day. "Guess I up and did it this time, didn't I?"

Lila shrugged. "Hens cackling in the yard. Don't pay them any mind."

"There didn't seem any harm in passing a little time with the boy. He's a nice kid, and he's always hanging around helping out with the chores."

"There's no accounting for what sets a righteous woman off," Lila said with a wry smile. "They're a mystery to me."

"I can't imagine why Cass wants to be one of them."

Lila looked around at the whinny of a horse. "Speaking of Cass . . . here she comes riding along with Preacher Pernell. This should be fun to watch. When that righteous broad gets an eyeful of the cozy way those two are looking at each other, she's like to blow the top of her head right off."

Sue chuckled wickedly. "I want to see that."

Cass did not react in as sanguine a manner when she got the drift of the ruckus. Poisonous glances sent her way from the Shelby women bore witness that she and Mr. Pernell had made matters that much worse. It was a dismal fall back to earth after an afternoon spent in the clouds.

"All I did with the boy was smoke a cigar with him and talk a bit," Sue told them. "We didn't do anything interesting. Honest, Reverend."

A shout of "The devil is among us," rose from the crowd of angry women. Mr. Pernell looked genuinely worried as he cautioned the ladies not to answer. Cass's heart sank. What she feared most had come to pass, and she was partly responsible. The good women of the Shelby train had divined the truth, and they were to be condemned before even starting their new lives.

Preacher Pernell heaved a sigh and squared his shoulders, as if girding himself to march into battle. When Cass started to march right along with him, he barred her path with an outstretched arm. "Stay here, all of you. And for God's sake, look humble."

Cass thought she heard him mutter "goddamnit" as he stalked toward the hostile mob, but she must have been mistaken. Surely Homer Pernell would never say such a thing.

"I'm humble," Lila said with an unconvincing shrug.

"Me too," Cass sighed.

"Just hope Frenchie doesn't come around," Sue said. "She doesn't know humble from a hole in the wall."

The women engulfed the poor preacher like quicksand closing around a sinking victim. He stepped up on Jed's stool to rise above them.

"Sisters, sisters, good sisters." He held up his hands as if in benediction, and the women fell silent. "What troubles your souls?"

"What troubles our souls is those hussies bringing God's judgment down upon us, Mr. Pernell," came an anonymous shout.

" 'Lead us not into temptation,' " cried another voice.

"They're tempting all the menfolk—men and boys. There's not a man here who hasn't turned his head to sniff after their wickedness."

Even the preacher, was the unspoken accusation. Nathan took a deep breath. "Sisters . . . will you judge those whom God has directed to you for instruction?"

Questioning silence.

"Did Christ turn away the repentant harlot and cast her

into hell? No indeed. He told her to go and sin no more. And that's what she did."

Eliza Jacobs objected. "The age of miracles is done, and if these tarts are repentant, then I'll eat my shoe!"

"How do you know the age of miracles is done?" Nathan demanded. "And who are we to judge these women, to say that God must withhold his forgiveness? How do you know that He didn't send them here to learn by the example of your virtue? Do you dare turn them out?"

Sue hugged her knees and chortled. "He's good. Damn he's good."

"Isn't he?" Cass sighed. Her heart had risen from the pit into which it had sunk. Her hero was saving the day.

Rachel wandered in, took in the scene, and raised a perfect brow. "What's going on?"

"Pull up a stool and watch the show," Lila invited. "We're about to become either pariahs or prodigal daughters. Depends if the biddies swallow the pap that Mr. Pernell is handing them."

"He's on our side?" Rachel asked.

Lila glanced at Cass with a smile. "I reckon he is."

They all turned their eyes on Cass and echoed Lila's knowing smile.

"Good work, baby girl," said Rachel.

"Yeah." This from Sue. "Keep it up. It never hurts to have a preacher on your side."

Cass refrained from comment. The ladies could make light of the situation if they pleased. But she knew that this was a very important juncture. Mr. Pernell was trying to save their butts, and he was laying his own reputation on the line to do it.

"Who among you," the preacher exhorted, "has never veered from the path of righteousness? Sometime in our sorry lives, we all need to wipe the slate clean and start again, and God makes this possible. Did not Saint Paul himself persecute Christians before God showed him the light and let him start again with a new spirit and a clean soul?" His eyes rose from the crowd and fixed unwaveringly upon Cass. "The Lord gives us all second chances, and third chances, and fourths. Redemption is a gift of heaven, and it is not our place to deny it to anyone."

Her heart soared. The message was for her. Her past could be wiped clean. She could be the kind of woman that a preacher could love. He was telling her that, speaking to her alone even while his words were directed toward others.

The crowd of women had settled, Cass was glad to see. Of course they had. What woman could resist the sound of Homer Pernell's voice? Jed Jacobs looked relieved, and some of the menfolk of the train cautiously came near to hear what the preacher had to say. It was obvious they wanted no part of their womenfolk when the ladies were in high temper. Effie Brown had joined the group to give huzzahs to the preacher, and Granny Decker had tottered out of her tent complaining of all the "infernal noise."

"Sounds like a bunch of cats squalling," she grumbled. "Body can't take a nap without someone raising a ruckus."

"Look humble," Lila reminded her charges as the knot of Shelby women started to disperse, some still grumbling and throwing poisonous looks their way.

"And contrite," Cass added.

"Do we have to lick boots for the rest of the trip just to make those cacklehens happy?" Rachel asked with an offended sniff. "If we do, I'm turning back. And forget looking humble. I'm not humble for any man—or woman."

When evening fell, Clyde Dawkins got out his fiddle and gave the camp some tunes. Ben Holden joined in with his banjo, and a few minutes later, the professor tuned in with his fiddle as well. The piano wasn't his only talent, and he brought the tunes from mere sawing on the strings, which was Clyde's specialty, to something more like real music.

The sound of cheerful music did much to lighten the still tense atmosphere of the camp, and when Effie and Matthew Brown stepped out to dance, the mood grew more cheerful still. Pouring coffee for Mr. Pernell, Eliza Jacobs made a sour comment about the levity.

"There's nothing in the Bible that forbids a bit of dancing," the preacher reminded her. "As long as the proprieties are kept."

She harrumphed and stood with arms crossed as more

couples joined the merriment. Amos and Amelia Byrd were quite graceful. Cory Decker led out his mother. Granny grinned like a girl but soon surrendered her son to his wife. The Decker children, a cherubic boy of ten and his five-year-old sister, joined with the Campbell toddlers to chase among the dancers in a game of tag. Young Faith Scott boldly dragged Amos Jr. into the dance, and the Sutters also joined in. The rest of the Shelby community stood by and watched, some smiling, some clapping in time to the music, some disapproving. Maude Atkins tutted at the levity, but when her husband, George, asked her to dance, she positively simpered.

Lila's group sat at their own cook fire, watching. Cass helped Luce with the supper clean-up. Rachel had her hands busy with her tatting. Frenchie hummed along with the music and tapped her foot in time, while Sue squinted at the stitching sampler Cass had given her—she had decided to learn to sew.

"I guess they're not quite the prissy pissants I thought they were," Frenchie observed. "Those Deckers can really cut a rug."

"As if we had anything as civilized as a rug out here," Rachel sniffed.

"Mr. Pernell is dancing with Granny Decker," Sue said. She laid the sampler in her lap and smiled wistfully at the dancers. "That's sweet."

"That preacher man's a good fella," Mama Luce declared with a sidelong look at Cass.

"He is," Cass agreed with a sigh.

Luce looked at Lila, and they both smiled.

Ben turned his banjo over to Aaron Sutter, who didn't play well but did play with enthusiasm. Then he headed straight for Rachel and made a courtly bow. "Dance, Miss Rachel?"

She hesitated, then smiled loftily. "I suppose."

"I suppose." Frenchie imitated the haughty tone of Rachel's words as the couple joined the dance. "Like she wasn't wishing him over here with all her might."

"Really?" Cass asked.

"Miss Innocence. Of course really. Where do you think

Rachel's been in the dark hours of every morning? She's been stepping out with that one."

"She's been milking a cow with him," Lila clarified.

Frenchie snorted. "That's a new name for it!"

"He is a handsome boy," Sue observed.

"He ain't no boy," Luce said. "And don' call 'im that in Miz Rachel's hearing, or you be minus some hair on yore head when she get done pulling it."

"Look who's coming this way," Frenchie said. "The preacher man himself. He ditched poor Granny fast enough." She sent a sly smile toward Cass. "Now, who over here do you suppose he wants to dance with?"

"Oh dear!" Cass fussed. "I'm a mess." She pulled her hands from the tub of hot dishwater and looked around for somewhere to wipe them.

"Goodness!" Sue teased. "Cass thinks he wants to dance with her. And I thought he was coming to court me."

The preacher gave them all a smile, but he had eyes for only Cass. "Will you dance with me, Miss McAllister?" he said very formally.

"Oh! My hands are wet."

Luce threw a towel at her. "Here you go, honey."

She barely managed to catch it. Usually she wasn't such a jitterninny, but all afternoon she'd been turning into a nervous Nellie every time she thought of Mr. Pernell—dropping things, forgetting what she was saying in the middle of a sentence. She'd even walked straight into Mr. Sutter's horse, causing the poor beast to spook and Mr. Sutter to almost get thrown.

Mr. Pernell gave her a heart-stopping smile and offered his arm. Cass ignored Frenchie's snicker as she allowed him to lead her off.

Cass had never before danced with a man. She had danced with women, mostly fancy ladies who'd amused themselves by teaching her dances that would certainly never be seen at any proper ball or neighborly barn dance. Lila had taught her the two-step and the waltz, so she knew what to do with her feet and her hands, but dancing with a man, she found, was entirely different from dancing with a sister. Entirely different. With Mr. Pernell's arm around her waist and his hand holding hers, Cass felt as if they were dancing on clouds, the stars above shining on them alone. She wanted to do more than dance; she wanted to sing, to cry out to the world that she was happy to be in this man's arms. A multitude of eyes followed them as they moved to the music. Cass could feel their impact. She glanced toward Lila, who smiled encouragement. Luce nodded, and Sue clapped in time to the music. Then she came face-to-face with Frenchie. The professor had put aside his fiddle and dragged her into the merriment. Frenchie winked, and then other couples came between them.

"Your friends giving you a hard time about dancing with a preacher?"

"They adore you," Cass told him with a smile. "You saved our bacon this afternoon. We can't ever thank you enough."

"That pretty smile of yours is enough thanks."

Cass blushed. Who would have thought that a preacher would employ such words. He made her feel special. Rational thought deserted her when he was close. This was love, Cass decided. And no wonder poets wrote ballads about it and singers sang of its glory. She was in love, and not all the prim Shelby hens nor her cynical friends could convince her that fate hadn't intended Preacher Homer Pernell especially for her.

Nathan suffered a similar affliction. Cassidy Rose McAllister made every fiber in his body stand up and salute. All the woman had to do was smile at him to make him come alive, and a casual touch of the hand produced desire so sharp it was painful. He'd vowed to stay away from her that very morning, and the afternoon had found him kissing her in a secluded glade, defending her right to stay with the wagon train, and now taking her in his arms and dancing in full view of a host of disapproving eyes.

Nathan's father used to say that his youngest son didn't have the sense God gave a grasshopper. Those had been the days before the war, when the world was fresh and innocent and Nathan had been as green as the family's rolling Tennessee pastures. The world had grown harsh and dan-

gerous, but obviously his father's words still rang true: he
still didn't have the sense God gave a grasshopper.

"You're very silent tonight," Cass observed. Her smile
lit up the gathering dusk and tripped a cord in his heart.

"Thinking about what the future holds."

"I would think your future is all laid out."

"Not at all. A preacher can't make his way just preaching. He has to do something useful, like farm or ranch or
run a livery. I've been a wanderer these past few years, but
the time has come to settle down and make a home somewhere."

"Surely you'll stay with your people."

"I said I'd stay with them to Oregon. After we reach
Oregon, who knows?"

Her gaze dropped, and a thick curtain of lashes veiled
her eyes. "You're thinking that they won't want you because you've been friendly with me and the other ladies."
She sighed. "Mostly because of me."

Friendly was a very mild word for what he felt in her
presence. "A man can't let his life be ruled by what other
people say."

"For a woman it's different. If a woman wants a husband and a home, children, a decent life, she has to guard
her reputation and be always aware of what other people
say about her."

"I don't think people in the far West are quite so per-
snickety, Cass. You'll be able to start over."

"I've always wanted a home and children. I've always
wanted to have people wish me good day when I sat down
in church, to be a part of quilting bees and ice cream socials. And if I have to cross rivers in that leaky wagon and
slog through mud and dust and fight Indians to get where
I want to be, then I'll do it."

"I'll just bet you will," he said with a chuckle.

The ache of desire that plagued him warmed a bit with
the longing to protect. Cass asked so little, yet so much—
to think that such a thing as a peaceful home and a quiet,
respectable life might be waiting somewhere for people like
her, and like him. Such a tempting dream wrapped up in a
tempting woman, a woman who looked up at him with ad-

miration in her eyes. And desire. She ached for him, just as he ached for her. The ache was in every smile of those delectable lips, every move of her lissome young body, every sparkle in her jewel bright eyes.

He drew her closer, proprieties be damned. She shivered. "Are you cold?"

She actually blushed. Who would think that a woman of her experience could still blush?

"I . . . yes. I must be cold. I should get my shawl."

"I'll walk you to your tent."

They didn't make it to the tent. As soon as they were in the concealing shadows of the wagons he swung her around to face him. "Cassidy Rose, you are a beautiful woman."

Her voice trembled. "Am I?"

"Oh, yes. You are."

He pulled her close, alert for any sign of resistance. She was perfectly willing, it seemed, because she all but melted into his arms. He took her mouth slowly at first, trying to be the gentleman she thought he was, but the part of him that was no gentleman demanded more. He probed with his tongue, and she opened to him, uttering a little cry of passion that almost did him in. It was all he could do to refrain from lowering her to the hard ground, rucking up her skirt, and taking her right there.

He wove his fingers through her hair and gently pulled back. They both labored for breath. Her lips were moist and seductively swollen, and the surge of renewed urgency made him groan. He pressed his mouth to her throat, murmuring, "Cassidy. Cassidy, Cassidy, Cassidy . . . We've got to stop."

"Yes," she breathed.

He moved to the soft lobe of one delectable ear. "We'll go too far."

"Yes."

Her hair was soft against his fingers. He buried his face in it, longing to continue this delicious exploration, to nuzzle her neck, her breasts, her . . . He didn't dare let his imagination wander farther. They would both be lost. With superhuman effort, he pulled back.

For a moment they both tried to get back their breath. Cass's dreamy expression slowly became worried. She bit her lower lip and apologized. "Mr. Pernell, I'm so sorry. You must think I'm . . . I'm . . ."

He finished for her. "The most wonderful woman I've ever met. I should be apologizing to you," he said with a rueful smile. How he longed to hear his real name on her lips. Nathan Stone. It would be music coming out of her mouth. "Cass, I love you."

She looked up at him with wide eyes.

"I love you, Cass." He realized suddenly that he meant it. "We've only known each other a few weeks, and I realize making a declaration is reckless, but it's only fair to warn you. When this trip is done, I mean to ask you to marry me."

Her mouth formed a perfect O.

"I don't want to wait, sweetheart. I'd marry you at the next outpost of civilization that has another preacher, but it wouldn't be fair to you. We've both got things to do before we can make a life together."

"Oh, my! Mr. Pernell—Homer." Her smile turned shy, and thick lashes lowered to veil her eyes. "It's only fair that I should warn you also. If you propose at the end of this journey, I'll say yes."

He was insane, and he knew it. But it just might work. She was desirable, courageous, passionate—the kind of woman to partner a man in the raw world for which they were bound. And she shared his dream of the perfect future—stable, honest, even dull. Dull would be a relief after the past few years.

Maybe his luck had changed.

Some hours later, Cass stood in heavy walking boots and nightgown with only a flimsy shawl protecting her from the damp night air, contemplating the dark looming form of a wagon. Mr. Pernell's wagon. Homer's wagon. What was she doing in this midnight hour far from her own blankets, shivering in the springtime chill, afraid to move forward but unwilling to go back?

Her life had changed so much in the last few weeks that she hardly knew herself. Who was this woman marching—or sometimes trudging—toward a bold and unknown future, who fancied herself in love, who prated to her friends about decency and propriety and then played the wanton herself? This midnight jaunt was indeed wanton, she told herself. There was no other word for it. Wanton. And no excuse for it either.

She waited for shame to settle in, to save her from the sin she was about to commit. It didn't. That in itself worried her. She should be ashamed, doing the very things for which she scolded Lila's ladies. Coming here was reckless, foolish, selfish, and indecent.

Wasn't it? Surely if she carried through her intention to go to her love, he would think her evil indeed.

Wouldn't he?

Yet she couldn't turn back. In the grip of something she didn't fully understand, she walked forward through the damp grass.

"Homer!" Her whisper sounded loud in the silent darkness, but not even a dog barked. "Homer!" He slept in his wagon, not a tent. The bowed canvas top was drawn shut and a flap was tied across the opening against the night chill. "Homer!"

The opening ripped open and an arm plunged out to pull her in. "Good God, woman! Will you wake the whole train?"

Inside the wagon, she could see him only dimly—a solid shadow silhouetted briefly against the starlit opening, then blending with the dark interior of the wagon. She tried to think of something to say, something that would justify this midnight visit. But no possible excuse presented itself to her mind except the real one.

"I couldn't sleep," she admitted sheepishly. "I got to thinking about so many things. About the trip ahead of us— the river crossings, the Indians, the sickness. So many rotten things could happen to either one of us before we reach Oregon."

A rustling in the wagon made her jump. Warm fur brushed against her. "Oh, my goodness! Dog! You scared the life from me."

"Out," the preacher ordered the mutt.

A wet tongue swiped Cass's hand, and then they were

alone. Very alone. Just her and this looming, warm, tempting man.

"Catch your breath," he advised. "Good Lord, are you crying? Here, sit down."

He guided her to a box where she could sit, then tenderly touched her cheek, which made more tears flow. Cass didn't know where the tears came from.

"Now, what are you talking about?"

"Suppose . . . suppose one of us doesn't make it to Oregon? We'll never be together."

For a moment he was silent, then his voice came out of the darkness. "Why would one of us not make it, Cass?"

"For all the reasons I just said. Savages. Sickness. Accident. Anita didn't expect to be killed by Indians, but she was. The Crespins' little boy died beneath the wheels of my very wagon. The cholera has been known to wipe out whole wagon trains, I've heard. I don't want to take the chance of never . . . of never being with you. Never . . . lying with you."

From the darkness came a deep sigh. "Cass . . . you tempt a man beyond reason."

"You must think I'm truly sinful. Here I talk of being respectable and, and—"

"No, Cass. Don't say it. How could I think you're anything but the best woman in the world?" His hand touched her hair. "Are you sure you want to be here with me?"

Her heart pounded, and some cowardly, cringing part of her shouted that she wasn't sure. But it was a small voice, drowned in the bliss of his touch. "I'm sure. Really."

Nathan could see her clearly. Her white gown seemed to glow in the faint starlight leaking through the canvas opening. Her face was pale, her hair was lost in the darkness of the wagon. She looked like a statue in marble or a virgin sacrifice, swathed in white and awaiting her fate.

But she was no virgin. Far from it. Cass was a woman, and she had decided to give herself to him. He could no more refuse the gift than a starving man could refuse a feast. More than lust drove him. He suffered a genuine need to make this woman his own, as if their coming together would somehow seal for them the future they both wanted.

He took her hand. "Come here, my love."

She rose, a pale wraith, but solid and warm beneath his hand. He kissed her slowly, then worked loose the buttons of her gown, one by one, with fingers suddenly grown awkward. Bit by bit it gaped open, and he wished he had a lantern to light the beauty only hinted at in the dark.

The gown fell, finally, and she seemed to fold inward, a show of modesty strange in one of her former profession. But Nathan was in no state to think on it more than a mere second. His hands touched what the darkness hid, and he altogether lost the power of thinking. Urgently he guided her toward the sparse straw mattress along one side of the wagon.

"Are you cold?" he asked at her shiver.

"I . . . I'm—"

"I know a way to keep you warm."

He wore only a set of long drawers, and he made short work of them so he could lie with her skin to skin. She was soft, fragrant, heaven in the form of a woman. With his hands and mouth, he made her very warm indeed, and if at first she stiffened at the intimacy of his caresses, she soon grew pliant and giving. A single cry of pain gave him pause, but the moment's surprise burned quickly away in the inferno of climax. Her cry of pleasure was as real and heartfelt as his own.

It wasn't until his world had settled back to earth that Nathan realized he'd courted and seduced an innocent girl.

Chapter 9

June 7, northwestward-bound along the Little Blue River—

This country is the most beautiful I've ever seen. Even after all these years of wagons traversing this very route, the grass in the river valley is still lush. Our mules are in heaven and grow more sleek and fat by the day. Firewood is easily had, and the Little Blue River is crystal clear, swift, and cold. The wonderful scenery relieves the tedium of our journey, and of great interest are the many names or initials of our predecessors carved into trees along the way.

One would not know that only two years ago the Sioux and Cheyenne spread fire and destruction throughout this valley, burning ranches and posting stations. Many are the burned-out ruins we have passed, grim reminders of a danger that is still present. All on the train speak of Indians with fear and loathing. A perfectly just person must have some sympathy for the Indians, I suppose. Even in Kansas we heard about the injustices visited upon the Red Man by the White Man—the massacre two years ago at Sand Creek being an example. Still, when one faces the danger of violent death, it is difficult to think upon one's enemy with any charity at all.

Before entering this lovely valley, we were required to cross the Big Blue River. The crossing was the most difficult so far of our journey, as the water was high and the current very swift. The Deckers lost their very nice buggy that was Mrs. Decker's pride and joy, and the Marches's cow was swept away. Our party came through the crossing intact, though damp. We re-caulked our wagon with pitch before the crossing, but the water managed to seep through. If not for the help of Mr. Pernell, we would have been much more than damp. The mules were required to swim and our wagon caught the current and threatened to spin about to tangle us all. Mr. Pernell and his splendid horse rode to the rescue along with Mr. Sutter, Mr. Campbell, and our own dear professor. We managed to complete the crossing with only dampened cargo and jangled nerves.

And that incident, dear journal, brings me to a most delicate subject. Even though these words are private, I hesitate to speak of what has occurred between myself and the brave Mr. Pernell, who serves as preacher and religious shepherd to our friends from Shelby.

Here Cass stopped writing. The light of her lantern shivered with the blustery drafts that forced their way into the tent, and the tent canvas rippled in the night wind. Close beside Cass, Lila slept. Her snores and the whine of the wind were the only sounds. The camp was silent, and in her little circle of light, Cass felt that she and her sister might be the only people in a vast, wide wilderness.

Yet still she felt too exposed to put to paper the extraordinary experience of three nights ago, when she had lain in Homer Pernell's arms and learned firsthand why love made people do foolish things. She remembered every feeling, every nuance of emotion that his caresses had evoked. She had always pictured the sex act as rather crass, something that men enjoyed and women simply permitted. But

what had happened between her and Homer had not been
crass at all. She had felt like a goddess, naked and free,
giving and receiving joy in the most elemental, natural way
possible. His touch was gentle and loving—and so blissful.
In the light of day, the memory of their congress should
bring embarrassment, but it didn't. The final act of intimacy
had brought her to a peak of happiness that was just short
of heaven. He had filled her with joy, and never, never,
never would she regret giving herself to him.

Yet her hands would not write the words in her journal,
even though no one but she would ever read them. So perhaps there was a small bit of guilt in her soul. They should
have waited until they were husband and wife in law as
well as spirit. But that smidgen of guilt could not oppress
her. Now that she had discovered the joys of love with
Homer Pernell, nothing could oppress her.

> *In summary,* she continued, *I shall merely say that
> Mr. Pernell has asked me to be his wife, and I have
> accepted. He is the most perfect man in all ways. Cer-
> tainly my situation will be better than I ever could
> have dreamed back in Webster, for I will be a
> preacher's wife, the very epitome of respectability.*
>
> *I fear that our respectable positions will have to
> be with a group other than the Shelby community,
> however, for since Mr. Pernell announced our inten-
> tion to marry at Fort Kearny, where we presume a
> clergyman can be found, his people have been openly
> disapproving. Many a foul look has been sent my way,
> and toward my friends as well. And though he hasn't
> spoken a word of complaint to me, I know that Mr.
> Pernell was roundly lectured by Mr. Jacobs, the com-
> munity leader.*
>
> *I am much more fortunate than he, because I am
> surrounded by friends who wish me well. Though
> Frenchie and Sue tease me unmercifully, that is their
> way of showing affection. Dear Luce is very happy
> for me. I can tell by the way she scolds, warning me
> to behave myself with Mr. Pernell until we are wed.
> In her words, I am "no loose-tailed layabout like some*

*others she could name." Luce seldom misses a chance
to toss an insult into the midst of Lila's ladies, but
they all know she merely blows smoke.*

*Lila seems happiest of all about the coming nup-
tials, save for myself. A girl falls in love for the first
time only once, she says.*

*For me, the first time will be the last. There will
be no other man in my life but Homer Pernell.*

"Dog, old boy, I'm a happy man." Nathan leveled the
sights of his rifle at a distant tree branch and fired. The
branch shattered in a most satisfying manner. Dog watched
placidly. "Yessiree, Dog. A happy man." He reloaded, raised
the rifle to his shoulder, and fired again. Another branch
dead.

He was happy, Nathan told himself, even if Dog seemed
to meet his declaration with skeptical looks. He was going
to marry a beautiful, passionate woman. He was leaving the
law far behind, along with his past. And old Jed Jacobs had
confided just that morning that they would leave discussion
of his future with the community until they got to Oregon.
That was just fine with Nathan, because once in Oregon,
he had no future with the Shelby community. They were
nice enough people, but he wasn't about to be a Bible
thumper the rest of his days. It was bad enough he had to
put up with a name like Homer.

"Things are going to work out fine," he told Dog, who
merely yawned. "So stop giving me those 'you ought to
know better' looks."

He stowed his rifle in its boot on Tiger's saddle, then
buckled his gunbelt around his hips and tied the holster to
his right thigh. "Close your ears," he told the dog.

His quick draw was less than quick, Nathan discovered
in the next few minutes. And his aim wasn't as true as it
once had been. That's what he got for not practicing. But
practice required riding far enough from the train so that
no nosy busybodies sauntered over to see what all the gunfire was about. He might have a hard time explaining why
a peaceful preaching man needed the skills of a gunslinger.

Nathan hoped he no longer needed such deadly skills, but he wasn't willing to bet his life on it.

"Rusty," he commented to Dog. "If any gunfights are waiting around the next bend, I'm likely to be a dead man."

After a few more minutes practice with the pistol, he cleaned his weapons, reloaded, and headed back for the train, which was camped down the valley a couple of miles. He passed the burned-out remains of a cabin—a blackened remnant of the Sioux and Cheyenne terrors of '63 and '64. It was a sober reminder that any man's future could be blotted out without warning.

His future, he reminded himself, might require some delicate diplomacy where Cassidy Rose was concerned. His intentions had been honorable enough. By the time they reached Oregon, any lawman who knew his face would have been a half continent away. He could have bid the Shelby community a friendly good-bye, married Cass with some assurance of a bright future, and she would have been perfectly happy as the respectable wife of a respectable rancher or farmer or lumberman. Preachers weren't the only men who were pillars of the community, after all.

But his intentions hadn't quite held up to the temptation of Cassidy's midnight visit. What man could have resisted those adoring, earnest whispers and that lovely young body? Maybe the real Homer Pernell would have sent her back to her own tent, if he were as pure in mind and spirit as a saint. But not Nathan Stone, who wasn't pure in any sense of the word. Nathan loved Cassidy Rose McAllister. He sincerely did. Not only did he love her, he craved her with the craving of a healthy man for a beautiful, loving woman. Who could blame him for jumping at what she offered. After all, it wasn't as if he were blazing a new trail.

So imagine his surprise when, at the critical juncture, Nathan discovered that he was blazing a new trail. Cassidy Rose McAllister was as pure as the driven snow. No matter what her sister and friends were, Cass had never sold her body, because her body was as fresh and virginal as the day she was born. At least, it was fresh and virginal before Nathan had put his mark upon her. He'd been surprised, but not surprised enough to back off before the damage was done. Someone could have whacked him with a board and he still couldn't have backed off at that point.

So the deed was done, and the only way to mend the situation was to marry the girl as soon as possible. Years had passed since Nathan had called himself a Tennessee gentleman, but, as low as he'd sunk, three rules of that gentleman's code he'd never broken: he'd never back-talked his mother, he'd never abused his horse, and he'd never dishonored an innocent girl. As soon as they could find someone with the authority to marry them, Nathan was going to do the honorable thing, and hope for the best. If the law caught up with him before he got far enough away, then he'd face that when it happened. Besides, the law wasn't going to catch up with him. He was officially dead, buried in a grave outside Silas, Kansas. And who would suspect a preacher traveling west with a whole community of churchfolk? He was safe. Getting married now was the right thing to do. It would give him that much more time to be with Cass.

Suddenly Dog stopped and whined, his ragged furry ears cocked in the direction of heavy brush just ahead. A frisson of alarm traveled down Nathan's spine. He'd assumed the Indians in these parts would hesitate to attack a man shooting off the amount of lead that he'd been shooting off. But he might be mistaken. Then a soft gobble made him smile, and he pulled his rifle from its boot.

"What do you say, Dog? Do you think my love knows how to dress and cook a wild turkey?"

Cass was a happy woman. Since her night of love, the sun had become warmer, the mornings fresher, her chores lighter, the mules sweeter-tempered. She scarcely noticed the small irritants of life such as mosquitoes, sore feet, smoky cook fires, and the occasional poisonous look from the Shelby women.

Today they had called an early halt, because the March baby had taken ill again, and little Mary Decker as well. Cass was glad to have the time to finish up the shirts she was making for Mr. Pernell. After making the bloomer costumes for Lila's ladies—which were lying ignored except for the two she had chosen for herself—she still had plenty of yard goods left over, and her dear Homer seemed to be a pauper when it came to clothing. He wore the same two shirts day in and day out. So she had decided to prove what a good wife she intended to be by making up the lack in his wardrobe.

"Aren't you a busy little bee," Frenchie commented as she poured herself a cup of coffee from the pot sitting on the fire.

Cass answered in the same tone. "It's nice to have someone to sew for who appreciates the effort."

"Cassie girl, I always appreciate your talent with a needle, as long as you aren't sewing something that makes me look like a frigging ten-year-old."

"That bloomer dress did not make you look like a ten-year-old."

"Close to it. But look who's coming—the lucky man himself."

"Oh, good! I can measure his sleeve length again. I may have made this too short."

Frenchie snickered. "His sleeve length, sweetie? Is that what you want to measure?"

Mama Luce came from around the wagon and gave Frenchie a stern look. "You behave yo'self and don't give the chile ideas. If you don't have anything to do but drink coffee and laze about like a no-account hussy, bring that basket and come wit' me. There's wild onions and garlic in the woods over here, and I mean to have 'em in tomorra's stew."

Frenchie tossed the dregs of her coffee and gave Cass a cheerful grin. "Have fun."

Frenchie and Luce had taken off to find the onions when Cassidy's love rode up and dropped a dead turkey at her feet. "You know how to fix a turkey?"

She smiled wryly. "This one looks past fixing, poor bird."

"I can see I'm going to have a smart-mouth wife," he said, dismounting.

His grin made her heart beat faster. She loved the way his eyes crinkled when he smiled. It was a smile that took up his whole face, not just his mouth. And she loved the

way his eyes looked as dark as deep midnight one moment
and as soft as sweet chocolate the next. How she wished
another preacher might ride up this very night so they could
be married. She wanted to lie in this man's arms every night,
to sit beside him in the daylight, and do all the little things
a loving wife might do—brush back the stray locks that always fell over his forehead, straighten the collar of his shirt,
give him a wifely peck on the cheek whenever she felt the
urge. Married life was going to be so sweet.

"So . . ." He raised a brow. "Do I have to pluck and cook
this myself?"

She came out of her daydream. "Of course not. I know
how to cook a turkey, Homer Pernell. Don't malign my domestic skills."

His eyes swept her from head to toe in a possessive manner that sent a flash of heat through her veins. "I wouldn't
dream of maligning your domestic skills, sweetheart. Believe me, I treasure them."

Embarrassed, Cass avoided his eyes and picked up the
bird by its feet.

"I gutted it already."

"How romantic."

Then suddenly, her sweet Homer Pernell with the soft
chocolate eyes was gone. Even not looking at him Cass
could feel the sudden chill of his transformation. When she
turned toward him, she saw a man she didn't know. His
eyes had gone hard and flat, as black and cold as last night's
coals, and the planes of his face had settled into an expression that sent an arrow of uncertainty into her happiness.

"Homer?" She set the bird onto their folding worktable.
"Homer? Is something wrong?"

When he said nothing, she followed his gaze. A stranger
had ridden into camp on a tired-looking chestnut horse. He
was bent from his saddle to talk earnestly to Aaron Sutter,
who listened then shook his head. Aaron called over Jed Jacobs, who joined the conversation and also shook his head.

Homer brushed past her and vaulted into the big wagon.
The word that he uttered was one that no preacher should
even know, much less use.

"Homer Pernell! What is the matter?"

"Quiet!" he demanded in a harsh whisper. "Tie up my horse behind the wagon."

Baffled, she did as he bid and looped Tiger's reins through an iron ring on the side of the wagon bed. Then she went back and peered into the wagon. "What are you doing?" He had his eye fastened to a small hole in the canvas that had not yet been patched.

"Cass," he said in a quiet, intense voice, "you're going to have to trust me in this. I'm not here. If anyone asks, I'm out hunting. Keep Tiger close to the wagon. Oh, shit!"

She gave him a stern gaze for the profanity, but he wasn't looking at her. His eye was still fixed at the rip in the canvas. Miffed, Cass left him alone and wandered closer to where Jed and Aaron conferred with the stranger, who had pulled a paper of some sort from his pocket and was showing it to the men. Others were paying attention as well, and a crowd began to gather.

Granny Decker plucked at Cassidy's sleeve. "What's afoot, missy? My hearing isn't what it once was."

"I don't know," Cass replied with a worried frown. "Let's move closer."

Lila and Sue joined them, followed by young Amos Byrd with Faith Scott trailing in his wake. Clyde Hawkins, Banjo Ben, and wagonmaster Charlie Morris now were staring at the stranger's piece of paper.

"We don't got no one here by that name," Morris told the man.

"That drawing could look like a lot of men," Jed observed. "Ain't much help."

Clyde Hawkins chimed in. "Everyone here's been with us since Shelby, Missouri, 'ceptin' a couple of wagons of women and their piano player. They sure ain't who you're lookin' fer."

Lila snagged the professor, who was just leaving the group of men. "What's going on?"

"Nothing much. He's a federal marshal on a manhunt. Looking for some lowlife who slipped out on his appointment with the hangman in Silas. Remember when old Sam Keller's store was robbed and the old man shot?"

"Cass was in the store when it happened," Sue reminded them.

No one needed to remind Cass of the incident. She was beginning to have a very bad feeling about this.

"They hanged those fellows," Lila said.

"One of 'em got away. Fella by the name of Nathan Stone. The marshal says he killed a Kansas girl back during the war, and it looks like he did in some fellow outside of Silas, too. Killed him, buried him, and left his own name on the grave."

Rachel walked up. "Wait till you hear what Ben told me!"

"We already got the story," Lila said.

Cass drifted away, feeling as though someone had dropped a ten-pound rock into her stomach. If not for Homer's peculiar behavior, she would scarcely have given the manhunt a thought. Even with her love acting in such a suspicious manner, she couldn't really believe this marshal had anything to do with a preacher from Shelby, Missouri. It just didn't fit.

Fighting a sense of doom, she marched toward their wagon.

"Homer Pernell, I need some answers."

"Quiet!"

"Do you know that man? He's a federal marshal."

"Shhhhh!"

"Don't 'shhhhhh' me! Do you know a man named Nathan Stone?"

His head snapped around, and the expression on his face scared her to death. But the beginning boil of anger fortified her courage.

"Well? Do you? And if you don't, then why are you hiding from that man out there who is searching for Nathan Stone?"

"Cass . . ." His voice was tightly controlled, quiet, and had a chill to it that froze and shattered any remnant of hope that he had an innocent explanation. "I will explain. I promise. But that marshal cannot see me."

Odd pieces of a puzzle fell one by one into place. A glimpse of him twirling a pistol around one finger with a skill that no preacher should own; a horse built for speed and beauty—so different from the usual modest hack that a preacher might ride; a certain worldly wickedness in his smile; an almost profane tolerance for a group of mostly unrepentant tarts. Then the last piece came clear, making the picture complete. His eyes. Why hadn't she recognized the eyes? Black and deep, fearful in their intensity. They were the eyes he had turned on her when she said the name Nathan Stone. And they were the eyes that had looked down at her from above a scarf that had covered the rest of his face. Homer Pernell wasn't Homer Pernell. He was a dangerous stranger named Nathan Stone, and he'd held her in his grip in Silas while his partners robbed and shot old man Keller.

The horror of the revelation made white lights burst in her brain. Despair rose in a flood and almost choked the breath from her lungs.

"Tell me that you didn't kill a girl in Kansas." Her voice was but a choked whisper. "That you didn't shoot the real Homer Pernell and bury him so you could take his place."

"Shit!" was the only answer he gave her. "Get out of my way, Cass. I'm going."

He jumped from the wagon, landing nearly on top of her, and yanked Tiger's reins from where she had tied them.

"You owe me an explanation! You can't just leave without telling—" She had to swallow the rest of her rant when he grabbed her and swooped down upon her mouth in a hard, fast kiss.

"I love you, Cass. I wish I had time to explain. But I don't."

Fury burst from her tattered heart and rushed outward to every fiber. She had given herself to a con man, an outlaw, a murderer. Her virtue was gone forever—the virtue she'd guarded so well during years spent in a world that destroyed virtue as it destroyed innocence, hope, and laughter. She'd wasted it on a devil who'd played her for a fool. No doubt he'd laughed all the while she trusted him. How he must have smiled at her innocent declarations of love, at her pathetic offering of her body. The very man who'd mauled her in Keller's mercantile.

He had one foot in Tiger's stirrup when she launched herself at him. "You worm! You piece of slime! Scum! Don't you dare leave before you give me some explanation of what you thought you were doing. How dare you lie to me and take advantage of . . . of a foolish girl's trust!" She pounded a fist on his back. If she'd had a stout stick at hand she would have whacked him. He had broken her dreams, and she hated him as she'd never hated anyone or anything in her life.

"Cass, for God's sake!"

"Don't you dare call on God, you hypocritical dog-turd. You—"

"Step away, ma'am," said a strange, flat voice. "And you, mister. You turn around slow like."

Cass's heart nearly stopped. She'd all but forgotten the federal marshal. Slowly, her preacher turned. But he wasn't her preacher any longer. He was a criminal named Nathan Stone. Even his face didn't look the same as her dear Homer's. The man she loved had never looked so hard, so cold, so desperate.

"I do declare," the marshal said laconically. He held a pistol steady and pointed straight at Nathan's heart. "It's the dog-turd himself. I have to agree with the lady's description."

Nathan ignored the gun. He gave the marshal a half smile. "Lawton, you're a persistent sonofabitch. I'll give you that."

"You'll give me a hell of a lot more than that."

"We'll see."

Beside Tiger, Dog whined. Tension and consternation mingled as an agitated babble broke out in the crowd that had gathered. Every soul on the wagon train was watching the drama, and as the facts became apparent, cries of alarm mixed with moans of dismay.

"You mean he's the man you're looking for?" Jed Jacobs demanded.

Questions and comments pelted in from all sides. "Homer Pernell's an outlaw?"

"Didn't you hear the marshal? Mr. Pernell's dead."

"Oh, my lord, the devil is among us!"

"Mr. Pernell's not dead. He's standing right there."

"Haven't you been listening?"

"I always figured there was something fishy about him."

"It can't be! I don't believe it!"

"The devil's among us!"

"There must be some mistake!"

All the while the lamentations swirled around them, Nathan Stone and the lawman stood with eyes locked, two wolves staring each other down. Cass was frozen in place, despite Lila motioning frantically for her to remove herself. She felt as though lightning had struck her, turning her into a statue.

"Enough!" the lawman finally bellowed. "You people quiet down and back off. You've been hoodwinked by this scum, and whatever he was to you, he isn't anymore. I'm taking him back to Kansas City. I suggest you go back to doing whatever it was you were doing."

Tight-lipped and still murmuring, the crowd started to loosen and back off.

"You, Stone. Unbuckle the gunbelt and drop it."

"Sure thing."

Before Cass knew what had happened, a steel-thewed arm shot out to circle around her neck, and suddenly she was back to front against a man who had become a stranger. A cold pistol barrel rested against her temple. Lawton's gun wavered, and gasps came from those who still watched. From the corner of her eye, Cass saw Lila rush forward only to be restrained by Rachel. Sue wrung her hands and moaned. Jed Jacobs's eyes grew wide, and even Eliza Jacobs, the old battle-ax, looked concerned. Everything was crystal clear and passed in dreamlike lethargy. Surely, Cass thought, this was a nightmare. None of it could really be happening.

Stone's voice rumbled against her back. "I'm leaving, Lawton. And if anyone tries to stop me, I'll put a bullet through her."

Cass closed her eyes and prayed. Suddenly religion had become very relevant. She heard a moaned "No!" from Lila. The rest of the encampment was still as death.

Stone's arm tightened around her. "Don't gamble, Lawton. If I'm the cold-blooded killer you think I am, then I'll do it, won't I?"

Cass opened her eyes to see Lawton lower his pistol. His face was flushed and angry beneath his sandy blond hair. "I'll catch up to you again, Stone."

"If you catch up to me while I still have her, she'll suffer for it. Now back off."

Lawton did as ordered.

Stone dragged her toward his horse. Cassidy's numbness was fading. Unless she did something fast she would be in very great trouble indeed. "Get on," Nathan ordered. Close against her back, he started to heft her into the saddle. With all her might, she sent a sharp elbow into his ribs. He oofed out a pained grunt, but grabbed her quickly with an arm around her waist. His pistol swung steadily to bear on Lawton, who'd taken advantage and surged forward. "Don't even think about it, marshal. And as for you, you little witch . . . no more tricks." He tossed her to the saddle. She landed stomach down, shrieking. He vaulted to the saddle behind her, pushing her back down when she struggled to sit. She ended up draped across his hard thighs with her head bouncing against his knee. Her uncomfortable position gave her an upside down jouncing view of the receding wagon train as Tiger took off at a gallop.

Chapter 10

Nathan drove Tiger as if the devil himself pursued them, and the devil probably did in the person of John T. Lawton. He'd known Lawton was somewhere in Kansas, and he'd figured the single-minded marshal was looking for him, but after all that had happened, he sure hadn't expected the bastard to ride into the Shelby wagon train and blow his new life all to smithereens.

Tiger lurched sideways and crowhopped in objection to Cassidy's struggles. The little she-viper wasn't making this escape any easier. She pounded futile fists against anything they could reach—Nathan's thigh, Tiger's shoulder and belly. Her legs flailed furiously.

"Settle down!" he warned her with a mild swat on her rear.

In response, she bit his knee.

"Goddamnit, Cass!"

She shouted a string of words that sounded like obscenities, but shouting into Nathan's leg, the saddle, and Tiger's shoulder at the same time she bounced on her stomach made the exact meaning unintelligible. Just as well, Nathan thought. When she made a grab for the pistol that rode his hip, though, that was the last straw. He hauled Tiger to a sliding halt, jumped to the ground, and pulled her after him. As soon as her feet touched solid earth she took a swing at him.

"Whoa! Who would guess that little Miss Respectable had such a temper?"

"Get your hands off of me, you maggot! I can't believe I was stupid enough to ever trust you!"

She connected with a fist before he could contain her flailing arms.

"Ouch! Quit your frigging tantrum, you hellion! Just—ouch!—quit!"

Cass continued to struggle, even after Nathan had both of her wrists secured in one big hand. His other hand searched the saddlebags for something to tie her with. But there was nothing in the bag but extra ammunition, a moth-eaten blanket, and the Bible Jed Jacobs had loaned him. He'd carried it everywhere, just for show.

She managed to stomp on his toe.

"Ow! Damnit!

"You lied to me! You lied to everyone, but you especially lied to me, you no-good snake. You took advantage of me, and I was stupid enough to let you. I can't believe I . . . I let you . . . I actually . . ." Her freckles swarmed into a solid stain of rage as she aimed a kick at his shin, which he just managed to dodge.

"Cassie, sweetheart, settle down. I can explain."

"Sweetheart? Sweetheart? You held a goddamned pistol to my head! You threatened to shoot me!"

He'd never before today heard her cuss, but he supposed the situation called for it.

"You were the scumbag in the Silas robbery! How did I not recognize you? You've been laughing up your sleeve this whole time!"

"Well, no. Really—ouch! Have you got lead in those shoes of yours? Damn!"

"Let me go!"

"No. Not until you calm down. Look, you're upsetting Dog. You don't want to get bit, do you?"

Dog had been regarding them with lively interest all the while. Now he lay down and yawned. Big help he was.

"Dog should be careful of the company he keeps. Even

a mongrel deserves better than you." The genuine pain in
her eyes reminded him that he wasn't the only one whose
life John Lawton shattered this day.

"Cass, I never meant for this to happen."

"I'll just bet you didn't!"

"You must have known back there that I wouldn't really
shoot you. My god, woman, I love you!"

"You lied."

"Not about the important things. When I said that I love
you, I meant it."

"Well, I don't love you!"

She was still angry, but at least she had quit beating on
him. Cautiously, he loosened the pressure on her wrists. He
should have known better. The little witch went for his gun
again, and this time she got it.

For a mere second time seemed to slow. Nathan could
see the lightning flash of expressions across her face—surprise, consternation, indecision. She regarded the pistol in
her hands as if it were a snake that might bite her. Then
she met his eyes with hers, and regarded him with the same
fearful expression.

"Cass . . ." He tried for calm in his voice, but he could
already almost feel a slug tearing through him.

She turned and fled, taking the pistol with her. Dog yipped
and bounded after her, no doubt expecting a game of chase.
With a curse, Nathan joined in.

She didn't have a chance against his long legs, and in
only a few seconds he grabbed her. She shook loose and
sprinted away until his flying tackle sent them both to the
ground. Dog bounded around them, barking with delight.

"Damnit, Cass! Give me the pistol."

"Get off me!"

"Not until you give me the damned pistol!"

Her writhing struggle made him angry, and it also aroused
him, which made him angrier still. She'd been beneath him
once before under much different circumstances—never
again, and Nathan didn't like the reminder of what he'd
lost.

"Hold still, goddamnit! And let me have the gun!"

He trapped the hand holding the pistol, and it went off.

Cass screamed, Dog barked, and Nathan became very still, waiting for a blossom of scarlet on her or an inkling of pain in himself. Neither happened. The pistol fell to the ground, and Cassidy's face crumpled.

"No, no, no, no, no!" she wept. "I don't want to love you, whoever you are. Stop looking like Homer, and smelling like him, and feeling like him. You aren't him."

"No," he said quietly, still pinning her to the ground.

"I want to love a peaceable, respectable man. Not you. Not you."

The words bubbled through her tears, but Nathan understood them well enough. She had felt it also—desire is not as easily changed as the heart. For a woman, who is supposed to love with the heart more than the body, passion for a man she had decided to hate would be the ultimate humiliation.

"You're right. You can't love me," he began in order to be kind, to break the bond forever and cleanly, but his words stumbled into his own bitterness. "You can't love me, Cass, because I'm not peaceable and not respectable. I'm a sonofabitch who's killed and seen more killing than any man should, who's burned, who's robbed, who's hurt innocent people. And that's what I'll always be, I guess." He got up and pulled her to her feet, at the same time grabbing the pistol before she could snatch it yet again. But most of the defiance had run out of her. As she stood there dirt-smeared, red-eyed, and tear-streaked, he couldn't resist touching her cheek. She flinched but didn't back away. "Turns out there's no such thing as redemption," he said sadly. "At least not for me."

Back in the saddle, Cass, ominously quiet, sat upright in front of Nathan. Tiger liked this arrangement much better, and he galloped off at a good pace to the east, toward a stage station they had passed the afternoon before. Cass would be safe there, Nathan thought. Not happy, perhaps, but safe. And since the coach route followed the same road the wagons used, she would have a way back to her sister and friends.

When luck ran out, though, it really ran out. Very little time passed before pursuit became obvious. Nathan peered through narrowed eyes at the small dust cloud a mile or so back—a one-horse dust cloud, if he wasn't mistaken. Lawton.

"Damn him!"

Cass smiled. He gave her a disgusted scowl. "You're really determined to see my neck stretched, aren't you? If not for you coming after me like a screech owl, I could have slipped away until the marshal left. Lawton never would have identified me."

"Tough."

"And your firing off my pistol might as well have been a signal for him to come looking."

She gave him a smug look. "You can't blame others when you have to pay the consequences for your crimes."

He checked the loading in his pistol, then the rifle that rode the saddle boot. "Want to see my blood, do you?" He kicked Tiger into a canter. "You might get your wish before the day's out."

They rode only far enough to find good cover. Even Nathan's proud Tennessee stud couldn't hope to outrun Lawton's horse carrying two on his back. They halted where the gentle crest of a small bluff combined with a stand of scrub to make a natural fortification. If he could hold Lawton off until nightfall, he might still escape.

"Behave yourself!" He pulled Cass from the saddle and set her on the ground with a stern look. "Things might get nasty, so just stay here and keep quiet. Don't even think of taking off. Dog might like you, but he'll fetch you back if I tell him to."

With a sullen hmmph she looked down her nose at him.

"And by the way, Miss Moral Superiority, just in case you're interested in the truth, John Lawton's after me for something I didn't do. I've done enough in this life to send me to hell several times over, but I didn't do this."

She hmmphed again. "Does truth ever pass your lips?"

"That does it!" From a scabbard at his belt he took a knife. Her eyes widened in panic. "Sit down!"

For a change she did as she was told, and when he cut two long strips from the hem of her petticoat, she looked relieved that he hadn't used the knife on her.

"I'm tying you up, you little troublemaker. Lawton out there isn't playing games, and neither am I. Now, you just sit here with Dog. Behave like a lady and hold your flapping tongue, or I'll cut another strip to gag you with. Understand?"

She nodded mutely, resentment burning in those bright green eyes that had once looked at him with such adoration. Nathan sighed. Life was a sack of shit. He tried to forget about her, temporarily at least, and positioned himself at the crest of the hill overlooking all possible approaches. He didn't have long to wait before Lawton showed up. When the lawman was still at very long rifle range, Nathan fired a shot in his direction. He didn't have a hope of hitting him at that distance. He wasn't even sure he really wanted to hit the guy. He just wanted him to go away. The marshal quickly took cover in a thicket of scrub oak.

"Stone, you chicken-shit, send down the woman and it'll go easier on you."

"Stow it, Lawton. If you cared about the woman you wouldn't have come after us. I told you what I'd do."

A shot rang out, and halfway down the bluff a rifle slug plowed into the dirt. Lawton was trying for range. Nathan fired off a reply in the direction of the thicket. At least he would show him he meant business.

"Head back where you came from, Lawton. Otherwise I'm going to do something we'll both regret."

Lawton moved, running like a streak to a swale that gave him cover. Nathan fired a shot, but it was a waste of ammunition, and he knew it.

"Missed, asshole!"

"You're taking chances with someone else's life, marshal."

"You won't hurt her yet. She wouldn't be of use to you dead, would she? You haven't had time to have your fun yet."

"What does he mean?" Cass demanded.

"Nothing. Be quiet." He fired toward the man's voice and saw his bullet dig up dirt at the top of Lawton's rise. At least the bastard was in range now.

The trouble was, Nathan was in range as well. Lawton's

next shot plowed into the hill just below the crest, and the next went clean over the bluff and hit a tree. Lawton appeared briefly from his cover to make another shot, and Nathan sent two rapid shots in his direction.

"Get down!" he ordered Cass. "Lie flat."

"What do you think you're doing?" she demanded frantically. "One of you is going to get killed!"

"That's the point."

For the next thirty minutes they exchanged sporadic shots, accomplishing nothing. The sun crept closer to the horizon, however, and Nathan began to hope that they could hold out until nightfall, when they could escape under cover of the dark.

"Mr. Stone," Cass said primly.

"What?"

"You tied me too tightly. It hurts."

With a sigh he scrambled the few feet to where Cass lay. The strips of petticoat had rubbed her wrists raw, and her ankles were starting to swell—both problems no doubt due to her trying to wriggle her way free. Still, he felt a twinge of guilt. Cassidy Rose McAllister was the last person on earth that he wanted to hurt, and circumstances were forcing him to do just that. He untied her and chafed her hands.

"Why didn't you say something earlier?"

"I was hoping Mr. Lawton would shoot you and set me free."

"Bloodthirsty little witch."

She flinched when he started to retie her. The flinch went straight to his heart.

"If I leave you untied, will you give your word to behave?"

She looked thoughtful.

"If you try to run, you'll just be stuck out here in Indian country with no food and no weapon. Lawton won't bother with you, believe me. The only thing in the world he wants is my neck in a noose, and he's not going to detour one minute for a woman he doesn't even know."

"Well then, I'd better behave, hadn't I?"

Nathan didn't much like her tone, but he left her as she was. "Watch her," he said to Dog. "She's tricky."

Dog obediently padded over and flopped down beside Cass. She smiled sweetly at him and scratched an ear. He half closed his eyes and whined in ecstasy. Nathan was about to think better of leaving Cass loose when another shot whined over the crest of the bluff and they all flattened themselves to the ground. When Dog started to get up, Cass reached up and pulled him down.

"He's come a bit closer," Nathan said, scrambling back to his vantage point. He looked at the sun. Wouldn't it ever set? He kept his eyes peeled, praying that Lawton would make a mistake and show himself again—this time long enough for Nathan to get in a good shot. He didn't have any burning desire to kill the lawman. Lord knew he'd done enough killing during the war to sicken any man, but experience didn't necessarily harden a man to the deed. But if he could send a lead message whizzing just past Lawton's ear it might make the marshal a good deal less bold. All Nathan needed was to hold out until dark. That was all he needed.

Cass crept up and lay prone on the grass beside him. The fool dog kept her company. "What do you see?"

"Nothing, right now. Get back to where you belong."

"I belong on the wagon train."

He sighed.

"Have you men given up trying to shoot each other?"

"No," he said curtly. "But the way things are going, no one's likely to shoot anyone. Once it's full dark, you and I are leaving."

"Is he so stupid he doesn't realize you'll do that?"

"Lawton's not stupid. He's creeping his way up the hill to do some close-in killing, I figure. He'd rather see me hang, 'cause it hurts more than a nice clean bullet, but if he has to shoot me point-blank to get the job done, he will."

"And of course you wouldn't dream of doing the same to him."

"I'm just defending myself."

"How could I have ever believed you were a man of God?"

A flash of fire erupted from a small thicket two hundred feet away, and a bullet hit sent a spray of dirt into their faces. Nathan shoved Cass even flatter. "Damn him to hell! He's going to end up killing you instead of me."

Then Lawton got overconfident. He'd chosen a thicket that didn't give quite the cover he thought it did. His blue shirt was visible enough that Nathan could pinpoint him exactly. "There he is, the sneaky bastard, and next thing you know, he's going to be right in our laps. Or at least that's what he thinks."

Nathan sighted carefully down the barrel of his Winchester. "This'll make him think."

He fired—just as a narrow-eyed Cass jostled his aim. "What the hell—?"

"You're *not* going to kill that man. Not while I'm watching!"

But the cry from the thicket indicated he might have. "You fool!" Nathan bellowed. "I was just going to wing him. You sent my aim off."

"Hah!"

From the thicket there was only ominous silence. "Now see what you've done, you meddling little witch!"

"What *I've* done, you villain?"

He pulled her roughly to her feet. "It's done, now. We're leaving."

"I'm not!" She kicked his shin and jerked away as he reacted. "I'm going down to help that man. Shoot me if you dare!" She marched halfway down the slope, then turned to taunt him. Spreading her arms wide, she challenged: "What's the matter, Stone? Is a woman too easy a target?"

Nathan ground his teeth and raised hands to the heavens. "What the hell have I ever done to deserve Cassidy Rose McAllister in my life?"

"Harlots! Jezebels! Devil's handmaidens!" came the cries from the little assembly of women gathered beside the unmoving wagons. Their menfolk drifted around the fringes of the crowd, some looking angry, most looking uneasy. The children of the train were quiet, sensing the general tension. Jed Jacobs stood above them all in the supply wagon from which Homer Pernell, or rather the outlaw impostor, had once preached. His wife, Eliza, stood beside him, looking harried and smug at the same time.

Lila and her ladies stood in a worried little knot beside their own wagons. Lila was pale and frazzled. She could break up barroom fights, confront brutal customers, and stand up to a few nights in jail without mussing a single hair or smudging the artificial rose in her cheeks, but Cassidy's abduction had sent her to pieces. She paid little mind to the ruckus raised by Eliza Jacobs and her morally superior sisters. Her eyes searched the distance for the return of John Lawton with Cassidy Rose safe in his care.

The other ladies were torn between concern for Cass and concern for themselves. None of them wanted to be on their own in dangerous, barely civilized country. What's more, they weren't women who heard fighting words without wanting to fight, and the insults rising out of the Shelby crowd were enough to spark a veritable war.

"I told you so, sisters and brothers," Eliza crowed almost joyously. "I told you we were headed for trouble the minute we took those women into our midst. We're walking the devil's path, and God has deserted us. And why shouldn't he? We shelter harlots among us. Now our own minister of God, the Lord's own mouthpiece, whose mission it is to anchor our faith and guide our footsteps on the paths of righteousness—our own minister is revealed to be the devil's own sword, a thief and murderer. I tell you, brothers and sisters, we have strayed far, far from God's garden, and He is letting us create our own doom."

"Amen!" cried Virginia March.

"Amen," came an uneasy chorus from the rest.

"She's on a roll," Frenchie commented.

"Why do you suppose she hates us so much?" Sue wondered.

"Probably she's never really had a good lay. I've heard it makes a woman cranky."

Rachel chuckled. "And what does having too much do to a woman?"

"Same thing," Frenchie opined.

"Now, Eliza dear," her husband said. "I don't think we can blame all of this on the McAllister party."

A few murmurs of agreement, both male and female, supported him.

"Can't you see?" Eliza hissed. "Are there scales before your eyes? We forfeit God's protection by breaking God's rules. What will happen next? Plague? Red savages swarming over us like locusts?"

"A bunch of claptrap if you ask me!" Granny Decker said.

"Mother!" her son warned.

"It's God's own truth is what it is," Eliza rebutted. "We must purge ourselves of sin, starting with the devil's daughters. Banish them! Brothers, turn your faces from their temptations, and sisters, cast your eyes not upon their sinful, fancy ways. Throw the strumpets out!"

The women, and some of the men, cheered, but a few voices rose above the din. Effie Brown's was one of them. "I say everyone should have a chance to improve themselves. Who are we to judge these women?"

"That's right," Banjo Ben agreed. "You can't leave a bunch of women on their own out here. Besides, they've caused no trouble, and they've shouldered their share of the work. Just because you don't like the way they dress and talk, and maybe their ideas of right and wrong are different from yours—that don't give no reason to leave 'em behind. They didn't have anything to do with the preacher tuning out to be an outlaw."

"There's something to what Ben says," Aaron Sutter claimed.

"He's just your hired man, Aaron. He shouldn't be talkin' like he was a white man."

A chorus of agreement met the older Amos Byrd's pronouncement.

"Well, I'm not anyone's hired man," the professor shouted. "And I'm as white as anyone here."

"The professor's gonna git himself in trouble," Luce predicted.

"Fool!" Frenchie said.

He strode boldly over to the crowd and, hands on his hips, looked them in the eye. "Those ladies over there might not be pure as the driven snow, but they're good women.

You've got no call to spit on them or turn them out. Just like you, they're headed to a new life. They've as much right to it as you do."

"Only thing worse than a whore is a man who works for a whore," said Amelia Byrd, standing close by her husband. If she'd left the insult at that, the insanity might not have erupted, for the professor was a mild sort of fellow and was used to insults from men and rejection from women. Mrs. Byrd carried her contempt a bit farther though, and spat at his feet.

For Frenchie, that was the last straw. She insulted the professor every chance she got, but it was a privilege she reserved to herself. She marched over to Amelia Byrd and glared at her. "You self-righteous pig-faced prig. You aren't worth the spit it takes to shine that man's shoes. If you had half the professor's character you'd be twice the woman you are."

"Slut! How dare you." Mrs. Byrd forgot her dignity and gave the smirking Frenchie a hard push. Frenchie shoved back, and Amelia bounced her backside onto the ground. Her husband, Amos, bellowed like a bull and jerked Frenchie back, and Amelia's friends swarmed around her like hornets. Sue dove in to help Frenchie. Rachel and Lila weren't far behind. The Shelby men waded in to rescue their womenfolk, and the throng became a roiling, shouting mass of communal fisticuffs. Aaron Sutter and Ben Holden tried in vain to separate the combatants, and Mama Luce tried also. But when Virginia March snatched the kerchief from Luce's head to yank her frizzy gray hair, the old Negro woman joined in the melee.

On the sidelines, Granny Decker climbed to the box of the Decker wagon and worked on her knitting while calmly watching the fray. Charlie Morris stood by and shook his head in disgust. Clyde Hawkins tried to be a wag by fetching his fiddle and striking up a lively Irish tune—one he thought was the perfect accompaniment to a bit of brawling. But his effort didn't last long. The mass of contenders drifted his way, and Clyde and his fiddle both disappeared into the fracas.

Still perched on the "preaching wagon" with his horri-

fied wife, Jed Jacobs sighed and prayed. "Lord, you shoulda'
warned me. Here I was thinkin' that Injuns were gonna be
the problem."

Cass shivered and hugged her knees to her chest. The shelter of leafy branches that Nathan had erected kept off the
misting rain that had settled in with nightfall, but it did little to keep out the damp cold. She had no shawl, and the
one blanket Nathan had found in his saddlebags was draped
over the unconscious John Lawton. Cass had cleaned and
bound the gunshot wound to his chest with more strips cut
from her poor petticoats. Soon she'd have nothing but her
flimsy cotton bloomers beneath her skirt.

Sitting across from Cass, Nathan Stone had been silent all
during their supper of roasted rabbit and the flat bread they'd
found in Lawton's saddlebags. Their small fire cast a ruddy,
flickering light on his grim face and made him look much
more fearsome than he actually was. At least, Cass hoped the
harsh, implacable cast of his face wasn't a true reflection of
Nathan Stone, in spite of the scathing accusations she'd sent
his way. With her life turned upside down, she didn't know
what to think anymore. On one hand, for weeks the man had
managed the role of a charming, amiable, cheerful, gentle,
helpful servant of God. Surely someone truly evil could not
have played that part so well. Yet he had held a pistol to her
head, kidnapped her, threatened to kill her, and almost had
killed a federal marshal. He wasn't exactly a Sunday school
teacher either.

A moan from the marshal brought her attention around.
When she crept near to check on him, she found him awake
and staring up at her with pale blue eyes. "Marshal Lawton?"

He answered with a pained grunt.

"How do you feel?"

"Unh!" He rasped: "How the hell do you think I feel?
I'm alive. I'd guess I have you to thank for that."

Across the fire, Nathan snorted. "You have her to thank
for being shot at all. I was aiming for a near miss. Wing
you at most, just to scare you off. If she hadn't knocked
my aim, it would've worked."

"I don't scare that easy, Stone."

"I guess you don't die that easy, either, Lawton. Far as I can tell, the slug missed your heart and lungs. You're not going to be giving me grief for a good while, though, and that's a fact."

Lawton turned his head slowly to meet Nathan's eyes. Cass could have chipped ice from the air between them. "Doesn't matter if it's this year or next, or even next decade, Stone. I'm not going to rest until I see you hang."

"That's what I figured." Nathan's mouth twisted into a humorless smile. "Should've killed you. She wouldn't let me."

That wasn't true, Cass knew. Nathan had followed her down the hill, but he hadn't tried to finish the job he'd bungled. He'd helped Cass stanch the flow of blood, cussing all the while, then carried the wounded man to this copse of trees, where he'd made a pallet and fashioned a shelter.

"He wouldn't have killed you in cold blood," Cass told Lawton, just to be fair.

Lawton closed his eyes briefly, as if overwhelmed by mounting pain. When he opened them, his lips twitched into a bitter smile. "You still think Stone's a decent human being, lady? Did he tell you about his brave exploits?"

"He robbed the mercantile in Silas. I was there."

Lawton grunted painfully. "Yeah, he did. But that's small change. Back in the war he rode with Quantrill."

Cass sent a horrified look Nathan's way. He sat staring at the fire, his features hewn from cold granite, his eyes flat and black.

"They ripped through Kansas, looting, burning, killing. If you had Yankee sympathies, then you were fair game. But they didn't really care. Mostly they raised hell for hell's sake alone."

"My sister and I were in Lawrence," Cass said.

"Then you know. I had me a nice farm. Didn't care much if Kansas was slave or free. Just wanted to be left alone to do my work. My brother went off to fight for the Yankees. My sixteen-year-old sister lived with me at the farm—until a pack of Quantrill's dogs came calling when I was gone into town. They killed a hired man, burned the barn, and took their turns on my sister, Amy."

Cass bit her lip and lowered her head to her knees.

"I came home in time to kill two of 'em. Another one got killed a week later in an attack on an armory. The fourth is serving ten years for assault and armed robbery in Kansas City. The fifth is our friend Stone."

Cass didn't want to believe it. What he'd done in Silas was bad enough, and she'd assumed he had other such robberies to his discredit. But this was monstrous.

"I never touched his sister," Nathan said in a flat voice. "I tried to stop what was going on. Even pulled a gun—but one of the others pistol-whipped me from behind. I'd just come to my senses when Lawton came riding in like the devil himself."

"Isn't a murdering, thieving scoundrel in the world who doesn't whine about being innocent."

"Was your sister still alive?" Cass asked in a small voice.

"She was. For two months she would hardly talk, and nights she'd wake up screaming. Then she found out she was pregnant. She quit eating. Said she hated what was inside her and hated herself for giving it life. By the time the baby was born, Amy was nothing but skin and bones. The baby was born dead, and she died three days later." He sent a look of incandescent hatred toward Stone. "You killed her sure as you slit her throat."

Nathan shook his head in silent denial, but he didn't speak. None of them spoke. The story of Amy's tragedy had filled the little shelter with a dismal heaviness.

Lawton drifted to sleep. His breathing was shallow and his color pasty, even in the firelight.

"I don't know if he'll live," Cass remarked to Nathan as he banked their little fire.

"He'll live. He's too damned ornery to die."

He'd dragged his saddle into the shelter and spread out both his and Lawton's saddle blankets. "Come lie down," he told Cass. "We might as well get some sleep."

"No, thank you," Cass said primly.

"Do as I say, Cassidy Rose. I'm not in a mood to put up with your lip."

"Where are you going to sleep?"

"Right here with you, sweetheart. You think I trust you not to go running off?"

"What do you care? You don't need a hostage anymore."

"There's all sorts of dangers out there for the unwary. I'm not going to let you go wandering off and get scalped by an Indian or eaten by a wolf."

She snorted. "I'd wager none of those dangers are as disgusting as you."

"Goddamnit!" He pulled her to the blankets and pushed her down. "Don't you ever give up?"

Resentfully, she did as he bid, enduring the stiffened sweat that caked the blankets, the overpowering stink of horse, and, worst of all, his company when he lay next to her. But when he circled her with his arm, she emphatically pushed him away.

"It's either this or have your hands and feet tied."

"I'm not going to run. I promise."

"Good girl. Then we can keep each other warm."

"You don't have to lie so close."

"The better to know what you're up to, sweetheart. And you'd better stop that squirming if you want me to remember I'm a gentleman."

She snorted sarcastically at that, and his temper reached the breaking point. Cass found herself pinned beneath him, looking into fathomless black eyes burning in a grim face.

"You listen to me, you stubborn little self-righteous prig. I lied to you about who I was, but no part of what was between you and me was a lie. I love you, goddamnit, fool that I am. And I meant to marry you and settle down with a home and family. What is so wrong with that? I was going to leave the wild life behind and do right by a wife and children. How is that so different from what you and your sister want to do?"

"Neither my sister nor I ever raped anyone and left them to die," she said coldly.

"Neither did I."

The silence between them was icy, yet she suffered waves of sensuous heat through the frightening tension. She was intensely aware of the man on top of her—the steel thighs that straddled hers, the hips that pressed so intimately, the broad chest that hovered just inches above her breasts. Her face heated. He saw. How could he help but see? The humiliation made her want to cry, but she refused to allow such weakness in the presence of such a hateful man.

With an inarticulate sound of frustration, he finally rolled off her. But his arms still held her prisoner. She huddled with her back to him, trying to keep tears at bay. It was a strange and bitter comfort to have his heat gradually warm her body. She remembered too well how comforting that heat could be, how enticing. She despised herself for the slow burn of desire that he could still inspire in her, even now that she knew what kind of man he really was. Why did something so beautiful have to turn so ugly?

At long last, she fell asleep, Nathan Stone warming her back and Dog curled at her feet.

Chapter 11

Cass rode stiffly upright on Lawton's mount, a high-strung chestnut mare who disapproved heartily of the makeshift travois she dragged. Every movement and moan from Lawton, who was tied onto the travois, made the horse snort and sidestep in distress. She wasn't used to being a draft horse. And Cass wasn't used to riding a high-strung mount. Lawton's horse was going to toss her off, Cass was certain—just one more thing to be annoyed about this morning. She would add it to the mud, the unseasonably cold damp, and her dour, dictatorial companion. All morning long he'd been ordering her about like a slave, not allowing a morning campfire, calling her a spoiled brat when she complained about the lack of breakfast, not letting her go into the trees alone to take care of personal business.

"There might be Indians about," he'd said when he'd stomped out her attempt at a fire.

"There might have been Indians last night," she pointed out.

"Last night was rainy and foggy. No one would have seen our smoke."

"Well then, I hope you like your rabbit cold."

"I gave the last of the rabbit to Dog."

Dog had looked supremely satisfied, and that had annoyed Cass even more.

But the lack of warmth and breakfast was nothing compared to being escorted to a wholly inadequate bush and ordered to take care of business.

"I can manage alone, thank you," she'd told him frostily.

"I'm not up to chasing you over hill and dale if you bolt," he'd said. "I'll just stay right over here. You have to a count of a hundred before I turn around."

She couldn't resist. "You can count to a hundred?"

"I've counted to ten already. You'd better hurry."

He had the nerve to laugh as she hurried behind the bush. "This isn't necessary!" she complained. "You're deliberately being difficult."

"I'm going to deliver you back to your sister in one piece, and I don't intend to chase you all over the territory to do it."

That was the one good thing about this morning. Nathan Stone had promised to take her back to the wagon train—her and Lawton both. There was no longer any reason for him to flee. The gravely wounded lawman wasn't a threat, and the scoundrel need no longer be burdened with a hostage. So back they went. Cass just wished he wasn't so adamant about escorting them. The sooner she was free of the man, the better she would like it. Every time she looked at him, heard his voice, saw the beginnings of a smile or the familiar way his brows drew together when he was deep in thought—every time he reminded her of the man she had loved, a knife stabbed through her heart. She wanted to be rid of all those reminders so that she could more easily hate him. Not that she didn't thoroughly hate him already. She did. She truly did. But she could hate him so much more easily once he was gone.

"You know," she ventured, attempting a reasonable, persuasive tone. "There's no need for you to take us to the wagon train. It's not as if the valley and the trail are hard to find. And once we hit the trail, there will be plenty of other travelers. You could be running off to wherever you plan to run off to. Getting a head start. You never know who else might be chasing you."

He gave her an irritating smile. "Don't get your hopes up. As far as I know, no one else is chasing me—yet. I said I'd get you back to your sister, and I mean to take you back."

"Well, aren't we the noble one!" she sniped.

"At your service, ma'am."

His refusal to be baited annoyed her even more.

They came to the well-worn wagon trail in the early afternoon, after a long morning of intermittent stops to check that Lawton was still alive and the jostling was not making his wound bleed overmuch. Cass didn't know how the man survived. His face was pasty white, his breathing shallow, his eyes, when he opened them, pale and lifeless. "He'll live," Nathan assured her when she stopped yet again to check his pulse. "I'm not lucky enough for him to die."

"What a cold-blooded wretch you are."

He sighed. "The marshal can live to be a hundred for all I care, as long as he leaves me alone. Enough people have died in the last few years that hell must be just about full. No sense in wishing for another useless death."

They had stopped to water the horses in a small creek when Dog and both horses pricked ears down the trail to the west. Like the hunted animal he was, Nathan was immediately alert. "Don't move," he warned Cass. "This draw hides us from most of the trail. Let me see what's spooked the animals." He drew his pistol and urged Tiger to the edge of the trees. Cass sat beside the travois and dribbled water between Lawton's lips from a soaked rag that had once been the hem of her petticoat. Wearily she wondered if this new alarm was Indians, more outlaws, another lawman, or just innocent travelers.

"My life has become a two-penny novel," she complained to the insensible man. "And I'm too tired to really care."

"Well, what have we here?" she heard Nathan say.

Somehow, Lila reflected, heading east in a wagon, back toward civilization, just didn't have the zest of heading west. The sense of adventure was gone, and hope of a new fu-

ture had gone with it. A pall of gloom had settled on their
two wagons, now alone on the trail except for sparse traffic heading west—one family that had given them curious
looks and a barely courteous greeting, and the regular stage
that had reluctantly stopped to answer Lila's inquiry about
Lawton, Stone, and Cass. No one had seen them, which
made Lila's heart sink even lower. She vowed to search
until she found her sister. Cass had been the one good thing
in her life since they were children, since long before their
parents had died. The red-headed, green-eyed imp had been
a bright spirit that livened a dull existence, and to protect
her, Lila had sacrificed just about everything a woman could
sacrifice. The very thought that her sister might be gone
sucked the life right out of her. Nothing else registered as
real—not Frenchie and Sue pecking at each other in the
back of the wagon, Rachel complaining about the injustice
of them being put out of the Shelby train, the professor trying to convince her to let him go after Stone and Cass, or
Luce bellyaching that they were cowards for turning around.

"You ain't even listenin' to me, Miz Lila," Luce complained.

"I don't need to listen. You've been saying the same
thing for the last hour."

"Then why don' you hear what I say, woman? Miz Cass
gonna be mad as a buzzin' bee when she get back to that
train and find we's not there."

"If we'd tried to stay with that train one more hour, they
would have lynched us, I think. I told Jed Jacobs we'd wait
at the Spring Ranch station. The marshal will bring her there,
I'm sure."

"And she's gonna wave that finger of hers right in your
face for headin' the wrong direction."

"In case you didn't notice, Luce, we got tossed out of
the train on our butts, bustles and all."

"Don't mean we cain't follow behind. So what if they
turn up their high-falutin' noses? We don' need their help."

"Yes we do. Besides, I've lost my taste for heading west,
and I don't think the others ever had much of a taste for
it. We'll wait for Marshal Lawton at the station."

Luce retreated into sullen silence. Frenchie and Sue still

sniped at each other beneath the wagon canvas—something about a comb that one of them had borrowed and broken, and Lila could hear Rachel cussing at the supply wagon mule team. Rachel didn't often cuss, but all of them were in a bad temper. Even the professor was out of sorts. When Frenchie and Sue weren't battling like cats, Frenchie and the professor were sparring, just to be ornery. If a band of Indians had come along at that moment, they would have been wise to give the McAllister wagons a wide berth.

Just as the thought of Indians passed through Lila's mind, a horseman emerged from the trees some distance ahead. Her heart gave a lurch. Had she conjured a horde of Indians into existence? Then she recognized the horse. Surely no other horse between Independence and Oregon had that proud head and sleek lines.

Luce drew the same conclusion. "It's Mr. Pernell, God bless him! Tol' you the whole thing was a mistake."

"Nathan Stone is his name," Lila said coldly. "God damn him to hell. What the . . . ?" Her heart filled when another horse appeared and the flash of coppery red hair against the green forest background unmistakably identified her sister. "It's Cass! Oh, my! It's Cass!"

She whipped the mules to a faster pace, and when the two parties met, she jumped from the wagon box and pelted toward her sister with all the speed her thirty-year-old knees would allow. At the same time, Cass slid from her horse and opened her arms in a welcoming embrace. The other women gathered around them in a group hug, exclaiming, questioning, laughing.

When Lila's eyes met Nathan Stone's, she saw something she didn't expect to see. The villain actually looked shamefaced. To a casual observer, he might look cold and closed, even a bit contemptuous. But Lila was a master at seeing through men's masks. Her profession had given her a lot of practice. Her anger at Nathan Stone sputtered. Now that Cass was back she could afford to reserve judgment.

She extricated herself from the mob greetings and fixed a steely eye on the outlaw, her arms folded sternly across her bosom. He gave her an apologetic grimace. "I wasn't going to hurt her, Lila."

"You did hurt her." She walked to Tiger's head and looked the ex-preacher square in the eye. "You hurt her bad."

His eyes examined the ground at his feet. "She'll get over it."

"Will you?"

Startled, he snapped his gaze back to hers. She held it a minute, just to prove she wasn't a bit intimidated by the events of the past two days, then glanced back at Cass, who was describing her adventures to the women and the professor.

"I knew you weren't going to shoot her," Lila said quietly, turning back to Nathan. "In my business a gal learns to recognize the murderous sort, and you aren't one. But you broke her heart, and then you dragged her into the middle of a fight where she might have gotten hurt in a dozen different ways."

"I didn't mean to break her heart. I didn't mean any of this to happen."

"We don't any of us mean for things to turn out like they usually do. I'm thinking, Mr. Tough Guy, that you hurt yourself as much as anyone else."

He answered with a curt shake of the head. "Don't waste your sympathy, Lila. Men like me don't have feelings. The only way we get hurt is if you shoot us."

"That could be arranged!" Cass had detached herself from the knot of welcoming friends and regarded him sourly.

Life came back into his eyes. He goaded her with a smile. "You'll have to get a lot better with a pistol than you are now, sweetheart."

"Don't tempt me to use you for target practice. You've delivered me and Mr. Lawton. Shouldn't you be headed for Mexico, or hell, or wherever?"

"Mr. Lawton?" Lila glanced around, and her eyes came to a stop on the travois. "Don't tell me . . . is that . . . ?"

"That's the hero himself," Nathan told her.

"He's not dead, is he?"

"Not last time we checked."

Lila rushed to the travois, which she had scarcely noticed in the joy of reunion with Cass. There lay a pale and sunken version of the vital, confident man who had ridden in to change all their lives just the day before. "My God! What happened?"

"Stone shot him," Cass volunteered.

Lila gave Nathan a horrified look.

"It wasn't my fault!"

Cass scoffed. "I wasn't the one who sighted down the barrel and pulled the trigger."

"No. But you were the one who stuck her nose in at the wrong time. Seems to be a habit of yours."

"Oh, quit it, children!" Lila scolded. "We need to get this poor man some help. Luce, Cass, help me untie these— Cass, goodness me! Are these strips from your petticoat? Never mind. Mr. Stone, if you would be so kind as to unfasten the travois and lower it gently to the ground. Professor, would you help him, please?"

Feeling herself for the first time since her sister's abduction, Lila organized her few troops like a general making camp. Tents sprang up, and a pile of wood waited only for a match to turn into a cheerful campfire. The professor stalked a wily rabbit in the forest beside the river, and Sue and Frenchie, more amiable now that they weren't jouncing along in an uncomfortable wagon, sat on the riverbank trailing fishing lines in the water.

Sacks of flour and rice and a barrel of salt pork had been shifted from the supply wagon to the big wagon to make room for the wounded man to ride. But for now, John Lawton rested in the coolness of the tent usually shared by Lila and Cass. Lila had changed his bandage, cleaned and poulticed his wound, forced water down his throat, and instructed Luce to boil millet into a soft mush that an invalid might be able to eat. Nursing was another skill that had come in handy during years spent in the oldest profession.

Rachel stuck her head in the tent and glanced at the patient. "You need help?"

"You could find some clean rags."

Rachel chortled. "I could tear up that bloomer dress Cass has been trying to get me to wear."

"That's a thought. We're going to need more clean bandages, or we'll have to put the laundry tub to boiling every night when we stop."

"He going to live?"

"God willing."

"Okay," Rachel said with a smile. "Just don't tell Cass I did the ripping. She's in a temper fit to rip somebody's hair right off the scalp, and I don't want it to be mine."

After Rachel left, Lila glanced down at the marshal. He would live, she thought, despite the fact that he'd been unconscious since Nathan Stone and Cass had dragged him here on the travois, despite his washed-out, bloodless pallor. He had a strong face, and Lila had always believed that a person's true character was reflected in the face. His face said he was strong enough to get through this crisis and become strong once again. It was a down-home face with traces of sadness. The lines carved around his eyes and on his brow spoke of determination and hard living, but the harshness there couldn't obliterate the basic honesty and a certain reluctant kindness.

Or maybe, Lila mused, his face was simply that of a man who'd gotten a bullet through the chest and bled most of his life onto the ground. And she was an over-the-hill whore spinning fantasies about any man with a nice face and a complete set of teeth.

From outside the tent came voices: Cassidy's edgy soprano followed by Nathan Stone's mocking baritone.

"Still here, I see," Cass grumbled.

"Don't call out the cavalry. I'm just resting my horse and mooching a little grub from Luce."

"I hope she told you we can't spare so much as a bean for the likes of you."

He chuckled. "Still holding a grudge, I see."

"I'd scarcely call it a mere grudge."

"What do you want from me, Cass? I told you I never intended to hurt you. I delivered you back to your sister. And I said I'm sorry."

"How big of you! I suppose you expect me to forgive you, to say everything's all right, don't bother your conscience about the little fact that you're lower than a worm in a dirty rain puddle."

Lila could hear the tears in Cassidy's voice. She wondered if Nathan Stone could. Apparently not, because his voice rose a notch in frustration.

"You might at least understand that I didn't mean for all this to come down around our ears."

"How noble! You intended to continue lying to everyone, including me, in order to save your worthless skin."

His sigh included a muttered curse.

"Look what you've done! We've been ousted from the train and now have no way to go west—no guide, no protection."

"That wasn't my doing! The truth is, Cassidy Rose, that you women would have been thrown out long ago if I hadn't stood up for you."

"Oh, yes! The great holy preacher and his great holy speeches. And all along you were nothing but a two-bit gunslinger slinking away from the law."

"I was trying to change all that," he reminded her stiffly. "Seems to me that someone who's trying to start over in life shouldn't throw stones at someone else doing the same thing. And as for lies, you weren't exactly truthful when you persuaded Jed Jacobs to let you join with his wagon train, were you?"

Lila heard hurt in the silence. Her usually sunny-natured sister was determined to maim Nathan Stone in any way she could, and she was willing to tear herself apart to do it. Love did that when it ended ugly, or so she had heard. Lila didn't know firsthand, because she'd never had the disease.

"Cass . . ." Stone's voice was conciliatory. "I want you to believe one thing before I ride out of here. John Lawton thinks what he says is true, God knows, but I didn't hurt his sister. I was there, and the devil himself knows I caused enough mayhem during the war and since to earn my place in hell, but I've never in my life raised my hand to a woman."

"Except me," Cass said quietly. And the quiet tone made her bitterness all the more sharp.

Poor Stone, Lila reflected. She could see him turning over a hot fire, spitted on Cassidy's ire.

"You're right," he finally admitted. "But you're rid of

me now. I'm headed to Mexico, because if Lawton survives, he'll be after me the minute he can drag himself onto a horse. And he won't stop coming until one of us is dead. I'm not sure even the Mexican border will stop him."

Cass was silent.

"Maybe you can ask him to report back to you, to give you details on just how he brings me down. Maybe it'll make you feel better."

"Maybe it will," Cass said defiantly, but her voice was troubled. "So good-bye. I've got better things to do than to stand here and wave a handkerchief as you go." Her footsteps marched away, then stopped. "Oh, by the way, Stone. Lawton's in that tent over there, just in case you want to put another bullet in the poor man before you leave."

Stone cursed, and Lila didn't blame him. She was going to have a talk with her sister about the virtues of forgive and forget. There was nothing like chewing on bitterness to poison a woman's soul.

Still thinking along lines of bitterness, Lila reflected on the dismal picture their future presented. They would trudge their way eastward to some town just like Webster or Silas. And what would they do, an ex-whore and a bitter young girl who'd lost her illusions even before she'd started to live? It was a dismal prospect.

Much later, Lila would tell herself that it was that dreadful expectation that sparked such a wild idea, for normally she was such a sensible woman, accepting grim realities for what they were and making the best of bad situations. But not this time. This time her mind protested the status quo with one hell of an idea. It burst upon her full blown, an explosion any wise person would ignore. But Lila didn't. Usually Cass was the one who thought up wild schemes to get them out of trouble—or into it, at times. But these last weeks trekking west had done something to Lila's good sense. Or maybe it had simply given her a sense of adventure.

Without a moment's hesitation she strode from the tent, and her eye fixed immediately upon her intended victim.

•   •   •

"Let this be a lesson to you, Dog." Nathan tightened the cinch on Tiger's saddle, which he had loosened to let the horse graze. "Women are trouble. Every last one of them. Any man who wants to keep his sanity should avoid them, one and all."

"I take that as an insult," said Lila, surprising him from behind.

He turned and gave her a chagrined look. "Oh, well—I didn't mean you, of course."

"You really are a shameless liar," she said sternly. "And where are you going, Mr. Stone?"

He saw trouble in the glint of her sharp hazel eyes. As if he didn't have enough trouble already. "Well, I figure Mexico is about the only safe place for me right now."

"Really? You're going to just ride off and leave us here?"

"Uh . . ."

"Let me tell you what I think, Nathan Stone, or whatever your real name is."

"That's the real one," he admitted cautiously.

"What I think, Nathan Stone, is that you owe us a trip west."

"Huh?"

"Cass and I and the rest of our party are alone in this hostile wilderness, without a guide and without companions. In short, sir, we're up a damned creek without a paddle, and it's all your fault."

"Now, Lila, that's not the way it is. And you know it."

"What I know is that you owe us a trip west. You need to stay and act as our guide and protector."

"You've got to be kidding!" His voice rose along with the level of his frustration.

"I heard you tell Cass that you wanted to mend your life. Well, sir, here's a start. Act responsibly and make some amends for getting us tossed out of the Shelby train."

"This is crazy! You and your sister are cut from the same cloth! Do you know that?" He checked the loading of his rifle, then shoved it back into its saddle holster. A sane man should not try to deal reasonably with women, Nathan thought irately. "Lila, in case you haven't noticed, I'm a man on the run from the law."

"Really?" She smirked—the same annoying expression her sister had perfected. "Seems to me the only law chasing you is flat on his back in that tent over there. And he's likely to be flat on his back for some time. I'd think you'd want to stick around and keep an eye on him—be ready for him when he gets back on his feet."

"You're insane."

"You could pretend to be a preacher again. No one would take a pious preacher for a wanted outlaw. Make up any story you want. We'll back you up on it."

"Woman, I've never been farther west than you have, and I'm not a damned trail guide."

She refused to give up. "The guidebook tells us the route and what to expect. What we need is a man with a strong arm and a steady hand on a gun. Someone who'll make the ne'er-do-wells we meet on the trail keep their distance. Someone who knows how to pull a wheel off a wagon and talk to a mule in his own language."

"Your friend the professor is a man."

She laughed. "That professor?"

With a reluctant smile, Nathan had to chuckle. "Lila McAllister, you can drive a man crazy."

"You have no idea how many men have said that."

"I'll bet. But you're not sucking me in to this. I don't know what you're trying to do, but whatever it is, it's no good for me."

She positively twinkled. "You might be surprised. You'll get points in heaven, you know. We can't go on without you—a group of defenseless women prey to every evildoer that comes down the pike."

"Lila, I *am* an evildoer—just in case you forgot."

"Well, you're not who I'm talking about. Don't you remember that family that we passed a couple of weeks back—they were traveling alone, a farmer, his wife, and two little girls. We came on them two days later and they'd been robbed of every coin they had, not to mention two good horses and the farmer's shotgun. You wouldn't let that happen to us."

He sighed, wondering if he should simply get on his

horse and ride off. That might get the point across to her. Then Cassidy's voice joined in.

"He wouldn't let what happen to us?" She came from around the wagon carrying a bucket of water, looking as if she might dump it over his head.

Lila smiled serenely. "He wouldn't let any of the rougher elements on the trail take advantage of us when we all head west."

"What?!" If her voice had an edge before, now it was a newly stropped razor.

"Nathan is going to help us complete our journey."

"The only journey he's taking is on the trail that leads away from us. Are you out of your mind?"

Nathan thought of concurring, but after the last two days, he hated like hell to agree with anything coming from Cassidy's mouth.

"Why not? He's the only one here who knows how to repair a wagon wheel. He's also the best hand I know for getting these fractious mules across a river." Lila smiled serenely her sister. "It's the perfect plan. We'd be fools to go on alone, and you must admit he owes us some help."

Cass uttered a word that she would have to forget if she were ever to become a respectable lady.

"Besides, what better cover could he have than traveling with us? And Mr. Lawton can come with us, where Nathan can keep an eye on what he's up to."

"Lila!"

"What?" She ignored her sister's horrified look. "You were the one so anxious to go west. Do you mean you would give it up just because of a little misunderstanding?"

"A little misunderstanding? Have you forgotten what he did? What he is?"

"It's not like you to be so uncharitable, Cassie. After all, he brought you back in one piece."

Cass looked ready to explode, and that in itself made Lila's offer—or demand—almost tempting. Sometime during the last two days, annoying Cassidy Rose had become entertainment. He'd enjoyed her in the role of lovestruck maiden, but the fire-eyed hellion struck more to the heart.

As things stood, the only time she would speak to him was when her temper was up.

"He's a thief, a kidnapper, and"—she gave him a dark look, but didn't go so far as to repeat Lawton's accusation—"and God only knows what else."

"Everyone deserves a second chance," Lila reminded her.

Nathan gave Cass a knowing smile as she ground her teeth, unable to refute her own favorite platitude quoted back to her. Suddenly, foolishly, he didn't want to walk away. He'd lost Cass, but he didn't want to give her up. Oregon was miles ahead. Who knew what might happen during such a long journey? Lawton might die, and Nathan would be a free man once again. He might still try for a new life. And Cassidy's temper couldn't burn forever. If he courted her as Nathan Stone, as an ex–bad guy seeking redemption, would he have a chance? Didn't every woman want a man she could change, save, or reform?

It was risky, he admitted. Lawton was a wild card. But if he played his hand right, Nathan might hamstring the lawman for a while, at least. Was a few more weeks of Cassidy's company worth the chance?

"I can't promise to stay all the way to Oregon."

Lila grinned, and he could see the triumph on her face. Cass opened her mouth, then snapped it shut with a furious scowl. He couldn't resist touching his hat in salute and giving her a grin. "Cassidy, sweetheart, you can't expect me to just ride away and leave you ladies in the lurch."

With a hiss—probably venting steam—she turned and stalked away. Nathan considered himself lucky that he hadn't gotten the contents of her bucket over his head. Lila watched her go, then gave him a look that held none of the good-humored wheedling she'd used on him so far.

"Hurt her again, Stone, and I'll get out the hanging rope myself. I'm gambling that you're a better man than even you think. Prove me right."

Supper that night was a lively affair. Nathan had bagged three quail to roast over the fire, and Luce cooked a pot of beans with salt pork and a tangy sauce whose ingredients she stubbornly kept a secret. The ladies were excited over the prospect of continuing their journey, in spite of all the complaints he'd heard from them in the weeks they'd traveled together. All regarded him with a reserved caution, but they weren't hostile or even aloof. Having lived on the underside of society themselves, they weren't anxious to condemn. Except, of course, Cassidy Rose. She alternately ignored him and sent him seething looks that should have scorched the hair right off his head. Lila had little to fear about him hurting Cass again. If Cass could kill with those dagger-eyed scowls, he wouldn't live long enough to hurt anybody.

Not that he really blamed her. Nathan could just imagine what his mother—that gracious Tennessee lady—would have said to any man who'd used a woman as he had used Cass. She would have invited him to leave the house in that soft honeyed drawl that was so sweet, and she would have punctuated the invitation with a load of buckshot.

After supper, Nathan was glad enough to escape Cass's barbed looks. He had a few things to settle with Lawton, and it was best done now, when Lila was with him to witness what was said. She'd taken her supper, along with biscuits soaked in broth, to be with her patient.

When he stuck his head in Lila's tent, she was spooning biscuits and broth into Lawton's mouth.

"I see you're still alive," Nathan said to the marshal.

Lawton gave him a cold look. "What're you doing here?" he rasped.

"Miz McAllister didn't tell you, eh? I'm the new trail guide around here." He grinned annoyingly. "We're going west together, Lawton. You and me. That is, I'm going. We don't know about you yet."

Lila gave him a warning look. "Nathan . . ."

"I'm not going to shoot him, Lila. You can stay right here and make me behave. In fact, I want you to stay. Lawton and I are going to have a little talk."

"You don't have anything to say that I want to hear," Lawton said.

"Then you're not as smart as I thought you were, because I'm the one holding the cards here, marshal."

Lawton's fingers flexed, longing for a pistol, no doubt.

"I'm going to help these ladies travel west," Nathan continued in a businesslike tone. "If you come with us, you just might get better. Personally, I don't care if you live or die. I just don't want you being the death of me."

The lawman was silent.

"So we'll do it this way. You swear not to breathe a word to anyone along the trail that I've got a price on my head—and that includes the bluecoats at the army posts along the way—and I won't use my influence with these ladies to leave you by the side of the trail with a horse you're too weak to climb aboard and a pistol you're too shaky to aim. We agree to a truce."

"You're a son of a bitch."

"Tch, tch. Watch your mouth. There's a lady present."

Lawton glanced at Lila, who definitely looked tense. "Do you know what kind of scum this is? You'd be safer making the crossing alone than having this . . . this sorry excuse for a human being along."

Lila gave him a stern look. "Mr. Lawton, sometimes we sorry excuses for human beings need to stick together. And sometimes people rush to judgment."

Lawton answered with a disgusted snort.

"Make your choice, Lawton. It won't hurt my feelings any to leave you here. You never can tell. Another wagon party might find you before you die. Or Indians."

Lawton's mouth thinned to a pained line. "Only to Fort Laramie. After then, all bets are off."

"Good enough. I don't suppose you'd care to shake on it."

"I'd rather shake hands with a rat."

Nathan took the barb with a smile. "Cheer up, Lawton. If you survive, you might get another chance to kill me."

"You can count on it, Stone."

Nathan had a bitter taste in his mouth as he ducked out of the tent. Lila followed him and laid a hand on his arm. "I suppose you had to do that."

"Yup."

"Do you trust him to keep his word?"

"Having second thoughts about having me along?"

"No. We need you, Stone. But I don't want to see you hanged because I lured you into staying."

Nathan sighed. "He'll keep his word. I've run with the hyenas long enough to know a noble lone wolf when I see one. He'll spit nails about it, but he'll keep his word."

She gave him a narrow-eyed look. "Would you really have left him by the side of the trail to die?"

Nathan smiled crookedly and turned away without answering.

Chapter 12

The day fit Cass's mood exactly—drizzly and chill, with an occasional rumble of thunder and flash of lightning. They were headed west again, but she couldn't be happy about it. From her perch on the wagon box, all she could see ahead was gloom—mud, rain, the aft end of mules, and gloom.

"You look sour as a crab apple, Miz Cassidy." Mama Luce rode beside her on the wagon box, braving the elements to keep her company. Cass would just as soon be alone. She felt like fit company for the cranky mules, but not for people. Especially some people. She resentfully eyed Nathan, who rode a short distance ahead with the professor.

"So that's how it is, is it?" Luce said with a knowing chuckle. "Lordy, lordy! Our baby's grown up an' discovered that love ain't no pretty storybook. Tch!"

Cass shifted her resentful glare to the old Negro woman.

"Don't you look at me that way, honey! Ain't ol' Luce who done you wrong."

"I wasn't looking at you any special way," Cass grumbled.

Luce snorted. "Sometimes those eyes of yours have teeth, girl. They purely do."

Cass wasn't in the mood to argue. At least not with Luce, who pursed her lips and glanced back and forth between Cass and Nathan.

"He look mighty good up there," Luce said. "He don't ride sloppy, like some o' these farmers you see. Him and that horse, they're like one high-blooded animal. You can tell that one was born a gentleman. Only gentlemen ride like that."

"You're right about the animal part."

"Tch!" Luce chided. "Honey, I can understand being peeved. Yes, I can. But sometimes a woman has to stretch her forgiveness with men. Especially if you find one that gets into your heart." Luce skewered Cass with a sharp eye. "Not to mention gettin' into other parts."

Cass glanced quickly away.

"Don't pretend you didn't hear, missy. I been in this world a long time. Longer than anyone in these two wagons, that's for sure. And I don' get no wool pulled over these old eyes by some young chile like you. It ain't no terrible sin, if you ask me. Not when you is in love. It happens just natural like. I ain't so old that I don't remember."

Cass didn't want to talk about it. Tears were too close to the surface, and she didn't want to cry. She'd already cried. Last night, relegated to Luce and Frenchie's tent while Lila kept watch over the marshal, Cass had cried until it hurt, bitter tears that she had muffled in her blankets. There had to be an end to tears. She didn't want to cry anymore. He wasn't worth it, the toad. And she didn't want to talk about it.

Luce went on. "If you ask me, Miz Cass, men are just naturally ornery critters. They give women fits. But then, I guess we give 'em fits right back. They can be stupid as those contrary mules up there, and just as hardheaded. But women ain't much better." She flashed Cass a grin. "'Ceptin' you and me, o' course."

"Nathan Stone isn't stupid. He's just rotten and wicked."

"Now I don't believe that, honey. I don't believe that a smart gal like Cassidy Rose McAllister gave her heart to a man who is rotten and wicked."

Cass shot a glance at Nathan, then focused again on the

familiar mule backside. "I gave my heart, I guess. Along with some other things. But I took it back."

Luce chuckled. "I guess that's something you ain't learned yet, chile. Hearts is easy to give, but they ain't so easy to take back."

At one time Nathan Stone's life had been fairly simple. Not happy, not productive, but simple. Life got that way, he had discovered, when a man focused on running and surviving. Those things didn't leave room for much else. Life was desperate, but it was simple.

Lately, though, Nathan's focus had slipped. Changing a name and identity was just a simple lie. That was easy. What had muddied the waters was people. He'd made the mistake of getting involved with people—Jed Jacobs and his battle-ax wife, the widow Scott and her pretty daughter Faith, the Sutters and Ben Holden, and Granny Decker, whose sharp old eyes and canny wit were a danger to anyone intent on pulling a fast one. But worst of all was Cass McAllister. She was a woman who could muddle any man's mind, but Nathan should have known better. She'd made him forget that he had a noose waiting to drop over his head. And he still wasn't cured of the lunacy, or he wouldn't be riding toward Oregon with a pack of ex-whores, an aging Negro cook, and a useless musician. He should have laughed in Lila's face when she spouted that nonsense about him owing them a trip west. But he hadn't. He was a damned fool, and he was headed for trouble.

Over the next rise he discovered how right he was, but the trouble wasn't exactly the sort he had feared. The moment he spied what blocked the way ahead, he wheeled Tiger and motioned the professor, who was somewhat behind him, to hold hard. "Get back to the wagons! Now!"

Cass pulled up when she saw them barreling toward her. On the supply wagon, Rachel did the same.

"Get the wagons in those trees over there." Nathan pointed to a grove fifty yards from the trail.

"What's wrong?" Cass demanded.

A worried Lila poked her head out from the back of the supply wagon. "Why have we stopped?"

"The Shelby train is just ahead, and they have Indian trouble. Get the wagons out of sight."

Neither Cass nor Rachel hesitated. The word "Indian" spurred them to action. It was too much to hope, however, that the ladies would cower sensibly in their wagons and be quiet. They demanded details, and when they heard them, they indulged the typical female instinct for trouble, Cass leading the way.

"We can't just huddle here and do nothing," she objected.

"I don't see why not," Rachel sensibly replied. "They've got God on their side, don't they? Let Him get them out of the mess."

"From what Nathan says," Sue commented, "their precious holiness isn't doing much of a job of saving them from the savages."

"What are the choices?" Lila asked.

"We can stay here," Nathan said. "Or we can try to detour around and hope the Sioux don't see us or pick up our trail. Or we can head back toward Spring Ranch station and take shelter there. Or . . ."

Lila raised a brow at him, and Cass gave him a dark look.

"Or," he continued almost reluctantly, "we could try to help."

"Which would you do?" Lila asked pointedly.

Nathan looked at the group before him—three ex-whores, their madam and her fractious kid sister, a Negro woman who was older than Methuselah, or nearly so, and a reed thin piano player who probably couldn't stand up in a stiff wind. The Sioux might die laughing if they charged to the rescue. That was certainly the best they could hope for. The only sensible thing to do was turn tail and run.

"Well?" Lila urged.

He just shrugged.

"You would help them, wouldn't you? If not for us, you'd already be riding in with guns blazing."

Not necessarily, Nathan thought.

"We have plenty of guns," Cass said, "and we're not the kind of people to ride off and let other people get scalped. Right?" she asked the others.

"Right!" Lila said with a smile.

Rachel looked worried. Frenchie lifted a brow and sighed. Sue murmured, "I guess so."

"Just gimme a fryin' pan," Luce declared. "I'll show those heathens a thing or two."

Nathan foresaw disaster. "Now wait a minute, ladies . . ."

In the end, Nathan won. There would be no heroic charge to the rescue. Instead, they would use their wits along with the element of surprise. He divided them into two squads. The professor took Lila, Rachel, and Frenchie. Mama Luce, Sue, and Cass went with Nathan. He intended to keep Cass directly under his eye. The thought of her roaming out of his sight with a loaded pistol scared him more than the Sioux did.

Before they parted, Lila gave him a broad grin and patted his arm.

"Still believe I'm some kind of a hero, do you?"

"Just a decent fellow," she answered. "That'll do."

Nathan kept his skepticism to himself.

He moved with his little troop toward the crest of the trail, which climbed a rise then sloped down to cross a stream. The stream had proved the Shelby train's undoing. It wasn't so much swollen as muddy. The banks on either side were little more than churned-up muck furrowed with the ruts of wagon wheels. Two of the Shelby wagons had gotten stuck on the far bank, dividing the train in two: thirteen on the far side of the stream and five still waiting to cross. A small band of Sioux had seen them in this helpless position and attacked. Not only could they not escape—at least not without the leading wagons leaving their companions to be slaughtered, but they couldn't even form a defensive circle. They were strung out, unprepared, and helpless before the onslaught of six shrieking mounted warriors. Gunfire from inside, behind, and underneath the wagons was enthusiastic but ineffective. The target practice since Anita's death hadn't made marksmen out of the Shelby men. Two wagons were burning. At least three mules had been slaughtered in their traces, and the surviving animals added to the confusion by their panic. Men shouted and women screamed.

The scene reminded Nathan eerily of war. It *was* war, only this time the enemy wore loincloths instead of blue jackets.

Nathan's plan was to make the Sioux believe a respectable force was coming to the rescue. Each person carried at least two guns, a third if they could manage it. They were to hide behind the crest of the rise and fire from spread-out positions, firing as rapidly as they could. Those who had some chance of hitting something were to try for a kill, but Nathan didn't have much hope that any of his little troop could hit a man on horseback careening along at a full gallop. Then again, they might get lucky.

Before he gave the signal to fire, Nathan asked Cass, "You did load your pistols, didn't you?"

"Yes," she snapped.

"You're sure." She treated guns as if they were rattlesnakes. He wasn't even sure she knew how to load.

"I loaded them for her," Luce told him. "All she gots to do is pull the trigger."

Cass glared at him. "I'm not stupid." A wry grimace. "At least not usually."

She didn't look a bit scared, the little fool. "If any of those Sioux charge up the hill at us, you women get off your best shot, then dive for cover. Pretend you're a rabbit and burrow, if you have to. Don't try to be heroines." He gave Cass a stern look, which she parried with a sniff of disdain.

Everyone was in position. When Nathan gave the signal to fire, the hill came alive with gunfire, staggered so that while some reloaded, others still fired. The ruse was a fair imitation of a dug-in troop of soldiers firing at will, and if the battle cries were a bit high-pitched, the Sioux didn't seem to notice.

Nathan brought one Indian down, and another fell from someone else's gun. Beside him, Cass fired at random, flinching with every shot, her eyes squinted nearly shut. When her pistol hammer clicked on empty chambers, Nathan took the gun and quickly reloaded it. When he handed it back to her, he carefully pointed it away from himself and toward the battle below. "That way," he told her.

She sent him a poisonous look and once again fired away.

The Sioux did not stick around to discover Nathan's ruse. With two warriors down, they lost interest in the hapless wagon train. Nathan signaled a cease fire as the Indians scooped up their wounded comrades and galloped off, sending random shots up the hill. General pandemonium broke out among Nathan's troops. From the celebratory dances, back-slapping, and strutting, one would think they'd defeated General Grant.

"Cass, Rachel—go get the wagons and meet us down there. Those people are going to need some patching up."

Cass had never before seen such devastation. The Shelby train stank of smoke and death. Groans and weeping, a woman still screaming, a child's wail—sounds straight from hell. The sights were worse. Many were dead— people with whom she had greeted the mornings, hauled water, gathered wood, complained about the weather. Now some of those people lay still and silent in bloody heaps. Others nursed frightening wounds. Cass stared around her, feeling helpless and numb. As ostracized as they'd been with the Shelby train, there was a connection between them. She knew these people. This sort of thing happened to strangers, not to ordinary people who were part of her everyday world.

Luce called her to the side of a singed wagon. She forced herself to respond, fighting down nausea and tears. The cook bent over Cory Decker, who at least was alive, if his cursing was any clue. Close by, his wife, Pamela, was smeared with blood. She sat on the muddy ground, weeping, rocking back and forth, and clasping little Mary and Thomas.

Luce was busy tying a tourniquet around Cory's thigh. She jerked her head toward the rest of the family.

"Mrs. Decker," Cass said, putting her arms around the woman and her children. "Are you hurt, Mrs. Decker?"

Pamela went on rocking without a pause. Little Mary sobbed into her mother's breast, and Thomas looked like Cass felt—stunned.

Cass fetched water and a towel from the Decker wagon, then wiped the blood from Pamela's hands, face, and arms. It was Cory's blood, for Pamela didn't have a scratch, and with the gentle soothing of Cass's attention, life came back into her eyes. Without letting go of her children, she leaned into Cass's shoulder and wept, then together they checked every inch of Mary and Thomas. Mary had a bump on the head where her father had pushed her down onto the wagon floor, and Thomas had scraped elbows and a sprained wrist.

Cory Decker had taken a bullet in the thigh. A fractured bone had him immobilized with pain. He might keep his leg, Luce told the women, if he were lucky, and if infection didn't set in. At least Luce had stopped the bleeding.

Other Shelbyites had suffered much worse. Clyde Dawkins was dead. No more would he entertain the train with his fiddle playing. His spinster sister, June, cradled his head in her lap, asking over and over again what she would do now. Matthew Brown was gone as well, leaving Effie a widow. Aaron Sutter and his wife, Susan, were dead. Their hired man, Ben Holden, had sustained a bad burn on his chest and arms trying to put out a fire in the Scott wagon. Rachel had rushed to give him aid the moment she'd spotted him lying beside the charred wagon. Amos Bryd, Sr., had his senses addled by a bullet that creased his scalp, and Amelia had promptly fainted at the sight of his blood. Granny Decker had survived in good form after taking up her son's rifle and joining in the fight. Only after the Sioux had left did her heart act up. She had collapsed trying to care for her son.

Jed Jacobs's jaw had been shattered by a bullet. Eliza Jacobs had proved her mettle by neither fainting nor screaming. She sat calmly with her husband, holding pressure against the wound to stanch the flow of blood until Hope Perkins came to her assistance in wrapping a bandage.

The man who should have taken charge—wagonmaster Charlie Morris—was among the dead. In fact, most of the men were either dead or wounded. As Cass moved along the line of wagons, helping where she could, her gorge rose more than once. The injustice of such violence made her want to cry and scream at the same time. Life shouldn't do such things to good people. Cass wanted to shriek her objection to the universe, to God himself, that the world should not tolerate such things.

God and the universe did not present themselves for her disapproval, however. Nathan, on the other hand, did. He had taken charge of the crisis, posting guards from among the few surviving men and organizing others, women included, in transporting bodies to where the professor, Ed Campbell, and the junior Amos Byrd were digging graves. His businesslike manner struck Cass as indifference. He lifted Aaron Sutter and Clyde Dawkins onto the death cart without so much as a flinch and firmly but gently separated Effie Brown from her dead husband.

Cass took Effie into her embrace and lit into Nathan with a vengeance. "You are a callous monster! Can't you just leave Matthew here for a while so Effie can say good-bye?"

His brows snapped together in a black scowl. "Weeping over her husband's body while he lies in a pool of his own blood is not saying good-bye. She needs to see him properly buried and then get away from the site of this goddamned massacre. Elsewise the nightmare just goes on and on."

"He's right," Effie choked out. "The best I can do for Matthew is see him put in the ground proper like. Dust unto dust." She disentangled herself from Cass. "I've got to fetch his Bible. He's got to be buried with his Bible," she said and stumbled off.

Effie's compliance with Nathan's tyranny just made Cass more furious. "How can you just hurry them off to be dumped into a hole?" She felt herself getting closer and closer to the edge of hysteria. "They're not just bodies! They're people! People we knew and danced with and . . . and crossed streams with. Matthew helped me hitch our team when I didn't know a chest strap from a headstall. Clyde tried to show Frenchie how to play the fiddle. They're not bodies, damnit! They're people. You can't just . . . just . . ."

"They're not people anymore," Nathan said coldly. "They're just bodies. The people are gone."

Her breath caught. His face was granite, his eyes black ice. "How can you not be moved?"

"I've seen a lot of death, Cassie. You get used to it. Or you give in to it and go mad."

Somewhere in those cold, flat eyes she detected a spark of compassion. Her heart melted just a bit at the thought of what sort of life accustomed a man to a scene such as this, where he could look upon the murdered bodies of friends and keep a calm face, think with a cool head. What kind of hell on earth did a man have to endure to become such a creature?

Tears rose dangerously close to the surface. Slowly but surely, control was slipping from her grasp. "I . . . I don't want to get used to it," she quavered.

"Sometimes life does that—throws stuff at us that we don't want to do, don't want to see. You know that, Cassidy Rose. You know that as well as I do."

The gruff understanding in Nathan's voice did Cass in. Tears flooded to the surface in an uncontrolled rush. Death, blood, pain, and grief crashed down upon her, a leaden, inescapable burden that choked the very breath from her lungs. All of life's injustices and miseries seemed crowded into that one moment.

Before she could flee, Nathan's arms surrounded her. "Cassie," he whispered low. "Cassie, don't." The comfort of his voice made her cry harder, for Nathan was one more thing she could weep for. She had glimpsed in his eyes the hell he had endured sometime, somewhere—a hell that had made him the man he was. She didn't want to feel for him. She didn't want to feel for Matthew, Effie, Ben, the Sutters, Jed, Clyde, the Deckers and all the rest whose lives had been taken or ruined that day. Feelings were too painful. Life was too painful. She almost felt sorrier for those left behind than those killed. How the survivors must suffer! Cass had lost no loved ones, suffered no wound, yet she grieved as though her heart had been cut open.

As she wept harder, Nathan held her tighter. Part of her wanted to sink into his embrace, and another part wanted to push him away. Torn between the man she had loved and the man who had betrayed her, threatened her, manhandled and mocked her, Cass could only stand in his embrace and water his shoulder with her tears.

"It'll pass," he assured her, his lips moving against her

ear. "It'll pass. Tomorrow it'll be better, and the next day, and the next."

With an anguished wail she pushed herself out of his hold. How dare he comfort her and pretend to have a heart! "Get away from me, Nathan Stone. Just get away." Feeling every inch a fool, she fled to the group of women that was gathering around the McAllister wagons.

June 17, camped ten miles northwest of Spring Ranch Station—

My heart is heavy as I write these words, dear journal, for the world has come to pieces. Or so it seems. Much has changed since I last wrote. I have been proven a fool, for the man for whom I had such an attachment, Mr. Homer Pernell, was revealed to be a fugitive from the law. His name was as false as the good character he pretended. Nathan Stone is his real name, and it is printed upon wanted posters throughout Kansas. I will not detail the frightening experience to which he subjected me, for it is something I do not wish to remember. Forgetfulness would be a welcome balm.

Shortly after Nathan Stone's unmasking, our little band of ladies was expelled from the wagon train. These Christian brothers and sisters could not countenance the presence of "fallen women" in their company. After our wagons left, their company suffered the fate that haunts all emigrant nightmares. While two of their wagons were mired in a stream, a band of vengeful Sioux spied their helplessness and attacked. The suffering the savages left behind is unspeakable. Many good, brave souls have departed this earth, and many are left behind to weep, their dreams ruined and their lives destroyed. The injustice of it all truly makes me want to shout to the heavens in complaint.

Fortunately, our little band came upon the battle and was able to drive the Indians away before the Shelby train was completely destroyed. I think none would have been left alive—men, women, or chil-

dren—had Nathan Stone not concocted a plan of rescue. For this, at least, I must give him credit. He did not run from the battle. So now we are rejoined with our former companions, but relations between the Shelby women and our band of ladies is understandably tense. Not only do we share a history of animosity, but the burden of gratitude lies awkwardly with those who once expelled us. A truce of sorts was in force as we buried the dead, tended to the wounded, and worked to bring some order to chaos. We offered comfort where we could, and it was well received.

Effie Brown particularly needed a shoulder to cry upon. She was passionately attached to Matthew and says she can't imagine life without him. At least she has a son in Oregon who awaits her arrival, so she is not completely alone in the world. Weeping along with Effie made me realize how fortunate I have been in my life. I am ashamed to say it, but sometimes tragedy striking another puts our own troubles in perspective. I suppose that failing is simply the human condition.

Granny Decker led a parade of Shelby women the next morning. The battered train, along with the McAllister wagons, had camped a scant three miles from the site of the attack after burying the dead, patching up the wounded, and freeing the two mired wagons. The night had been an evil one. People were understandably nervous, and the fall of darkness magnified the jitters. Every rustle in the grass or hoot of an owl had sent people jumping for their guns. In the absence of healthy men to stand sentry, women had volunteered, including Granny, who had recovered quickly from her "spell," as she called it. "I can pull a trigger good as any man I know," she claimed. "And an old crone like me don't need much sleep. Soon enough, I'll be sleeping in a pine box, so I might as well be useful while I've still got my legs under me."

So Granny had stood a four-hour shift of guard duty, along with Eliza Jacobs, Pamela Decker, Frenchie, and Cass.

Amos Byrd, despite his creased scalp, stood a shift as well. And Nathan Stone had patrolled on both shifts.

Despite lack of sleep, however, Granny Decker was bright-eyed and bushy-tailed at the head of the delegation of Shelby women who came marching to the McAllister fire, where Nathan sat with Mama Luce drinking coffee.

"Lordy, lordy," Luce muttered, eyeing the women balefully. "What now? They gonna shoo us away again after we saved their sorry butts?"

"Morning, Mr. Stone," Granny said. "Morning Luce."

"Morning," Nathan replied evenly.

Lila stuck her head out of the supply wagon to eye the women suspiciously.

"Morning, Lila," Granny said brightly. "How's Mr. Lawton this morning?"

"He'll do."

"Glad to hear it. My Cory is right grateful for that poultice you put on his leg. The blood's still a nice healthy red this morning, and he's not feverish at all."

"Glad to hear it."

"Get down to business, Granny," Amelia Byrd demanded.

Nathan put down his coffee mug. "What business would that be?"

"Serious business, Mr. Stone." The old woman pulled up a stool, claiming the privilege of old age. "You don't mind if an old woman eases her bones, do you?"

"Make yourself at home," Luce replied.

"Now, boy—Mr. Nathan Stone—do we have your real name this time?"

"That's the one my mother gave me."

"Good. I'm glad we have that settled."

Nathan sighed. He wished the old woman would get to the point. He was tired and not a little cranky. In the last three days he'd gotten almost no sleep. He'd been chased by a bloody-minded marshal, nearly shot by the woman he loved, duped into taking charge of two wagons full of whores, and dragged into a battle with scalp-happy Indians. On top of that he'd had to bury seven good men and one good woman while watching their friends and families grieve. He was not in a mood for idle chatter.

Not that Granny Decker was giving him idle chatter. That old woman didn't have an idle bone in her body. One look at her sharp gray eyes told Nathan she was softening him up for something.

"Granny, you can call me anything you want. Now, what serious business do you have on your mind? I know you didn't all come over to drink Luce's coffee." He gave them a challenging glare, one by one—Eliza Jacobs, Amelia Byrd, Pamela Decker, the widow Scott, her sister Hope Perkins, Grace Campbell and her eldest daughter Sally, Effie Brown, Clyde Dawkins's sister June, and Granny herself.

"Truth is, young man, we're in a pickle. Here we are in the middle of going to Oregon, just a few days from the great Platte River, and now we got no menfolk. They're all buried or laid up, the wagonmaster buried with them."

There were no comforting words Nathan could offer. The truth was hard, but it was the truth.

"So we want you to head up this train, Mr. Stone. We women got enough pluck to do the chores, drive the wagons, and care for those that are hurt. But we need a man to head us up. Someone who knows mules and wagons and how to fight, if need be. We need a good man to be wagonmaster, at least until some of our own menfolk are on their feet again."

Nathan flinched. First Lila, now Granny. Did he have a sign painted on him—sucker for hire? "Now Granny, I'm not a good man. Besides, you've got Amos Byrd and his boy, Ed Campbell, who isn't in bad shape, and a few others."

Amelia Byrd snorted. "Amos is a good farmer. But that man couldn't organize ants marching toward an anthill. And my boy is only sixteen. He's got his head so far in the clouds he can't see where his feet are going."

Grace Campbell just chuckled at the notion of her husband taking charge.

Nathan felt the walls closing in on him, not to mention a noose tightening around his neck. It was bad enough Lila had talked him into taking on her herd of whores. He was not taking charge of twenty wagons full of starchy Bible thumpers who knew he was a wanted man. They were an "eye for an eye" sort of people, and some of them might be glad to turn him in and see him hang.

No one, positively no one, had a glib enough tongue to talk him into this one.

Chapter 13

"I can't believe I let that old biddy talk me into staying," Nathan groaned, sitting hunched on the wagon box of his wagon, which still had his few possessions inside it. In the short time he'd been gone, it hadn't been touched. Neither had it been damaged in the Sioux attack. His shirts were here. His extra work gloves. His blankets. The wagon was an uncanny symbol, waiting for him to come back, a sign he was supposed to come back and take up the reins as if nothing had changed. But things had changed drastically, and he did not want to stay. Taking on Lila's little group was one thing. Taking on the whole Shelby crew— every one of whom knew he had a price on his head—was something entirely different.

He snorted in disgust and let his head drop into his hands. A man could excuse himself for being sold a bill of goods by a beautiful woman like Lila, especially when she had Cass to dangle subtly as bait. But to be hornswaggled by a sly old biddy like Granny—that was a damned disgrace.

Beside him, Dog whined plaintively, catching Nathan's mood.

"You can say that again," Nathan agreed.

A deep rumble of laughter answered. "Mr. Stone, you

look like you were the one who got all his chest hair singed off—and then some—instead of me."

Nathan raised his head to find Ben Holden leaning against the wagon. "I wish to hell people around here would stop calling me Mr. Stone," he grumbled. "Makes me sound like some sort of damned banker."

Ben grinned. "We all know you ain't that."

"How you doing?" Nathan asked.

"I'll live, I figger. I look like raw meat under these bandages, but it'll heal. Miz Lila knows poultices and such, and Rachel's watching me like a hawk to make sure I don't fester. That woman has a bossy side to her."

"Miss Rachel's a woman with some class."

"She ain't the only one of those gals that has class."

Nathan didn't want to be reminded. "Yeah. I know it. What do you need, Ben? I've got a load of self-pity to wallow in, and that's better done alone."

The big Negro laughed again. "Now you don't want to do that, do you? You're a lucky man. These people think God is just workin' in strange ways by sending you back to deliver them from their trouble."

"Goddamnit! Not you, too! Does everyone here think I'm a goddamned hero? That I'm some kind of a do-gooder? Why the hell don't I just saddle up my horse and get out of here?"

"Because they need you."

Nathan snorted. He should have listened to his better judgment. He and Tiger and Dog—that was the way it should have been. The three of them headed for Mexico. No women. Absolutely no women.

"Or maybe you stay for the same reasons you took Lila's group on. Good cover." Ben flashed a grin. "And a good heart."

Nathan glowered at Ben as if the man had called him a bad name. "I do not have a good heart!"

"Good cover, then."

"Not that good."

"You were willing enough to take 'em on as a preacher."

"That was before they knew the truth. Ben, any one of

those people could slip a word in the wrong place and put a noose around my neck."

"They won't do that. They're fractious folks, and a bit starched up for most people's taste, but their word is good. They won't give you away."

"Is that so? What about all the other problems—me not knowing anything about the trail, the shortcuts, the fords, the Indians? Not to mention the possibility I might not make it alive from one day to the next. There's a green-eyed red-head on this train who'd love to see me swinging from the nearest tree. She's almost been the death of me twice. Next time I give her the chance, she'll just out-and-out kill me."

Ben guffawed. "Miss Cass is your problem. The other problems I can help you with. Listen, Mr. Stone. Nathan. You don't have to know anything about the trail."

"Good. I don't."

"Or wagons or river fords or watering holes in the desert. I made my way west when I was twelve and ran off from a Louisiana plantation. I know the tricks of the trail, or most of them at least. I can take these people west, but you know as well as I do that they're not going to be led anywhere by no Negro."

"What's that got to do with me?" Nathan wondered how Cass felt about them joining forces with the Shelby folk. All through Granny's sales talk she'd had the strangest look in her eye. Was her anger burning down? Or was she plotting some way to make him regret not being killed by the Sioux?

"You're not listening, Stone."

"Huh?"

"I say it's got a lot to do with you. All you have to do is front for me, and I'll take this train west."

Nathan sighed.

"I'll take the train west, and the train will take you west, far away from any wanted posters and zealous lawmen."

"Except John Lawton."

"Lawton's just like Cass. Your problem."

"Between you and Granny, you wear someone down to the hilt."

Ben grinned. "You're a good man, Nathan Stone."

"I wish you people would get it through your thick heads! I am not a good man!"

"You're a good man, Nathan Stone." Cass mimicked the words she'd heard Lila utter that very morning when their "wagonmaster" had stopped by to help them doctor a mule's foot. "Good man, my piddling foot!" She sloshed the water from her buckets into the water cask fastened to the side of the big wagon. Her arms ached, but not as much as her feelings. Five days had passed since the Sioux attack, and everyone else seemed to have forgotten that Nathan Stone was a liar, a villain, a taker of innocents, and a fugitive from justice. The Shelby people had given him back his wagon, fed him at their cook fires, and treated him like a prodigal son. Even Eliza Jacobs tiptoed around him as if afraid a cross word might drive him away. Sue and Frenchie, freed of the false notion that he was a holy man, teased and flirted in a manner that made Cass's stomach turn.

"Well, you don't want him," Sue had commented two days ago. "It would be a damned shame to let him go to waste."

"Have you forgotten what he is? What he did?"

"Baby girl, it's a downright sin to hold a grudge. Besides, as far as I can see, Nathan didn't hurt one hair on your head. And he's been real gentlemanly about the low tricks you've been plaguing him with. If he were really a bad one, he'd have thrown that hot cup of coffee in your pretty face last night."

"He didn't know it was me that put salt in it."

"The hell he didn't."

Cass's lips twitched into a smile as she remembered how he'd choked. It couldn't have happened to a more deserving man.

"One more load," she muttered, picking up the empty buckets and heading for the creek. When they got settled in Oregon, she was never going to carry another bucket of water. She was never going to tramp through mosquito-infested woods to find firewood. She was going to buy a feather bed and never again sleep on the ground. And never,

never was she going to eat salt pork and beans. Even Luce's good cooking couldn't make that palatable.

The luster had definitely faded from her dreams of going west. Not only was her heart broken, her fingers were worn to the bone. Frenchie, Mama Luce, and Cass carried most of the burden of daily chores these days. Sue had taken to helping Effie Brown, who was now alone with a wagon and team she scarcely knew how to drive. Rachel was with Ben Holden more often than not. She used the excuse of tending his burns. But really, Cass thought uncharitably, just how often did the man need to be poulticed and bandaged? Lila was unavailable night and day, it seemed. She was with them and yet not, spending most of her time with the injured lawman. It was looking as if Lawton might live. Cass sincerely hoped so, not only because she admired the man, but he seemed to be the only one besides her that wanted to see Nathan Stone get his just deserts.

She filled the buckets and sloshed back toward the wagon.

"Mornin', Miss Cassidy." Young Amos Byrd emerged from the trees, stealthy as any Indian. "I'd offer to carry those buckets for you, but I'm on duty." He proudly indicated his father's carbine that rested in the crook of one arm. "I'm watching the creek and the north approach."

"That's good, Amos. I feel very safe."

They never stopped these days without a guard being posted—Nathan's orders. The shortage of healthy men dictated that women and half-grown boys take their turn. Even Granny Decker stood a shift. Cass had volunteered, but Nathan had just looked at her and laughed. "I know how good you are with a gun," he'd chortled.

"If I thought I had a chance to shoot someone worthwhile," she'd replied churlishly, "maybe I'd become a marksman."

He had just laughed. Cass hadn't been assigned a shift as sentry.

Young Amos was obviously very proud to be doing his part. His chest was puffed out, his eyes bright with fervor. "Is that your last load, Miss Cass? Mr. Stone said we was to stop foolin' around in the morning and get on the trail earlier."

She was tempted to say what she thought of anything Nathan Stone had to say, then considered the youth of her listener. "This trip ought to do it, Amos."

He tipped his battered straw hat. "You be careful now, ma'am."

Cass was still smiling about the boy's fledgling manliness when she heard weeping. It came from the Jacobs's wagon. She immediately leapt to the worst possible conclusion, for last she'd heard, Jed Jacobs had been feverish and weak from his wound. A Sioux bullet had shattered his jaw, hitting nothing mortal, but leaving him in great pain and danger of infection. Lila had offered to help, of course. Running a brothel had given her a good working knowledge of patching up wounds of all kinds, and when she wasn't busy with Lawton, she was doctoring the victims of the Sioux attack—all but Jed Jacobs. Eliza had refused to let Lila taint her wagon by stepping over the threshold or corrupt her husband by touching any part of him.

Cass set down her buckets and scratched on the wagon canvas. "Mrs. Jacobs?" No answer. "Mrs. Jacobs, is everything all right?"

Eliza stuck her head out. Her eyes were red and swollen, and her graying brown hair, usually rigidly confined in a bun, straggled around her face in dreary, lank strands. "What is it?" she demanded fiercely.

"Eliza, is Jed all right?"

"How *could* he be all right, with all that's happened? What do you want?"

"I thought I heard you crying. Can I help?"

Eliza's answer was a bitter laugh. "Help? You? Wicked creature! You and your kind brought this upon us, and now you offer help? Devil's daughter! Begone!"

Eliza's curse pushed Cass over the limit. From the very start of this trip she had meant nothing but good. Good for Anita, who'd been killed in a most horrible way. Good for Frenchie, Sue, and Rachel, who did nothing but laugh at her efforts to make them respectable; good for Lila, who regarded their future with nothing better than a calm sort of boredom; good for Homer Pernell, who turned out to be a false scoundrel whose very name was a lie. She'd wanted everything to be so right for everyone, and in return she was snickered at by her irreverent friends, spit on by the respectable Shelbyites, and betrayed—even threatened—by the man who'd taken her heart, not to mention her virtue. Now Eliza Jacobs had the nerve to call her wicked when all she'd done was offer help. It was all too much, and Cass didn't intend to stand still for any more.

"Mrs. Jacobs! I am not wicked, and I am the daughter of an Iowa farmer, not the devil! My sister and I have done nothing to you other than offer help and compassion. It's you who are being wicked in denying Jed the care he needs. But no! You'd rather let him die and then complain that we brought more of God's wrath down upon you. You're bringing God's wrath upon yourself, madam, because you'd rather have something to whine about than have your husband alive and healthy!"

"Well, I never!"

"Well, you should have!"

An unintelligible cry from inside the wagon grabbed both women's attention, and Eliza looked so anguished that Cass regretted her burst of temper. Temper was the curse of her life.

"Please," she said softly, "let someone help."

Eliza clasped her hands together in a grip that looked painful. Tight-lipped, she gave Cass an agonized look. "Tell your sister, if she would care to come, I will not forbid her."

Lila knotted the ends of Lawton's clean bandage and contemplated her chances of hog-tying him. There was nothing more difficult than a patient just beginning to recover.

"You're looking mighty grim this morning," he said.

"Only because you're one of the most stubborn, bullheaded men I've met. And I've met a few."

"I reckon you have," he agreed.

"Quit trying to move that arm. Don't you know the arm muscles are connected to the shoulder muscles, and the shoulder muscles hook up with the chest muscles? And your chest has a hole in it, in case you haven't noticed."

"I've noticed. But it goes against the grain for a man to get food spooned into him like he was a baby."

"You rip open that chest wound and you're not likely to need food much longer. You got lucky once. If I were you, I wouldn't push it."

Lawton grunted his disdain, but Lila thought she saw a twinkle in those blue eyes—a sign of returning life if she'd ever seen one.

"Eat the rest of this and I'll let you have a few bites of Luce's gooseberry pie."

He reluctantly opened his mouth for the spoonful she held. Foolish man. He wasn't out of the woods by any means. She'd seen bullet wounds nearly mended suddenly fester and turn mortal. But she didn't know a man in the world who didn't somehow, deep down, believe he was invincible. And the marshal was no different from the rest of them. He would be up and walking around soon if she didn't sit on him.

"Enough! Enough!" he complained between mouthfuls. "What is that stuff?"

"Boiled oats. It's good for you."

"Have I been eating this all along and just now realized it tastes like—I can't think of a description tame enough to speak in front of a lady."

Lila laughed. "Mr. Lawton, if you still believe I'm a lady, you have been in another world these past few days."

"How about some good solid bread smeared thick with butter?"

"Maybe one of Luce's biscuits," Lila conceded. "And I think Rachel churned some butter from the Sutters' cow. But you get only a little, mind you. And a bite of pie. Let's not overtax your vitals."

He gave her a half smile. "Miss McAllister, just looking at you could overtax any man's vitals."

She laughed again. "You *are* getting well, aren't you!"

The amiable mood fled when Nathan Stone stuck his head in the wagon. He gave Lawton a flat glance but spoke to Lila. "Lila, who's driving your other wagon? We're ready to roll."

"Cass is."

"Where is she?" His voice grew sharp, as it always was

when anyone mentioned Cassidy. Speaking of bullheaded, Lila thought, those two took the prize.

"She went to fill the water casks while the professor hitched her team."

He muttered an unintelligible word as he left. Lila was pretty sure it was a curse. When she glanced at Lawton, the look on his face gave her a chill. The amused slant of his smile, the twinkle in his eye—they were gone. In their place was a knife-sharp focus. He looked like a man sighting down the barrel of a rifle.

"John Lawton, no man should allow himself to nurse that sort of hatred."

He jerked out of his near trance. A dark sorrow replaced the deadliness of his expression. "You don't understand."

"I think maybe you're the one who doesn't understand."

That statement earned her an annoyed look, but she persisted. She liked this man, but hatred tore a person apart. It leached joy from life and goodness from a heart. John Lawton was a good man, she sensed, and for him to destroy himself in that way would be a crime.

"Lila, you don't know Nathan Stone."

"Oh?" She propped him more upright so he could drink a mug of coffee. "Cassidy told me what you think he did."

"What I think he did?" He grunted. "Dash it all, I can sit myself up, woman! Stop treating me like an infant."

"I'm not treating you like an infant, but like a man who took a bullet in the chest. Stop treating yourself as if you're expendable."

He mumbled a protest, but took a swallow of coffee when she held the cup to his lips.

"And yes, I repeat: what you think Nathan Stone did. Did you actually see him attack your poor sister?"

"I saw that piece of shit face-to-face."

Lila shook her head. "Did you see him attack your sister?"

"He was there. If you think any man watches something like that without unbuttoning his own trousers, then you don't know men."

"I know men. Good and bad, gentlemen and brutes—I

know men. And that's why I can't believe Nathan Stone would do something like that."

A scratching on the wagon canvas preceded Cass's entrance. "I'm back. Do you need anything before we go?"

"Nathan was looking for you."

Cass grimaced. "I know. Our high-and-mighty 'wagonmaster' thinks someone has appointed him tyrant. I'm glad to see you're getting better, Marshal Lawton. And if it means anything, I think you're right on the money where Stone is concerned. He's a skunk."

"Cass . . ." Lila warned. Sometimes she wanted to grab her little sister and shake her until she showed some sense.

"Well, he is! The marshal knows it, and so do I."

"You should remember that ladies do not eavesdrop." She sent Cass a pointed look. "Marshal Lawton is listening to the bitterness of his own loss, and you're nursing a grudge and acting like a ten-year-old. And I'm tired of both of you. Cass, you put Nathan Stone in peril of his life by taking after him like a jaybird when he was trying to hide. And after that, he brought you back without hurting a hair on your head. Didn't he?"

Cass pouted. It made Lila madder.

"I'll admit you have reason to be disappointed, but I expect more from you than turning petty. Putting salt in the man's coffee was not funny, and spilling cold water down his back last night when he was sitting at our fire was something I'd spank you for if you were ten years younger."

Cass tried to hold her pout, but a chuckle broke through. "You must admit it was funny when he shot up like he did—tripping over that big dog of his and landing in the dirt like the pig he is."

"Cassidy Rose McAllister, the next time you cause something like that to happen to that poor man, I will spank you. I don't care how old you are, you're acting like a wicked child!"

The pout came back to her face. "Strange how everyone thinks a criminal is the salt of the earth and I'm nothing but wicked. Which reminds me—I stopped by the Jacobs' wagon. Eliza also thinks I'm wicked, by the way." Cass lifted her chin defiantly. "Jed's pretty bad, I think, and Eliza said if you'd care to look in on him, she wouldn't object. I'll be up on the big wagon, driving, in case you need anything from this wicked child."

Lila shook her head as Cass huffed away. "The older I get, the less I understand people. Cass has a heart as big as the sky. She wants good for everyone—and yet that same heart can hold such a grudge."

"You can't blame her," Lawton said.

"Yes, I can," Lila snapped, turning her vexation in his direction. "And you're nursing the same kind of grudge. The difference is that Cass gets revenge by putting salt in the man's coffee and pouring water down his shirt. You want your revenge in the shape of a noose. You'd better be very, very sure, John Lawton, because an innocent man's death is a heavy thing to carry on your conscience."

At the nooning, Lila made time to visit Jed Jacobs. There wasn't much to be done for the poor man other than make sure his wound was clean—which it was, for Eliza Jacobs was nothing if not meticulous. She'd scarcely left the back of her wagon, which young Amos Byrd drove for her so she could tend her husband around the clock. Lila complimented Eliza on her excellent caretaking, which softened the older woman's manner not one jot, then brewed willow bark tea for the suffering man. Scientists had concocted a new fancy-sounding medicine from willow bark. It had been available for over ten years, but not in out-of-the-way little towns. Plain old willow bark tea had served Lila well in the past, and it was, she figured, basically the same thing. Then she left Eliza instructions for a poultice that would help draw out the infection.

"Change the poultice every four hours, and give him the willow bark tea at the same time. And you might try praying," Lila advised with a touch of irony.

"What would you know about praying?" Eliza scoffed.

"You'd be surprised. Prayers from us sinners add a bit of spice to God's day, don't you think? Otherwise, think how bored He'd be." She gave Eliza an amiable wink, then left before she could reap the response to that remark. She suspected Jed Jacobs would pull through just fine. In order to live with a wife like Eliza, the man had to have a heaping share of fortitude.

The wagon train crawled slowly toward the Platte—crawled at a pace of less than ten miles per day, for women drove the wagons and tended the stock, and many of them were used to leaving such chores to their husbands. In addition, they had all the housekeeping chores that normally kept them busy—cooking, laundry, mending, child care. The few healthy men were spread thin. Amos Byrd's creased scalp was mending nicely, and he and young Amos helped out wherever they could. Virginia March's husband, Simon, did what he could, but with Virginia tied up caring for their new baby, he spent most of his time dealing with his own wagon and team. The professor also tried to help, but oftentimes his "help" was more akin to hindrance. One afternoon when he spelled Cass, the team grew so fractious from his awkward handling that Frenchie, who rode shotgun with a carbine in her lap, had wrested the reins from his hands.

"Honestly!" she declared. "You need someone to take care of you. It's a good thing you play a mean piano, because if you had to do something useful for a living, you'd starve." She thrust the carbine in his hands with a warning: "Try not to shoot yourself, okay?"

Banjo Ben couldn't do much physical work while his burns healed. If he tried, Rachel sat on him until he promised to behave himself. He was able to help Nathan scout for campsites and bring down enough game so that their food supplies didn't become depleted. Staples were available at various ranches and stage stations, and at Fort Kearny and nearby towns such as Valley City and Dobytown, but no one could afford to pay the inflated prices.

The train crawled, and none of Nathan's imprecations about crossing the far mountains before the snow flew could make it go faster. His objection to stopping on Sundays fell on deaf ears. The Shelbyites felt that risking any more offense to God might well be a mortal blow.

Their last Sunday on the Little Blue River demonstrated how close to mortality they still were.

Chapter 14

The day started off with a war, the first skirmish of which was fought at the McAllister cook fire, where Mama Luce served up griddle cakes and coffee. Nathan joined them, as had become his habit, though he was careful not to turn his back on Cass. The morning began innocently enough, with birds greeting the rising sun. The air was fresh and cool, and a morning fog hung in the hollows, making the world look soft and new.

Cass took coffee to Lila, who was still in the tent with Lawton. Nathan's eyes followed her. Cass resented the way she felt his every glance, every smile or scowl. Even when she couldn't see him, she sensed him. The brush of his eyes warmed her skin. A smile made her heart beat faster. This very morning he'd had the nerve to wink at her, and before she'd recalled her contempt and revulsion, she'd almost caught herself in a smile.

The injustice of it soured her morning. That her senses were still so attuned to him, as if they were still lovers and he wasn't the scum of the earth—such a thing just wasn't right. It made her want to punish him yet again—dump his bedroll in the next stream or put a mule turd in his boot—childish, but satisfying. Lila wouldn't stand for any more pranks, though, and Cass knew her sister was right.

When Cass returned to the fire, Nathan was gone. On his stool sat fifteen-year-old Faith Scott, who had dropped by their wagons more than once in the past week, first to gush her thanks for their intervention in the Indian attack, and then simply to pass the time of day. This morning she was having an animated discussion with Frenchie about hairstyles.

Faith and her widowed mother, Alice, along with Alice's sister Hope Perkins, had seen their wagon and most of their goods burned during the Sioux attack. They'd moved into Clyde Dawkins's wagon with Clyde's sister June, but life was hard for poor Faith, with an uncertain, scary future and no better companions than three older women who had long forgotten what it was like to be a young girl. Whenever she came around Lila's ladies, they went out of their way to be friendly.

"Good morning, Faith," Cass greeted her.

"Hullo, Miss Cass. How is the marshal doing?"

"He's feverish, and his wound has started to fester, but I'm sure Lila will see him right again."

Sue snickered. "If she doesn't kill him first. I think Lila talked that man right into a fever. Anytime he's awake they're spitting at each other like cats and dogs. He complains about having to stay still, and she threatens to tie him. He complains about that pabulum she feeds him, and she just keeps filling him up with oats and broth and willow bark tea. And anything Lila has an opinion on—"

"Which is everything," Cass interjected.

"—the marshal thinks something different."

"Lila can work any man into a fever without half trying," Frenchie said with a suggestive grin.

"You mind that mouth o' yours," Mama Luce warned her.

"Well, I think it's very romantic," Faith gushed. "A wounded hero, fallen in the line of duty, and a beautiful woman nurses him back to health." She sighed. "Do you think they'll get married?"

Laughter and snorts answered her question. "Lila get married?" Rachel scoffed. "Not in this century."

"She's too independent to turn her life over to some man," Frenchie said.

"Oh, I don't know," Sue argued. "Just because she's thirty doesn't mean she can't find a good man to share her life with." She pushed out her bosom. "Not all of us wither as we get older, you know."

The notion of a respectably settled Lila brightened Cass's morning. "I agree with Faith," she said to the others. "It's very romantic."

They all laughed, and Faith beamed. "I'm almost old enough to get married, you know. My ma got married when she was sixteen and birthed me when she was just seventeen. But Ma won't tell me nothing about how to get my man. She says if a match is made in heaven, it just happens."

Frenchie snorted, and Luce sent her a warning glare.

Faith's expression became wistful. "You ladies all look so pretty all the time. And men look at you like . . . well, they look at you, you know? I wish someone would tell me how a woman gets a man to look her way," she hinted broadly.

Rachel laughed. "You wouldn't be setting a hook for young Amos Byrd, would you, Faith?"

Faith blushed a rosy red.

"Now there's a young man any gal would hanker after," Frenchie said.

Faith completely missed the teasing in Frenchie's voice as she positively beamed. "He's wonderful, isn't he? Maybe you could show me how to fix myself up so he'd notice me. Not anything big, you know. Ma would have me memorizing whole Bible chapters if I did something wild like rouge my cheeks. But there must be something . . ."

"Honey," Luce broke in, "you take ol' Luce's advice and forget about the boys a while yet. You wanna be old and tired with a baby on each hip afore you're twenty? You jest enjoy bein' a little girl while you can. If any of these ladies here had a lick o' sense, they'd tell you the same."

Faith stuck out her lower lip. "I'm not a little girl."

"You listen to Luce," Rachel advised, her voice serious

now. "Believe me, honey, once you start lettin' men into your life, things become a lot more complicated."

"An' don't tell your ma you been talking like this," Luce warned, "or she'll—"

"Faith Elizabeth Scott! What are you doing here?"

The demand came from Hope Perkins, Faith's maiden aunt. And one look at the woman, Cass thought, would tell anyone why she was a spinster. She must put a lot of effort into looking drab, for surely no woman with such regular features, thick brown hair, and buxom figure could look that way naturally. Cass scolded herself for such uncharitable thoughts, but Hope promptly proved she deserved every one. The skirmish had begun.

"What do you think you're doing, you wicked creatures? Trying to seduce a poor fatherless girl into the ways of sin? I told my sister Alice it was a mistake letting such women into our company!"

"We weren't seducing Faith into anything!" Cass snapped. If she was called wicked one more time on this trip, she was simply going to explode.

"Aunt Hope! I wasn't doing anything wrong."

"Just talking to these women is a sin," Hope told her niece. She snatched her up from the stool and gave her a pinch. "Evil rubs off, young lady. Wait until your mother hears about this."

Faith wailed.

Frenchie responded by grabbing Hope's arm. "Leave off there, sister."

"Yeah. Take it easy," Rachel said. "She didn't do anything wrong."

Hope pulled away. "You creatures don't know right from wrong. Maybe if someone had taken a strap to you when you were young, you wouldn't be on the path to hell."

Sue feigned innocence. "I thought we were on the path to Oregon."

"Watch out, Faith," Frenchie warned with a smirk. "Drab rubs off too. I wouldn't let that woman touch you, if I were you."

Hope flushed. It was the only hint of color in her face. "You . . . you . . ."

"Slut?" Frenchie suggested. "Afraid to say the word?"

"Yes! You are. All of you. We all know it." She grabbed Faith's arm once again and dragged her away.

"Aunt Hope!" Faith moaned a series of fading protests as her aunt dragged her back to reluctant respectability.

"So much for gratitude," Rachel commented wryly. *"You're sluts, and we all know it!"* she mimicked.

"They save their gratitude for Nathan," Sue told her. "It's easier for them to stomach a criminal than a soiled woman."

Frenchie snorted. "It's harder for a whore to get into heaven than for a camel to stick a needle in its eye."

Luce banged the dishpan onto the worktable. "What nonsense you talkin', gal?"

"Isn't there something like that in the Bible?"

"Not in no Bible I ever read. But speakin' of heaven, they're gatherin' for services over there."

"How can they have services?" Cass asked bitterly. "Their preacher turned out to be a fake."

Luce filled the dishpan with steaming water from the kettle. "They don't need no preacher's blessin'. They'll plumb talk their own way into heaven."

"Spare me a morning listening to all that singing," Rachel said. "I think I'll look in on Ben."

Frenchie's eyes glinted at Rachel's mention of singing. "I think it might be nice to attend their services. After all, those generous ladies took us back into the fold and treat us in such a mannerly way. We should show how thankful we are."

Cass didn't like the look on Frenchie's face. "I think we should stay here and mind our own business."

"I'm going to Sunday services," Mama Luce told her. "Lookee there at the preachin' wagon. Ol' Eliza Jacobs is standin' right up there with a Bible in her hand, just like a preacher herself."

"This I just have to hear," Sue said.

Rachel changed her mind. "Maybe I'll go after all. This could be interesting."

"If you ain't going," Luce told Cass, "you can pick up these cups and plates and wash 'em up. Got the water all soapy and hot right here."

So Cass washed the morning dishes while the four women marched off to church services—quite a reversal of how things used to be. "Behave yourselves!" she called after them. She ought to go with them to keep trouble from erupting, but she was getting tired of making herself the lid on top of a volcano. Some mountains were just meant to explode. Cass couldn't make herself care terribly about whatever trouble the ladies might cause. Things just didn't matter as much anymore.

She muttered to herself as she threw tin coffee mugs and dirty plates into the dishwater. Self-pity congealed to a lump in her chest. She didn't like the feeling, yet she couldn't seem to get away from it. One part of her stood apart, scolding as she wallowed in the injustices visited upon her. It was easier to feel sorry for herself and angry at Nathan than to accept the fact that she'd been a gullible fool. All her life she'd been the competent one, the sensible one, running the details of their lives while Lila did what Lila did best—charm men and make money. She'd been condescendingly virtuous, Cass admitted painfully, and self-righteously prim. Now she was the one who had stumbled, and to preserve any shred of dignity, she had to blame anyone and everyone but herself.

"Lord in heaven!" She threw a cup into the dishpan so hard it bounced right out and into the dirt. "I don't even like myself anymore."

A piteous whine answered her. She looked down to find Dog sitting beside the supply wagon and looking at her with melting eyes. Her world brightened just a bit.

"Run away from your evil master?" she asked the animal.

Dog held up a paw and whined again.

"Something wrong with your foot, sweetie?"

Cass wiped her hands and sat down on the grass beside him. When she sat, the dog's head topped hers by a good six inches. Yet big as he was, he wasn't fearsome in the least. His master should be so gentle.

His master had been gentle once, Cass remembered reluctantly. But it had been a masquerade. Men were not as simple or honest as dogs.

"Let me see what the problem is." She took the offered paw and cautiously felt the hard pads. No thorns, no cuts, no sharp grass seeds working their way into the skin between his toes. "I think you just want the leftover griddle cakes, you wicked dog."

He slurped out a tongue to lick her face. She laughed and batted him away. "You sneaky mutt!"

"Taking out your aggravation on my dog?"

Nathan's voice made Cass jump. He pulled up a stool and grinned at her. "What's the matter? Is Dog the only one on the train who'll listen to you?"

"You are abominable."

"That's a good one. Pretty soon you're going to run out of names to call me."

"Not likely." Why couldn't he look like a villain? Cass wondered sourly. It was unjust for a man with such a winning smile and seductive eyes to be scum.

"Any of Luce's good coffee left?"

"If I'd known you were coming, I would have poured it out."

"Or down my back, more likely."

"That's a thought. Don't you have someone else to bother? Why don't you go over to the Sunday services? They might even let you preach again. They seem to have forgiven you everything else."

He glanced across the circle of wagons to where Eliza was exhorting her flock. Cass saw a flicker of regret in his eyes and suffered a moment—just a brief moment—of fellow feeling. False as he was, Nathan Stone had, like her, hoped for a resurrection of sorts, a new life that wiped away the taint of the old. As long as John Lawton was alive, he had much less chance of carrying it off than she and Lila did.

"They don't seem to lack for a preacher," he said with a smile. "Eliza's preaching up heaven and casting out devils, looks like."

Cass shot him a look, and he raised a hand to ward off the obvious comment. "Don't say it!" he warned. "I tried hard enough to cast myself out, sweetheart, but your sister

and Granny between them made it clear that leaving would
make me an even bigger villain than I am."

Hymn singing commenced, and "Rock of Ages" floated
upward from the circle along with the campfire smoke. Eliza
directed the hymn in the same manner as she preached, waving the Bible in time with the words and glaring at any inat-
tentive soul who wandered off key. Most of her glares shot
toward the group of four interlopers from the McAllister
wagons.

"By the way, how's Lawton?"

"His wound is running pus and he's running a fever. That
should make you happy."

His mouth slanted upward in a wry smile. "Too bad your
sister's such a competent nurse. With my luck she'll set him
right in no time."

"You're odious."

"Another good word. Where do you get all these?"

"I read. Everyone should try to improve themselves. You
should give it a try."

"I tried to improve myself. It didn't work. Had a beautiful woman all ready to marry me and make me a respectable man." He gave her a look that seared straight to
her bones. "It almost worked."

She tried to dredge up another name to call him, but
made the mistake of meeting his gaze. Try as she would,
she couldn't quite find the scoundrel she despised in the
dark depths of those eyes.

The growing swell of noise from across the circle finally
intruded. Cass jerked her eyes away from his.

"Your friends have voices like screech owls," Nathan observed.

"That's not true. Frenchie is good enough to sing on the
stage."

Nathan laughed. "Not like that."

He spoke the truth. The singing had turned into a raucous contest, with the Shelby women competing with
Frenchie, Sue, and Rachel to see who could send God the
loudest hymn. The two groups had drawn apart like two op-
posing armies, glaring as each tried to outdo the other. Eliza
waved her Bible to and fro, trying to keep some semblance

of control. Frenchie and her little troop were holding their own and more, but then, they were used to being raucous. The Shelby women were newcomers to such boisterousness.

Cass hurried across the circle, visions of a free-for-all in her head. Nathan wasn't far behind her, grinning as if the whole thing was just good fun.

"It's all that old biddy's fault," Mama Luce complained to them. "First she ups and quotes every verse in the Good Book that takes after harlots. Then she tries to chase us away. Says our ladies put a sour note in God's music."

Cass could scarcely understand Luce's disgusted account over the singing, which had deteriorated into little more than a shouting match, each faction trying to drown out the other. Wringing her hands, Eliza Jacobs shouted an appeal to Nathan. "Mr. Stone! Do something!"

With a grin, he vaulted to his former place in the "preaching wagon" and raised his arms for quiet. False prophet or not, he'd lost none of his power over the crowd. The tumult died a ragged death.

"You ladies are not behaving like ladies," he chided, cocking a brow, first at Frenchie, then at Eliza.

Eliza stiffened her already straight spine. "These are private services, Mr. Stone. You're supposed to keep the peace in this wagon train. Tell them to stop intruding where they're not wanted."

Luce objected. "Ain't nothing private under God's wide open sky, missus. If you want to be private, you stuff your backsides into one of them private wagons. You tell her that's right, Mr. Stone."

"It does seem that an open-air service should take all comers," Nathan agreed. Before Frenchie's troops could gloat, however, he went on. "It's also true that those attending Sunday services should show some manners and respect. Back when I was a boy in Tennessee, my mama always told me, if you can't behave anywhere else, you'd better behave in church."

"Amen!" Luce said fervently. "Now let's get on with it."

"The service is over," Eliza declared frostily.

"No, it ain't!" Luce denied. "What kinda service has only one bit of singin'? And where's the prayin' and the amens?"

"What's the matter?" Sue taunted. "Afraid we'll outpray you?"

"Like we outsang you," Rachel added.

Cass touched Frenchie's arm and pleaded. "Come on, Frenchie. Let's go back to our own wagons."

"No, sirree! We're staying right here and getting ho-lified." She gave Cass an impish grin. "Isn't that what you wanted, Cassie girl?"

Eliza opened her Bible and began to read from Revelation. Cass sighed. The Apocalypse seemed an entirely appropriate subject for this particular service. She sent Nathan a sour look as he climbed down from the wagon. "You didn't make things any better."

He tipped his hat to her—mockingly, she thought. "Why, Miss Cass, I'm just an abominable odious snake, remember? Not a saint. Besides, I doubt Jesus himself could keep these two bunches of hens from pecking at each other." He sauntered away. Dog stayed with her, sitting sedately at her side. She scratched his ears and sympathized. "I don't blame you. I'd disown him too."

The war ended in a draw, with no blood shed, but much worse was yet to come. Everyone went about the drudgery that could only be done on days when they weren't travel-ing. The water near their campsite was a miserable spring that took ten minutes to fill a bucket, but the laundry still had to be washed, so buckets had to be hauled, and refilled, and again refilled. The afternoon grew hot and muggy, and Luce grew cranky with the heat as she baked the loaves of bread that would carry them through the next week. No one wanted to be near Mama Luce when she was cranky, so Rachel grabbed her tatting and took herself off—toward the Sutter wagon, Cass noticed, which had fallen to Ben since the Sutters had both died in the Sioux attack. Sue took their pile of laundry and combined it with Effie Brown's. The two women made the unpleasant chore a joint effort. Cass resigned herself to stitching a torn harness—not exactly the fine needlework on which she prided herself. Not a breeze stirred the air, and sweat ran down her forehead and drib-bled into her eyes, making the task harder. She felt sorry for Lila in the tent with Lawton. Surely in this heat they were both cooking.

Later in the afternoon, dark clouds gathering to the west promised cooling breezes. The present hour, however, was still a steambath. When Cass checked on Lila, she and her patient were both sweating enough to break any fever.

"Maybe you should move him outside," Cass suggested. "There's a little shade by the wagons."

"No. Everyone knows fresh air is bad for someone with a fever. I'll just keep putting these cool cloths on him."

"Is he getting any better?"

"I think the inflammation is down, and the poultices are drawing the pus."

"Lovely," Cass said with a grimace.

"Poor man hurts so. I've been giving him some laudanum to help him rest. I blame myself for not keeping the wound clean enough. But with all this"—she waved a hand, indicating the campsite and wagons beyond the canvas of the tent—"this dirt, mule filth, close air, and scarcely any clean water for washing, I suppose infection is almost a certainty."

Cass detected more than weariness in her sister's eyes. John Lawton, she realized suddenly, was more to Lila than just a patient. She'd never pictured her sister holding any one man in her heart. Perhaps she didn't know Lila quite as well as she thought. "You look really tired," she said. "I told Sue and Effie I'd help them finish the laundry, but when I'm done there I'll come sit with the marshal. You deserve a break."

"I'm not doing anything but sitting here."

"Don't argue. I'll be back."

When Cass did come back an hour later, she got no argument from her sister. Lila was done in. The late afternoon had turned suddenly cool, and the concern now was to keep Lawton warm.

"Give him the laudanum if he gets restless," Lila told her. "It'll put him out, and he needs the rest. Call me if you need anything."

Cass didn't mind sitting with Lawton. As the sun went down, she enjoyed the cool breezes that sneaked in through the tent flap, and even though she kept the patient bundled, to her the refreshingly chilly air was welcome. Distant thunder promised rain, and for once the thought of rain was welcome. She hoped someone remembered to set out the open water casks.

She also enjoyed the solitude. These past days she had shared Luce and Frenchie's tent, and while she was very fond of both of them, Frenchie talked a lot, frequently late into the night. Lawton, poor man, was the ideal tentmate. He didn't talk at all, because the fever and laudanum together had knocked his senses right out from under him. Poor, poor man, Cass reflected—another one of Nathan Stone's victims. He looked very noble lying on his pallet suffering, his sandy hair disordered and damp with sweat, his skin flushed, an unhappy cast to his expression even though he slept. Cass diligently kept cool cloths on his brow. She hoped Nathan was right when he proclaimed Lawton too ornery to die. She'd never seen Lila look at a man with quite that soft expression in her eye.

When the sun was well down, Lila brought Cass a dish of stew and a mug of tea. She approved of Lawton's condition—his fever was finally abating—and offered to resume her duties.

"You go eat your dinner in peace," Cass told her. "I'll stay here a couple more hours."

Lila brushed back the hair that had fallen over Lawton's brow. "He's improving, bless him. And he should sleep like the dead until morning. If anything changes, give me a call."

"Don't worry. I will."

After Lila left, Cass wrapped herself in a blanket and made herself comfortable on Lila's bedroll. She didn't intend to drift off, but the day had been such a weary one, and slumber was so tempting.

When a crash of thunder woke her, she shot up, confused and muzzy with sleep. Evening had darkened into full night, and the wind flapped the tent canvas and sent fingers of chilled air through the tent flap. Another crash of sound made her jump. Thunder? Or a lightning strike? The explosion had been so close it was hard to tell. She fumbled for the lantern, finding it only with the help of lightning

flashes. Its wavering light showed Lawton still fast asleep—
that laudanum was strong stuff.

She checked the poultice, which was still in place, and
bundled him more tightly in his blankets. The unhealthy
heat had left him almost completely. Lila would probably
show up any moment, Cass thought, and she would be happy
with her patient's improvement.

She'd no more than completed the thought when a bright
white explosion accompanied another blast of thunder. The
earth shook beneath her.

Cass hugged herself tightly. She hated thunderstorms.
Lord knew she had endured enough of them since setting
off on this journey, for in Kansas they always came roar-
ing in with the spring. She had sat in their porch swing in
Webster watching tornadoes snake their way across the plain.
But huddling in the dark while the wind howled and the
thunder crashed was far worse. One never knew what lurked
in the darkness, wind, and fury. A tornado could be bearing down on the hapless campsite, and no one would know.
There would be no warning. Cass had heard of whole wagon
trains turned to splinters by tornadoes, or deluged in sudden torrential rain and literally washed away.

The thunder was almost continuous, and beneath the con-
cussions, the howl of wind was a constant whine. Cass
doused the lantern as the tent bucked and flapped, fighting
the stakes that held it to the ground. With a snap, something gave way and the canvas partially collapsed on itself.

Cursing all the while, Cass unlaced the opening and
dashed out to repair the damage. The wind immediately
ripped her hair loose from its knot and tried to tear the very
clothes from her body. Flashes of lightning gave the scene
a hellish glare, but at least the eerie light enabled her to
find the damage. Two wooden stakes had pulled up and now
whipped back and forth in the wind. More were threatening to pull loose. In a few minutes the tent would be around
their ears.

"I need a hammer!" she shouted uselessly. "Damn it all!"
The battering of the wind and the tumult in the sky terrified her. And terror made her angry. She took off a shoe
and tried beating the remaining stakes more firmly into the

ground, then tried to grab one of the loose stakes that danced in the vicious wind. It eluded her.

Someone grabbed her, shouting in her ear. "Let me do that!" Cass clung to him, beyond thinking.

"Hold on to me!" screamed Nathan.

Within moments he had the loose stakes, along with all the others, hammered firmly into the ground. Driving rain began to sting them with bulletlike drops, and they both sought the shelter within the tent.

Cass groaned and shivered, hugging herself with cold and vexation. She owed Nathan thanks, but what came out of her mouth was pure spite. "You're not staying here, are you?"

"You're welcome," he said with a crooked grin.

Cass took a breath and reconsidered her mean-spirited remark. "Thank you," she said reluctantly. "Thank you very much. Don't feel you have to stay. I'm sure you have others to see to."

"Not really. Things are pretty much under control now. Eliza Jacobs's cow broke loose and trampled through Ben Holden's tent, but we managed to catch her. She stepped on your friend Rachel's hand."

"Rachel was in Ben Holden's tent?"

Nathan's eyes twinkled. "Seeking shelter, no doubt."

"Of course."

"The Byrds lost the top from their wagon. The Scott ladies lost their tent. The fools hadn't staked it at all. They were afraid their wagon was going to tip over, so they're huddled in with your sister and Luce."

She couldn't help a tentative smile. "That could be more dangerous than the storm."

"Could be." He grinned. "You all right?"

She would be better if he weren't filling the tent with his presence, calling to mind another night when they'd shared the darkness, isolated from the rest of the world by an arch of canvas. If he would go and take those memories with him, she would be fine.

"I'm perfectly all right," she lied. "Do feel free to leave."

"Lawton?"

"He's better. Don't feel you have to stick around."

"Your tent seems secure enough now."

"I'm sure it is. Aren't you needed somewhere else?" The dark seemed so confined, the tent so small, and he filled so much of it. Worst of all was the lingering desire to jump into his arms each time the lightning flashed and thunder rolled.

A clap of thunder made her jump, and the rain pounded down with punishing force.

"You wouldn't send me out into this flood, would you?" Nathan asked.

"Yes."

"It's cold, and I could catch pneumonia and die. Then who would be your fearless trail guide?"

"You're not *my* trail guide!" Cass grasped at a straw. "And what about my reputation? Suppose this downpour lasts all night. Everyone will think . . . will think we . . ."

He grinned wickedly, which tempted her to use main force to toss him out of the tent and let the deluge drench his evil grin. "You are . . . are . . ."

"Abominable?"

"Exactly! Please leave!"

"Don't worry about your reputation. After all, we have a chaperon." He pointed at Lawton.

"Some chaperon. If this thunder and lightning haven't wakened him, do you think anything could?"

A crack of lightning struck somewhere very close, and the sound nearly deafened her. She jumped and found herself enclosed in Nathan's strong arms.

"Do you really want me to leave, Cass?"

"No," she squeaked. Tears leaked disgracefully from her eyes. "I'm afraid of storms," she admitted in a quavering voice.

"I figured. Otherwise you wouldn't come within ten feet of me."

Cass's courage deserted her as the barrage grew more intense. She willingly settled with Nathan on Lila's bedroll and hid her face against his shoulder. He held his silence, for which she was grateful. She didn't think she could stand it if he chose this moment to gloat. The shelter of his arms felt so very good, so very right, as did the comfort of his broad shoulder, the warmth and hard strength of him. She was such a ninny. Her head knew very well that Nathan Stone was the worst kind of scoundrel, but her heart, hurt as it was, still softened every time she saw him. Now the rest of her was melting as well, breathing in the wind-fresh scent of his skin, listening to the beat of his heart beneath her cheek as if it were some kind of lullaby.

His hand stole around and cradled her head, fingers lacing through her windblown hair. The gesture should have been intrusive. It should have been offensive. It was neither. She should have shook him off and pushed him away. She didn't.

"I never meant to hurt you, Cass. I hope someday you realize that's the truth."

Nathan's voice was little more than a whisper, but somehow she heard it above the battering of rain and the crash of thunder. She didn't answer, because she didn't know what to say. Instead, she allowed herself to go to sleep.

Lila emerged from her tent to a wet, cool morning. She stretched mightily, feeling more refreshed than she had in days, despite the storm and an undercurrent of uneasiness about how Lawton had done during the night. And despite spending the night crowded together with Luce, Alice and Faith Scott, Hope Perkins, and June Dawkins. Frenchie had huffed off to sleep with Sue when they had appeared, but the arrangement hadn't been that bad. Faith was a giddy kind of sweet. Her mother, Alice, was plain and quiet, and June Dawkins was a sturdy, independent soul that Lila found herself actually liking. Even Hope had been at least civil— a good thing, since she was depending on Lila's hospitality to keep her out of the rain. When the Shelby females weren't running in a pack, they were almost like real women.

The camp was more or less a disaster. Two wagons had lost their canvas tops. One of the tops was plastered against one of the other wagons, along with the Scott tent. Still, the morning was sunlit and beautiful, and Lila felt just fine. There was something to this business of starting over after all. Or maybe, she thought, glancing toward the tent where

Lawton lay, something else was making her feel like a new woman.

Mama Luce emerged from the tent behind her, followed by Alice and Faith. The little tent seemed to spill out women in an endless stream.

"I reckon all the firewood is soaked through," Luce complained. "Won't be no hot coffee and biscuits this morning."

"We have some firewood stored in our wagon," Alice said timidly. "Maybe it stayed dry. We could use that."

A big grin grew on Luce's face. "That'd be right neighborly of you, missus."

"It's the least we can do, after your help last night."

Five minutes later the cook fire was built and water was starting to heat. Lila headed toward her own tent to check on Cass and Lawton when out stepped none other than Nathan Stone. She stopped in her tracks. He gave her a faintly guilty-looking smile before heading toward the damaged tent and wagon cover. Cass appeared next and stood at the tent entrance with a rumpled dress, wild hair, and an uncertain expression. She seemed not to see Lila. In fact, she seemed not to see anything other than Nathan Stone walking away from the tent.

Luce came up beside Lila. "Don't you tease that girl, Miz Lila. She been cranky enough as it is."

"I wouldn't dream of teasing her," Lila said, a satisfied smile on her face. Sometimes things just had a way of working out.

Chapter 15

"Civilization at last!" The town before them earned every bit of the cynicism in Frenchie's voice. Dobytown, sometimes known as Kearny City, was hardly what anyone would call civilization. It was the stepchild of Fort Kearny, the lair of sharks and opportunists who fed on transient emigrants—no place for a lady, or for anyone not wanting to be quickly parted from their money.

Still, after weeks spent living out of a wagon, no real woman could resist a chance to go shopping. Lila, Cass, Sue, and Frenchie were no exceptions. They'd walked the little distance from camp to town in high spirits, armed with a fair amount of cash from Lila's nest egg and a long list of needed items.

"It's not much, is it?" Cass said as they walked into the town. Spread over the prairie was a haphazard jumble of buildings. No discernible network of streets brought order to the random arrangement. Buildings sprang from the prairie like weeds in a field, and were certainly no more attractive. Some were timber, but most were sod. Wagons, horses, and people had trampled the coarse prairie grass into dust, which swirled in choking eddies from beneath the brisk traffic. Not only emigrants flocked into Dobytown for supplies and entertainment, but soldiers and railroad workers as well.

"Well it can't be all bad." Frenchie cocked an artfully plucked brow. "Most of what I see is saloons."

"I could use a drink." Sue's voice was hopeful.

Cass said primly, "That's not what we're here for."

"It might not be what you came for . . ." Frenchie teased, chuckling.

"No boozing," Lila warned sternly. "Cass is right. Now listen, ladies. I know you can behave with decorum, because back in Webster you acted like ladies of refinement every night when the doors of Lila's Place opened to admit our gentleman callers. The only way you can expect to be treated with any kind of respect is to mind your manners. That means no cussing, no drinking, and no giving the eye to any men."

"Hear, hear!" Cass seconded.

"Well, hell!" Sue objected. "What's the use of even coming in to town?"

"We're here to buy supplies," Cass declared, "to get a nice glass of lemonade, if this town has heard of such a thing, and to remind ourselves that there is life beyond trudging along a trail all day."

Dobytown made the little town of Webster look like a metropolis by comparison, but that didn't keep the women from having a good time. At a sod grocery store they paid outrageous prices to restock their supplies of flour, coffee, and sugar. Baking powder was a luxury not to be had. For the past week they'd been eating bread made from sourdough and soda, and it appeared they would continue. Cass bought tea, a new tin mixing bowl for Luce, and some writing paper to continue her journal. Frenchie paid dearly for a bonnet she wouldn't have looked twice at back in Kansas, and Lila was able to replenish her medicine chest with laudanum, calomel, paregoric, and arnica. More and more their traveling companions were depending upon her to treat their sprains, bruises, and the other ills. Most of her patients were doing well. Lawton was on his feet part of the day, and Jed Jacobs was eating soft foods. Even Cory Decker was walking about with the aid of a cane that Nathan had cut for him.

Cass was recovering as well. Though she'd had no physical injury that could be poulticed or bandaged, she was every bit as wounded as those who had suffered in the Sioux attack. But since the stormy night spent cringing in Nathan Stone's embrace, something inside her had begun to heal. The future once again seemed brighter. People were worth the effort of a smile. The sights of the trail and the tenor of her thoughts were once again worth noting in her journal.

She didn't know what had lifted the dreadful weight she had carried in her heart. Nothing had changed, really. For the most part, the people she saw every day still looked down their noses at her and Lila. The trail was still difficult, the danger of Indians, sickness, or injury was very real, the ground was still a hard bed, and sand was still a part of everything they ate. Moreover, Nathan Stone was still scum who'd broken her heart and made her feel like a fool. But after the night of the storm, they'd reached a truce of sorts. He didn't provoke her, and she didn't needle him. They tried to be polite. Life was more pleasant that way.

"Look, Cassie," Sue exclaimed. "There's sewing needles. Do you need some more sewing needles?"

Lila laughed. "Don't encourage her to sew up any more bloomer dresses."

"For your information, this bloomer dress is very comfortable, and it allows you to sit astride a saddle without being immodest. You don't know what you're missing,"

Frenchie chuckled and lowered her voice. "There's a fellow I wouldn't mind riding astride."

Cass elbowed her in the ribs, but she did follow Frenchie's gaze to the tall cavalry officer who perused the boots lined up for sale. "Behave yourself!" she whispered. "If you know how."

At that moment the officer caught Frenchie's eye and touched his hat. Before Frenchie could respond, Cass grabbed her arm and headed for the door. "Come on," she called to the others. "I can do without the needles."

Frenchie laughed as they stumbled out the door. "You don't trust me?"

"Does she look like she was born yesterday?" Lila asked, following behind them.

"Not anymore, she doesn't," Frenchie replied.

Cass grimaced, but she was able to chuckle at the gibe. She'd fallen from her pedestal, and her friends weren't going to let her forget it.

They wandered through the labyrinth of shabby buildings. The saloons did a brisk business, even in the middle of the day. In one or two of them, piano music tinkled from open doors and windows.

"I'm glad the professor didn't come with us," Frenchie said. "It would purely break the man's heart to hear a piano abused like that."

"He could probably get a job," Cass noted. "Sounds as if they need someone who can actually play."

"He doesn't want a job," Sue said with a smirk. "He wants to go west with Frenchie."

Frenchie rolled her eyes.

Most of the people on the street were men, many sunburned, bewhiskered, and travel-stained. A good number seemed to be drunk. Blue-coated soldiers from Fort Kearny were here and there. A boardinghouse sign boasted that it housed officers of the Eighteenth Infantry. It was one of the few respectable-looking buildings in the town.

A few other emigrant women braved the town to shop, but most of the women in Dobytown were there to service the men. And a ragged bunch of whores they were. Not at all up to Lila's standards.

"We could make a fortune here," Sue speculated. "There isn't a single girl in this town who doesn't look like a raggedy old alley cat."

"Take a look at their clients," Frenchie advised. "They're a good match for the ladies."

"Some of the soldiers aren't bad," Sue said. "And they get paid regular."

Lila scoffed. "For every soldier, there's a dozen muleskinners, shysters, gamblers, and randy men from the wagon trains who haven't bathed in weeks. Those three who just came out of that saloon, for instance. I wouldn't have let them in the door of Lila's Place if they offered twice the price. They look as if they should be dipped as well as bathed."

The three men she spoke of had stumbled out of the Lucky Lady, a sod shanty whose bawdiness was evident by the sheer volume of noise coming from the open door. They'd had a good time, it appeared, because they grinned, slapping each other's backs and chortling at some private joke as they weaved into the street. One of them spied the four women and elbowed his companions in the ribs.

"Frenchie," Sue warned, "don't look like that."

"Like what?"

"Like you always look when a man looks your way. Like that!"

"I don't look like anything."

"Yes, you do. See, they're coming this way."

They were indeed. Their aroma preceded them, making the women flinch.

"Well, lookee here," the leader said through his grimy beard.

"Jus' what we was wantin'." His friend gave the women a leering once-over and scratched his paunch. "Yer in luck, girlies. We just won big, an' we aim to have some fun."

"Bully for you," Frenchie said. "Move aside, gents. We've got places to go."

The women tried to dodge around the men, but the one who seemed to be the leader, a barrel-shaped ape whose greasy hair matched his greasy beard, grabbed Sue by the arm. "What's yer hurry? We tol' ya that we got money."

"Yeah!" Paunchy said. "You'll get paid."

The third man in the trio didn't say anything. He just stared at them with his mouth half open.

Frenchie stepped between Greasy and Sue. "Let her go, lamebrain. We aren't for sale. And even if we were, we wouldn't be to the likes of you three."

"Hey!" Greasy's brow beetled at the insult. "Who do ya think y'are?"

"A lady with some taste," Frenchie said haughtily. She pulled Sue free and all four of them hurried down the street. For a moment, the three amorous revelers huddled in a grumbling trio. Then they followed, throwing insults.

"Pretty full of yourself, ain't ya?"

"Bitches!"

"What'sa matter, sweetheart? 'Fraid to open your legs for a real man?"

"That's enough!" Lila stopped and turned to face them down. In her hand was the small palm pistol she'd taken from her reticule. She never went anywhere without it. "You gents are offensive. Now just turn around and leave us be, or I'll be forced to call the law."

The men looked at her popgun and laughed. "Whazzat? Hell, lady. You couldn't stop a mosquito with that."

Lila's eyes narrowed. "You think not?"

Their predicament had drawn some notice from others on the thoroughfare, but no one seemed inclined to intervene. Frenchie and Sue definitely looked the part that the men had assigned them—therefore forfeiting any gallantry their gender might have inspired—and by association, Lila and Cass were cast in the same role.

"Just go away," Cass pleaded with them. "There are plenty of women in this town that would be glad of your money."

Paunchy grunted. "Now you done been so uppity, we ain't even gonna pay. Not unless you're real, real nice."

Greasy moved faster than any of the women could have expected. Lila's little pistol went flying, and Lila shrieked as his big, dirty hand closed around her wrist. Cass flew to her sister's defense, grabbing the ape's arm and kicking his shins. The silent one grabbed her in turn, pulling her back against a meaty chest. Frenchie and Sue both jumped to the rescue, but four women—no matter how determined—were no match for three big men who fought like gorillas. Greasy simply picked up a flailing Lila and headed for the nearest alley. His friends dragged Cass and Sue in the same direction, with Frenchie riding the silent one's back, pounding on his head. He merely laughed, ignoring the few onlookers who were beginning to show alarm.

Then something caught him at the knees and knocked him to the ground. Frenchie and Cass hit the ground beside him. When Cass picked herself up, she was amazed to see the professor squaring off with their three assailants.

"Hey, hey!" Greasy shouted.

The three toughs grinned fiercely, eager to fight—espe-

cially since the beanpole musician waving his fists at them
presented about as much challenge as a flea.

"Watch out, Professor!" Frenchie cried as one of the men
took a swing at him.

Their would-be savior dodged the first blow, but the second caught him square on the chin. He windmilled with his
fists, and the three louts laughed. They were drunk, but not
drunk enough to be brought down by this puny excuse for
a man, even with the women joining in, which the women
eagerly did. The louts easily tossed aside Lila and Cass. Sue
landed a kick on Greasy's knee and got bounced on her
backside in the dust.

The professor stayed in the fight gamely, awkwardly flailing his fists and once using his head as a battering ram. He
might as well have slammed his skull against granite for all
the good it did. The three men simply toyed with him, despite the shrieks and forays of the women, and soon he
sported one eye swollen shut, a bloody nose, a gashed cheek,
and a useless arm. When he collapsed in the dust and they
began kicking him, Frenchie managed to put an end to the
massacre.

"Take this!" she shrieked, and beaned Greasy over the
head with a cast-iron skillet. Paunchy turned to look and
got the skillet full in the face. He collapsed in a heap with
a smashed nose and a surprised expression on his face. The
silent one saw the ferocity in Frenchie's eyes and ran off,
leaving his fallen comrades to the women's mercy.

Cass picked herself up from the dirt. "Shoot, Frenchie!
Where did you get that?"

The answer came from the aproned shopkeeper who
dashed out of the dry goods store next to the alley. He raised
a fist and shouted at Frenchie. "You can't come in here and
run out with my goods! That skillet cost fifty cents, woman!
Come back here!"

Frenchie shrugged, sauntered up to the balding, rotund
little man, and gave him back his skillet.

"It's got blood on it!" he objected.

"Tough!" Frenchie said. "It was for a good cause. What
kind of town is this where respectable ladies can't walk the
streets in broad daylight without being set upon by no-goods

like these." She sniffed and brushed the dust from her silk skirt. "When these louts wake up, tell them to pick on someone their own size next time. Maybe they'll have more luck."

Cass laughed. Frenchie laughed with her. Between them, they hauled the professor to his feet and propped him up as he regained his balance. Then all four women gave the shopkeeper charmingly benign smiles as they and the professor threaded arms and marched off.

"Ladies, ha!" the little man shouted after them.

Cass heard the insult, but for once she felt no shame.

Their knight errant was in no shape to walk very far under his own steam, but the wagons were close by, camped alongside several other emigrant parties on the broad, rutted prairie.

Luce was the first to hail them from the camp.

"What's you got here? What happened?"

Rachel and Ben hurried over as well. "What in high heaven happened to you?" Rachel demanded. Ben helped the women lower the fallen hero to a stool beside Luce's fire. Effie Brown and Granny Decker came over to see what was up. Pamela Decker wasn't far behind. She gasped at the sight of the professor's purple eye and bloody face. "Oh, dear Lord! The poor man!"

Frenchie took her handkerchief—embroidered linen with delicate lace—dipped it in a bucket of water, and began to wipe the blood and grime from the professor's face. "This stupid fool thought he could take on three drunk toughs by himself."

"The professor?" Rachel exclaimed. "Fight?"

Cass, Lila, and Sue provided the details of the story while Frenchie fussed over the professor, doctoring his hurts even while she scolded him unmercifully.

"Who do you think you are?" she asked scornfully. "Some knight riding to rescue the damsels in distress? Didn't you think we could take care of ourselves, you fool?"

"We weren't doing a great job of taking care of ourselves," Cass commented, getting out tin cups for coffee.

"If Frenchie hadn't been giving the eye to every man we passed, maybe they wouldn't have taken us for whores," Sue complained.

"I certainly didn't give the eye to *those* louts."

The professor tried to say something, but his swollen lip slurred his words past recognition.

"You just be quiet," Frenchie warned him. "I've never seen a man with less sense. You truly do need someone to take care of you. Who taught you to fight like that, anyway? Whoever he was, he was an idiot."

"Poor man," Effie sympathized. "Do you think that gash on his cheek should be stitched? I have some fine silk thread."

"Oh, leave it," Sue suggested. "The scar will make him look dashing."

"Who attacked you?" Pamela Decker asked.

"No one," Frenchie told her. "Just some drunks who thought we were setting ourselves up for business." Her expression softened. "You are a fool, Professor, but you're a sweet fool. I don't think I've ever had a man dive in and try to protect my virtue before."

"Me neither," Sue admitted.

"It was *very* sweet," Cass agreed, a smile tugging at the corner of her mouth.

Lila watched the scene in silent amusement.

"What are you all looking at?" Frenchie demanded. Sue smirked, and Frenchie actually blushed. Cass couldn't remember a single time in the past that she'd seen Frenchie blush. "Go on, all of you," she said belligerently. "Don't you all have something better to do?"

"What's all the fuss?" The new voice came from none other than John Lawton, pale, scarecrow thin, but upright on his feet and walking about, although a bit gingerly.

"Frenchie clucking over the professor like a hen over an egg," Sue said with a wicked grin.

"I am not!" She looked around at the interested faces and grew even redder. Abruptly, she stood and threw the wet, bloody hankie at Steamboat Sue. "Here! You patch him up if you think it's so funny. Or let him take care of himself, the idiot. I don't care!" With an indignant glare, she flounced off.

Lila looked from the professor to the fleeing Frenchie

and shook her head, smiling. "You watch out, Professor. You've got a real fighter hooked on your line."

The professor could only groan. Lawton moved to where he could get a look. "Looks like he got a real fighter real mad. What happened?"

"The professor very gallantly rescued four of us ladies from the unwanted attentions of some drunks in town. And he paid for it."

"Ouch," Lawton said in sympathy.

"Stew's done," Luce announced loudly. "Come git it! Professor, I'm boiling up some millet for you."

This inspired a louder groan than any of his injuries.

"You'll eat it an' be happy about it," Luce advised. "If you didn't go stickin' your face in front of other men's fists, you could'a eaten this rabbit stew." She smiled up at Lawton. "Howdy, Marshal. You're lookin' fit as a flea."

"And not much stronger," Lila added. She reached up to place a hand on his brow, then smiled. "No fever. But don't overdo," she warned sternly. "Or back to the tent with you."

"Yes, ma'am," he said dryly, then advised the professor: "Don't let this woman get her hands on you, friend, or you'll have to get her permission to so much as scratch your nose."

Lila laughed, pulling up a stool for him by the fire. "If men had the sense God gave a woman, we wouldn't have to treat you like babies every time you stub your toe."

Cass ate her dinner silently and enjoyed the sounds of happy conversation around the fire. Frenchie had slipped back into the circle at the call for dinner, still looking miffed but casting concerned glances at the professor. Lila beamed at Lawton, who was exceedingly polite with all of the women, just as if they were real ladies. Rachel and Ben sat close together, and from the way Ben looked at the beautiful octoroon, Cass figured the man was planning a future around her.

Strange how things worked out, Cass reflected. Everything had been so dismal—not only for her, but for all of them when they'd set out from Webster. Now look at them, sitting happily around the campfire, talking, teasing—she glanced at Lila—maybe even loving. The warmth in her heart made her smile. Maybe they were going to make it after all.

Dusk brought a coolness to the air. A little distance away, the Shelby people celebrated their arrival at the Platte by building a huge bonfire. Earlier that day Granny Decker had invited Cass and "your sister and all those silk-wearin' peacocks you call friends" to join them. Surprisingly, Alice Scott seconded the invitation. As soon as dinner was done and the dishes washed, there would be singing and maybe even some dancing to celebrate their arrival at such an important milestone.

As if he'd been especially invited, Dog trotted up to join the McAllister group, meticulously doing the rounds to give each person an opportunity to get rid of unwanted morsels. Lila chuckled at his blatant begging. "Who invited you?" She threw him a piece of sourdough biscuit.

Cass's heart sped just a bit, for where Dog was, usually Nathan wasn't far behind. As expected, there he was, coming for a bowl of Luce's stew, his tall frame outlined in fiery orange from the bonfire behind him. Cass was about to speak a greeting—not too friendly, of course. After all, Nathan was still scum, and she wouldn't want him to think she was even close to forgiving him. But he stopped in his tracks, little more than a dark silhouette against the Shelby fire. Cass could almost feel his eyes lock with Lawton's. Nathan turned around without a word and walked in the other direction. Dog looked after him a bit wistfully, but stayed to mooch.

For just a moment before she caught herself, Cass actually felt sorry for Nathan Stone.

For all that she thought the idea very pleasant, Cass did not go to the Shelby bonfire. She stayed behind to draw up dress patterns fashioned after the ready-made dresses she'd seen in one of the Dobytown stores. Lila, Sue, and Rachel went to the bonfire with Effie Brown and Granny Decker. Frenchie stayed behind, ostensibly to help Cass with the patterns, but really to keep an eye on the professor, who had retired to his pallet in the big wagon, a cold compress on his face. Usually he made up a pallet beneath the wagon, but tonight he'd felt the need for privacy.

"I'd like to see old Eliza's face when she sees our girls sitting around the fire singing hymns with the rest of them," Frenchie chortled.

"She's been polite ever since Lila was such a help to Jed."

"I guess you could call it polite. I saw Jed up messing with their mules this morning. Cory Decker's hobbling around fine, and Amos Byrd's quit having his dizzy spells." She sent Cass a sly look. "Pretty soon they won't need your Nathan Stone to be head man around here."

"He's certainly not *my* Nathan Stone," Cass said calmly. Only too well did she know Frenchie's game of striking a match to the fuse of emotional dynamite, and she wasn't going to play. "And when he's no longer needed, I'm sure Mr. Stone will be more than happy to leave us in his dust." And why did that thought make her feel suddenly empty? She wanted nothing more than to be rid of the man.

"Don't you think that neckline should be cut a little lower?"

Cass sighed patiently. "We're trying for respectability, Frenchie."

"You'd never catch me wearing something like that. Honey, if you're a woman, you ought to advertise it."

They argued amiably over the cut of Cass's designs. Down the line of wagons, voices raised in praise of God's goodness. A few notes of a banjo accompanied the songs.

"Ben's trying to get his fingers to play again."

"He's healing nicely."

"Thanks to Rachel. That girl's as easy to see through as crystal. She claims she's just friends with that big Romeo, but she's over the moon about him."

"Ben's a good man."

"I'm not saying he's not. But he won't give her what she wants."

"Sometimes people change what they want to fit what they have."

"My, my. Aren't we the philosopher tonight?"

Cass smiled wryly. "Yes, aren't I?" She wondered where that gem had come from, and was she talking about Rachel or about herself?

Then the words of a song reached her ears, not the hymn the Shelbyites sang. The voices were rough and the words rougher.

"What the—?" Frenchie's exclamation was cut off by two figures lurching from the dark—Greasy and the Paunch. Paunchy's nose was a bit flatter than it had been that afternoon, and purple bruises beneath both eyes rivaled the professor's. They were both staggering drunk, singing an off-tune, off-color song that had something to do with a pig and the pig-farmer's wife.

"Not you jackasses again!" Frenchie moaned.

"We foun' 'em," Greasy hiccuped. "Here they are. The one wit' da red curly hair and the one wit' da big tits." He hiccuped again.

Paunchy wagged his finger at them. "You girls . . ." He swayed. "You girls did . . . done . . . You girls done us wrong."

"Tha's right. We don't take that from . . . from bitches."

Frenchie laughed. It was hard to be alarmed by two such pathetic figures. "What's the matter, boys? Wouldn't any of the local whores take your money either? Maybe if you took a bath once in a while . . ."

"Frenchie . . ." Cass cautioned. "You men get out of here. All we have to do is call out and every man in the camp will be here." Maybe, if they could hear anything over all that singing.

"Oh, come on, Cass! Look at them! They're so drunk they couldn't pull the wings off a fly. Even the professor could probably kick their butts."

Frenchie was wrong. With a suddenness that startled both women, Greasy pulled a knife. "You laughin', bitch? I don' take no laughin' from no one, 'specially a bitch!" He burped a cloud of alcoholic fumes, which set his friend to laughing. Cass didn't think it was funny at all.

"Get out of here!" she warned them. "Now! Or we'll scream."

"Scream," Paunchy invited woozily. "Tha's what we want. Scream yur little butts off."

Greasy lunged. Frenchie and Cass both shrieked. The knife came within a hair's-breadth of Frenchie's breast. Cass thought desperately of the guns stored in the back of the big wagon, just steps away.

Paunchy laughed as they backed away. Frenchie was spouting every vile word she'd learned during her long tenure in a vile profession.

The professor's head poked through the back opening of the canvas. "Whagonon?" he mumbled from his swollen mouth. His eyes were mere slits in a swollen face. His appearance made their assailants even more gleeful.

"C'mere, bitches!" Greasy called, brandishing the long-bladed knife. "You din't want me, so take this instead."

"I don't think so," came Nathan's voice from behind them.

Greasy turned, swinging the knife in an arc. Nathan grabbed his wrist, twisted hard, and the ape hit the ground with a scream. Paunchy attacked like a huffing locomotive, but met with a boot in his oversized stomach. Nathan shoved him back. He stumbled over a stool and into the fire. Shrieking, he rolled to put out the flames, then lay sobbing in the dirt.

"Can't you two stay out of trouble for even an hour?" Nathan inquired.

"Whagonon?" the professor was still mumbling.

A bubble of laughter rose inside Cass's chest. Now she had something else she had to thank Nathan for. Was there a number of rescues that would balance the huge black mark he'd earned?

"Well, that was a timely entrance," Frenchie acknowledged in a quavering voice, then "Watch out!" as a shadow launched at Nathan from behind.

Both women screamed as the third man from the trio—a latecomer—charged like a bull buffalo and tackled Nathan, carrying them both to the other side of the campfire. Nathan ended up on the bottom, flattened like a pancake while the tough grabbed his hair and proceeded to pound his head against the ground. Cass clawed at the man's back, but he easily threw her off. Frenchie picked her up and they both charged, but the charge wasn't needed. Lawton's voice cut through the ruckus. The click of his pistol's hammer as he pulled it back got everyone's attention.

"Stop," Lawton said simply.

The man stopped.

"Get off him."

He got off.

"Now take your friends—I don't care if you have to drag them—and go sleep it off where you won't bother anyone. Understand?"

His mouth hanging open, the lout nodded.

When they were gone, Cass and Frenchie picked Nathan up from the ground. He held his head and groaned. "Damn! I hate like hell to have to thank you of all people, Lawton."

Cass knew exactly how he felt.

"Where'd you get that gun?" Nathan asked suspiciously.

"From the back of the wagon."

"That's my pistol," Cass said.

"It was the only one handy." Lawton handed it to her.

"That gun isn't loaded," Nathan pointed out. "Cass is scared of loaded guns."

"I know that." Lawton jerked his head toward the darkness where the trio from hell had disappeared. "They didn't."

"I have to give you credit for nerve."

The ruckus had attracted an audience from the bonfire, Lila among them. "John Lawton, are you overdoing it again?"

Lawton smiled and shrugged. He might be able to face down a bully with nothing more than an empty gun, but there wasn't a man alive who could face down Lila when she had that glint in her eyes.

"He was pulling my bacon from the fire, Lila," Nathan said. Then grudgingly to Lawton. "Thanks."

"It's amazing you've survived as an outlaw as long as you have, if that was an example of how tough you are." Lawton let Lila take his arm and lead him toward his tent. But at the edge of the firelight he turned and scowled. "Don't get the idea I would have cared if that piece of vulture bait had split open your head," he said to Nathan. "I just don't want someone else to get a pound of your flesh before I get mine."

•   •   •

Lawton put up with Lila fussing over his bandage and checking for signs of renewed bleeding. Finding no damage done, she handed him back his shirt. Her lips curved in a smile, and her uncharacteristic silence made Lawton uneasy.

"What are you looking at me like that for?"

"Like this?" She raised a brow, smiling.

"Yes. Like that. If you're going to harp at me for stepping into that fight, then get it over with."

"Me? Harp?"

He rolled his eyes.

"I'm very glad you charged to Nathan Stone's rescue. Especially since he had just rescued my sister and one of my best friends. I would have been upset if he'd had his brains splattered all over the ground, and I think everyone else would have been, also."

"Well, don't get the idea I think he's anything other than a neck looking for a noose. I just stepped in because the women were in trouble."

Lila shook her head and laughed softly. "Oh, it hurts, doesn't it?"

He narrowed his eyes suspiciously. "What hurts?"

"When doubt enters into hate. Hate is such a comfortable feeling, once you get used to it. It's so certain. So all-consuming. But it's hard for a good man to hang on to."

It was his turn to chuckle. "You've got it wrong, Lila." She was one delicious-looking woman, but she had the strangest notions. It came from having a woman's soft heart hidden beneath all that bluster. "I'm not a particularly good man, and I don't have a doubt in the world about Nathan Stone."

"You are a good man, John Lawton. And you have to put up with all the baggage that comes with that." She reached out, almost as if to touch his face in a caress, then dropped her gaze and lowered her hand. "Sleep well, Mr. Lawton. Tomorrow we're on the road again."

Chapter 16

Nathan looked at the women gathered in an attentive little knot on the prairie just outside the circle of wagons. They looked back at him expectantly. Almost every woman on the train was there, clad in a sunbonnet and prim dress of brown or gray. Cassidy Rose looked equally prim in her practical bloomer costume, and even Frenchie, Sue, and Rachel looked almost respectable. No doubt they didn't want their bright silks soiled by what they were about to do.

All were armed with baskets or flour sacks, and their expressions ranged from amused to disgusted at the prospect before them.

Nathan mumbled a complaint to Ben, who stood beside him. "This is a hell of a way for a Tennessee gentleman to make an honest living."

Ben grinned. "I'm thinking you ain't been no Tennessee gentleman for a while now."

"I haven't made an honest living in a while, either." He looked at the wide prairie spread out before them—the flat river plain, the grassy sand hills. Grass, sand, river, and mud. For as far as the eye could see, there was not a tree, a stump, a branch, or a single stick of wood. "I suppose we should just get it over with."

Ben chuckled. "It's a long, long road, Nathan Stone.

We're gonna stack, burn, and breathe this stuff for weeks to come. It ain't gonna be over for a long, long time."

The train was four days out of Fort Kearny and halted for a long nooning. Their hoarded supply of wood from the Little Blue River valley was exhausted, and now they had to seek other fuel for their fires. The Platte River Valley hadn't seen a stick of burnable wood in years. What little had grown on this grass-covered prairie had been used long ago by the first emigrants to roll down the trail. Now the only fuel available was provided by the buffalo—in the form of dried droppings. One of the few things that the Shelby women and Lila's ladies agreed upon was the utterly disgusting nature of the fuel Mother Nature so abundantly provided.

"Buffalo crap?" Frenchie had asked in amazement when Nathan had announced that morning that a collection troop would be organized at the nooning. "You expect us to collect and burn buffalo crap?" She glanced with a hint of apology at Effie Brown, who'd been sitting at their fire. "Sorry, Effie. Buffalo chips. By any name, it's just as disgusting."

"It's the only fuel available out here," Nathan had said. "Didn't you read your guidebook?"

"I don't read the guidebook," Frenchie had said.

"You don't read, period," Sue teased.

Frenchie ignored her. "I don't have to read the guidebook. That's your job, Nathan. So I think you should collect the buffalo cr—chips. Have fun."

Nevertheless, they were all there. At least the women were there. The men, except for Ben and the younger Amos Byrd, stayed behind to "guard" the train. Collecting turds was definitely women's work.

"Come on, ladies," Nathan said, trying to sound enthused. "Let's get to work."

The little knot of women stayed together as they moved out. No one wanted to be first to find a gem for her sack. Ben was there to point out the do's and don'ts of chip collecting. He was the only one who'd traveled this trail before.

"You don't want 'em if they're wet," he explained unnecessarily, pointing to a recent deposit that had flies buzzing around it. "The drier the better, and even the little ones will burn good. 'Course they don't often come small. Here's a good-sized chip that's just perfect."

The women gathered around the fine example with varying expressions of distaste on their faces. Faith Scott didn't hesitate to put her thoughts to words. "Eeewwww!"

"Now, Miss Scott, it ain't that bad," Ben denied. "These things hardly stink at all once they're dry, and they make a nice, hot fire with almost no smoke."

"Eeewwww!" Faith repeated.

"Eeeewww!" several of the women imitated with self-conscious giggles.

Eliza Jacobs lent her authority to the undertaking. "Enough frivolity, ladies! We have work to do." She didn't, however, volunteer to be the first to pick one up.

Ben smiled. "I tell you what, ladies. Just to show you how innocent these things are, Mr. Stone here will pick up this big one here, break it in half, and stuff it in his sack. And he'll smile all the while, won't you, Nathan?"

"Uh . . ." Nathan squared his shoulders, eyed the buffalo pile suspiciously, then glared at Ben. "If it's so clean and harmless, why don't you pick it up?"

"Why, Mr. Stone," Ben said, all innocence, "a black man picking up that big turd isn't going to convince any of these ladies that the stuff isn't so bad. Anyone can tell you that Negroes are made to do dirty work."

Rachel slid Ben an annoyed look, but he just grinned. Out of the corner of his eye Nathan saw Cass smirk her amusement.

"He'll even take off his gloves," Ben offered. "Just to show that it ain't really that messy."

"You're going to pay for this," Nathan promised as he took off his leather gloves and opened his sack.

Ben just laughed. Nathan girded himself, held his breath, and did the assigned deed, hearing Cass's laughter in the background as he did.

"Oh, the look on his face!" Cass chortled.

Everyone joined in the general laughter. Even Eliza smiled a bit.

"Well, that's not so bad!" Granny Decker declared. "You women act like you ain't never gutted a chicken or cleaned a pigsty." She selected a medium-size chip and unhesitatingly stuck it in her basket.

"I seen men more disgusting than these things are," Sue said, following Granny's example.

Most of the Shelby women looked at Sue aghast, but Granny only laughed. "So have I, dearie. So have I."

July 4, Willow Island Station—

We camp tonight beside an unprepossessing stage and mail station by the name of Willow Island—merely an adobe hut, corrals, and a wood frame house. Where they got the wood is a mystery, for we haven't seen a tree in miles, and in fact have gotten quite accustomed to collecting and burning dried "chips," which are the leavings of the buffalo that roam these plains. We have seen a great number of these animals. Mr. Stone, Amos Byrd and his son, and Ben Holden shot one a few days ago, and we discovered the meat to be delicious. Everyone in the train took a share, and Mr. Holden showed us how to salt and dry the meat that couldn't be eaten immediately. The buffalo is a welcome change from salt pork, quail, rabbit, and beans.

We see many other travelers every day, now that we are on the Great Platte River Highway. All trails traveling west converge upon this route, for it is the easiest way to cross what has been called "the Great American Desert." This is no desert, though, but a vast plain with abundant grass and rolling sand hills that rise on both sides of our wide ribbon of river bottom. Sometimes the trail traverses the hills, which makes the going more difficult. Often, also, we bounce across the numerous buffalo trails that cut perpendicular to our path. The peculiar beasts travel from the river to the sand hills in single file, cutting deep and narrow ruts across the trail. Walking or riding beside the wagons is much more comfortable than bumping along on the wagon box over the rough road.

Now that Lila is not constantly caring for Mr. Lawton, she often relieves me in driving the big wagon.

Our party is much changed from the little group that set out from Webster. Frenchie is quieter. I think she is weary from the drudgery of travel. Lila, on the other hand, glows with more life than ever. She weathers every difficulty with cheerfulness and youthful energy. I hope it is the prospect of a new life that makes her seem so young, and not the attentions of John Lawton, for it appears they have become very good friends. For propriety's sake—and this is the first time in years that Lila has paid mind to propriety—the marshal spends his nights on his pallet in the supply wagon now that he is more alive than dead. I have moved back into the tent with Lila. It is nice to have her company again, but I think she misses him. They often sit by the fire until late, and usually I am fast asleep by the time Lila comes to sleep.

Rachel has abandoned her genteel affectations and actually asked me to make her a bloomer dress like the one I find so comfortable. I believe the first one I gave her was ripped up for bandages. Sue has struck up a close friendship with Effie Brown, a very kindly lady who was widowed in the Sioux attack. Effie has been teaching Sue housekeeping skills, while Sue has helped Effie with the difficult chores of handling the mule teams and the wagons. Sue offered to cook a special dinner for our group last night. I'm sure Luce enjoyed the respite, but the rest of us had grave doubts about surviving the meal. To our surprise, though, supper was very good. Effie, who joined us, says Sue has great talent as a cook. Sue seemed very proud of herself. She was once so concerned about age stealing her looks that she would sulk all day if she discovered another new crease around her eyes. But her mood has improved greatly since becoming friends with Effie. I think she might realize now that she has assets more lasting than beauty.

Effie Brown is not the only Shelby woman who occasionally joins our fireside. Granny Decker is often there, sometimes with her daughter-in-law Pamela. Faith Scott often drifts by to say hello, though I believe her mother and aunt disapprove. But even they have been more civil since taking shelter with Lila the night of the storm. Amelia Byrd has also thawed a bit. Her son, Amos, often comes by in the evening to help us with chores, though I believe that is with his father's approval more than his mother's.

All in all, however, the tension has relaxed quite a bit. The Shelby women are happy, I'm sure, that their men are recovering so well. All are on their feet again, though Cory Decker will always walk with a limp, and Jed Jacobs bears the disfigurement of his shattered jaw.

Surprisingly, the Shelby people seem content to retain Nathan Stone in his position as "wagonmaster," even though the Shelby men are once again capable. The man is of gravely flawed character, but he is a natural leader. It is no secret that Ben Holden knows the ins and outs of the trail much better than Mr. Stone, but it is Nathan Stone who has the natural authority to lead. Almost everyone seems willing to forget that he is a condemned felon. Perhaps it is just as well. Even I find comfort in his confidence with firearms and his careful planning for all types of possible dangers. At Fort Kearny we heard fearsome stories of Indian trouble on the trail. At Fort McPherson, we're told, wagon trains are not allowed to proceed unless they have at least fifty wagons. Though we have seen only occasional sign of Indians, we all live in fear of a similar disaster. Nathan Stone is a man comfortable with violence. He has survived in a violent world, and perhaps he can manage our survival as well. It would be too cruel a fate, I tell myself, to be starting a new, respectable life and have that life snatched from me by an Indian bent on slaughter. It doesn't bear thinking about.

On the subject of our new life, dear journal, I conclude with news of a momentous decision. At Fort Kearny I had a letter waiting for me from my good

*friend Martha Tremaine—now Martha McCannes—
who traveled by coach to Denver some time ago. She
is enthusiastic about our decision to come west, and
begs us to make Denver our destination. Lila and I
have decided to accept her invitation. No one awaits
us in Oregon, and Denver is a growing town with
many opportunities. We will stay with the Shelby train
until the trail splits, and then follow the Platte south
to Denver. What our friends will do I cannot say,
though I hope they decide to come with us.*

*I have told myself I don't care what Nathan Stone
will do. Any day he might leave for Mexico, for he
is, after all, still a fugitive, and though he has struck
a bargain of some sort with Marshal Lawton, who
knows if that bargain will hold now the marshal is so
much better? I am truly a fool to even care what happens to such a man. The Shelby people might forget
what he is, but I have not. And neither has the marshal. They eye each other like dogs circling for a fight,
their snarls silent but the need for battle plain in their
eyes.*

*I do hope, however, that the battle waits until they
have both left our company—and that I never hear of
the outcome. No matter which of them wins, I will regret the other. Yes, even Nathan Stone. I admit it.*

"Hello," Faith greeted the group of ladies who sat around
Mama Luce's cook fire. "Isn't it a nice evening?"

"It is if you like flies buzzin' around your beans," Luce
said, swatting at her food. "When the sun is out, it's the
flies. When the sun goes down, it's the mosquitoes. The
bugs around here are either eatin' my food or eatin' me. I
don' know which vexes me the most."

Faith laughed shyly. "The flies must have heard about
your very good cooking."

"Why, ain't you a sweet one? It's not like I get any ap-
preciation from these others."

Lila chuckled. "We only kneel down every day and give
thanks for the best food on the whole wagon train."

"Everybody else says that too," Faith was quick to add.

"She's a sweet child," Luce cooed. "You want a biscuit, girl? With honey?"

"That would be lovely. Thank you." She demurely took a seat beside Effie Brown, who joined Lila's group almost every evening. She and Sue helped Luce with the cooking chores, and Effie had thrown her supplies into the pot with theirs.

Effie smiled at the girl. "How are your mother and aunt, Faith? Your mother is looking very tired, I think."

Faith lowered her voice. "Mother was having a very bad time of month. But she's feeling better now."

Lila joined in. "Tell your mother if she'd like some willow bark tea, I have plenty. It does wonders for such things."

"Yes, ma'am. I surely will. This is a wonderful biscuit, Miss Luce."

The conversation continued in this polite but extremely dull vein until Effie Brown excused herself to consult with Ben Holden about a sick mule. With only Lila's group remaining, the young girl's face grew brighter. She immediately put forth her request. "Miss Frenchie? I saw you cutting Miss Rachel's hair yesterday. Miss Rachel, you have really glorious hair!"

"Thank you, Faith."

"It always looks so pretty, piled up in curls or just swinging real stylish on your shoulders. My hair would never do that." She touched her thick braids with a finger. "It's never been cut, you know. It's down to my knees when it's loose, but I never wear it loose, because it's ugly and frazzled on the ends. Would you cut it for me, Miss Frenchie?" The last sentences rushed out of her in one breath, as if she hurried to get out her request before losing courage.

For a moment Frenchie's eyes glinted. She liked nothing more than to fuss with hair or face paints. Then she shook her head. "What would your mama think, Faith?"

"She wouldn't mind! Really. But she's busy, and she doesn't know anything about hair at all. Pleeeaaase!"

"I did just sharpen my scissors yesterday."

"Frenchie," Lila said, "you'd better ask the girl's mother first."

"She won't mind!" Faith assured them. "Really, she won't."

No one believed her, including Frenchie. But working with such promising raw material was hard to resist. Faith was a pretty girl, but that prettiness was hidden behind drabness—tightly braided brown hair, plain, shapeless dresses, and a complexion dulled by harsh lye soap.

"Well, I suppose a little trim couldn't do anyone harm," Frenchie said. "Let's go into the tent over there and take a lantern. It's getting dark, and I wouldn't want to chop off the wrong thing."

"I'll come and help," Rachel and Sue offered at the same time.

Faith could scarcely contain her joy. Lila and Luce both shook their heads ominously.

"I want no part of this," Cass said with a chuckle. "I'm going to wash the dishes. When her mother comes storming in, you tell her it was all your idea."

Frenchie grinned. "You're a coward, Cass. We're not going to make her look like a fancy lady. But we might touch up her face a bit too, just to see how pretty she's going to be when she gets dressed up someday."

"Oh would you?" Faith breathed ecstatically.

Frenchie was an artist with scissors, and she got bolder as she worked. The first couple of inches that came off Faith's head of hair made no difference at all other than to eliminate the worst of the split ends, so more came off, and then more. Faith begged her to cut it to the middle of her back, and Frenchie finally gave in.

"You have beautiful hair," Rachel told the girl. "You should brush it at least a hundred strokes every night and when you wash it, rinse it with vinegar. It'll make it shine like the sun."

"Would you show me how to wear it up like you wear yours?" Faith pleaded. "Please?"

"Why don't we find a nice soft way for you to wear your hair?" Sue suggested. "Something that goes with your fresh young face."

Frenchie laughed. "And something that won't give her mother a heart attack."

They worked on, all of them giggling like young girls, and finally declared Faith's hair perfect—trimmed, tamed, and fastened at the crown to fall in a soft and girlish cascade down her back. Then they began to consider her face.

"You have stunning eyes," Rachel said. "They're blue as the sky. No man should be able to resist those eyes."

"Even Amos Byrd?" Faith asked.

Sue scoffed. "He's much too old for you."

"Lamebrain," Frenchie laughed. "She means the young Amos, and if that boy can resist you, then he's crazy."

"He seems to appreciate Miss Cass just fine."

"One of the first things you learn about men," Rachel advised, "is that they're always attracted to what they think they can't have. Your boy Amos knows that Cass won't give him anything more than the time of day. So he's safe. That's why he moons over Cass."

Faith brightened. "Then maybe if I make Amos think I don't give a fig for him, that I wouldn't walk with him or dance with him or even talk to him, even if he asked me, then he'll be attracted to me."

"Like a fly to molasses," Frenchie assured her.

"Can you teach me how to use the cheek rouge and that stuff you put on your eyes?"

All three of the older women took a long, assessing look at their subject. Frenchie drew a line with her finger along Faith's cheekbone. "Maybe just a bit here," she speculated. "What do you think?"

"And a dab of powder?" Rachel suggested.

Suddenly the tent opening ripped apart. There stood Alice Scott and Hope Perkins, charging to the rescue of their innocent girl. "Faith Scott!" Alice growled. "What have I told you about coming over here and bothering these people?"

Faith turned, looking defiant, and Hope gasped. "What have you done to your hair?"

"Frenchie trimmed it for me."

Frenchie refused to be intimidated by their scorching disapproval. "Just look how beautiful she is!"

Gaining courage from Frenchie, Faith set her chin stubbornly. "There's nothing sinful about cutting hair. Or even using rouge and powder. Plenty of women in the Bible did it."

Hope sniffed scornfully. "The Bible is full of strumpets

and whores. Rouge and powders are not for innocent young girls."

"Just looking pretty doesn't make a woman a whore!" Faith insisted, her lower lip trembling.

"Of course it doesn't," Sue said. "But your aunt is right, Faith. A fresh young thing like you doesn't need paints and powders. You're perfect just as Mother Nature made you." She sighed. "What I would give to have that natural young glow again." Quickly she backpedaled. "Not that I'm a crone yet, mind you."

Alice folded her arms across her bosom and sighed. "Faith, I just don't understand why you keep coming over here searching after face paint and fripperies when you've been brought up to be modest and sober and plain, like a godfearing woman ought to be."

"There's nothing in the Bible about being plain," Frenchie said.

"And how would you know?" Hope Perkins sneered.

"Because if God liked plain, he wouldn't have made flowers, or hummingbirds, or rainbows, or . . . or beautiful young girls like Faith."

"That's right," Sue concurred. "And I can see where she gets it, too. Mrs. Scott, did you ever try fixing yourself up a bit? You wouldn't be a widow woman for long."

"Th-that's ridiculous!" Alice stammered. "Why would I want to paint myself like a . . . like a harlot? A woman's true beauty is in her virtue, not her face."

Frenchie and Sue scented yet another project in the offing. Resurrecting Faith's hair had put them in the mood. "You wouldn't have to use paint," Frenchie said. "Wellll . . . maybe just a touch. But if we plucked the brows a tiny bit, some witch hazel around the eyes, or maybe use Rachel's special mud mask that makes the skin glow so nicely."

"This is absurd!" Alice insisted. "I'm taking my daughter and—"

Sue made a circle around the embarrassed woman. "You have a very nice figure, Alice. If you would just wear something a bit more flattering . . ."

"I never—"

"Flattering doesn't have to be immodest. And Hope . . ."

All three ex-harlots surveyed Alice's sister in frank appraisal. "Hope Perkins," Rachel said, "I know women who would give a right arm to have your skin. It must run in the family for you ladies. With a little care and a bottle of Madame Jeannette's Soothing Complexion Creme, you could glow like a gentle sunrise. And your hair—my goodness, it's as long as Faith's was. What do you ladies have against scissors? Look at how thick it is. With some of the weight off, she'd have a lovely bit of curl, don't you think, Frenchie?"

"Certainement!" Frenchie said with her old French accent.

"Frivolous!" Hope scoffed.

"Preposterous!" Alice agreed.

But both women glanced in the looking glass that Frenchie held up, straining to see the charms that these outsiders saw in them.

Within a few minutes, the tent was full of exclamations, laughter, and downright giggles. A passerby might reasonably think a troop of young girls were having a gossip fest. Attracted by the commotion, Pamela Decker drifted over. Virginia March was suitably horrified when she learned what was going on, but she also was seduced by advice on how to cure the dry spots on her scalp. June Dawkins learned how to use her hairstyle to make her nose look shorter, and Amelia Byrd, at first determined to bring her godfearing sisters back to their senses, ended up memorizing the recipe for Rachel's revitalizing mud mask.

The tent bulged at the seams. Up to her elbows in soapy water and dirty dishes, Cass watched the influx of women with a wondering shake of her head. The men of the Shelby train were in for a surprise.

Nathan tugged off his shirt and tossed it to the ground. He had sweated it through. The sun had slipped below the horizon, leaving a dusky golden glow shimmering over the plains. But it was a hot dusky glow, and shovel work had never been one of Nathan's favorite chores.

Just the same, the well had to be dug. In the near distance, the Platte River was a ribbon of gold glistening in the waning light, but the reality of the river was mud. In

many places the Platte was a mile wide but just inches deep.
Along this stretch it was nothing more than mud and quicksand boasting a few channels of thick, sandy water. It was
hardly fit for the buffalo to drink, much less people. Shallow wells dug some distance from the river almost always
yielded potable water, though. They were digging three.
Amos Byrd and Ed Campbell wielded a shovel a good
stone's throw downstream. Ben Holden and Cory Decker
dug upstream. And Nathan dug in the middle. The work
would have gone faster with more hands and more shovels,
but for all that they were mostly up and walking, many of
the Shelby men weren't quite up to hard labor.

As if Nathan was. It was a hell of a way for a Tennessee
gentleman to make a living.

"I remember," he told Dog, "just a few weeks ago we
were shivering night and day, and wet down to our skin
from the rain. What I'd give for some of that nice cool air."
He tossed a shovelful of dirt, another, and yet another, then
paused to wipe his brow. At the sight of the man walking
toward him, he sighed and lifted his eyes to heaven. "Hallelujah! Just what I need."

Dog barked a greeting as John Lawton strolled up. The
marshal had a shovel in his hand.

"Looks like you need help."

"Lila sees you with that shovel, she'll drag you off and
tie you to a tentpost."

Lawton had long outgrown the invalid stage, but his right
arm was still stiff and weak from the muscle damage in his
chest. Lila seemed mortally afraid he would bust something
wide open if he did more than sit around looking puny, but
then, women were that way.

"I need the exercise," Lawton said. "Sticks in my craw
to be lying around while there's work to be done. I'll pull
my weight."

Nathan waved his hand toward the hole he'd started.
"Dig your own grave, for all I care."

Lawton gave him a look, but started digging. Nathan
joined him, and soon they had a rhythm going. Dig, throw,
dig, throw, first Nathan, then Lawton, and on and on as the
hole grew deeper. Lawton sweated and turned pale, but he

didn't stop. He wouldn't, Nathan knew, as long as Nathan kept on. That was the manly way. A man just didn't admit he was weaker than an enemy.

He knew what else stuck in Lawton's craw, now that he had his feet firmly planted among the living. What truly struck in his craw was hanging like a leech on this wagon train while every fiber in his soul wanted to be sticking a pistol barrel up Nathan's nose and hauling him off to the nearest outpost of the law. The only thing that kept him from doing it was the bargain they'd struck. Nathan was lucky that Lawton was an honest, noble sort of fellow. It would be a real shame to have to kill such a paragon.

Nathan puffed out a weary breath. "Rest a minute," he said. No sense in letting the man kill himself with a shovel.

Lawton dug a few more shovelfuls—just to prove he was the better man, Nathan figured. Finally, he stopped and leaned on his shovel.

"I have to admit you're a rare man, Lawton."

Lawton regarded him through narrowed eyes. "How's that?"

"You honor your word—whether or not you think that word might be a mistake, or even a dereliction of duty. There aren't many men in this world who are that god-damned noble."

Lawton scowled. "You say noble as if it means stupid."

Nathan shrugged.

"I'm not so stupid I can't bring you down, Stone. But if a man's word isn't good, then he isn't either."

"Spoken like a true hero."

Lawton stabbed his shovel into the hole—no doubt wishing it was Nathan's skull. "I'm going to enjoy seeing you hang someday."

Nathan grinned. "I figure you would. I figure someday you'll be the death of me, Lawton. That's why I enjoy causing you grief now and then."

The marshal's eyes went black and hard as slate. "You've already caused me enough grief to last a lifetime."

Nathan met the deadliness of his gaze without flinching. "That's where you're wrong, marshal. I know what you believe, but I didn't lay a finger on your sister. If I could have stopped what happened, I would have."

Lawton's expression didn't change.

"You don't believe me. Guess you never will."

"You're right. And all bets are off at Fort Laramie."

Nathan shrugged. "Then it's catch me if you can."

"I'll catch you, Stone. And I'll see you hang."

"Maybe. Or maybe, if you catch me, you'll just have to kill me yourself. Those hotheads in Silas were going to hang me, sure. But if they'd waited for the circuit judge, he'd have just packed me off to prison. All my killing was done during the war, my friend, and in spite of that bastard Quantrill, I never hurt a hair on a civilian's head. Not that I know of, at least. No one's going to hang me for a few penny-ante holdups in Kansas. No one except you."

Lawton snorted in disgust.

"It's the truth, Lawton, and you know it. So you come after me, Mr. United States Marshal. If you haul me back to Kansas, I'll rot in prison for a while. But if want to see me hang, you'll have to do the job yourself."

"Damn you, Stone! You think I wouldn't?"

Nathan smiled slowly. "I don't know. Do you have the stomach for cold-blooded murder?"

Lawton just stared at him.

"Think about it, lawman. Just how cold-blooded can you be?"

Chapter 17

Nathan dipped a towel in the very small amount of water in the bottom of the wooden bucket. The sweat expended in digging the well made him aware of just how precious that water was. He wrung the towel over his head, letting the water—what little of it there was—run through his hair and drip down his bare torso. It was full night, but the air was still warm and muggy. The humidity held the day's heat like a sponge.

He soaked up another towelful and, with a weary sigh, trickled water down his neck and chest. Dog tired was hardly the right expression for how he felt, because Dog, the big furry leech, had loafed all day. But Nathan was tired. Grit tired from eating dust all day on the trail. Dirt tired from digging that damned well. And butt tired from pounding leather while leading a hunting party that afternoon to a small herd of buffalo in the sand hills.

As soon as word of the buffalo had spread—Ben Holden had found the herd while scouting out a campsite—the Shelby men had wanted to bring one down. Jed Jacobs, who still couldn't decently chew his oatmeal, much less a buffalo steak. Cory Decker, who couldn't ride a horse with that bum leg any better than he could walk without a limp. Amos Byrd couldn't blame his lack of marksmanship on anything

but his own poor eyesight. Nathan was discovering that leading the Shelby wagon train was easier when the Shelby men
were prostrate. Now that they were recovering, they were
more nuisance than help.

He emptied the rest of the bucket over his head and went
rummaging in his wagon for a clean shirt. What came to
hand was a shirt Cass had made him back in the days when
they were hoping for a future together. He resisted the instinct to stuff it back into the box that held his clothes, to
get it out of sight so it wouldn't bring to mind the things
he'd lost. Instead, he pulled it on. It was the only clean shirt
he had.

As if the shirt had been a warning, when he climbed
down from the wagon, he spied Cass. She was a mere silhouette against the McAllister cook fire, but he recognized
those curves, that profile, the faint sound of her humming.
She was alone. Her friends were having some sort of noisy
hen party in one of the tents, leaving Cass alone by the
McAllister cook fire, busy with the washpan. The sight of
her made his gut churn. Still, that didn't keep him from sitting on the back dropgate of his wagon, watching her.

All his life Nathan Stone had wanted things he couldn't
have. Growing up on an affluent horse farm in Tennessee,
he'd longed for adventure. During the war, when adventure
had exploded into violence, he'd dreamed of peace. After
the war, he'd wanted his old life back, complete with parents, brother, and the humdrum everyday sameness he'd
once despised. And only weeks ago, running for his life,
he'd wanted nothing more than to lead a peaceful existence
where he didn't have to depend on a gun and he didn't have
to live every day in the shadow of prison—or worse.

But more than anything he'd ever wanted, he wanted
Cassidy Rose McAllister—another thing beyond his reach.
Cass despised him, and he didn't really blame her. She
wanted a solid citizen for a husband, even though she'd be
miserable with a respectable community pillar. Cass had too
much life in her to marry someone who would try to squeeze
her into the mold of a proper woman.

Of course, Cass would never believe that.

Nathan could understand, he supposed. He wanted to be

something that he wasn't cut out to be, also. He hoped Cass would have better luck at it than he was having.

He was about to go back into his wagon, close the canvas opening, and try to think about something else, when Cass had a visitor—young Amos Byrd. Tall as a sapling and just as skinny, Amos was a sixteen-year-old bundle of developing male urges. Nathan knew the stage well. Lately he had thought he might still be in it. Amos had a bad case of puppy love—a puppy as big as a bull buffalo in this case. For weeks he'd been sniffing around Cass like Dog sniffing at a hambone.

The boy ambled up to the McAllister cook fire, hands in his pockets and elbows sticking out like wings on a plucked chicken. He said something. She said something back. Nathan could hear their voices, but he couldn't quite make out the words. The boy twisted the toe of his boot in the dirt and mumbled. Cass laughed, a gay sound full of music. Nathan remembered that laugh so well, how the sound of it had always made him smile. Then Amos bent over, leaning close to her.

What the hell was the kid doing? Nathan wondered. Whispering in her ear? Pecking her on the cheek? Whatever it was, it was much too familiar. Who knew better than Nathan what such proximity to Cassidy Rose McAllister's tender self could do to a man's self-control? And a kid Amos's age didn't have any self-control. He jumped down from his wagon and strode to the McAllister fire with thunder crashing in his soul.

"Amos!"

The boy jumped at the sound of Nathan's voice.

"Amos, do your ma and pa know where you are?"

"Mr. Stone! Hi. Uh . . . uh, well . . . no." He dug the toe of his boot deeper into the ground. "I guess they don't."

"It's after dark, Amos, and you should be with your folks, not hanging around here."

"I . . . uh, yeah. I guess so. G'night, Miss Cass. G'night, Mr. Stone."

"Goodnight, Amos," Cass called after the boy as he scrambled away. When she rounded on Nathan, however, her voice was frosty. "Just what are you doing?"

"Better question," he countered. "What were you doing?"

"What do you mean? I'm drying the supper dishes. What do you think I'm doing?"

"You know what I mean. I thought you wanted to start a new, respectable life. Does respectability include leading on boys who aren't even dry behind the ears?"

"What?"

"You heard me. The small talk. The girlish laughter. And what the hell was he doing bending over close enough to bite your ear?"

"Bending over to . . . what are you talking about?"

"You know damned well what I'm talking about."

She looked at him through wide eyes for a moment, then laughed. "You're jealous! Jealous of a sixteen-year-old wet-behind-the-ears boy who's all elbows and knees."

"Of course I'm not jealous."

"You're jealous," she said confidently.

"All I'm trying to do is keep peace in the train. The Byrds aren't happy about their son sniffing around the company of loose women."

"Loose women?" Her voice sharpened with both hurt and indignation. "Of all the nerve! Talk about the pot calling the kettle black!"

He'd gone too far, Nathan sensed. "Not you personally!"

"Yes. Me personally, you arrogant sack of manure. I wasn't what you'd call loose before I met you, but I guess I fit the description well enough now."

"That isn't what I meant, and you know it."

"I know no such thing."

"God! Why are women so damned difficult?"

"*Women* difficult?"

"That boy has been sniffing around your group—mostly you—ever since Webster. And you've smiled at him and let him do chores and carry your sack when you gather chips. Don't you know what he's thinking?"

"Amos is a sweet boy." Cass put the last clean plate into the storage crate and hung the dishtowel to dry by the fire. "You're the one with the wicked thoughts, Nathan Stone. Jealous of a kid like Amos—that is really pathetic."

"I am not jealous."

She gave him a superior smile that drove his temper up a notch.

"And if you think young Amos Byrd is nothing more than a sweet boy, you know nothing about men."

Her eyes narrowed. "On the contrary, I know entirely too much about men, and very little of it is good!"

"Then maybe you should be more careful not to lead them on."

"Lead them on?" The fire banked in those green eyes exploded. She advanced ominously upon Nathan, a finger pointed straight at his heart like the barrel of a pistol. "Let me tell you a thing or two, Nathan Stone. I have never led any man on. Not that boy. Not you. I am not a tease. I am not a flirt. I am a decent, respectable woman, in spite of living in goddamned whorehouses most of my life, and in spite of falling prey to an immoral, lying, womanizing scoundrel like you!"

"I didn't say—"

"And another thing, Stone." She was close enough now to poke him with the lethal finger, backing him against the wagon. "You've got no call to spy on me or say anything to me about what I'm doing or who I talk to. If I wanted to take up with a man, it would be none of your business, now, would it? Hell! You said yourself I'm a loose woman. Why not spread the wealth around a bit? You had *your* fun, after all."

Nathan's temper rose. Just the thought of Cass lying with another man made him want to shake her until her teeth rattled. "You shut your mouth, Cassidy Rose McAllister."

"And you mind your own business."

"You are my business, goddamnit!" He confiscated that annoying finger that drilled a hole into his chest and engulfed the rest of her hand along with it. She tried to jerk away, but he held on. Abruptly he used the leverage to swing her around, putting her where she'd pinned him, flat against the side of her wagon.

"Let me go, you worm."

"No. I have a thing or two to say."

She pushed at him, but he didn't budge.

"First of all, I didn't call you a loose woman. You have

fun twisting my words, but don't start believing your own mischief."

"You are—"

"Abominable. I know. Second, you were not my 'prey.' I never meant to make love to you until after we were married. You came to me that night, if you will remember. And Cass, sweetheart, no man this side of ninety could resist what you offered. Especially a man in love."

"Love!" she scoffed. "A heck of a lot you know about love!"

"I know a hell of a lot more than I want to know, thanks to you." He grasped her jaw, forcing her to meet him eye to eye. Then very deliberately he lowered his mouth to hers. She was rigid as wood, but only for a moment. A tiny moan of passion too long denied rose from her chest to vibrate against his mouth, and that one small sound nearly undid him.

She melted, inviting him to deepen the kiss. He softened, threaded his fingers through her hair, gently holding her head as he feasted upon her, pressing her against the wagon until he possessed not only her mouth, but every inch of her warm, womanly softness. Her arms clutched his back and shoulders, her body strained against his with an urgency that made him ache, and her mouth fed upon his even as he devoured hers.

But heaven lasted only a moment before Cass wrenched away. Gasping for breath, she stared up at him, the moon turning her face pale and striking silver glints in the hair that had tumbled free of its sedate bun.

"Not again," she declared, her voice a shaky whisper. Fear warred with passion in her eyes. "I will not fall for you again."

Nathan cupped her cheek and ran a thumb along her swollen lips. "You make me lose control."

Her face twisted as she tried to hold back a sob. With both hands, she shoved him away from her and fled for the refuge of the wagon. He stood staring after her, gut and emotions both churning, until a shy feminine voice jerked him out of his stupor. Faith Scott's greeting came from behind him.

"Hello, Mr. Stone. Are you all right?"

He turned, and his eyebrows nearly shot from his face. "Faith?"

She smiled coyly. "Do you like it?"

Any man would like it, Nathan thought. Someone had taken the plain little brown wren and turned her into something definitely not plain. Her hair had been cut to mid-back length. The front and sides were softly pulled back and fastened at the crown, and the rest tumbled softly down her back. Brows that had met above her nose had been tweezed into naturally arched accents that set off her eyes. She still looked innocent and fresh as a fifteen-year-old girl should be, but she was a beautiful innocent and fresh.

"I . . . I like it very much."

"Really?" she said uncertainly. "You're not just saying that?"

"Really."

She grinned. "Have you seen Amos around?"

"He was here not too long ago. Now he's probably at his folks' wagon."

"Good." She gave him a coy smile and a little wave. "Bye now."

He'd no sooner recovered from Faith's appearance than Alice Scott, Hope Perkins, and Amelia Byrd emerged from the tent where he'd thought a hen party was going on. Was it just the moonlight, or did all of them look about ten years younger? Stranger still, the habitually sober, quiet women were whispering among themselves and laughing like girls.

"Hello, Mr. Stone," Alice called.

He could swear that Amelia Byrd batted her eyelashes at him, and Hope Perkins was actually simpering.

Women! Nathan thought as he stalked toward the safety of his wagon. He'd be willing to bet that not even God understood them.

The Shelby train made good progress now that most of the Shelby men could once again drive and take care of the teams. Tension between the travelers had eased, and it was a happier group that now made its way west along the south bank of the Platte. A stranger would have had trouble differentiating the two groups that had once been so distinct and separate. The flamboyant plumage of Lila's ladies had faded with the miles. Rachel now wore a bloomer costume similar to Cassidy's. Sue was more often at the Brown wagon than with the Webster group. Frenchie had abandoned her elaborate curls for a simple chignon that confined her hair from the wind, and her lace and silks were relegated to a trunk somewhere in the wagons. Never one to bow to conventionality, however, she now wore what she called a split skirt—in reality little more than loose-fitting men's trousers—and often rode astride the professor's horse. The professor had thrown her a censorious look or two, but lately a smile from Frenchie was quick to quiet his scoldings. He didn't criticize her for her pokes at propriety, and she, in turn, no longer needled him with her sharp tongue.

John Lawton grew more dour with every mile west they rolled. During the day he rode his horse when he wasn't driving the big wagon with Lila at his side—Lila, who wore a permanent smile and seemed to grow younger each day. Lawton pulled his share of the load on the train, helping in wagon repairs, livestock care, digging the shallow wells that so often provided them with their water, and standing regular sentry duty at night. With so few men on the train, Nathan and John Lawton had to work side by side with uncomfortable frequency. Neither of them liked it. Both wore hard faces and spoke only single-word sentences when they were together. Fort Laramie was a constant promise in Lawton's eyes, defiance the reply he got from Nathan.

More than once Nathan thought about taking off in the middle of the night, abandoning his promise to the Shelby people, and let Lawton catch him if he could. He knew the Tennessee stud could outdistance and outlast Lawton's mare, and before him was a whole wide, almost deserted country to hide in. It wasn't his promise to the Shelby group that kept him with the train, Nathan admitted to himself. It was Cass who kept him riding west. He didn't have a thing to offer her. He didn't have room for her in his future, which would be short indeed if John Lawton had his way. And he certainly didn't deserve her. Cass herself would be the first to agree with that.

The sad fact was that Nathan had already lost her, but he couldn't quite give her up.

Two days east of Fort McPherson, Nathan rode beside his wagon, which was being driven by the younger Amos Byrd. Once again Nathan contemplated the pros and cons of striking out on his own, leaving Lawton behind and getting Cass out of his sight, if not out of his mind. In the days since he'd kissed her the old awkwardness between them had returned full force. Cass avoided him whenever possible, almost as if she were afraid of seeing him. She'd even left the McAllister supper circle one evening when he'd showed up to eat. After that he started taking his meals at the Shelby fire.

Nathan's reflections were cut short when Ben Holden came galloping in from scouting the trail ahead. He wheeled his horse to come up neatly beside Nathan. Then his eyes darted among the wagons until he found Rachel. When he saw she was watching him, he smiled and waved.

"All that to show off for a woman?" Nathan inquired dryly.

Ben gave him a half guilty grin. "That one's worth showin' off for."

Nathan took a quick glance at Rachel, who was driving the smaller McAllister wagon. No matter how dusty the trail or miserable the weather, that one always looked as if she stepped out of some genteel parlor, even in that ridiculous bloomer dress that Cass had convinced her to wear. "You are a damned lucky man, Ben."

"Not lucky yet," Ben replied with a chuckle. "But I'm workin' on it."

"So, besides showing off for your lady love, what sends you back here riding like your horse's tail is on fire?"

"There's a burned-out Indian camp up ahead. Looks like a Pawnee camp."

"Sioux raiding party?"

"That'd be my guess. Looks pretty recent. Maybe this morning."

"We'd better keep our eyes open and set an extra lookout tonight. No camping outside the circle. All firearms kept loaded, just in case."

"With all the white folks around here to hate, you'd think those Sioux would leave their fellow Indians alone."

"These tribes have been fighting each other probably for as long as they've been here. Lucky for us. We wouldn't want them to have to rely on scalping us as their only entertainment."

They camped not far from the scar on the plain that had lately been a Pawnee village, and once the livestock was secure and sentries posted, many went to sightsee. The village was a sad sight, even for those who regarded Indians as vermin. Some spots still smoldered. Here and there a few tent poles still stood, covered with scorched hides, looking skeletal and grisly. A few baskets, a broken pot, a child's stick doll were all that remained of the community. Fortunately for those who poked around the pathetic remains, there were no bodies.

"There must have been survivors," Ben said. "They took their dead with them."

"This place smells evil," Jed Jacobs complained. "It's the den of the devil."

Nathan knew only too well what the odor was. He'd smelled it too often during the war. "Scorched flesh," he told Jacobs. "I'd say not everybody got out of the fire. I wouldn't go poking too deeply into those ashes."

Dog was not subject to human squeamishness, however. He did go nosing deeply into the remains of teepees and piles of ashes, and it was he who uncovered the lone survivor.

Suspiciously, Nathan went to see what caught the dog's attention. "What've you got there, boy?" He knelt down and looked, and his gut clenched.

Dog had uncovered a tiny, filthy, but very much alive infant wrapped in blankets and hidden beneath a singed buffalo hide. It squalled loudly at the attentions of Dog's seeking tongue.

"What have we here?" Nathan gently unwrapped and checked the baby. He was greeted by an explosion of odor that overpowered all the other unpleasant odors in the camp. "Whew! I think someone needs changing!"

The baby stopped wailing and looked solemnly up at him.

"Oh, my lord!" came Cass's amazed cry from behind him. "It's a baby!"

"A very dirty baby," Nathan noted.

"Well, take it out of those filthy blankets!"

"Me?"

"Oh, move aside! I'll take care of it!"

The moment Nathan was out of the infant's sight, it squalled again. Nathan had heard that Indian babies were trained to keep quiet so they wouldn't alert an enemy. Apparently this one had missed that training.

Cass discarded the filth-encrusted blankets, but the naked infant struggled and screamed loudly enough to bring the cavalry thundering to the rescue if they were anywhere in the vicinity. When Nathan offered it a finger and a soft word, it immediately hushed.

"She likes you."

"She has good taste," he said with a grin.

"She has woefully low standards. Take off your shirt so we can wrap her."

Nathan grimaced. "She's covered with . . . with . . ."

"I know what she's covered with. I'll wash your precious shirt. We don't have anything else to wrap her in."

Only after the infant was wrapped in Nathan's shirt and held in Nathan's arms did she stop crying. A crowd had gathered around them by now, attracted by the wails. The men regarded the baby suspiciously while the women, for the most part, averted their eyes. Not until Eliza Jacobs pushed her way to the front and fixed her offended gaze on the baby did anyone dare voice what was on many of their minds.

"That's an Indian," she pointed out in a sharp voice.

"Yes." Nathan grinned as the little girl grasped one of his fingers with pudgy, awkward hands and dragged it into her mouth. "Ouch! She's got teeth!"

"Just what do you think you're doing?" Eliza demanded. "Don't tell me you're thinking of trying to save it?"

A man in the crowd spoke up. The voice sounded like Simon March's. "I'd sooner save a rattlesnake."

The crowd muttered agreement.

"It's a heathen and a savage," Eliza declared, "sprung from the loins of barbaric, filthy murderers."

"It is neither heathen nor savage!" Cass countered. "It's a baby, not even a year old. We can't leave it. It'll die."

"Good riddance."

"That's a horrible thing to say!"

Effie Brown came hesitantly forward and regarded the baby with a mixture of sympathy and pain. "Poor thing. So little."

The baby gave her a suspicious glance, then cooed up at Nathan.

"What would we do with a Pawnee child even if it survived?" Effie asked hesitantly. "If the Pawnee discovered we had the child, they would surely attack us to get it back. They might even believe we kidnapped the baby."

"It's true," Amelia Byrd concurred. "It would bring the savages down upon us."

By now everyone had crowded around Nathan and the infant, hovering in a solemn jury. The baby girl looked back at them, equally solemn.

"Put it back where you found it," Amelia urged.

The older Amos Byrd joined in the sentencing. "If you want to be merciful, put it out of its misery."

"But it's just a baby," Virginia March said, horrified.

"It's a child of the devil," Eliza pronounced. "Leave the little demon to God."

"To the wolves, you mean!" Granny Decker, flanked by son Cory and his wife, Pamela, elbowed her way to the front of the circle. She squinted at the baby girl, at Nathan, at Cass, then back to the hovering onlookers. "I cain't believe you people. Hate has truly taken root in your hearts if you're making war on babies."

Most of the circle had the grace to look abashed. Not Eliza Jacobs. "Granny, it's a filthy Indian. Do you remember what the Indians did to my Jacob, to your Cory, to Clyde, Matthew, Aaron and Susan Sutter?"

Granny gave her a sly smile. "This little baby did all that?"

"You know what I mean!"

Nathan spoke up. "It wasn't even the same tribe, Eliza. And even if it were, this is a baby. All your arguing is useless, I'll tell you right now, because I'm not leaving this baby to die. I've done some things that I'm ashamed of, but I've never deliberately hurt a child."

A snort of derision came from a little way off, where John Lawton watched the little drama with a skeptical look on his face. Beside him was Lila, and the snort earned him a poke in the ribs from her sharp elbow. Nathan smiled. Lawton could snort all he wanted, but Nathan was not going to let anyone hurt the little bundle of life resting in his arms. And even if he hadn't been determined to defend the little tyke, Cass looked as though she might take a pistol to anyone who had other ideas.

"That's settled, then!" Granny declared.

Nathan hoped that Cass knew something about taking care of babies.

"What do I know about taking care of babies?" Cass asked a smirking Lila.

"You were the one so anxious to save the kid."

"You felt the same way. If no one else had defended little July here, you would have."

Lila gave a noncommittal "hmmm."

They sat beside the fire in camp. Cass bounced the baby gently in her arms, cuddled her against a shoulder, kissed her, sang to her—but nothing stopped the kid from crying. She'd been crying since they took her from the ruined Pawnee camp. She wouldn't eat the warm broth or the soaked bread they offered her. She wouldn't sleep. She wouldn't do anything but cry, cry, cry.

"You need milk for that chile," Luce told her.

"Sutters' cow dried up. The only cow in camp that's got milk belongs to the Jacobses."

Luce shook her head. "That woman has a heart hard as stone."

"Harder," Rachel said. "Ben tried to talk to her, and she was downright nasty to him."

Sue came out of the dark with a little crock in her hands.

Effie was right behind her. "I mashed up some soaked dried peas," Effie said. "Maybe little July will like those."

Little July didn't. The peas ended up all over Cass's bodice.

"The color looks good on you," Lila observed dryly.

Luce chuckled. "Here come Daddy Nathan. Baby didn't cry like that when he was holdin' 'er."

"Well then, here!" Cass shoved the howling kid into his arms. "Take her, *Daddy Nathan.* I have to clean myself off."

The sudden silence was almost deafening.

"Lord! That's a relief," Frenchie said. "I knew there was a reason I don't like kids."

Lila smiled. "She certainly likes you, Daddy Nathan. She won't stop crying for anyone else."

Nathan growled at the new title. "She'll have to learn. I don't know anything about babies."

"Not much to them, is there?" Frenchie opined. "They cry, sleep, eat, puke, and crap. What's there to know?"

Cass paused from dabbing at the peas to send Frenchie a dirty look.

"She done all of that so far," Luce said, " 'ceptin' sleepin' and eatin'."

Lila got a twinkle in her eye. "Maybe if Nathan took her into our tent where it's quieter, Cass could get her to eat a bit."

"She needs milk," Rachel reminded them. "And Eliza isn't going to volunteer her cow."

"Just try it," Lila urged.

Nathan balked. "Now wait a minute . . ."

Cass was suspicious of her sister's manipulations, but she ended up sharing a tent once again with Nathan. Lila moved in with Luce and Frenchie, and Cass and Nathan spent the night trying to get the little Pawnee waif they called July—after the month—to eat. The baby was quiet as long as Nathan held her, but she wasn't interested in anything they had to offer.

After a few grumbled objections—mostly for form, Cass thought—Nathan settled into his role as surrogate father. The baby took to him so because Nathan was the one who pulled her from that fearful pile of blankets, hides, and ashes, Cass told herself, but she was surprised at how gentle he was with the infant. He wasn't above making funny faces to get the little girl to chortle, or singing a soft tune to encourage her to sleep—not that she did sleep. But his lullaby, Cass mused somewhat reluctantly, was flawless. If she'd been that baby girl lying in his arms, she certainly would have fallen to sleep with a smile on her face.

They had help throughout the evening as one by one or in pairs the women of the train succumbed to the lure of a baby in their midst. Alice and Faith Scott, both looking quite fetching since they submitted to Frenchie's "fashion advice," were the first to come. Faith cooed over the baby while Alice dispensed advice about infant stomachaches and sleeping schedules. They were followed shortly by Hope Perkins, who regarded the baby suspiciously, then, when the kid smiled at her, downright wistfully. She asked to hold her, but July wasn't ready to be that friendly. At her sudden wail of distress, Hope handed her back to Nathan.

Granny and Pamela Decker came and stayed almost the whole evening. And even Amelia Byrd marched in, glared at the infant as though determined to despise the little tyke, and ended up trying to sweet-talk her into a spoonful of broth.

Cass watched them come armed with their prejudices and suspicions and one by one fall under the baby's spell. She herself had been entranced the first moment she saw the child. With her abundance of straight black hair and her huge dark eyes, the baby was the most beautiful little girl she'd ever seen. And the sight of Nathan making a fool of himself for the child's benefit was one of the sweetest things she'd ever seen. It was tempting to forget Nathan's shortcomings and let her heart soften toward him just a bit. A tiny bit. How could a woman despise a man who could laugh about a baby peeing on him?

Still, with all their good intentions, they made little progress toward getting the baby to eat until Steamboat Sue, Effie Brown, and Alice Scott made a triumphant entrance into the tent late in the evening. Sue held up a bucket. "Milk!" she proclaimed.

"Oh, my goodness?" Cass said. "How?"

Sue smirked. "Effie and Alice and I taught Eliza a little lesson in Christian charity."

Alice smiled. "I had at least twenty Bible verses up my sleeve that she couldn't argue with. Even Jed joined in to persuade her."

They fashioned a nipple from the finger of a glove. July had no trouble recognizing what was required. Giving them all a look that clearly said "What took you so long?," she greedily sucked down as much milk as her little stomach could hold, emitted a noisy, contented burp, and promptly fell asleep in Nathan's lap.

"Well, how about that?" Nathan said softly, as if he'd just witnessed a miracle.

The night was long, but it was still too short. Nathan had seldom felt so at peace with the world and himself. Even though it was a false peace, doomed to shatter with the morning light, it still settled deep into his soul like a soothing balm.

He looked down at Cass, who lay beside him, curled on her side with her forehead resting on his arm. His arm was going numb, but he wouldn't move it for the world. She'd finally surrendered to sleep after a long time just staring at the baby and smiling that secretive smile that women get when a baby is within reach. Her objections to spending the night with Nathan in the tent had been easily overcome. She'd already spent too many nights with him, she'd said, then laughed when he pointed out that they had a chaperon—a much prettier chaperon than the one they had tolerated last time they'd been together in this tent.

They had talked a bit—friendly words in low voices. July's presence seemed to make discord impossible. Nathan had told her a bit about prewar Tennessee, the fine horses, the genteel life, his ornery, stubborn father and tolerant, gracious mother. She had told him amusing stories from her travels with Lila. Sometimes, Cass related, she thought there were no good memories in their path from a poor farm in Iowa to the decadent opulence of Lila's Place in Webster, Kansas. But they were there if she looked hard enough, she admitted.

They hadn't talked long before Cass had fallen asleep. He'd eased her down beside him, July between them. Nathan didn't want to sleep, though. He wanted to savor every minute of this peculiar feeling that had come over him. Peace, warmth, a peculiar contentment. In looking at the two of them, woman and infant, Nathan suffered an intense longing that Cass was his woman and this infant was their child. How sweet such a thing would be. How sweet, and how impossible.

In the midnight darkness, surrounded by the scent of warm baby and warm woman, listening to their quiet breathing, nothing really seemed impossible.

Chapter 18

July 9, Fort McPherson, Nebraska—

After being on the trail so many weeks, absorbed in our own problems and our own small community, the bustle of this place seems strange. It is not an impressive outpost—only a stockade enclosing five or six buildings made of cedar along with three barns and various corrals for stock. Four companies are stationed here, two of the cavalry and two of the U.S. Army volunteers.

Yet the place seems like a great town, with comings and goings and crowds, wagons, mules, cattle— even chickens and pigs—everywhere. Because of trouble with the Indians on the trail ahead, no wagon train of less than fifty wagons is allowed to progress past this post. So those of us with small trains must wait until enough wagons join us to make up such a large force that the Sioux and Cheyenne would not dare attack. All of us are grateful for the respite but anxious to be on our way. Most here are on their way to California or Oregon and must cross the mountains before the early snow flies. Waiting here while precious time passes, we endure a barrage of rumors

of trouble ahead—settlers murdered and trains deci-
mated, but the truth of such stories is hard to judge.

For myself, I am glad of the rest. I have charge
of a Pawnee infant we found in a burned-out village
several days back. As I write, the precious little girl
sleeps on a pad of blankets in the back of the wagon.
Though she is a darling, she does keep me from sleep-
ing much at night. July, as I call her, is much taken
with Mr. Stone, who rescued her from certain death.
The first night she would not rest unless it was in his
arms. I must admit that he dealt with the situation
quite admirably.

Cass put down her pen and sighed. Sitting in the shade
of the big wagon, trying to set her thoughts in reasonable
order, she wasn't sure she wanted to think overmuch on
Nathan's obvious affection for July. More content now, the
baby didn't scream when they were separated, but no one
could make her smile or chortle like that man could.
Strangely enough, Nathan seemed to enjoy the baby as much
as the baby enjoyed him. Every evening he sat at the McAllister fire to be with the little girl. In fact, the McAllister
fire was the center of activity on the train these days, because few women managed to resist the lure of July. Even
Eliza Jacobs had grudgingly dropped by a time or two,
though she looked at the child with an obvious expectation
that it would sprout horns and grow a tail. Yet even Eliza,
it seemed, had come to realize that a baby was a baby
whether it was white or red. The project of feeding July,
dressing July, arguing over the best ways to care for July
had accomplished the impossible of molding the women of
the train—all the women of the train—into a sisterhood of
sorts. A sometimes fractious, squabbling sisterhood, but a
sisterhood all the same.

Things have changed so much, Cass wrote, biting her
lip in thought. *I look forward with great regret to the*
prospect of leaving this company, as we soon must do
if we are to go to Denver. I am uncertain who will
come with us. The women of our once isolated group

have formed other attachments. Yesterday Rachel confided to me that Ben Holden proposed marriage to her, and she has accepted. He is a far cry from where she had once set her sights, but she seems very happy, and Ben is a good man. Steamboat Sue's friendship with Effie Brown has given her new confidence and taught her that life does offer opportunities other than selling herself. She has not complained of her age in some time. I am very happy for her, but if she decides to continue on to Oregon with Effie, we will miss her sorely.

And Frenchie—if Frenchie has been changed at all by this experience, she won't admit it. God bless her, she is a good woman. She enjoys being "on the game," as those in the profession call it, but that doesn't change the goodness of her heart. I think the professor loves her dearly and is gathering his courage to propose. He asked me this morning to coach him on how a man should put that all-important question to a woman. As I have had only one proposal—and it made under false pretenses—I couldn't be of much help. I wish him luck, though. Since the professor came to our aid in Dobytown, Frenchie has paid him more attention—caustic attention, at times, but that is simply Frenchie's way. Mismatched as they are, I believe somehow that our brave musician and the outrageous self-proclaimed strumpet would make each other happy. They deserve to be happy. Quite honestly, I believe that we all deserve to be happy. Even, perhaps, Nathan Stone.

Groaning, Cass furiously scratched out the last sentence. All avenues of thought eventually led to Nathan Stone. When would she stop being a fool?

"You could have knocked me over with a feather," Frenchie told Cass. "The man is such a fool. I don't know why I put up with him."

"Because he's a man," Sue said with a sly wink.

"And you're a woman," Rachel added.

They were in a half-empty storeroom off Fort McPherson's mess hall, where very shortly Frenchie and Rachel would star in a double wedding ceremony. For this special day the ladies had claimed the storeroom as a dressing room. Cass had worked all the night before, and all day as well, putting together two very special gowns for two very special women to wear at their wedding. Now she and Lila did their best to create suitably elegant hair to go with the bridal dresses.

"Frenchie, will you hold still?" Cass complained.

"I can't believe I'm doing this," she grumbled.

"Well, you are. So hold still and let me pin these curls."

"The man is a fool," she repeated. "I warned him. I'm a whore, I said, and it's the only thing in this world I'm good at."

"That's not true," Lila told her.

"Really? What else? Lila, you're a natural business-woman. Cass can sew well enough to open her own shop if she wanted to. Rachel can read and write. Sue learned cooking from Effie Brown. She could cook for a king and not get any complaints, I swear. But what's my talent? I'm a whore. It's what I'm good at."

"Well, now you're going to be a wife."

Frenchie snorted. "Lord help me. I must be desperate. I like my men big and broad, not puny and timid."

Cass laughed and playfully yanked a piece of Frenchie's hair.

"Ouch!"

"Don't talk that way about your groom. The professor's not timid. He had the nerve to propose to you, didn't he?"

A small but revealing smile curved Frenchie's mouth. "Yeah. He did. And while he did it, the dolt burned my ears about the words I use, the clothes I wear, and the way my hips sashay back and forth when I walk. I spent a lot of time working on that sexy walk, you know. But the damned man's always lecturing me about one thing or another. Do you know what he said to me when he proposed? He said it was time someone took me in hand. And then he said that I'm like a rose in a thicket of thorns. A man gets stuck a lot before he sees how soft and fragile the flower is. Do you believe he said something stupid like that?"

Nevertheless, Frenchie seemed engrossed in the image. Her eyes softened dreamily for a moment, then, catching herself, she snorted. "The man's full of shit. He needs someone to take care of him. Keep him out of trouble."

"Well, there you go," Cass said, pinning the last sausage curl into place. "You'll be very good at that."

The answer was another snort, but Cass thought Frenchie looked quite pleased with herself, all the same.

The mess hall filled with people eager to witness the weddings. The trail west was hard, problems many, tragedies all too frequent. No one wanted to pass up an opportunity for such a happy celebration, whether or not they knew the celebrants. Cass, Lila, Luce, and Sue sat in the front row of benches that had been arranged for the occasion. John Lawton sat next to Lila, and Nathan sat in the row behind, keeping an eye on Lawton. Most of the Shelby company were there and smiling, even Eliza. Faith sat thigh to thigh with young Amos, and when the boy scooted away to get some space for himself, Faith followed, sticking like a leech. Faith was as pretty as she could be, with her new hair and a dewy, fresh appearance helped along by just a touch of rosewater and Madame Jeannette's Soothing Complexion Creme. Amos's resistance seemed more a matter of form than fact.

A considerably softened Hope Perkins cradled little July in her arms. Hope, along with several of the other Shelby women, had taken Frenchie's advice to heart. She'd arranged her hair softly caught back with combs instead of the usual stern bun, and the effects of a nightly dose of witch hazel and complexion cream had made a noticeable difference. Lately she had been almost cordial to Lila and her ladies, and her sister Alice had been downright amiable.

Frenchie looked radiant while the preacher—a man traveling to California to find, as he put it, new pastures to plow for the Lord—read the words of the marriage ceremony. Despite her earlier protestations and a skeptical grimace during the words "love, honor, and obey," she knew exactly what she was doing. Cass couldn't help but feel a bit sentimental about Frenchie finally finding her knight in shining armor, unlikely a knight though he was, and the professor winning the woman he had loved so long from afar. She did adore happy endings.

Not to be outshone by Frenchie, Rachel also looked the part of the radiant bride. But then, Rachel almost always looked radiant, whether or not she felt radiant. It was a matter of pride with her. Cass thought her state of mind today probably was in tune with her glowing appearance. She looked at Ben Holden with an expression close to adoration. An ex-slave certainly wasn't what Rachel had set out to find, but Ben had made her happy.

Perhaps, Cass thought, no one knew what would bring happiness before he or she actually found it. Perhaps all their goals and imagined needs were as empty as air—Rachel's, hers, everybody's. Did Cass really know what she wanted out of life? Did Lila, or John Lawton, or . . . Nathan?

There was Nathan again in Cass's mind. Listening to the drone of the marriage service, she could feel his eyes on the back of her head, feel his gaze almost as if it were a physical touch.

Beside her, Sue gave a squeak of laughter when the preacher called the professor by his real name—Ezra Jonathan Doolittle. Frenchie laughed also, irreverent as always. Up to this moment, none of them had ever called the man, so constantly present in all their lives, anything but the professor.

"Ezra Jonathan Doolittle?" Frenchie chortled with amazed glee.

The professor gave her a stern look, and she subsided to a mere smile, though her eyes twinkled dangerously. A few hoots of laughter from the audience elicited a glare of admonishment from the preacher.

"The professor has her obeying already," Sue muttered in Cass's ear. But she said it with a smile. Everyone, it seemed, was anxious to be happy. Weddings did that to people.

Cass suddenly suffered an intense longing for what could have been. Had John Lawton not come along and exposed Nathan's true nature, she would have been the one standing there before the preacher, becoming a wife and promising her love. Maybe she could have gone through life never knowing that the Reverend Homer Pernell was the outlaw Nathan Stone—a man too familiar with guns and blood and violence. Maybe she would have been happy, birthed and raised children, and grown old with a man who had a past she didn't know about. Would that have been so horrible? Did the past really mean so much? If you loved the man he was now, was the man he had been so important?

Of course it was important, Cass told herself. She shouldn't be thinking such foolishness.

After the wedding there was dancing at the campsite. Simon March scraped away at a fiddle. He wasn't nearly as good as the professor, or even poor Clyde Dawkins, but everyone had such a good time that they paid little attention to the barely tuneful squeaks. People from other trains soon joined them. One of them brought his fiddle, and soon they had real music.

It was a special occasion—so special that Cass scarcely thought twice about dancing with Nathan when he asked. It wouldn't be long, after all, before she was rid of the man forever.

"This is the only wedding I've ever been to," she told him as they two-stepped their way through the throng of other dancers.

"That's hard to believe."

"The local madam and her sister don't generally get invited to such social events."

"Well, now you have."

In a sudden awkward silence, Cass recalled once again that today might have been their own wedding day. Or perhaps they would have found a preacher at Fort Kearny and be old married folks by now. She would know what it was like to wake up beside a man every morning, feel his bearded face brush against her cheek, feel his cold feet against her bare calves. He would have learned that she was often cranky in the morning. Maybe he was a morning grouch as well. She would never know.

"My brother had the world's fanciest wedding," Nathan said. "Back before the war in Tennessee. I swear everyone from the county came. The shindig afterward was the social do of the season."

"It must have been splendid."

"From my mother's point of view it certainly was. She and the bride's mother planned the whole thing. I don't think my poor brother was ever asked his opinion. He and Clarissa—that was his wife—just went along with anything they were told."

"Where are they now?"

"Richard, my brother, was killed at Antietam. Clarissa remarried shortly after the war ended. Some carpetbagger from New York."

"I'm sorry. What about your folks?"

"My father died of gangrene in a Northern camp after he had been taken prisoner. My mother just sort of faded away after I got home. There wasn't anything left for her."

Sorry seemed an inadequate expression for the destruction of a whole family, so Cass didn't say anything at all.

"That whole world is dead," Nathan said pensively. "The whole world that was the South. It was a good world in a lot of ways. I don't think it deserved what happened to it."

They danced in silence for a moment. But silence left too much of Cass's attention for the feel of Nathan's arm around her, his hand splayed at the small of her back, his chest only inches from her nose. She tried to think of how he'd lied to her, betrayed her, used her, but the old anger wouldn't ignite.

"A life like you once had in Tennessee—is that what you want?"

He smiled grimly. "All the time I was growing up, that's what I wanted to escape from. I didn't know how good it was."

"And now?"

"Now I just want to go somewhere and make my own life. Quit running. Never lift a gun again unless it's to bring down a deer. After I hooked up with the Shelby folks, I thought I had a chance at it." He looked down at her with a wry smile. "I thought I could offer you a life, Cass, until Lawton came along."

Had he been thinking of all the "could have beens," as

she had? To divert a rush of maudlin regret, she changed the subject. "What will you do now?"

"Head for Mexico, though I'm not quite sure when I'll take off. These folks don't need me now that they'll be trailing along with all these other wagons, but it might be safer for me to stick around where I can keep an eye on Lawton. He's hamstrung until Fort Laramie, but I have an idea if I go riding off, he'll take that as calling quits to our little bargain."

Cass wouldn't be with the group when they got to Fort Laramie. She would probably never know what happened to Nathan and Lawton. Probably it was better if she didn't know.

"Mexico," she half whispered, acutely aware of his body heat seeping into her veins, his breath ruffling the stray tendrils of her hair. "I hope you make it, Nathan."

"Do you?"

There was more being said here than their few words, and suddenly Cass lost the desire to dance. She wasn't sure she wanted to discard her anger this easily, if that was what she was doing. "I have to check on July. She's been passed around all day. Right now Alice has her."

Nathan didn't protest. Perhaps the merriment had gone from him as well.

July was fine—warm, sleepy, and smelling of sweet milk and clean baby. Alice was reluctant to give her up. "Go dance," she told Cass. "You're only young once, dear. When we're back on the trail there'll be little enough time for having fun."

Sooner or later, Cass knew, she would have to think about July's future, but tonight her mind was too crowded—with weddings and leave-takings and Nathan Stone—to hold yet another problem.

So without thinking, she allowed herself to be escorted through the dark by Nathan. And without thinking, she found herself walking beside him toward his wagon. She should not allow herself to be alone with him, Cass thought. She should be back at the dancing, celebrating with Rachel, Frenchie, their friends, and the dozens of other emigrants who had come to dance and clap and sing with the newly-weds. But the thought didn't have much effect.

Nathan's wagon loomed up in the dark. Too many memories haunted it. She remembered when she had crept out of the morning mists to petition the handsome Mr. Pernell to preach up her friends and put them back on the right path. Instead she had ended up spying on a half-naked man shaving off his morning beard. That had been the morning that poor Anita was killed.

And then there had been the time she came to that same Mr. Pernell with the heart and intentions of a wanton, so afraid that he might reject her, find her wanting, or that God might strike her dead on the spot for leading one of his servants astray. God hadn't struck her dead, and the man inside the wagon hadn't really been a servant of God. But he had been a gentle, wonderful lover. By morning she had been so consumed by passion that she'd thought nothing in heaven or earth could ever change her feelings for the man she loved. Nothing.

How wrong she'd been. Or had she? In the recesses of her heart, did she still love that man?

She was surprised from her musing by the brush of his hand against her hair. Was his touch inadvertent? She turned away and tried for an impersonal subject. "It's nice that they gave you back your wagon."

"Very nice, since it had my belongings in it."

And memories. Were the memories important to him?

"Young Amos drives it for me usually. I have things to tend to with the rest of the train."

Like scouting, hurrying up stragglers, refereeing squabbles, finding a little Pawnee baby and defying the whole wagon train to keep her alive. Was this really the man who had so heartlessly betrayed her?

"It's good for sleeping, though. Keeps out the wind and rain if not the dust."

His hand glided over her shoulder and down her arm, an action removed from their inane conversation. Two things were happening here. One was simply polite, meaningless small talk. The other she didn't understand. Why was she standing in the dark with this man?

"Cass." His voice slipped into a different register entirely. No longer casual, it brought her face around to confront his. "Sometime before I leave, whenever that will be, if you could say that you forgive me, the words would take a weight off my conscience."

Any other time she would have snipped that men like him didn't have a conscience. Not tonight. Tonight, his hand rested warmly at her waist, and perversely, she liked it there.

"Nathan . . ."

"Just think about saying it, when you can mean it. Think about it."

"Nathan . . ." She decided to be honest. "I . . . I think I'm afraid to forgive you. I don't want to let myself remember how much I cared for you before I knew who you really were."

The hand moved along her back, softly caressing, warmly soothing—temptation itself. The irony of her own statement jarred her, or was it that slowly moving hand that caused the surge in her blood? How could a woman truly care for a man when she had no idea who he really was? She had loved a fantasy, a man she had concocted in her own mind to meet her own wishful desires. The lie had been only partly Nathan's.

"Now I know who you are," she continued softly. "It would be dangerous and foolish to let myself care for the real Nathan Stone."

"Yes," he agreed, his face disturbingly close to hers. "It would be dangerous and foolish."

Dangerous, Cass thought, because they had no possible future together. Foolish because Nathan Stone was not the man she needed or wanted. Besides that, he was a desperado, a fugitive, and a liar. And according to John Lawton, he might very well be a man who abused women for his own pleasure. Though day by day, as the real Nathan Stone revealed himself by his actions and words, that accusation was getting harder and harder to believe.

Her voice came out a breathy, hesitant whisper. "Just because I've been polite lately, it doesn't mean I care for you." She really ought to put some space between them, but his body was like a magnet that drew her in. "What we had back then was a lie." She couldn't resist the temptation to touch the broad chest that hovered so close. His shirt was warm from his heat. It was the shirt she had sewed for him.

"It wasn't all a lie, Cass." His hands cupped her face, thumbs brushing the corners of her mouth. "Hardly any of it was a lie."

Nathan's lips came gently down upon hers, and Cass didn't resist. After a moment she quit trying to resist, accepting finally that she wasn't going to listen to her own good sense. She wound her arms about his waist and leaned into him, engulfed by his scent, his taste, the rasp of his rough cheek against hers, the delicious sense of surrender to something stronger than herself and supremely male.

They surfaced for air, breathing hard, but he didn't let her go. "We could discuss this in the wagon," he suggested hoarsely.

"We shouldn't," she breathed. "We really shouldn't."

But they did. The inside of the wagon was warm and close, with barely enough room for them to move. The wind played a little melody on the taut canvas cover, making the darkness hum. It seemed very cozy. Very intimate. Too intimate. But Cass made no attempt to leave. She sat on a wooden locker, attempting to be prim. "We have no future together," she reminded him.

"No, we don't."

"Even if you were free."

"If I were free, Cassidy Rose McAllister, I'd do my best to give you the world." Slowly, one by one, he flipped open the buttons on her bodice.

"This is wrong." She sighed.

"Yes." He continued to unfasten buttons.

"And just plain stupid."

"Can't argue with that."

But he didn't stop, and when he eased her dress from her shoulders, she helped him. And when he opened the ties on her corset and slipped his hands inside to fondle her breasts, liquid fire poured through her veins. Of one accord they moved to the thin straw mattress that served as his bed.

Cass had only dreamlike recollections of the first time they had made love. This time, however, a heightened aware-

ness infused every fiber of her body. She felt every caress
clear through to her bones. The heat of his passion burned
away every inhibition. She willingly, eagerly gave him every
part of her body without hesitation. And she took every part
of him that he would give her. Around them, the night
glowed. In an impossible blend of animal satisfaction and
spiritual joy, Cass knew that she would never be quite the
same. She'd given part of her soul to a desperado and taken
part of his in return.

For most of the night they lay in each other's arms, not
wanting to waste any moment of this unexpected interlude
on mere rest. But finally, the world came back to claim
them. Exhausted and sated, they slowly became two people
once again, two people without a future together. One, perhaps, with no future at all.

"I don't know what happened," Cass whispered, still nes-
tled in the circle of Nathan's strong arms.

Nathan kissed the top of her head.

"I'm supposed to despise you."

"Yes."

"But I can't."

He smiled. She could feel the movement of his lips
against her temple. "Good."

"We shouldn't have done this."

"Probably not."

Her hand traveled up his torso, over the washboard of
his stomach, over the flat, hard muscles of his chest. She
simply couldn't resist. "I am a wicked creature."

"You could never be anything but an angel. A busybody
angel who tries to run people's lives. A dangerous angel
when you're riled. And a very, very sexy angel. But an angel
just the same."

She laughed. "I don't know how you ever passed yourself off as a preacher. You have a sacrilegious soul."

He just smiled.

Slowly, her lightheartedness faded. "This won't ever happen again." She meant the statement to sound determined,
but it only sounded mournful.

"No," he agreed with a sigh, twining a lock of her hair
around his finger. "It won't."

"It was foolish."

"Foolish."

"And stupid."

"Very."

She swallowed hard. "You are not what I want, Nathan Stone. I have a goal, you know, and you're not it."

"I know."

She lied, and she knew it. He had to know it too. But when the morning light came, when the world was once more normal, she must do her best to make that lie the truth.

The scratching at the tent flap and the soft hail from outside woke Lila. The night was inky dark and the air chill. She mumbled a word she wouldn't say in public and fumbled for the lantern. Cass's blankets were still neatly tied into their roll, Lila noted as she fumbled with the ties that held the tent flap closed.

"Nathan," she grumbled, pushing back the tangled fall of her hair and squinting at him. "It's the middle of the night. What are you doing here?"

"It's morning," he said.

"Until the sun comes up, it's night as far as I'm concerned."

"I'm leaving, Lila." His horse's reins were looped in his hands.

"Early morning hunt?"

"No. I'm leaving."

The finality in his voice brought her all the way awake.

"I wanted to let you know. So you can tell . . ."

She finished for him. "Tell Cass."

"Yes."

Lila glanced back at the rolled blankets. "I have an idea you could have told her yourself."

He had the grace to look guilty. "It'll be better if you tell her."

"Don't think you could look her in the eye and then go riding off into the sunrise?"

"Something like that."

She sighed. No sooner did things start going well than

someone had to get squirrelly. "Nathan, come into the tent. Let's discuss this."

"I've got to get going."

"This isn't right. You can't just ride off."

"The train doesn't need me anymore. They're going to be part of a big group that has guides who actually know what they're doing."

"What about Cass?"

He was silent a moment, his mouth grim. "Lila, I'll be honest. I'm crazy about your sister, but I have nothing in the world to offer her."

"Why didn't you think of that before you let her spend the night in your wagon?" Lila knew how to be as stern as a mother superior when she had to be. And right now she had to be. "And this isn't the first time. Don't think I don't know what went on when you were still wearing your preacher face."

"That's the most important reason I've got to go, Lila. I've got no right to her. But where Cass is concerned—well, she makes me forget what I have a right to and what I don't."

"And what if she's got your baby growing in her?"

His jaw went slack. Lila shook her head. Why didn't men ever think of the obvious? "It was only twice," he said, as if that made a difference.

"Nathan, honey, all it takes is once."

"Jesus!"

"He's not going to help you. Nathan, don't run out on Cass. She needs someone in her life who can make her lose control. She loves you, honey. And I think you love her."

His face went through contortions of indecision, then became granite. "The best thing I can do for Cass is to take off and quit hurting her. I can't give her what she needs, Lila."

"Nathan, you *are* what she needs."

Stony silence.

"At least meet us in Denver. If she turns up pregnant, you can lend her your name. You owe her that much. I'll tell John that you took off for Mexico."

He stared at the ground for an agonized moment, then

looked up. "He might believe you. He'd expect me to head down there anyway."

"He'll believe me. John trusts me."

The morning was still midnight black when Nathan rode quietly away, but soon the beginnings of the new day would lighten the east. Soon after that, Lawton would notice that his prey was absent, and it wouldn't take him long to realize that Nathan Stone had flown the coop for good.

Lila shivered in her nightdress and the flimsy blanket she'd wrapped around herself. She didn't look forward to the lie she had to tell, but sometimes a woman had to take a hand with Fate to make sure that everything came out as it should. Nathan would be hard to track. He was no amateur when it came to running. And Lila was no amateur at plotting.

He would be all right. They would all be all right.

But would John Lawton, upstanding beacon of the law, ever forgive her for the way she was about to deceive him?

Chapter 19

Cass leaned against the big wagon wheel, tears running down her cheeks. She was not good with good-byes, and there had been too many in her life lately. When loved ones left, the leaving tore such a hole in a person's soul.

Only a week ago she had awakened from a night of—what was it? Love? Passion? Pure damned foolishness? Whatever had transported them that night, Cass hadn't expected to wake and find Nathan gone. Gone for good, Lila had told her. Maybe you'll see him again, her sister had said, and maybe you won't. If things are meant to be, then they'll work out. Cass had refused to admit she was shaken, but Lila was impossible to fool. She was glad to be rid of him, Cass told herself over and over again. He had lied, taken advantage of her, and betrayed her. She was well rid of the man. Very well rid of him. Cass had as much trouble fooling herself, however, as fooling Lila.

Everyone else was leaving as well. Lawton had left the minute he realized that Nathan had flown the coop. Lila, the traitor, had told him that Nathan had headed for Mexico—not that Lawton couldn't have deduced that for himself. He and Lila had had a long private good-bye, and Lila had been upset afterward, though she denied it. Some of the life left her when the marshal rode off.

Frenchie and the professor—rather, Mr. and Mrs. Ezra Jonathan Doolittle—had also left them at Fort McPherson. They had bought a wagon at the fort and headed east, bound for the big cities of the eastern seacoast where they could make their way as entertainers. The professor itched to get his hands back onto the piano keyboard, he told the group, and Frenchie intended to try her luck as a professional singer.

Now the final blow fell, where Cass and Lila would go their separate way and everyone dear to their hearts would go theirs. Here at the upper ford of the South Platte, wagons bound for Oregon and California must cross the river and head northwest—toward the North Platte, Fort Laramie, and points beyond. Lila and Cass, along with three other families that had joined them at Fort McPherson, would follow the South Platte to Denver, now just a week or two away if they made good time. Steamboat Sue was continuing to Oregon with Effie Brown and, surprisingly, faithful Mama Luce elected to go with them. The three women planned to open a boardinghouse and public dining room at their destination. Rachel and Ben were heading to Oregon also. And they had convinced Cass to let them take July.

"She'll be raised in a loving family, I promise," Rachel told Cass.

"And we'll give her brothers and sisters to play with," Ben had added, looking at his wife with a twinkle in his eye.

Cass didn't want to give the baby up. She loved her not only for herself, but for the tenuous link the infant had forged between her and Nathan. But she couldn't deny the little girl two parents and a family who loved her.

Rachel gave Cass a reassuring hug. "We'll take care of July. Don't you worry. And we'll write when we get settled."

"Be happy," Cass said tearfully.

"We already are that."

Luce had tears running down her seamed black face. She gave Cass a fond embrace, the last of many they'd shared in their years together. "Honey lamb, you behave yourself in Denver town. Find yo'self a good man and be happy.

And take care o' that sister o' yours. I been doin' that for all these years, and now it's up to you."

"I will," Cass choked out.

Luce and Lila looked at each other. They'd been together since Lila had bought the old woman from a flesh peddler in Missouri, where she'd been worked unmercifully and kept in quarters a dog would have shunned. Lila had immediately set her free, but they'd been inseparable up to this day of parting.

The two women looked at each other silently. Neither could speak what they felt. Finally, they clutched each other in a desperate hug.

"When you get where you're going," Lila said, "send us a message care of Martha McCannes. She'll know where we are."

"You take care, girl," Luce whispered. "You take care."

Even the farewells with the Shelby women were emotional. Faith Scott cried. Her mother, Alice, gave Cass and Lila a hug and wished them luck. Hope Perkins hemmed and hawed, but she ended up giving them a hug as well. Cass knew she would miss all of them, especially Granny Decker, who patted her shoulder and said in her ear: "Buck up, dearie. He'll come back. If he's worth anything, he'll come back for you."

Cass was taken aback. "I'm glad he's gone."

Granny just shook her head and smiled.

Jed Jacobs shook their hands gingerly and wished them luck, and even Eliza was civil. "I may have been a bit harsh in my judgments at times," she admitted reluctantly, giving them a stiff smile. "I owe you gratitude, Lila, for helping with Mr. Jacobs."

They stayed until all their friends had safely forded the river, which was a particularly difficult crossing. The current was swift, the bottom uneven and treacherous, and the river wide. But finally all were across, wet but unharmed. By now they were very experienced at such crossings. The Denver-bound travelers waved to their counterparts on the north bank and shouted well-wishes, even though they couldn't possibly be heard over the quarter-mile stretch of muddy water.

"Oh, I hate good-byes," Cass said to Lila.

"Life's full of them," Lila said in a melancholy voice.

Jody Grier, who headed up a family of two wagons, five children, a wife, and a brother-in-law, rode along the Denver-bound wagons with the order to move out.

Lila sighed. "Let's go," she said to Cass. "We've got two wagons to drive and still a lot of miles to go."

July 29, Denver—

Our journey is finally over, and we are comfortably settled with the McCanneses, my good friend Martha and her husband, George, who is a very respectable, very kind man. Martha adores him, and I understand why.

Their home is one of the more substantial houses in the town. It is a brick two-story with a wide covered porch in front. There are six rooms downstairs, including a very nice parlor, a dining room, a library—which is Mr. McCannes's haven—a lovely breakfast room overlooking the garden, and a very large sunroom which can be used for quilting bees or socials. Upstairs are five spacious bedrooms. Lila and I each have a room to ourselves, which is unbelievable luxury after weeks spent in cramped wagons and tents. Indeed, Martha's beautiful house is just what I pictured for myself and Lila back in the days when achieving respectability was still just a dream.

I must admit, however, that in my dreams of respectability, Lila and I were always respectable in some peaceful, settled little town, with church socials and quilting bees, tree-lined streets with friendly folk sitting on their porches or strolling to take the evening air. Denver certainly is not any of that. Set at the confluence of two unpredictable rivers—the South Platte and Cherry Creek—it is a new, raucous town, filled with overflowing energy but very little peace. The inhabitants are rough frontier citizens, many of them miners seeking a quick fortune from gold and silver. Others are sharpsters seeking a quick fortune from the miners. Every man one meets upon the street car-

ries a loaded gun, and some of the women also. Slap-dash frame buildings are everywhere, and more seem to sprout up overnight like weeds. The business district boasts new brick structures only because of the fire several years ago that swept away the wooden shanties. The streets are often ankle deep in mud, for we've had rain almost every day. Trees are rare, and everything has a very temporary look. The town has been here for not even ten years, so I suppose I expect too much. If it survives to become a settled city, it might one day be very beautiful, with the vista of the nearby mountains and the wonderful clear air that affords views of a hundred miles or more.

George McCannes is an unprepossessing sort of man, rather middle aged, with thinning hair and thickening middle. He has a very keen wit, however, which has served him very successfully in business. Currently he owns a hotel and several eating places in the busiest part of town near the stage depot. Martha is the apple of his eye, and he is determined to make her comfortable, even in this rough frontier. Looking at Martha now, a respected wife with many friends among the "upper set"—if such a set can exist in a town of a mere 3,500 people—I find it difficult to remember when she came to Lila's Place, a bedraggled and desperate new widow without a penny to her name, willing to do anything to feed herself. It simply proves that one can advance from the dregs of society to the cream. Lila and I will be living proof, just as Martha is.

We already are living proof, in fact, for how different our lives are now than they once were. And they continue to change. We are searching for a house of our own and may end up building one. There is property not far from the McCanneses' that is within walking distance of the business district but still affords a fine view of the mountains. Mr. McCannes is using his contacts in town to try to get us a good price. We are very fortunate that Lila put away so much of the money she made during her years in the

*business. She is also exploring the possibilities of in-
vesting in the McCanneses' businesses as a silent partner, though I'm not so sure how silent my sister could
be.*

*Lila seems absorbed and happy in the business of
making a new life, but at times she is broody and far
away. I suspect she thinks often about John Lawton.
I'm quite sure she is in love with him. She and I do
not seem very wise about the men we choose to love.*

*As for myself, I try diligently to be happy, for I've
gotten exactly what I wanted. I miss our friends, and
every time I look at the mountains, I fear for their
safety in crossing such a barrier and carrying on
through the deserts and wastes on the other side. I
gave Rachel the McCanneses' address and made her
promise to write, but not nearly enough time has
passed. It is a long trek from the ford of the Platte to
Oregon. I pray for them every day.*

*In fact, God has been inundated with my prayers
these past weeks—for my friends, and for Nathan. His
leaving was unexpected, and it embroiled me in confusion. No sooner did I discard most of my bitterness
and anger than he left. I admit, dear journal, that I
succumbed once again to the temptation of intimacy
with the man, and this time I didn't have the excuse
of expecting marriage. It was a wicked thing to do,
but I can't regret it. For all my declarations that I
wanted him gone, I miss him terribly. On the journey,
even if we were battling, at least I could see him every
day, hear him speak, know he was safe. Now I have
none of that. Neither do I have realistic expectations
of seeing him ever again. Lila, my most perceptive
sister, senses my distress and its cause. She tells me
that if a thing is meant to be, then it will be.*

*Ironic, is it not, that I, who have always been the
busybody telling people how to live their lives, now
am in need of advice myself. When did I realize I was
still in love with Nathan Stone? I don't know. Perhaps
that love never deserted me. I just didn't recognize it*

until Nathan was beyond reach. And yet, wasn't he be-
yond reach even when we were together?

All this is meaningless, of course, because he is
gone. Like Lila, I have decisions to make and a life
to build. She manages to live with a bruised heart,
and so shall I. Tomorrow, the McCanneses are host-
ing a social evening to introduce us to their friends,
and I vow that I will smile and dance and look for-
ward instead of backward. That is the way life should
be lived.

The McCanneses' affair was more like a fancy fairy-tale
ball than a mere social, as far as Cass was concerned. A
small orchestra—or at least the closest that Denver could
manage—played in the sunroom, where the entire wall of
French doors were thrown open to the patio and garden.
The ladies were dressed in silks, jewels, and feathers, and
the gentlemen strutted about in tailored evening coats and
silk embroidered vests. Extra kitchen staff hired just for the
occasion had prepared enough food for the entire town, and
it seemed to Cass that the entire town was present—at least
the part of town that bathed more than once a month.

"Martha, this is simply incredible," Cass told their host-
ess.

Martha giggled. "Isn't it?"

Then they giggled together, like two alley urchins spying on a swank ball.

"I don't think I'll ever get used to it." Martha sighed.
"The fancy food, the dresses, the house, a man I love who
loves me no matter what. But it is so nice that you and Lila
are here. I've longed to have someone around who I don't
have to watch my manners with."

"Oh, Martha! You're so every inch a lady that you positively ooze class."

She laughed. "Oh, my dear, how easily you are fooled!"

Cass winced at the unexpected reminder. How easily she
was fooled. How easily she was made a fool. Or perhaps
she'd been a fool all along, thinking she could ever fit in
to this kind of life. Standing here all fancied up with the
cream of respectable Denver society all around her, she felt

suddenly as if this wasn't what she wanted at all. Only months ago she had stood peeking into the Webster Community Hall at Ethel James's birthday party. Back then her highest ambition had been to mingle with those proper ladies and gents, to have people nod and smile at her without turning up their noses, to have some young man think she was the loveliest girl in the room, ask her to dance, and come to think what a suitable wife she would be. She remembered the fantasy she had woven—herself fetching glances from all in the room in a stylish green dress with matching green ribbon wound through her hair.

That party seemed a thousand years ago, and that girl peeking through the window seemed a silly child. Yet here she stood, wearing almost precisely what she had envisioned in her dream, a dress the color of her eyes and hair ribbons to match. But she had changed. Perhaps she had grown up. Had she worked so hard to change her life only to realize that the change didn't bring her any closer to happiness?

"Excuse me," said a nervous masculine voice. "Mrs. McCannes introduced us at the beginning of the evening."

Cass searched her memory. "Of course. Mr. Bartlett."

"Please call me Ted. Would you care to dance?"

Cass smiled and gave him her hand. This was what she had wanted—a clean-cut, honest, decent young man looking at her as if she were enthroned on a pedestal. Why did the triumph feel so empty?

"I'd love to dance," she said.

For the entire evening Cass was in great demand as a dance partner. She danced until her feet hurt and her back ached, until she had to excuse herself to bolster her strength with punch.

"Allow me," her dance partner, a young man in the freighting business, said. "I'll fetch whatever you like."

"Thank you." Cass tried to keep from wincing. Her feet didn't want to take one more step in her ridiculous dancing slippers. "But please don't trouble yourself. I see my sister over there calling me. I should go talk to her."

Lila wasn't really summoning her. She and George McCannes were deep in conversation, but they both looked up and smiled when Cass limped up.

"If I could walk halfway across the country without collapsing," Cass said, "you'd think I could dance for a few hours without crippling myself."

McCannes grinned. "Everyone wants to dance with you, Cassie. I warned you that you would be the belle of the ball."

Cass smiled weakly, and Lila raised a meaningful brow in George's direction. Tactfully, he made an excuse and left them alone.

"Let's get something to eat," Cass said with a sigh.

"Wear yourself out?"

"These Denver fellows sure like to dance."

Lila smiled. "I'm glad you're having fun."

They loaded up two plates with cakes, candied fruits, and a confection of chocolate and sugar that Cass couldn't put a name to—but it was delicious—and found seats at the elaborately decorated tables on the patio. Cass avoided male attention by simply refusing to meet anyone's eyes.

"I have good news," Lila announced when they were seated. "George and I have reached agreement on a partnership. I'm going to be a truly respectable businesswoman from here on out."

"Lila, that's wonderful. I'm so happy for you."

"Me too. I didn't realize how relieved I would feel being out of the 'business' and challenging myself with something that doesn't raise eyebrows. And I owe it to you, Cassie."

"You owe it to yourself."

"Don't go modest on me, baby sister. You've always been the busybody who's nagged and pushed to make me change. Now I'm glad you did"—she grinned—"annoying as it was at the time."

Cass grinned back. "I thought I was subtle."

"About as subtle as a locomotive." She reached out and squeezed Cass's hand. "I hope you're glad we came here. I worry about you."

"I'm having the time of my life."

Lila looked skeptical. "You can't fool me. I'm your sister who raised you. Remember?"

"Don't worry about me. I'm grown up now, Lila, and

I've just realized that reaching a dream maybe isn't what I thought it would be. I'll adjust."

"Will you?"

"Oh, sure. After all that happened on the way here, being so respectable just seems a bit boring. The men I dance with seem like . . . like boys."

"Because they don't have a noose around their necks and a vengeful marshal on their tails?"

"No," Cass said too quickly, and not very convincingly. "Because they . . . they seem soft." She grimaced and lifted one shoulder. "Boring."

"Uh-huh." Lila didn't sound like a believer.

"They're nice. Very polite, respectful." Cass grimaced. "Hovering. Maybe I just don't like being treated as if I were some sort of fragile flower."

"Women are supposed to be flowers, Cass. Forget you can doctor a mule, shoot at Indians, and drive a wagon."

Cass grinned sheepishly. "I didn't do any of that very well."

"Well enough. We're here, aren't we?"

"We're here."

"Where we wanted to be. So enjoy yourself, baby sister. And think about what you want to do with your life. This is a new place, a new start, and a wide-open town. You could start your own shop. Or you could help me in the business, like you always have. Only this time it's a different business. Or . . ." She looked beyond Cass's shoulder. "You could get married, have kids, be a genteel wife with a cook and three maids and a butler. Here comes a nice-looking candidate now. I hope your feet are rested, because he looks determined."

Cass sighed.

Three days later, Cass sat at her dressing table, scowling at her reflection in the mirror. Lila stood behind her, pinning up the thick red curls she'd just produced with a curling iron.

"This isn't going to work," Cass said dismally. "I'm sick. I can't go."

Lila showed not a trace of sympathy. "You can go. You just have panic stomach."

"Do not."

"Yes, you do. Look at how pale your face is. I'm going to have to use rouge."

"No. Respectable ladies don't use rouge."

"You'd be surprised what respectable ladies use. Calm down, sweetie. It's just dinner."

"With a man. At a real restaurant. Where everyone in town can see us. Are you sure this is proper?"

"It's very proper. George and Martha both vouch for this fellow. And I like him too."

"You don't know him."

"I talked to him at the dance, and I liked him. I'm a good judge of men. With my experience, I ought to be."

"Ouch! You're pulling."

"You think that hurts? Wait until I tighten your corset."

"I thought respectable women didn't have to go through this sort of thing."

"One doesn't have to be drab or dowdy to be respectable, dear. The one essential difference between a decent woman and a whore is price. The price of a whore is a few coins— quite a few coins, if a gentleman patronized my house. The price of a decent woman is a wedding band. You still have to dress up the product to make the sale."

"Lila!"

"It's true."

"I'm not going to marry this fellow."

"Perhaps not." She smiled her older, wiser sister smile. "But you could do worse. He's very handsome," Lila continued, "and very well mannered."

Cass just sighed.

"If you don't like him, why did you agree to go to dinner with him?"

"I like him," Cass said in a rather truculent tone. "He's very nice."

"Not to mention rich."

"That doesn't matter."

"It never hurts." She pinched Cass's cheeks.

"Ouch!"

"Well, if you won't let me use rouge, then you have to endure some pain to get roses in your cheeks. Relax and enjoy yourself." She grinned. "Just don't do anything I wouldn't do."

"That's not much," Cass gibed.

Lila gave her a playful push. "Go on, you disrespectful child. I'll bet he's waiting for you downstairs."

He was, and Cass put on a smile when she saw him. Daniel Steele was his name. He really was very nice, very handsome, and quite well off, just as Lila had said. At the McCanneses' social he'd determinedly plucked her away from Lila and the refreshments and practically dragged her on to the dance floor, and he'd danced with her until the party ended. Cass hadn't minded so much. He was more interesting than any of her other dance partners. But dining alone with him in public seemed going a bit far.

Daniel took her to the Mountain View Restaurant, which was one of George's dining establishments. It was on Larimer Street, one of the busiest thoroughfares in town, and while it didn't really afford a very good view of the mountains, the food was good and the clientele smelled better than the run-of-the-mill Denverite.

Aren't we getting a bit picky, Cass thought to herself, *for a girl who has spent her life jumping from brothel to brothel?*

The maitre d' recognized them both—Daniel Steele as one of the town's bankers, and Cass as the restaurant owner's houseguest. "Mr. Steele, Miss McAllister," he oozed. "How good to see you both. I have a lovely table for you by the window."

Daniel slipped a greenback into the man's hand. "Thank you, Charles. That would be lovely."

How very civilized, Cass thought. *How extremely respectable.*

"Cassidy Rose," Daniel said to her once they were seated and left alone with their menus. "You are absolutely the freshest, most beautiful rose that's ever blown into Denver."

"Thank you, Mr. Steele."

"Tch, tch! Didn't we agree that you would call me Daniel?"

Cass smiled. "Thank you, Daniel. You're very flattering."

"I'm very truthful. For my own selfish reasons, I hope
you grow to love Denver and decide to stay. I know it's
very rough, from the viewpoint of a lady such as yourself . . ."

*A lady such as myself. A lady. Lord, if Daniel Steele only
knew!*

". . . but the town has such potential. Not just the min-
ing. But commerce, ranching, transportation. Denver isn't
going to be a boomtown that's dead in ten years. No. I'm
convinced that someday it will be a great city, sitting as it
does at the very gateway to the Rockies. But, I apologize."
He gave her a smile that she thought was just a little bit
condescending. "This is talk to bore such a lovely lady."

"No, please go on. You must know that my sister is going
into business with Mr. McCannes, so we have great interest in this town."

"No, I hadn't heard that. Your sister is a wise woman to
make such an investment. I'm sure George will make her
a great deal of money."

Lila had already made a fair amount of money on her
own, but Cass wasn't about to go into details about that.
She couldn't help wondering how he would react, though.
George McCannes loved Martha even knowing all about her
past, including the short interlude working for Lila. Would
Daniel Steele react as generously if he knew that "the freshest, most beautiful rose that had ever blown into Denver"
had been business manager and maid of all work—except
the work most central to the house—of the fanciest whorehouse in Webster, Kansas?

The thought left a sour taste in Cass's mouth, and she
suddenly realized that maintaining respectability would require denying her past for the rest of her life. This new circle of "friends," with the exception of George and Martha,
would cringe in disgust if they knew who and what she
really was.

Dinner continued over conversation that was fit for a
lady's ears. She told him something of the journey across
the plains, leaving out some of the more earthy details.

Daniel didn't impress her as a man who wanted to hear about bloody Indian attacks and the art of burning buffalo dung. The food at the Mountain View was excellent. The atmosphere was as close to civilized as Denver could offer, and the company was genteel. This was just the sort of thing that Cass had dreamed about every time she had ever been shunned, spat upon, ignored, and ostracized. Now that she had it, why did this genteel respectability feel so shallow?

The hour was not late when they left. Respectable single women did not keep late hours, it seemed, and Daniel had promised to have her back at the McCanneses' residence at an appropriate time. The street was quite dark, but enough light spilled from the doorway of the restaurant for Cass to recognize the man who stood watching the restaurant. He turned quickly and began to cross the street, but not before Cass saw his face. She stopped in her tracks, stunned, but only for a moment.

"Wait!" She pulled away from Daniel, who'd placed a chivalrous hand on her arm when she had stopped so abruptly. "Wait! You there!"

The man ignored her, hastening his step, but she shot after him, leaving Daniel's protest behind her. Boldly she caught the man's arm. He stopped, turned, and smiled sheepishly.

"Nathan," she breathed, scarcely believing her eyes. "You're here."

"Hello, Cass."

"What are you doing in Denver?"

Nathan turned his eyes to Daniel, who had come up beside her. The young banker fairly bristled with possession.

"Cassidy Rose?" Daniel prompted.

Cass blinked in surprise. She'd all but forgotten her escort. "Uh . . . Nathan, this is Daniel Steele, who is vice-president of the Stockman's Bank. Daniel, this is Nathan—"

"Sutherland," Nathan provided quickly. "Nathan Sutherland. Miss McAllister and I met on the journey out here."

Cass fell in with the deception. "Mr. Sutherland was our wagonmaster."

"How interesting," Daniel said, obviously not interested

at all. "But Cassidy Rose, why are you so surprised to see him here?"

"Oh! I . . . I thought he—"

"She thought I was headed to Oregon. We parted company at the upper ford of the South Platte. But the wagons I had charge of joined with another train, and I decided to see what Denver is like."

"Well," Daniel said with false heartiness, "welcome to our fair town."

How smoothly Nathan lied, Cass noted. He'd done it so often that he was an expert. What had really brought him to Denver when he should be sweet-talking the senoritas in Mexico? How she wished Daniel were not here. If she were alone with Nathan, she'd wring the truth from the scoundrel.

The more she stood there, looking on while the two men politely sparred with words, the more angry Cass got. Nathan had come to Denver, knowing she and Lila were here, and had not even bothered to find her, if only to tell her he was still among the living. She had fretted day and night about his fate, and here he was, the jackass, right here under her nose and not bothering to relieve her mind. He must have known that she would worry about him. After all, the last time she had seen him they had been in his wagon and . . . God help her, she didn't even want to think about what they'd been doing. Her frustration exploded from her in a loud sigh.

"Sorry, darling," Daniel said solicitously. "We're boring you."

Since when had Daniel been calling her "darling"? Cass wondered. Nathan bristled at the possessive endearment, then put on his granite face.

"Come along, dear. I promised George I'd have you back at an early hour."

Cass glared at Nathan. She wanted to upbraid him, to grill him with questions, to leap forward and take him in her arms and at the same time kick him in the shins for being such a blockhead. But she could do none of that with Daniel standing there watching her every move.

Nathan smiled and touched his hat, just as if she were

some mere acquaintance he'd met on the street. "Nice to see you again, Cass."

"Drop by the McCanneses' house and tell us what you've been up to," she said as politely as she could. "Anyone can tell you where it is."

Nathan just smiled as Daniel urged her away. And he stood watching as the impeccable, respectable young banker handed her up into his carriage. He was still standing there as they rolled past him.

Daniel smiled at her and shook his head sympathetically. "One must put up with all kinds, I suppose, on a wagon train."

Chapter 20

"You knew Nathan was in Denver and you didn't tell me?" Cass sent a simmering glare toward her sister. At the same time, she wore a back-and-forth path in the rug. Directly after Daniel Steele had delivered her to the Mc-Canneses' residence, she had rushed up to Lila's bedroom, snatched a Jane Austen novel from her sister's hands, and revealed the amazing news that Nathan was in town—only to discover that Lila had known all along. "Why did you do that? You knew I was worried about him."

"I thought you despised the man," Lila said with airy innocence.

"You know better than that."

Lila avoided Cass's eyes and toyed with the lace on her dressing gown. "Really?"

"Oh, come on!"

With a shrug, she gave in. "All right. You were worried about him, but I thought he should be the one to tell you he was here."

"He sought you out, yet he didn't even send me a message, or a 'hello, how are you?' How could he do that after . . . after . . . well, shoot!"

Lila was sympathetically silent. Cass was getting sick and tired of sympathy.

"Cass," Lila said gently, "if Nathan wanted to face you, then he would have come to you."

Cass blew out a *pfuuft* of disgust. "Did he say why he's here?"

Lila's mouth drew into a line.

"You're giving me the silent treatment. Why?"

"If he wants you to know—"

"He'll tell me," Cass mimicked. "All right! Fine! Where is the jackass?"

Silence.

"Come on, Lila! Whose side are you on?"

"I'm on your side, believe it or not."

"Then point me in his direction. I need to talk to him."

Lila was dubious. "Baby sister, if he deserves you, he'll have the backbone to come to you."

"Oh, for heaven's sake! He's a man! You expect him to have that kind of sense?"

Lila considered. "Maybe not."

"Tell me then."

After a moment, Lila sighed. "He works at the livery down the street from the Mountain View. I think he sleeps there too. He probably saw you go in with Daniel, and that's why he was standing there watching."

"He was watching me, so he must care some about me. Mustn't he?"

Lila made a face. "That's not the most important question, Cassidy Rose. The question is, do you care about him?"

Cass bit her lip.

"Do you love him, Cass?"

"Love," Cass sighed, and again worried her lip.

"That's what I asked. Do you love the man, warts, wanted posters, and all?"

Cass's brow puckered. She marched to the bedroom door and opened it, but before going out, she turned. "That's a good question. Thank you, Lila."

That night, Cass didn't sleep. She lay in her feather bed, staring into the dark. Lila's question rang in her mind, making rest impossible. She'd asked the same question of herself, time and time again, since the day she'd awakened in

Nathan's wagon to find Nathan gone. But when someone else posed the same question, it had more impact, ringing impact, like a bell clapper clanging in her head, going on and on until she found the true answer.

Did she love Nathan Stone, warts, wanted posters, and all? Would life with a lying, deceitful worm of an outlaw be better than a proper, respectable life hostessing quilting bees and prancing about on the arm of some pillar of the community?

She couldn't help but compare Nathan to Daniel Steele— handsome, proper, affluent, law-abiding, chivalrous, mannerly Daniel Steele. Beside Daniel, Nathan looked very rough indeed, with a slight stubble shadowing his lean cheeks and his clothes showing obvious signs of having been on the trail too long. Out of habit Nathan's hand hung close to where a holster might be, whether or not he wore one. His eyes, black as night itself, were ever watchful.

Daniel Steele, on the other hand, was sleek and polished as a newly minted coin. His hands were smooth and soft. His face so cleanly shaven that his cheeks positively glowed. His suit was the best, both of fashion and tailoring, and his eyes hid nothing. Daniel Steele was as honest and open as the day was long. Everything he had was up front. There were no layers to peel and then peel again to find the real man.

Nathan Stone, unlike Daniel, hid nearly everything. Where was the real man beneath the facade of frontier preacher, gun-toting desperado, long-suffering trail guide, savior of Indian infants, and gentle, generous lover? Had she found the real Nathan Stone yet? Had she peeled away all his masks? Or was the real Nathan Stone still to be revealed?

Cass realized there was really no comparison between the men. Daniel Steele was by far the better catch. But if she had to choose, Nathan would win hands-down. Nathan of the broad shoulders and capable hands, Nathan of the rare smiles that, when they came, heated her blood, Nathan of the wary eyes that could melt in a moment of passion, Nathan of the wisecracks and yes, the lies and desperation. Her Nathan. She did love him. And she knew that in spite of everything, the core of him was solid, unadulterated gold. Somewhere inside her she had known that all along, but her pride and hurt feelings got in the way. She loved Nathan Stone, God help her. Respectability and quilting bees be damned. She was going to find out exactly how he felt about her, and if he didn't admit to loving her, she was going to let him know just what a fool he was.

The livery barn was warm with the smell of horse, hay, grain, and aged leather. The morning stars were just beginning to fade, but Nathan was already at work. He squatted beside a livery horse tethered in the central aisle, examining a rear leg. From a nearby stall, Tiger snorted and tossed his head.

Nathan looked up at the Tennessee stud and grinned. "Jealous?"

Tiger stomped.

"We'll see if we can't find some time for a run today. Just you and me and the mutt. How about that?"

The horse didn't answer. Neither did Dog, who was curled in a corner on a comfortable pile of straw.

"You lazy animals don't know when you have it good."

Nathan had just picked up the rear leg of his patient and rested it on his bent knee when Tiger snorted in alarm and Dog lifted his shaggy head. Nathan looked up to see a woman slip through the barn door and close it firmly behind her. The lantern light glowed in coppery hair. Cass. Nathan's heart skipped a beat.

She walked down the straw-littered aisle, skirt swishing the floor in time to a determined stride. A few feet from him, she stopped and fixed him with a level regard that sent a small quiver down his spine. There was nothing more dangerous than a determined woman.

She didn't say anything, and neither did he. The silence stretched out, punctuated by the restless stomping of the horses and a quiet whine from Dog. Here was trouble, Nathan reflected—trouble, temptation, and bother. Here was also a balm to his weary spirit, for though the sight of her filled him with unwanted cravings, it also soothed him with much-needed comfort. Ever since he'd left her, Cass had ridden stubbornly in his mind and heart, plaguing his dreams, making his body ache with memories. And now here she was, breasts rising and falling as if she were winded from a long run, eyes sharp as cut jewels, jaw firm as iron. She had something to say, but it was something difficult, for she was having one heck of a time getting the words out.

"Well, if you're just going to stand there," Nathan finally said, "at least help." He thrust the horse's leg at her. "Hold this while I get the salve."

She took the leg without a word, bent down and balanced it on her knee, but her eyes flickered with a moment's hesitation, as though she'd like to run.

He rummaged around a bucket for the tin of salve. "See the cut right below the hock?" he asked.

"Yes."

"Hold the leg so I can smear this stuff on that gash . . . there! Good job." He eased the leg from her hold and patted the horse on the rump.

"You work here?" she asked.

"For a while."

"How long have you been here?"

He smiled. "For a while."

"Blast you, Nathan! Don't get smart with me! I came for some answers."

Here came the explosion. Nathan did love the way her eyes glinted when she was mad. Heaven knew she'd been mad most of the time they had been together. "Answers to what, Cass?"

"What are you doing here?"

"Working at a livery."

She looked as though she might hit him. "You know what I mean, you arrogant worm. I thought you were headed for Mexico."

"I am. Eventually."

"Then why aren't you there? Do you want John Lawton to drag you to the nearest hanging tree?"

"He won't do that. Even if he knew I was in Denver, it would take him a while to find me in this town."

"Oh, right. You're Nathan Sutherland now, not Nathan Stone."

He grinned. "My mother's maiden name."

"As if that's going to fool him."

"I won't be here long."

"And you are here because . . . ?" she prompted, her eyes flashing.

"I have to clean Belle's stall here before I put her away." He grabbed the pitchfork that leaned against the wall. "Bring along the wheelbarrow, will you?"

Uttering a word that a lady shouldn't use in public, she grabbed the barrow and followed after him. "It's a good thing for you that I didn't see that pitchfork first."

"That's what I figure."

She regarded him sourly while he pitched the used straw into the wheelbarrow and spread fresh upon the floor of Belle's stall. He feigned unconcern while her eyes bored twin smoking holes through him—through him and through every story he considered to innocently explain his presence in Denver. Cass was the kind of woman you could lie to once, then she saw through every little fabrication you tried. Women like her could be a great inconvenience.

"I guess you're not going to be satisfied until I tell you," he admitted.

"That's right. I want to know why you left so suddenly without a word—not a single, blessed word! And I want to know why you're risking your fool neck in Denver instead of holing up in Mexico."

He leaned on the pitchfork. "The truth is, Cass, that I left early that morning because I knew if I stayed, I'd take advantage of you again, and again, and as long as I had you within reach. As I told you once before, you make me lose control, woman. And you deserve better than to be seduced by some raggedy-tailed outlaw on the run for his life."

She lowered her eyes for the first time. "You could have at least said good-bye."

"I couldn't have said good-bye," he told her. "If I'd tried, I would have stayed."

She digested that for a moment. The slightest of smiles touched her mouth, then fled. "So you left," she said with a sigh. "Why didn't you go to Mexico?"

"Well . . . that was because of your sister."

"My sister?" Her eyes snapped up. "You're here for my sister?"

"Not *for* Lila. Because of her." Women, Nathan noted, were certainly quick on the draw when another woman's name entered a conversation. "Lila pointed out that I hadn't always acted in the gentlemanly manner a decent girl like you deserves."

Cass colored and managed to look indignant at the same time. "How did she know?"

"Your sister sees a lot just by keeping her eyes open," Nathan said.

"Go on."

"And, uh, she pointed out that there might be results from my less than gentlemanly behavior. She suggested I'd want to be around if you turned up in trouble."

Cass looked at him quizzically, then her eyes widened. "You came to Denver to find out if I was pregnant?"

Nathan hesitated. You'd think a woman would be grateful for a man's help in such a situation. But then, who understood women? Certainly not him. "Uh . . . yes."

"You're here just to be sure you didn't make a baby," she ground out, as if such a thing were unbelievable. "You didn't risk coming to Denver because you wanted to see me, or because you . . . you cared for me. You just came because Lila cracked the whip and said I might be pregnant."

"I wouldn't put it quite that way." It appeared he'd set the tinder to Cass's temper. The pitchfork would not be adequate defense.

"You're not only a fool," she growled, "you're a jackass. First you lie about who and what you are, then you hold a damned pistol to my head and threaten to shoot me—"

"I wouldn't have shot you, goddamnit! I thought we'd settled—"

"And then you come back and convince me all over again to fall into your arms like the fool that I am, and what happens? You hotfoot it off, letting me think you were on your way to Mexico, never to be seen again, and now you show up here, risking your damned neck! Not because you care about me, but because my busybody sister made you feel guilty about me."

"Cass, you're twisting this every way but straight."

"Ha! I'm twisting it how I see it, that's what!" She took out the lethal finger, her deadliest weapon, and pointed the business end in his direction. "Well, Mr. Fake Sutherland. For your information, I am not in the family way. Lila could have told you that when we first got here and saved you the trouble of hanging around to shovel horse manure. Not that the job isn't suited to your talents."

"You're not going to have a baby?" Only two days ago Lila had said she wasn't sure. Nathan couldn't decide if he was relieved or disappointed.

"No. No baby. So you can just pack up your horse and your mangy dog and get on with your life."

Nathan began to feel just a bit put upon. He'd tried to do the right thing, for a change, and Cass could do nothing but call him names and look at him as if he were three-day-old coffee. She was about to execute an indignant flounce toward the door, but he put an end to that performance with a hand on her arm. "Just wait one minute, Cassidy Rose."

She glared at him over her shoulder.

"Now we've settled the question about why I'm here. Why are you here?"

"What do you mean?" she asked too innocently. "I live here now."

"You don't live here in this barn. It's the crack of dawn, when all respectable young ladies are safe in their houses, doing whatever respectable young ladies do at this hour, and Cassidy Rose McAllister is tramping through the morning dew to hang me by my toes in a livery barn. Explain."

"I don't need to explain anything."

He smiled complacently. "If you don't want to spend the rest of the day shoveling manure, you do."

"You wouldn't dare."

"I'm still bigger than you. And remember, I'm a man with no scruples."

"You certainly are that."

He raised one brow, refusing to release her arm. She was

as stiff as a ramrod, and for a moment, her eyes met his
defiantly. There were faint shadows under those flashing
green eyes, he noted.

"You're being very unreasonable," she grumbled.

"That's something I'm good at."

"And just plain cruel."

He squeezed her arm—not enough to hurt, just enough
to remind her that he had the upper hand for the moment.
"Tell me, Cass."

"Oh, all right! If you're satisfied with nothing less than
my complete and utter humiliation, I'll tell you. When I saw
you here, I thought you'd come because maybe you just
couldn't live without me. Isn't that incredibly stupid? And
even stupider—I was going to say that I love you. That respectability is for the birds, and I don't . . . didn't want to
live without you either. Doesn't that make you want to throw
up with laughter?"

"Cass . . ." His grip on her arm tightened. He felt as
though Tiger had kicked him in the chest. He had figured
she cared for him, but love was a big word. She loved him
enough to throw aside her dreams, to give up on quilting
bees and church pews. That thought made his heart expand,
after it started beating again. "Cass . . . you shouldn't love
me, but I'm glad you do, because I never stopped loving
you. I think I started to fall in love the first time I noticed
you spying on my wagon. You ran like a deer the minute you
realized I'd seen you. After that, I never quite got control
of myself where you were concerned."

Her mouth fell open, and the tight-wire tension in her
body eased. "You've loved me all along?"

"I'm surprised you ever doubted it."

Her face lit a delighted smile. "You truly, truly love me?"

"I do."

She leapt at him and wound her arms around his waist.
"Then I forgive you."

"For what?"

"For everything. Do I need to go into detail?"

"You'd better not."

"And we'll go to Mexico together."

He snorted. "Like hell."

"Why not?" She tilted her face toward his, a face almost impossible to refuse.

"Cass, running to Mexico—that's no life for a woman."

"You don't know how tough I am."

"I know how tough you are. I don't want you to have to be tough."

"That's my choice."

"I love you, and it's my choice."

"If you love me, you won't force me to live without the man I love." She pushed him back into the stall, an impish smile on her face. "Do you think Belle can do without her nice clean stall for a while longer?"

"Cassidy Rose, what are you doing?"

"Showing you how very much I love you."

"Cass . . ."

She deftly unbuttoned his shirt, then attacked his belt buckle.

"Cass . . ."

"Don't interrupt, Nathan. I'm busy."

Lord, but she was busy! He put hands on her shoulders, telling himself he should get her under control. But he ended up caressing her instead. They collapsed together, laughing, to the clean straw. She landed on top of him, still struggling with his belt and trousers. But he rolled them over and pinned her beneath him.

"Woman," he said with a chuckle, "you need to be taught a lesson."

She gave him a sultry smile that could have made a saint jump out of his pants. "I need a lot of lessons, Nathan. Teach me."

The last was an invitation he couldn't resist.

An hour later, poor Belle still waited for her stall while Cass and Nathan lay on their backs in the straw, exhausted. If the town hadn't been starting to stir, promising business for the livery, they might have spent the whole morning there. Nathan had long since realized he had met someone more stubborn than himself. He raised himself on one elbow and teased her nose with a piece of straw.

She gave him a cat-in-a-bowl-of-cream smile. "You have to marry me now, you scoundrel."

"Do I?"

"Of course you do. I might be pregnant again, and Lila would fairly kill us both."

He chuckled. "You are a very wicked woman."

She laughed and attacked him. And Belle had to wait still longer for her stall.

Two days later the McCanneses hosted a very small wedding. The only guests other than the preacher and his wife were George, Martha, and Lila. The bride wore a pale green dress that she herself had designed and sewn. The color set off her copper hair and sparkling emerald eyes to perfection. And the eyes did sparkle like finely cut jewels. No one who saw her could doubt that this was a woman who had gotten her man.

The groom wore a new, stiffly starched shirt and trousers fresh from the general store. Like most grooms, he looked a bit flustered. But he spoke his vows in a firm, steady voice, and he kissed his bride in a manner that left no doubt that he was a man who had gotten his woman.

When Lila embraced her sister after the ceremony, she smiled and said quietly, "You've done the right thing, baby sister. All the respectability and security in the world can't make up for not having love. He loves you a lot. I can see it in his eyes. Always could."

Cass squeezed Lila's hands. "How I wish you could have the same."

Lila smiled sadly. They both knew to whom Cass referred. "Honey, I'm a whole different case than you. I'm older, and I've learned to roll with the punches. Don't you waste a minute worrying about me."

When Lila gave her new brother-in-law a hug and a peck on the cheek after the ceremony, she whispered in his ear: "You made a far better preacher than this dull fellow."

Nathan laughed. Cass turned a curious look on the two. "What?"

"Your sister was just reminding me of my past sins."

The preacher pulled a stern face. "Not too many of them, I hope, sir."

"Too many to count, sir. But from now on I'm going to

lead the dullest, most upright life a man can lead. I have a wife to keep me in line."

"In Mexico," Cass reminded him, just a hint of worry drawing a crease between her brows.

"In Mexico," he agreed.

Martha dithered. "I'd certainly feel better if you two were taking the stage instead of traveling horseback. The Cheyenne have been kicking up such a dust lately."

"Don't worry about us," Cass said. "We'll be fine."

"Typical woman," George commented with a chuckle. "Now that she's landed her man, she thinks the world is her oyster."

Cass smiled. "It is."

Scarcely an hour from the end of the ceremony, Mr. and Mrs. Nathan Sutherland were on their way south on Tiger and the best horse that George McCannes could buy—his wedding present to Cass—and a laden pack mule. Cass had followed Frenchie's example and made herself up several divided skirts for riding. Propriety no longer concerned her. Lila and the McCanneses watched and waved until the pair disappeared into the midday traffic of wagons, horses, and pedestrians.

"I wish they were going by coach," Martha said yet again.

"Too risky," George said. "Too many people, all of them nosy. They'd leave too much of a trail."

Lila and Cass, with Nathan's permission, had confided the problem to the McCanneses, who were very sympathetic.

"God grant that they'll be able to come back someday," George said. "The war ruined many a good man. I can tell just by the way he treats Cassidy Rose that her Nathan's a good man, despite this nasty business of him being in trouble with the law. Maybe the scalawag marshal who's after him will give up and go back to Kansas."

Lila sighed, still gazing in the direction that Cass and Nathan had gone. "Nathan is a good man. Quicker on the draw than he should be, maybe, but a very good man. Trouble is, John Lawton's a good man too." A shadow of regret clouded her face. "A very good man. And he isn't the sort to give up."

• • •

Nathan and Cass spent their wedding night under the stars. That wasn't a new experience for either of them. Yet this night was different, Cass reflected as she sat on a roll of blankets and stared into the fire. They had no circle of wagons for security, no people milling about, no teams of mules—and husbands—braying for their dinner. This was truly just her, Nathan, Dog, and wild Colorado. The scrub grass was their mattress and the brilliant, star-studded night sky their only ceiling.

The night was beautiful, undisturbed by the presence of people and untarnished by untidy civilization. Yet isolation brought a hint of danger. They trespassed where wild animals and hostile Indians ruled. Those who traveled alone risked much.

Yet Cass was happier than she'd ever been. The reason sat beside her, his arm holding her close. Her entire life she'd been searching for something. She had thought it was respectability and stability, but all along it had simply been a man to love her. Her and her only, in all ways, under all circumstances, good or bad. As long as she had that, nothing could ever make her truly unhappy.

"You're very quiet," Nathan observed. "If you've changed your mind about marrying me, woman, it's too late. I've got you now."

She laughed. "You've got me? I was the one who had to throw myself at you to get you to the altar. The truth is that I've got you." She raised her index finger and blew away imaginary gunsmoke. "The west's most elusive outlaw, brought down by my relentless pursuit."

"Seems to me I did most of the pursuing."

"Well, maybe we caught each other." She smiled. "And we'll hold on to each other."

"Just try to get away." He turned for a moment to check the loading of their pistols and his rifle. When he joined her once again on their blankets, he caught a glimpse of concern on her face before the expression disappeared. "Don't worry, Cassie. We'll be all right."

"I know we will."

"We're in a nice little hollow here, and I don't think anyone but the stars overhead can see our fire. There's only one approach, and the animals will let us know well ahead of time if someone's coming down the draw."

"I'm not worried." She trusted Nathan to keep her safe, and she trusted herself to be able to deal with whatever their lives held in store. She was no longer a girl peeking through a window at life and building fairy-tale dreams. In one summer she had grown into a woman. "I'm not worried," she repeated, an impish glint in her eye, "except about how you intend to keep me warm tonight."

"Is that so?"

She smiled enticingly. "It's been two whole days."

"You're shameless," Nathan said with a chuckle. "I've been told, you know, that once a woman becomes a wife, she loses interest in such things."

She feigned indignation. "A proper woman doesn't have any interest in such things before she gets married. As for the rest of us"—she slid him a mischievous sideways look—"well, I guess it depends on the man."

"And just what can the man do to keep a wife interested?" He drew a finger down the column of her throat, over her collarbone, and on a straight path toward the treasure hidden beneath her shirt. He didn't let the shirt stop him, but unfastened the buttons one by one, tantalizing her with gentle brushes of his roughened skin against the softness of her breast. "Do you think this might keep her interested?"

Cass caught her breath at the flood of heat his touch sent through her body. "It might." She sighed.

"Or maybe this." He spread the two sides of her shirt and leaned over to nuzzle at her chemise. The touch of his warm breath made her melt. Her head tipped back, her eyes closed, and her mouth drew into a smile. If she'd been a flower, she would have opened her petals to gather in the heat of his attention.

"Do you know how much I love you?" he murmured against the cotton of her chemise.

"Mmmmm," she replied. "Don't stop."

"Greedy woman." He lowered her to their blankets, where they both worked at ridding themselves of every stitch that separated them. They had all the hours until dawn, and they

used every one of them, neither counting sleep among the
necessities of that first night together as husband and wife.
The stars wheeled silently above them. The fire died, and
they didn't bother to add wood to the coals. The heat they
made together was quite enough to keep them warm.

Chapter 21

John Lawton had never been a man to give up, and he wasn't ready to give up even now, after scouring every route to Mexico and even dipping into Mexico itself without finding so much as a hint that a black-haired, black-eyed gringo on a flashy blood bay stallion had been anywhere near. Now, as a new day dawned, he rode northward, retracing the most common route between Denver and Mexico, just in case Stone had come farther west before heading south.

Lawton felt as though he'd ridden the entire great Southwest, and both he and his horse were the worse for it, bedraggled and worn out, dirty and discouraged. Someone in this benighted country must have seen the bastard. No man could miss that Tennessee stud, and few women could see a man like Stone—with his brooding dark looks and dangerous charm—and not remember. But everywhere he asked in this sparsely populated territory, every stage station, dusty town, and ranch, every traveler and settler—no one had seen a trace of Nathan Stone or any man who fit the description. The wanted poster he carried in his pocket was so creased and dirty that the drawing on it was scarcely recognizable as a human being, much less a specific man. But Lawton could describe his prey down to the last detail. He'd had

the picture in his head since the day he'd found his battered, weeping sister. Every line and plane of Stone's face
was burned into his memory, and every shadow in the bastard's black soul.

He would never forget, Lawton swore, just how black
that soul was. Stone could work his charm on gullible women
and ingratiate himself with good men, convincing them to
ignore his past villainy. He might even convince a sensible
woman like Lila McAllister. But not John Lawton. That sort
of chicanery didn't work on John Lawton. He was stead-
fast in his path, certain in his hatred. He'd been on the hunt
too long to let doubts fuzz his mind, in spite of Lila's notion that his antagonism toward the man had softened. Lila
McAllister—she'd been convincing in her certainty that
Stone was bound for Mexico. But perhaps Lila had lied,
and perhaps Lawton's judgment had been clouded by a pretty
face. From the very first Lila had tried to influence him in
the man's favor, pointing out that he might have jumped to
conclusions about Stone's villainy, trying to convince him
that his certainty was wavering. Lila flat didn't believe that
Stone was guilty of brutalizing any woman. The sonofabitch
was good at pretending to be a good guy.

Lawton tightened his resolve, refusing to yield to doubt.
When he caught up with Nathan Stone again, the bastard
wouldn't have any women or gullible do-gooders to defend
him. It would be just Lawton and Stone. All the cocky charm
in the world wouldn't do the scoundrel any good.

A growing irregularity in his mare's gait made Lawton
stop to inspect her feet. He found a stone in the left rear.
It had bruised the tender frog of the mare's hoof, and if he
didn't want to make her seriously lame, she needed a rest.

"Damn! Just my luck." He gave the mare a pat on the
shoulder and looked around. To the southwest of him, the
lofty peak named after Zebulon Pike rose into a mass of
thunderheads that threatened afternoon rain. To the west
were pine-clad slopes cut by canyons, and to the east was
the rolling, seemingly infinite prairie. Just ahead the land
rose gradually to a piney ridge. But nowhere in this landscape was any living being except John Lawton and a lame
horse, and nowhere was so much as an outrider's shack.

The stage road was in sight to the east, but it was empty. The closest station was a good many hours away.

"Well, old girl. We walk side by side, I guess. You can't say I don't treat you like a queen."

It was just minutes after they started walking that Lawton noticed movement in the brush and trees to his left. The mare snorted and balked as five copper-skinned Cheyenne warriors rode from the tree cover and galloped toward him. Suddenly all Lawton's other problems seemed insignificant.

Sunrise found Nathan and Cass already an hour on the road. This was no leisurely honeymoon journey. Both were anxious to be in Mexico, where they could start a life free from shadows of the past.

They set a good pace, but Nathan reined his impatience to travel even faster. Cass had to be tired after the night before, though she didn't seem tired. Her horsemanship had improved since those early days when he had used riding lessons as an excuse to be with her. Then she was just as likely to bounce off a horse as stay on it, but now she perkily sat astride her little brown mare, chattering happily about setting up a home in old Mexico, about how they could use her share of the McAllister savings to buy brood mares and start a horse farm like the one where Nathan had grown up.

Nathan didn't want Cass's money, and the more they rode, the more he suffered from a guilty conscience about what he had done. Mexico really was no place for a young, beautiful white woman, and he'd had no business marrying Cass no matter how much he loved her, no matter how much she insisted that she would go anywhere with him. It was a selfish deed, and no way for a Tennessee ex-gentleman to behave.

But it was done now. He could either make sure that Cass never suffered for the vows she had taken, or he could ride to the nearest stage station and pack her back to her sister in Denver. Nathan didn't think he could accomplish the latter, and Cass herself might have a thing or two to say about it. He doubted she'd be very polite on the subject.

Her mare trotting up beside him, Cass shot Nathan in the

heart with a bright smile. The sun caught fire in her hair and
made faint freckles swarm across the bridge of her pert nose.
The day was warm, and she'd left her shirt collar open a
bit. The innocent vee of bare skin tempted his imagination.
Even after a whole night spent in lovemaking, he hadn't had
enough. He would never have enough of her, and, selfish
though it was, he couldn't give her up. So much for the last
remnant of his claim to being a Tennessee gentleman.

"If you're tired, we could stop for a bit," he offered.

"Me, tired?" She laughed. "I've barely started."

The sun was well overhead when they smelled the fire—
the barest whiff of woodsmoke carried by a breeze from
the south.

"A homestead," Nathan speculated. "Or a campfire. But
why have a fire in the middle of the day?"

In this dangerous country, nothing could be taken for
granted. They proceeded with caution, watchful eyes scan-
ning the landscape ahead. A short time before, they had
crested a tree-covered ridge, and now the trail descended a
long slope into rugged country cut by numerous draws and
small canyons. On the west, mountains closed with their
trail, climaxing at the southern limit with spectacular Pike's
Peak. To the east the piney highlands gave way to rolling
prairie. And directly ahead they spotted a thread of smoke
rising from a dark seam in the landscape.

"I'd better see what it is," Nathan said. "You stay here
with the pack mule."

"I'm going with you," she said.

"Cass . . ." When he saw the stubborn set to her face, he
didn't bother to continue. He'd married himself a wife who
didn't know the meaning of wifely obedience.

Twenty minutes later, they were looking into the forested
draw from which the smoke was rising.

"Great," Nathan whispered. "Just damned great."

"Is that who I think it is?"

"None other."

"What do we do?"

If they had an ounce of brains between them, Nathan
thought, they would ride on quietly and leave John Lawton

to the mercy of the five Cheyenne braves who had him bound hand and foot and tied to a tree.

"Wellll . . . ," he ventured, "we could ride on."

She gave him a scandalized look. He hadn't thought she would go for that and, to tell the truth, it didn't sit too well on his mind either.

"Or I could shoot the poor guy to spare him further torture. He looks pretty poorly used, but I don't think they've gotten around to the really serious stuff yet."

She dismissed that idea with an unladylike snort.

"Well, hell!" The prospect before him wasn't a happy one. There were five prime Cheyenne warriors down there, any one of whom could probably take him apart. And even if they managed to rescue the marshal and not get themselves tied to a tree for Cheyenne entertainment, what could they do with him? Lawton would probably string him up from the nearest tree.

Still, Nathan had faced worse odds a time or two in his life and come out on top. He might be able to pull it off. Whatever the outcome, though, Cass shouldn't be anywhere near.

"Cass, go back to where we left the mule and stay there. If I'm not there in an hour, go back to Denver."

She actually laughed—a quiet laugh, but a laugh, nevertheless.

"I'm serious, Cass. Do as I say."

" 'For better or for worse,' " she reminded him.

"This is a whole lot worse that it ought to get. Now go."

"Do you remember the Sioux attack on the Shelby train?"

He knew what she was getting at, but he didn't like it. There were only two of them, and even if the Indians believed they were being attacked by a larger force, they would likely kill their captive before fleeing. "Damnit, Cass, I don't want you to have any part of this. It's too risky."

"Life is risky."

"Do you know what those Cheyenne would do if they got you?"

"I won't let them get me. Nathan, if we rode off and left Lawton here, I couldn't live with it, and neither could you. And I would rather be in the thick of things than waiting somewhere, wondering if you're dead, wondering if I have to spend the rest of my life without you. I'm not going to do that."

He clenched his teeth, vacillating between frustration and admiration.

In the end they compromised. Nathan circled around the draw and came at the camp from the trees behind Lawton. Cass stayed where she was, having promised to take refuge in a hidey-hole that Nathan had found for her if the Cheyenne started coming up the slope after her. The plan was for Nathan to sneak up behind Lawton, cut the man loose, and give him a gun. If the marshal was in good enough shape to defend himself, the odds would be only two to five—tough, but not impossible, especially once Cass opened fire from above, making the warriors think it was a concerted, organized attack.

They had at least a small chance to succeed. The Cheyenne were busy celebrating, no doubt anticipating the fun of causing Lawton a good deal of misery in the slow process of dying. Nathan didn't blame them all that much. There'd been a time or two when he himself had fantasized about the same sort of thing where Lawton was concerned.

It took him nearly a half hour to steal through the woods with sufficient stealth so that he wouldn't be noticed. In that time the warriors had jabbed at Lawton a couple of times with their lances, no doubt to give the man a taste of what was coming. From what Nathan could see, Lawton was taking the abuse like a man. Of course he would, noble, upstanding lawman that he was. Nathan had to wait, huddled in the brush, until the warriors turned back to their own pursuits. They wore no war paint, so most likely they were a hunting party that happened on a lone enemy and took advantage of it. He hoped that meant they wouldn't have much taste for standing off gunfire from multiple directions.

After what seemed like forever, Nathan saw his chance. The Indians' backs were turned. One of them was holding forth quite seriously to the others about something. Nathan hoped the subject was spellbinding, whatever it was. He crept forward on his stomach, rifle in one hand, pistol in the other, and a knife clenched in his teeth. To Lawton's credit, he didn't so much as make a sound when Nathan started sawing through the rawhide cords that bound his hands. The marshal's wrists were raw, the hands swollen. Nathan hoped Lawton could pull the trigger of the pistol thrust into his right hand.

The Cheyenne still hadn't noticed, so Nathan slid completely out of the brush and started work on the cords that tied Lawton's ankles. The savages had made damned good and sure their captive wasn't going anywhere.

Just as the cords parted, one of the warriors turned their way. All hell erupted. Gunfire from Lawton's pistol exploded in Nathan's left ear. One of the warriors fell, his face registering surprise.

Nathan started pumping his rifle and, at the same time, gunfire blossomed from the hillside. Cass was doing her work, although if her shots landed anywhere near the campsite, they certainly didn't hit anyone. In fact only the one Cheyenne was dead and one other wounded, despite all the gunfire, when the warriors decided that they would do well to fight another day. They scooped up their casualties, sprinted for their horses, and galloped down the draw.

When nothing could be seen of the Cheyenne other than the dust of their departure, Lawton wasted no time expressing his gratitude. "My thanks," he said and started to turn. "I owe you, mister . . ." His words choked in his throat when he realized who had come to his aid. "Hellfire!"

Nathan grinned. "Kinda sticks in your craw, eh, Lawton?"

Lawton stood like a statue, blood oozing from shallow cuts that the Indians had made in his chest and arms, his whole body aching from kicks and blows. But he was alive and for the most part whole, contemplating the irony of being rescued from certain death by the one man in the world whom he really wanted to kill.

They both had weapons, Lawton the pistol that had been thrust upon him, and Stone a rifle balanced easily in his hands. Both were poised, alert, their blood still running hot from their battle with the Cheyenne. It would be easy to end their long enmity right here, to blast away with the guns and find out who would be left standing once the smoke

cleared. To hell with the law. To hell with anything that restrained the need for vengeance, for action that would somehow wipe the pain of his sister's miserable death from his
soul. He'd always believed that bringing the last of that vicious gang to justice would lay her ghost to rest and give
him back his life.

The hell of it was that every time he turned around,
Nathan Stone was poking holes in his single-minded con-
viction that he was a villain who had no good purpose on
this earth. All through the journey west with that damned
wagon train, all through having to watch Stone day and
night, working with him, once even fighting beside him, all
through his lonely search along the routes to Mexico, Lawton had held on to his hatred. Or at least he'd tried to. Now
the bastard up and saved his goddamned life—and stood
there grinning at him as if he didn't know good and well
that Lawton was just a hair's-breadth away from pointing
a pistol at his heart and pulling the trigger.

Stone continued to smile. "So here we are, Lawton. You
and me. Guess this is it."

"You never did head for Mexico, did you?" Lawton said
bitterly.

"Nope. I didn't."

A crashing in the brush made both men swing around,
weapons ready, but it was Cass, not an Indian, that burst
into the little hollow. Her breath came in great heaves and
a smudge of pitch on her cheek spoke of a ricochet off a
pine tree during her race through the forest.

"What the hell?" Lawton demanded.

Still gasping, Cass pointed back and forth between the
two men. "You two aren't going to behave like idiots, are
you?"

"Miss McAllister! What are you doing here?"

"Mrs. Sutherland," she corrected huffily. "And this is my
husband, Nathan Sutherland. You might think he's someone
else, but he isn't. He's Nathan Sutherland, law-abiding family man. And he just took time from his honeymoon trip to
save your life—at great risk to his own."

Lawton clenched his teeth. "You married this . . . this . . ."

"Yes, I did."

"Lila let you marry this man?"

"She encouraged it, in fact. And why wouldn't she?"

The world had gone mad, Lawton decided. Outlaws were marrying good women and risking themselves to save lawmen. Lila McAllister, a heretofore intelligent, honest woman in spite of her former profession, had let her kid sister marry a piece of slime, and she had bald-facedly lied to a U.S. marshal in order to foil justice. Worse, she had lied to John Lawton, who loved her.

"Why wouldn't she?" Lawton asked bitterly. "Because this man is a fugitive from justice, and you both know it. Your sister aided a known felon by lying to me."

"She thought I was going to Mexico," Nathan said.

"Bullshit."

Cass stepped between them, her expression determined. Her strength reminded Lawton of her sister. "My sister is the best person on the face of the earth. You, sir, wouldn't know an angel if you tripped over her wings. And you don't know a good man when you're staring him right in the face. Nathan just saved your contrary hide. Isn't that worth something to you?"

Nathan moved her gently aside. "Cassie, sweetheart, go over there by those trees. Lawton and I have something to settle." He squeezed her hand. "Good try, though."

Cass was not so easily dismissed. "Don't be stupid about this, Nathan. There's just one of him, and he's in no condition to take you on. We saved his hide. Now just take the gun away from him and let's go."

"No. I'm tired of this damned cat-and-mouse game. Are we going to do this for the rest of our lives?"

"If we have to."

"Cass, go over by the trees."

The tone of his voice drew a simmering look, but she obeyed.

Nathan turned his attention back to Lawton. "How are we going to settle this? I'll let you choose, Lawton. Pistols? Knives? Fists? Hell, I'll even give you an hour or two to regain some strength."

The proposition was tempting. Lawton itched to lay his knuckles across Stone's face and discover if seeing the man's blood would make him feel better. Or put a bullet in his gut. Or feel the steel of a knife sink into his flesh.

"'Course you'd rather see me choking on the end of a rope, but that would be a mite unfair, don't you think? Hanging just isn't a two-man sport."

"Nathan! You idiot! Would you—"

Stone silenced Cass with a gesture.

"If you win, Lawton, I expect you to see my wife safely back to Denver."

"I'll skin him first! I'll make him wish those Indians had—"

Both men gave her a look, which silenced her but earned them both daggers from dangerously narrowed eyes. But Cass's face softened as her husband continued to look at her. Lawton tried not to believe the light in Stone's eyes. The bastard truly did love her. What right did he have to love and marry this girl when he had left Lawton's sister weeping and shattered like a discarded, useless rag doll?

Or had he? Could a man who spoke to a woman through his eyes like Stone spoke to Cass be brutal enough to abuse a waif like Amy? Had Stone tried to stop the gang rape, as he claimed? Had Lawton turned a petty outlaw into a monster simply to have one more object to take vengeance upon? Lawton shook his head, and in that moment his world seemed to shift. He had finally surrendered, he realized, and the surrender made him a free man at last. A man could hate only so long. He flipped the pistol in his hand and offered it butt first to Stone. "I think this is your Colt, Mr. Sutherland."

Stone's jaw dropped, and Cass blew out a long-held breath.

"You're not the man I thought you were," Lawton said, looking at Nathan, then at Cass, and back to Nathan. "Mistaken identity. I thought you might be that penny-ante scoundrel Nathan Stone. But now I remember he got himself killed a few months back. There's a grave outside Silas, Kansas, that bears his name."

With a delighted shriek, Cass launched herself at Lawton and wrapped him in a fierce hug. Then she did the same to her husband, and added a kiss as well.

"I get no kiss?" Lawton chided.

She bounced back to him and planted a chaste peck on the cheek. But Stone regarded him warily. Lawton didn't blame him. He was in no position to trust the law, especially the law as represented by John Lawton. And to tell the truth, Lawton still couldn't look at the man without his gut clenching. He might have finally surrendered to reason, but emotion took a long time to die.

"Why the sudden change of heart?" Nathan demanded.

"Like I said, you aren't the man I was looking for. You might have trampled on the law a time or two, but you're not the sort who picks on helpless women. And from what I've seen," Lawton growled, "you're not cut out to be a crook." He stabbed the man with his eyes. "Truth, now. You ever get away with much by riding on the wrong side of the law?"

Nathan snorted derisively. "Damned little."

"Ever shoot up innocent bystanders?"

"Not my style."

Lawton grunted. "The way I figure it, marrying this red-headed curmudgeon here is sentence enough for your crimes."

"If I told Lila you said that," Cass huffed, "she'd come after you with a stick."

Lawton smiled, thinking of bossy, brassy, gentle-hearted Lila. "She just might," he agreed. "But then, I might take after her with a stick myself for sending me on a goose chase these last weeks." He smiled again, feeling as free as a man who has just been released from chains. "Maybe I should just ride up to Denver and have a word with her."

Cass's eyes twinkled. "Maybe you should do that."

Lawton looked at Stone. "The Cheyenne took my horse. If you could see your way clear to giving me a lift to the road, I'll flag down a coach to Denver."

Nathan regarded him assessingly, as if he expected any moment for Lawton to make a grab for the gun he'd handed over just a minute ago. As Lawton's eyes held his, the tightness in Nathan's face relaxed. A faint grin curled his mouth. "We might see our way clear."

"And then maybe, you being a law-abiding citizen who

can go where he wants and do whatever he pleases, you could take your wife back to Denver, and she could try to keep her sister from peeling the hide from my back when I see her."

Nathan's brows shot up curiously. "She's the one who lied to you."

"Yeah. But women are good at turning the blame around on a man. You know?"

Nathan glanced at his wife. "I know." Then he grinned.

Someday, Lawton mused, he might even get to like Nathan Stone. Not right now. But someday.

Denver, November 1866
Dear Ethel,

Your letter, which I received two days ago, was a welcome reminder of the happy friendship we shared for so long. I am glad you found my account of our journey exciting. The delightful thing about letters is that one can eliminate the tedious and concentrate on the interesting.

News of your wedding is good tidings. I'm sure you will have every happiness with Tom. How I envied you last spring when you told me of your engagement. But I am wed now also, as I wrote you, so we are both happy.

And now the surprise—my sister Lila has also wed, just today, to the U.S. marshal of whom I wrote. Mr. Lawton has left his job as a lawman and has taken up the profession of building houses, at which he is very good. I have never seen Lila so happy. She glows like the sun. Perhaps being a wife will get her out of George McCannes's hair. I'm not sure the man bargained on her being quite so active a partner when she invested in the restaurant business. George and Lila do get on well together in the business, though, however George complains.

Happy events, it seems, come in threes, for yesterday I received a letter from my good friend Rachel in Oregon. She and her husband, Ben, have been very busy building a cabin before the winter sets in. Ben

*has found employment with a logging enterprise, and
Rachel has stayed very busy with little July. Soon July
will have a brother or sister. I am very happy for
them. Rachel deserves happiness. She writes also that
Luce, Effie Brown from the wagon train, and Sue have
found a place to open a boardinghouse (a legitimate
one, this time) and public dining room—with a bit of
help from Effie's son. The little settlement where they
landed is so anxious for their business to open that
the community has pitched in to renovate a building
that was once a saloon. Some irony there, I think.*

*As for the third happiness, dear Ethel, that one be-
longs to Nathan and me. The owner of the livery where
Nathan works is in poor health (that in itself, of
course, is not good news, for he is a nice man) and
has offered Nathan a partnership. Nathan is considering starting a freight run from Denver north to
Cheyenne, for everyone is speculating that the Union
Pacific tracks will go through there instead of Denver. We are also buying brood mares. If we put
Nathan's Tennessee stud to work, we could breed the
best horses east of the Mississippi, I do believe. We
are building—or rather John Lawton is building us—
a lovely house on our land west of town. It should
make a wonderful place to raise horses and children.*

Cass chewed on her pen, wondering if she should add a
fourth piece of good news. No, she decided. She wasn't
sure yet. Almost sure, but not quite. And Nathan should
know he was to be a father before anyone else knew. With
a smile, she wondered how best to tell him.

"What is that mysterious smile on your face?" Nathan
asked as he came into the room they rented in George Mc-
Cannes's hotel.

Her smile grew wider. "Just thinking of that lovely house
we'll soon be living in. Fit for a Tennessee gentleman."

"And his lovely lady."

She scoffed. "Lady?"

He lifted her from her chair and gave her a kiss on the
end of her somewhat freckled nose. "Lady in the very best

meaning of the word. Are you sorry you're not a preacher's wife?"

She grinned up at him. "I'd rather be your wife, you scoundrel. And do you want to know the truth?"

He kissed her soundly. "What truth?"

With her eyes twinkling, she whispered in his ear. "Nathan, my love, you really weren't cut out to be a preacher."

National Bestselling Author
Katherine Sutcliffe

☐ **RENEGADE LOVE**   0-515-12453-2/$6.99
On a wagon to Texas, a young woman meets a stranger who unnerves—and fascinates—her. Embers of desire flare into passion as wild as it is forbidden when she discovers that this irresistible man is none other than the infamous outlaw "Kid" Davis.

☐ **HOPE AND GLORY**   0-515-12476-1/$6.99
Nations tremble before mercenary Roland Gallienne. Now, weary of war, he seeks peace at the healing hands of the Chateauroux monastery healer.

The lovely woman is the child of his enemies, and tries to kill him—but to everyone's surprise he shows her mercy and takes her with him.

Their attraction can't be denied, and now, at the brink of a new battle, they must both struggle with an inner war—of the heart....

☐ **DESIRE AND SURRENDER**   0-515-12383-8/$6.99
Her father murdered, her home burned to the ground, Angelique DuHon left New Orleans with her mother—fleeing to the home of wealthy relatives in Texas. But against all odds, Angelique would do anything to save the greatest happiness she had ever known—even at the risk of her own life....

☐ **JEZEBEL**   0-515-12172-X/$6.50
☐ **DEVOTION**   0-515-11801-X/$6.50
☐ **MIRACLE**   0-515-11546-0/$6.50
☐ **MY ONLY LOVE**   0-515-11074-4/$5.99
☐ **ONCE A HERO**   0-515-11387-5/$6.99